# Book 1

# of

# The Ingenious

# Trilogy

# The Ingenious

## and the Colour of Life

J.Y. Sam

This is a work of fiction. Names, characters, organisations, places, events, and incidents are either products of the author's imagination, or are used fictitiously.

www.jysamofficial.com

Paperback ISBN:  978-1-8382436-0-9
eBook ISBN:  978-1-8382436-1-6
Hardback ISBN:  978-1-8382436-2-3

Cover design by David Prendergast

**First edition**

# DEDICATION

To Franco, Isabella, Marco.

# CONTENTS

# ACKNOWLEDGEMENTS

Thank you to everyone who has accompanied me on my journey to publish my debut novel. Firstly to my long-suffering family – Franco, Isabella, Marco – who have endured so many bouts of my writing fervour – often I was around in body but not always in mind! Always understanding of my need to get this book published. Also a big thank you to all those who have supported my journey – the Lucas family who have always cheered me on to publishing my manuscript, even when I lost faith in myself and my writing... Thank you too to Jess Lucas who was alpha reader, Beth Moyse and Mary Sergeant for being unexpected beta readers (and excellent grammaticians/English language extraordinaires), Naomi Garrido for her lovely creature graphics, and David Prendergast for interpreting my muddled instructions and producing a gorgeous cover design. How wonderful to have beautiful music linked to the book – Peter Wright's especially. And I'm so appreciative of my dear friends who may not have known about this project, but whose love and kindness have buffered the knocks from this journey – Yong, who is like a little sister to me, and her two children, Nok Lam and Nok Hang, Atsuko, Kamila, Iwona, and of course Stephen Wright – one of the best bosses ever. I'm grateful for all those who have been my pre-publication reader guinea pigs! And I want to mention too the enduring kindness of my brothers, Dave and Mike, and their other halves, Sandra and Jenny, and their children, Meliha, Jonathan, Matthew, and Peter (and their other halves); all dear family members. The Italian side of my family are very special too – Pino, Laura, Caterina, Pasquale, and their spouses and children. Remembering especially dear Michele, his life tragically cut short – he is sorely missed, and our prayers and thoughts are with Cristina and his children. And last, and most of all, I'm so grateful to my wonderful God, who has given us so, so much. More than we ever deserve.

'I also observed this about wisdom under the sun—
and it impressed me:
There was a small city with a few men in it; and a
mighty king came against it and surrounded it and
built great siegeworks against it. In it was found a
poor but wise man, and he saved the city by his
wisdom. But no one remembered that poor man.
And I said to myself: "Wisdom is better than
mightiness; yet a poor man's wisdom is despised, and
his words are not heeded."
Better to heed the calm words of the wise than the
shouts of the one ruling among fools.
Wisdom is better than weapons of war...'

Ecclesiastes 9:13-18

# PROLOGUE

Innocence is a beautiful thing.

But 13-year-old Jemima Jenkins should have learnt by now to be more suspicious of strangers. She had never really grown out of that youthful virtue of trusting everyone without question – yet there was an unspoken charm to her idyllic little world and her complete obliviousness to anything that could taint it. It was a utopian bubble that her loved ones, least of all she, dare burst. Perhaps it was because her parents indulged her, or simply because she was made that way – but such naiveté did not bode well for those rare crossroads moments in life that had potentially life-changing consequences...

And so, when Jemima awoke in the shadowy dark of night, soft and warm in her bed – she yawned, pulled a scruffy teddy to her chest, and blinked up at the strange woman that was sitting at her side. The girl murmured sleepily, 'Are you the night nanny?'

The woman – whose pale skin and weary eyes made her look much older than she was – just raised an eyebrow, and chewed her gum.

Jemima thought nothing of this as she yawned again and rolled onto her side. Thought nothing of the fact that the woman's mane of glossy hair did not look real, her make-up incongruous. Never wondered why her coat and gloves were still on, despite the stifling heat in the room.

There were just the two of them alone in the still house. Woman and child. Around them hung the silence peculiar to night, broken only by now-and-then sounds of floorboards creaking spontaneously, and, outside, branches that softly clawed against window panes.

Jemima wrinkled her nose, and kicked off the bedcovers to reveal floral pyjamas. 'So hot,' she huffed. 'Can you open the window, please?' The girl's eyes – the colour of deep sea – rolled back irresistibly, her eyelids already bobbing up and down with sleep.

The woman hesitated, but then decided why not. After all, she too was hot. As she walked over to the large sash window on the far wall, she looked around. The space was large and pristine, and in the dim light of the night lamp, she saw a room that would not have looked out of place in a reference library. Instead of dolls, toys, games, and childish paraphernalia common to girls her age, there were rows and rows of packed bookshelves.

Distractedly, the woman rattled open the window lock, pulling up the pane. She breathed in the fresh air for several seconds, before curiosity got the better of her – and, drawing closer to the shelves, she squinted at the felt-tip scrawled labels stuck on each book, colour-coded in rainbow hues. Tilting her head, she read some of the spines – 'From Pythagoras to the 57th Dimension' by Clifford A. Pickover, 'Our Mathematical Universe' by Max Tegmark, Jon Butterworth's 'A Map of the Invisible'. She stared blankly at them, none the wiser – and, giving up, drifted over to the large desk, littered with various gadgets: an electronic book reader, a digital camera, a tablet, and a state-of-the-art laptop still open with the screensaver swirling in softly-glowing colours. She stroked a finger across the smooth trackpad, and the screen switched to a bright white page packed with lines of text – the title bar at the top displayed the words: "Cherry $\pi$, the sweetness of equations in everyday life', by Jemima Jenkins'.

The woman attempted to read several lines, mouthing incomprehensible words, but quickly tired. Instead, she moved silently back across the room to the object of her work. The girl. She was fast asleep – and as the woman stood over her, her hand creeping into the messenger bag by her side, she stared, not quite at the child, but through her. There was an odd feeling of déjà vu, a sense of seeing the same thing but from a different angle – a parallax – and her eyes glazed over, as she remembered...

That's it, it was her last one-off job.

She had posed as a stand-in nurse in a retirement home, and sat, bedside, next to the wispy-haired old man, as he lay unconscious from the chloroformed gauze that she had just clamped over his mouth. The sweet smell of it mingled with the jarring stench of dried urine and bleach. As was her usual way, she extracted a syringe and a bottle of pentobarbital from her messenger bag, and pierced the needle into the amber liquid, smoothly drawing up the plunger until it reached the 5 ml mark. Holding it up to the light, she flicked it lightly to diffuse the air bubbles – and then sunk it, with all the finesse of a grave-digger, into the man's sagging, liver-spotted arm, swiftly pushing the plunger into its barrel. The old man awoke, startled, and tried to shout out, but she immediately covered his mouth with a rolled-up cloth, and held it firmly down as he struggled. His limbs began flailing, and his torso thudded heavily on the bed, again and again – the towel muffling his broken screams. When eventually his body stilled, the woman released, and bubbles of saliva seeped from the side of a twitching mouth – his lifeless eyes, wide in disbelief.

The intruder remembered all of this, as she looked down at young Jemima, sleeping innocently before her – golden hair billowing around an angelic face. The woman's own expression was stony and soulless, as she felt inside her bag and pulled out the bottle of chloroform and a cloth.

She paused for just a moment to examine her own feelings – for the slightest hint of compunction perhaps, a modicum of emotion, or remorse. But there was nothing, not a twitch. And so the woman continued dousing the gauze with the clear, sweet-smelling liquid.

As she glanced at the girl, she thought to herself how different this job was to all her previous ones...

She had never had to kill a child before.

J.Y. Sam

# THE GREY

*'At pivotal moments throughout history, there have always been grey areas, and there likely will be in the future. Courage now lies not in the black and white, as in the past, but in the grey.'*

Safak Pavey

# 1 CRANE FLY

Young Milly Bythaway lived with an unusual phenomenon. Every day, her dead mother talked to her.

It alarmed her, at first – but then, in time, she began to understand what was happening. The voice was a symptom of her special condition, and had nothing to do with madness, or schizophrenia, or ghosts, not that she believed they even existed.

It was all the work of her mind.

Her extraordinary mind.

So strong, so powerful, was Milly's memory of her mother, that the woman's entire maternal persona lived on in the girl's psyche. Residing there as the other person in her head. An inner voice. Time did not allow the memories of her beloved mother to fade, as it does with normal people. And hers was definitely not a normal mind.

Her mother's voice – which came as a whisper in her ear – seemed so solid, so clear in Milly's mind, that it was like insects preserved perfectly in amber. The warmth of her mother's breath, the whiff of the peppermints she sucked, and the light tickle of her hair – all perfectly encapsulated in her cerebrum.

And so as the girl blossomed into a teenager, she had by now learnt to live with this condition, and soon came to appreciate the specialness of it. Even dead, her mother would always be there. With her.

That, she supposed, was one of the upsides.

The downside was that memories of her mother, so easily conjured, also brought with them the searing sting of her death, on a daily basis. As if a sadistic universe found pleasure in wrenching off the sutures from her heart, only to sew them back again, stitch by agonising stitch.

But what could she do, but bear it? And so that was what Milly did every day. And that was why this 15-year-old girl threw herself into her schoolwork, and non-stop reading, studying, learning – keeping herself busy in every way.

The one lifeline she had, her raison d'être, was her father. He grounded her, and was the thing that kept her from going insane from the monotony that was her life. And monotonous was definitely how she would describe it.

For years she had been told to blend in with others at school, and be an average student, achieving only middle-of-the-road grades.

Don't go anywhere near the Gifted and Talented club.

Fade into the background.

Be invisible.

And with the same lacklustre performance that Milly wittingly put into schoolwork, her teachers responded with equally dull reports. *'Must apply herself to homework to improve poor test grades, participate more in class discussions, stop day-dreaming,'* were some of the usual comments in her reports. Most parents would have reacted abrasively to such criticism, but her father welcomed them, with great relief.

And so, when Milly clattered carefully into her father's tiny home office, balancing an uncertain teacup and saucer with one hand, and a crumpled school report clenched in the other, the girl knew very well what was coming.

Brian gratefully took the tea from his daughter, though it almost dropped. 'Whoops, sorry! I'm so clumsy,' he said, just as Milly saved the cup from falling. Together they placed it carefully on one of the many piles of paper that covered his desk.

He was a freelance accountant, and the spare room in which he worked – no bigger than a large cupboard – was itself a reflection of the state of the man. His battered desk creaked from the weight of an old beige computer. An ancient but reliable printer straddled two sets of dented filing cabinets. Box files were wedged haphazardly on dusty shelves that, over time, had bowed, creaking and groaning with overload. The room's ambience was depressed and grey. And incessant drafts from a splintered window were the room's involuntary sighs.

Milly hugged her father from behind, resting her chin on his shoulder. Mildly interested in the spreadsheet displayed on the screen, her green eyes zigzagged across the rows of numerical data, and returned to rest on one of the cells. 'The formula in G16. It's wrong,' she told him, tapping the screen with the corner of her envelope. 'Inside the brackets it should read 'B11 to D16', and outside it should be multiplied by twenty percent, not seventeen point five.'

Her father peered over the top of his glasses. 'Ah yes, of course.' And he quickly righted the mistakes, not even bothering to check them himself. He looked at the envelope in Milly's hand. 'What's that? A report?'

Milly let go of her father, and sat on the edge of an old chest of drawers. 'Yeah,' she said.

'What are they complaining about now?'

His daughter sighed. 'Mrs Tilman caught me "doodling" during class.'
'Doodling?' he asked, puzzled. And then it dawned on him. 'I'm
guessing notes in another language, or complex equations?'

'Sanskrit,' she said, looking up at him, excited to talk about her latest
interest. 'Just learnt it recently. Took me a while – actually about two
days. It's really good for poetry and philosophy. The script is so beautiful
that it's used for calligraphic paintings, which look like fine art but with
hidden aphorisms. I could show you some on the internet if you like, when
you've finished with the computer...'

Brian swivelled round in his chair to face her. She looked so small in
her school clothes – they always bought a few sizes too big, to save money.
'That'd be great, Milly,' he said, and then glanced away briefly – it was
still unsettling to see his dead wife so vividly in Milly's expressions. The
girl was the image of her mother.

He took her hand in both of his, and squeezed them warmly. 'And I'm
sorry to keep harping on – but it's really important that you stay below
the radar and don't draw any attention. It's for your own good. You
understand, don't you?'

Milly spread a smile on her face, as she always did. ''Course,' she lied
brightly. She'd had years of practice hiding her emotions. Quickly, she
changed subject. 'I'm going to start on tea, and I'll leave it out before I go,
okay?'

Her father thought about this.

'It's Wednesday,' she reminded him. 'The animal centre's today,
remember?'

Brian nodded, 'Yes, of course.' He swivelled side to side in his chair,
antsy. He had a ton of work to complete before the day was over.

Milly pushed his chair right round, so that he faced his screen again.
'Get back to work,' she said, and pecked him on the cheek. 'Love you, Dad.'

'Mm-hm,' he mumbled distractedly, already clacking at the keyboard
and glaring at the computer.

Milly started walking out, but she stopped and turned at the doorway,
resting her head on the flaked paint of the doorframe – breathing in the
familiar sight of him: the back of his head of thick hair bobbed from
calculator to notes to receipts, hands moving mechanically, bathed in a
faint triangle of ochre light. Milly offered tea to the back of him, chatted
to the back of him, said good night, good morning, goodbye to the back of

him. It was as if he were trapped, held hostage by the lopsided equation of inadequate earnings against the greater and often unpredictable outgoings. Somehow their house and expenses haemorrhaged money.

Milly turned away, sighing. And, realising the time, she jogged downstairs, and busied herself in the kitchen. Rummaging around in the fridge, it offered her only three slices of bread, a carton of margarine, some milk, a bit of hardened cheddar, three eggs, and three black bananas. Cheese omelette on toast was the obvious choice. And so she set about making it – and finished by covering the food with an upside-down plate, balancing one of the over-ripe bananas on top. Ready for whenever he emerged from hunger. She took another banana for herself, unpeeled it, and ate as she got ready to go out again. The last banana she put in her rucksack to snack on later.

She reached for her precious old beanie, carefully handling it as if it were made of spun gold, and pulled it over a mass of messy brown hair. Swinging her rucksack over a shoulder, she shouted goodbye to her father, and heaved on the front door. The door had been sticky since forever, and it took several tugs before it opened, and then closed shut. She stopped to catch her breath, and that was when she noticed – in the top right corner of the lintel – a taut spider's web, vibrating from an insect struggling to break free. It was a crane fly – its long legs glued to the unforgiving silk. Delicate cross-veins on its wings quivered with frustration.

'Hey there,' Milly murmured to it, drawing closer to examine the situation. 'You poor thing.' Reaching up, she carefully broke off sticky threads with all the concentration and precision of a surgeon in an operating theatre. When at last it was free, and clinging to her index finger, she found a twig, and used it to pick off remnant web strands, squinting, almost boss-eyed, as she worked.

The little creature sat quietly, its palp warily tasting the air, somehow knowing that good was being done to it.

'All done,' said Milly, pleased with herself, looking over the little thing. She lifted her finger skyward. 'Go on then, off you go.' But it did not move. She blew a gentle puff – and at last it took off, bouncing and fluttering clumsily in the air, rising higher and higher.

Milly watched it disappear with satisfaction. Then turned round, swung her backpack over her shoulder, and set off, wending her way through the roads that led to Acton High Street. She went past the run-down house where the old man, who nobody ever saw, lived – and reached the town centre bustling with chaotic traffic and passers-by. It was a colourful melting pot, with ethnic shops elbowing their way in between the older, established ones. The window of the local Polski sklep brimmed with poppy-seed cake, plum doughnuts, and smoked sausage. And, as usual, Ming's Restaurant was a-clatter with spatulas scourging woks. She passed too the Irish Pub, sign-posted by a golden four-leaved clover. Mobile phone shops-cum-internet cafes, were proprietored by men in flowing sarongs and koofiyad caps. Kohl-eyed women floated along in their black hijab. A pensioner, sporting blue-rinsed hair and a lilac scarf, shuffled by so slowly it was as if she were in her own time-warp. And children skipped beside frazzled parents, begging for a toy-laden Happy Meal.

It was spring, but the weather firmly ignored the time of year, and decided instead to be cold, grey, and drizzly – which surprised no-one.

Fortuitously, the bus arrived just as Milly approached the stop, and she hopped on, pressing her oyster card against the reader with a beep. It would take her through the next two towns, to Hanwell – Acton's older brother. Here Milly worked every Wednesday at the animal centre for pocket money, helping maintain the rabbits, muck out the enclosures, feed, and generally take care of them. It was a chance to commune with nature, which she hadn't realised how much she loved until she started working there. The centre contained only a handful of species, including exotic birds and spiders, mongooses, monkeys, apes, goats, and a large variety of rabbits of every size, breed, and colour – which is why the small zoo was affectionately called the 'bunny park' by locals.

It was just two hours before closing time, and visitors were already dwindling. After waving hi to George – the resident animal-keeper, who was as old as time itself, near-deaf, and went about his duties with silent deference and a smile – she changed into overalls and wellies, stuffed the banana in her pocket, and crunched across gravel paths to the rabbit enclosures. As she walked, she noticed a little boy, probably three years old, olive-skinned, with a lick of hair tightening on his forehead from the damp. His large, grey-blue eyes, as if undecided as to which colour they should become, shone with the thrill of nature. Beside him stood his young, pretty mother – she threw her head back and laughed at the boy's comical reaction to the meerkats.

When Milly reached her assigned enclosure, the rabbits – who were scampering about or lazing in their hutches – immediately gathered around her feet as she refilled their food and water. Meanwhile, the little boy and his mother walked past her again. But the woman was no longer laughing, because by now, the child was mid-tantrum, angered that his snacks had been confiscated – to save his appetite for dinner, his mother kept telling him. He huffed and glared up at her as they walked towards the primate section – both as determined as each other: the boy to get his own way, and the mother not to give in.

Milly did not know why, but at that moment, her mother's voice whispered in her ear. 'Interesting,' was all she said. And Milly wondered.

She found herself walking out of the enclosure to follow the couple from a distance – the air heavy with the scent of damp grass, clover, dandelion, and thistle from surrounding fields. Milly watched as they disappeared into the small building that held the chimpanzees, and she followed them inside. The querulous boy's defiant voice echoed, and she found them watching the apes, next to a Polish couple and a Japanese family with young children.

Suddenly, the boy grappled with his mother, trying to reach inside her tote – eventually he pulled out a small plastic bag, triumphant, and held it to his chest. His red-faced mother ordered him to give it back, and she tried to swipe the bag from him, but he was too fast. He ran backwards, stumbling into the Polish couple, and their SLR camera inadvertently let off a bright flash, the dim corridor struck with lightning.

Inside the enclosure, the chimpanzees screeched with fright. One of the hairy creatures jumped away, and swung up onto a ledge close to the ceiling, while the other tumbled backwards, dazed, its full weight crashing against the door to the enclosure, which rattled weakly in return.

Everything happened so fast – but Milly saw it all, as if in slow motion. The boy dipped next to the floor-to-ceiling safety railings that were set about a metre away from the glass of the enclosure. He managed to scramble between a warped iron post, and, safe behind the bars, he poked his tongue out at his mother, and waved the trophy bag of nuts just out of reach.

One of the chimps caught sight of the little boy on the other side of the glass, and stopped to watch him, cocking its head sideways.

Enthused by the creature's proximity, the Polish couple took more photographs, flashing again and again. The Japanese children, with great excitement, started banging on the iron railings – all making the chimpanzee screech wildly.

Milly turned to the Japanese family and spoke urgently to them in perfect hyōjungo, 'Please stop your children from making noise! They're frightening the animals.' And to the couple she switched to Polish, 'You must stop the flash. It's making them go wild!'

But one of the creatures had already worked itself into a frenzy, shrieking and battering fists against the door. Suddenly the door broke open with a loud smash, and the chimpanzee stumbled out, just metres away from the boy. It was huge.

The mother gasped, and Milly sprinted across to them as the chimp jumped onto the child and grabbed his arm. Whimpering, the boy clenched the bag of nuts firm against his chest. The excited ape screeched and pulled him round in a slow dance – and then sunk jagged teeth into the plump flesh of the boy's upper arm.

The child howled.

Blood splattered out in whorls.

The mother screeched and cried hysterically, 'Yarmetîm berê! Yarmetîm berê!!' She couldn't speak a word of English.

Milly's heart thudded as the hormone epinephrine cascaded from the medulla of her adrenal glands into her bloodstream, sparking billions of neurons in the Wernicke part of her brain – so that she immediately recognised the language. Quickly, she grabbed the mother's shoulders, and spoke to her in Kurdish. 'Stop screaming! You're frightening them.'

The mother ripped unbelieving eyes away to glance in desperation at Milly. Silenced, she turned back to her son, and fell to her knees, gripping the metal bars, as the chimp continued his attack. She begged Milly in Kurdish, 'Help me please! My son...'

Milly had already whipped out a bunch of keys from her pocket, and was turning one into the lock on the iron grid. She stepped in, trembling, quickly locking the door behind her, and shouting out to the boy in his language, above the high-pitched screeches of the distraught ape, 'Throw me the bag of nuts. Throw it to me now!!'

Something in his brain clicked, and he hurled the bag at her. She plucked it from the air, the dry plastic crunching in her palm – saw the beady eye of the chimp as it followed the arc of trajectory – and she ran into the main enclosure. The other chimpanzee, watching from afar, swung down from rope to branch, landing with a heavy thud on the ground next to her. He too was large.

The female, no longer interested in the boy, hobbled back after Milly, her teeth drenched in blood. She bashed the back of her knuckles against the ground, throwing up plumes of dust. Milly could smell the thick stench of the creature's breath.

Outside, the mother sobbed, as she held the bars of the cage, helpless. On the other side, the boy whimpered pathetically, cradling his arm, too afraid to move.

Milly was small and defenceless, standing between the two fearsome creatures. Though her heart raced, she planted feet squarely on the ground, raised her chin, and glanced from male to female – a shine of sweat on her forehead.

The male swiped at her, and Milly flinched, but he only grabbed the banana from her pocket. Plonking himself on the ground, he started peeling it. On Milly's other side, the female's eyes were still fixed on the bag of nuts, and Milly threw it as far as she could into the enclosure.

The chimp hobbled after it, and Milly quickly ran back through the door, slammed it closed, and, leaning her full weight against it, threw the keys to the mother. She told her to unlock the outer gate to extract her child. When they were clear, Milly herself darted out of the iron gate, and twisted the key firmly in the lock. She tested the gate, just in case, to satisfy herself that it was secure. Turning round, Milly heaved a massive sigh of relief.

But the boy had passed out, and his mother was rocking him in her arms, crying. She fell to her knees and bent over him so that her cheek brushed his lips. There was no breath.

Milly's mother whispered in her ear. 'It's been about four minutes.' And Milly knew that if the brain is deprived of oxygen for six minutes, it could mean permanent brain damage. She had to act fast. Taking off her belt, she tied it tight around the boy's upper arm to stop the bleeding. Then she took the boy from his mother and placed him flat on the ground – tilting his head back, lifting his chin up, and opening his mouth. She pinched his nose, and bent over to give him mouth-to-mouth resuscitation, pausing to watch his chest rise, and then giving 30 quick chest compressions. Milly repeated this until he began to breathe on his own. Then she sat back, and they both stared at the boy, as if their combined will could somehow revive him.

At last he stirred. He started whimpering, and held his hands out to his mother. Milly sat back on her haunches and sighed with relief. 'I think he's going to be alright...' she said in Kurdish, smiling weakly.

The mother fell upon her little boy, and sobbed.

Eventually, the park rangers appeared all of a sudden, one of them holding a phone pressed against his ear, speaking urgently to the emergency call operator.

As the sound of the ambulance sirens got louder, the rangers peered through the bars, and watched in amazement as the two chimpanzees sat meekly around the plastic bag, quietly picking fruit and nuts from the dust, as though nothing had happened.

Paramedics appeared, quickly assessed the situation, and began cleaning the bite wound on the boy's arm. Despite the teeth incisions, there had been minimal blood loss – the worst of it was the bruising that would soon cauliflower into bright green and purple welts. After a shot of tetanus, antibiotics, and a mild analgesic for the pain, he would live to tell the tale with great embellishment, it transpired, to friends and family.

The mother's eyes were still damp with tears as she turned to Milly before they left. 'Sipas dekem,' she said, placing a hand on her arm. 'Thank you. And God bless you! You saved my son's life.'

Milly's father had been called, and he drove over immediately, only to find his daughter sitting wrapped in a blanket, looking small and pale, staring into space.

He came running to her. 'Milly!' he breathed, and started fussing.

She got up and said, 'I'm fine, Dad. Don't worry.'

Brian looked at her arm. 'So what's that bandage?'

'Oh that,' Milly remembered. 'Feel a bit stupid, but after the thing with the chimps, I tripped on my own feet and fell over... It's just a graze.'

'Sounds about right,' Brian said, relieved. 'The daughter of a clumsy idiot like me.' He hugged her for some time, and then whispered, 'Love you, stupid.'

Milly melted in his arms. 'Love you too, idiot.'

One of the park rangers, who was going around speaking with everyone concerned, interrupted them. He explained that he thinks old George had forgotten to feed the chimps for the past day or so, and so the combination of hunger, mixed with the fright of the camera flashes, had spooked the animals into a frenzy – and that was why they were so fixated on the little boy and his bag of nuts...

When at last father and daughter arrived back home, Milly could only mutter something about wanting to go straight to bed. Her father – knowing his teenage daughter well by now – resisted the urge to follow her, and stood in the hallway to watch her drag one foot after another up the stairs.

Safe inside her bedroom, Milly looked over its comforting familiarity, breathing it in. It was her sanctuary, where she no longer hid what she really was. Where she could take off the mask of the dumbed-down teenager, and at last let out the animal – her intellect.

Milly paused to scan the walls of her room in the dim light, eyelids half-closed from fatigue. Every inch of wall space was slathered with scribbles in different languages, as well as equations, formulae, references, quotes, and diagrams. It was a textual explosion in black marker, now faded to grey. Only the white of the ceiling was bare – unable to be written on for the crumbling artex.

Her eyes flit over some of her calligraphy and artwork:

*'For once you have tasted flight you will walk the earth with your eyes turned skywards, for there you have been and there you will long to return,'* a quote from her beloved Leonardo da Vinci, written in meticulously neat cursive script.

*'ds = (del)q/dt'*, the elegant and robust second law of thermodynamics.

A sweeping spiral of numbers, *'0, 1, 1, 2, 3, 5, 8, 13, 21, 34...'* – Fibonacci's eponymous sequence.

Then there were artistic brush-strokes, Milly's own worthy reproduction of Da Vinci's *'Head of Leda'*: a lovely face, three-quarter turned, eyes downward-slanting, and framed by snaking braids and wispy spirals of hair.

Milly was so tired she could cry. She lay down on her bed without changing. Carefully she pulled off her old, bobbly hat, feeling the prickle of tiny electric charges, and then smothered her face in it. Of course, by now, the smell had long since disappeared, yet her incredible mind was able to bring back the exact scent it once held – of musk laced with jasmine, a hint of gardenia, and middle notes that in time gave way to an earthy, woody base. It was a scent that invoked her mother, was her mother.

She saw her now, in her mind's eye.

Savannah Bythaway.

Sitting up feebly in that metal-framed hospital bed. Her face, grey and ashen, and ravaged by sickness – yet her eyes were still beautiful, sparkling like polished emeralds. A scrawny nine-year-old Milly sat at her side, watching with fascination as her mother clacked knitting needles. Her long pale fingers moved with painful slowness, resting every other stitch from exhaustion. Struggling for air. But mother smiled down at daughter. She always smiled. And little Milly smiled back at her.

As Milly lay alone in her bedroom, she placed that precious old hat gently on the wooden knob of her bedstead, lay back, and closed her eyes. She felt the soft dampness of her mother's kiss on her cheek. Listened as her mother recounted her favourite bedtime story, the one that retold Milly's entry into the world, somewhat elaborated into 'The Birth of Princess Melody', and woven into the fabric of a fairy-tale. Her mother's reassuring whispers were soft as gossamer.

'...*The long-awaited baby princess was delivered by Mr Stork to two adoring parents, who loved the child even before she arrived. The princess was a pearl in the king and queen's eyes. And after much thought, they finally decided on a name. Princess Melody. It suited the infant perfectly, they thought. A name that hummed with a rhythm they knew would enhance their lives – something beautiful and beguiling, floating like a refrain always in the back of the mind...*'

Her mother's breath warmed her ear, the tickle of hair against skin. '*Goodnight my dear, sweet Milly,*' her mother murmured to her.

'Goodnight, mum,' whispered Milly back at her, speaking out loud to an empty room.

On the walls, her own curlicued writing and sketches bore down on her from all around – they blurred as her eyes magnetised closed, eventually becoming part of her dreams, and leaping to life as she slept.

And as Milly slipped into the depths of unconsciousness – sweet respite from the daily onslaught of an overcharged mind – a spindly crane fly floated down from the gap at the top of the window, onto her hair. It batted its wings slowly, flirting. And then drifted across to the curve of her shoulder – the delicate tibia of its long forelegs twitching on her sleeve. The insect turned to the lamp on the nightstand, attracted as it was to the light, but it resisted the urge to fly towards it. Instead it settled down, resting its abdomen against the warmth of her, tarsomeres burrowing deep into cotton fibres. It watched over the girl, a silent and serene guardian, with large compound eyes that glimmered like oily petrol in the dull light. Fine remnants of spider silk still clung to its trembling wings. But it paid no heed. Awed by its proximity to this giant being. It itself did not understand fully these feelings. Did not know the order of things, its life so tiny and insignificant in comparison. All it knew was an overwhelming sense of something, perhaps devotion, maybe allegiance – a concept barely comprehensible, yet there.

It settled itself down, this tiny watch-guard, and waited.

## 2  BEAUTY AND THE BRAINBOX

Calista Matheson was in a quandary. She could not decide which subjects she should study for her A' Levels.

All she knew was one thing. That she had to choose the easiest courses, that required the least possible work – because thinking in any depth was far too much effort, and therefore to be avoided at all costs. She had no aspirations of becoming someone, or achieving something – and wasn't bothered when nasty people whispered 'dumb blonde' about her. Though it didn't help that she thought 'euthanasia' was a Far Eastern country, wondered why the Pope lived in the '16$^{th}$' Chapel, was sure strawberries grew on trees, and kept mixing up small but critical words, like a.m. with p.m., up with down, left with right. (Friends soon learnt never to ask her for directions...)

Calista's saving grace was that she was beautiful. Strikingly so. And as such, she couldn't care less if people thought she was shallow. Her trump card was her exquisite beauty.

At the same time, her life was incomplete without the holy grail of *Celeb* magazine – and she only wore market-bought designer bargains labelled 'Chivenchy', or 'Salvatore Ferragano', and felt naked without her 'Guchi' lipstick and brow definer.

She was the type of person that girls loved to have as a friend, and boys were besotted by.

Yet, she never dated casually. Didn't sleep around like some of her friends, or spend entire nights on raves and binge-drinking – because (a) it wreaked havoc on her complexion and figure, and (b) because she was strict on morals. 'I've got princey-pals' she often told boys who persisted in trying it on with her. But then, when she spied the Adonis recently enrolled at her college, suddenly all her princey-pals, or even her principles, crumbled.

Jake Winters, a new boy in town, was quiet and intense, with a tousle of unkempt mahogany hair. 'Like a young Heinztein,' Calista thought to herself wistfully (vaguely divining that 'Heinztein' was a really lit scientist who probably invented baked beans). The boy's grey eyes simmered as he studied, his chiselled face frowned with concentration. And despite being the 'most handsomest' boy she had ever seen, he himself was completely oblivious as to how good-looking he was.

Most worrying of all, he was really, really clever.

Sadly for Calista, and very unusually, he didn't even notice her – and it dawned on the girl that the tables had turned, and for once it might be her doing the chasing...

For days she deliberated on how she could get his attention. But bright ideas and witty one-liners were not her forte. She even bought a notebook, like the one she saw him scribbling in. But after writing at the top of the first page 'IDEAS', and thoughtfully underlining it several times, the rest of the page remained disconcertingly blank, even after much wracking of her brain, and scratching of her beautifully coiffured head.

By the third day she had more-or-less given up (perseverance was never a strong point), and began wallowing in self-pity. For the very first time in her life she experienced the pangs of unrequited love – the wretched, self-inflicted torment that every teenager must at some time or other experience.

But then, one grey, rainy, October afternoon, she found Jake Winters sitting in the corner of the canteen by himself at lunchtime – leafing avidly through the pages of a thick technical book, drinking a cup of something steaming hot. She watched from afar as he pored over the book, intermittently blowing on his drink, and bending down absentmindedly to scratch an ankle (she noticed with amusement that he wore mismatched socks). Then, quite suddenly, he glanced at the canteen clock, frantically packed away his belongings, and ran out of the hall. Inadvertently leaving the book on the table, still open.

Calista walked cautiously over, and tilted her head to read the title at the top of the page. '*The Binary System and its Evolution toward the Era of Digitisation* – by S D Browning'. She mouthed each word slowly, intrigued, though still with no idea what the book was about, yet hugely impressed that the boy could even comprehend such thingummy systems and evolution digi-wotsits. She glanced toward the door, and, satisfied that he wasn't going to come rushing back, furtively swept it into her DKNI handbag, and made a speedy exit.

In the bright light of her student digs, she hunched over the book on her bed, and Calista's worst fears were confirmed: it was nearly impossible to understand. Packed with complicated words, zero pictures, no pretty colours, it was so very different from her glossy beauty magazines. She retrieved her dictionary from the floor (it was being used as a doorstop), blew off the dust, and began looking up the first word. At last she took out the pristine notebook, leafed past the bare 'IDEAS' page, and with her feather-topped pen, wrote down: 'WORDS', again giving it satisfying importance with multiple underlines. She meticulously copied out the first unfathomable word, followed by its definition – then did the same for the next word, and another – until, about half an hour later, she finally began to understand, dimly, what the first sentence was about. To her credit, she managed to stick with it for hours.

Two days later, when she had just begun translating the second page, she herself was sitting at one of the tables in the college canteen, sipping budget lemonade through a straw, and poring over the pages of her dictionary. A shadow fell across her table, and she turned to find *him* standing there. The straw dropped from her lips, plopping into the liquid with a fizz. She slapped her notebook shut.

'One of my favourites, that,' said Jake, nodding down at S D Browning's voluminous work. His expression of surprise in finding *her* reading it was quickly replaced by a friendly smile.

Unusually for motor-mouthed Calista, and perhaps for the first time in her life, she was at a loss for words.

He smiled at her – a lazy, lopsided smile. 'Cat got your tongue?'

Calista desperately tried to think of something clever to say. 'Y-yeah...' was all that came out.

He looked over her shoulder. 'Brilliant, isn't it?'

'Um, yeah, it's sick!'

'I see you're on the first chapter, the synoptic history of computers. What d'you think of it? The punch-card data-saving method was crazy, don't you think?'

Calista wasn't too sure. Didn't understand a word he just said. She just stared up at his devastatingly handsome face, unable to stop herself grinning.

Jake laughed nervously.

At last Calista tore her eyes away, finding eventually coherent words. 'Yeah, all that,' she said. 'Actually, I found this book here, in the canteen. Been reading it ever since. It's *so* interesting – can't get enough...' Her cockney was a stark contrast to his refined English.

Something suddenly dawned on Jake, and his eyebrows furrowed. 'Hang on a minute. I lost *my* book a few days ago – been looking all over for it. Perhaps it's mine?' He leant over her and flicked to the inside cover; unashamedly, Calista breathed in the warm musk of him.

'Well I'll be darned!' he said, after spotting his own handwritten initials 'JW'. Organised as he was, he had methodically initialled all his books. 'It *is* mine. I've been looking all over for this.' He sat down on the chair next to her, and scratched his head, looking over her face as if for the first time realising how exquisitely beautiful she was.

'Sorry!' grinned Calista, cheekily. 'Losers weepers...'

Now it was Jake's turn to be at a loss for words.

Calista laughed. 'I'm joking! Here, take it – it's yours.' She shut the book and handed it to him.

He took it and wrapped his arms around it against his chest. 'Thanks...' he said, trailing off.

Calista thought of something. 'I... I was just about to get something to eat,' she said. 'Found exactly £1.63 worth of coins rifling through drawers and pockets, as you do. And there's a special offer of a pot of tea and a sandwich – for £1.50. So if you fancy some lunch, and don't mind sharing...' Calista's eyes widened, hopeful.

'Hmm, dare I take food from a poor, starving student?' He thought for a moment. 'Sure, count me in!' It wasn't every day that he was asked to lunch by a beautiful girl.

Their ensuing conversation was awkward, stilted, but nevertheless they enjoyed each other's company. The tea and food was meticulously divided – and though they lingered, it came to a finish far too quickly for Calista's liking. Her brain went into overdrive trying to think of a way to engineer seeing him again. 'Erm, er, hmm...'

Jake looked at her, and eventually nodded over to his book on the table. 'So, I'm guessing you're joining Computer Sciences?' he asked.

That had never even entered Calista's mind. After all, you had to be really, really clever for that. And she most definitely was not. Still, she looked from the book to his stunning face, and found herself saying, 'Mm-hm, sure am...' – hypnotised.

'Great. Well, I'll see you in class then,' he beamed.

And that was how Calista Matheson eventually decided to study Computer Sciences, Programming, and Networking for her A' Levels – all the same classes that Jake had enrolled in. And it had nothing to do with the subjects...

••—————————————————••

The couple soon became inseparable.

They started saving seats next to each other in class. And at lunchtime they got into the habit of putting their loose change together, counting it out, and seeing what they could afford. They knew every bargain in town, collected every voucher, used their student discount to the full – all in order to spend as much time as they could together. A shared latte macchiato could buy them 30 minutes inside Starbucks. Buy-One-Get-One-Free vouchers gave them 15 minutes in the local supermarket. And £1 bought them a good hour at the internet café, huddled next to each other in front of a computer.

Proving that chivalry was not dead, Jake always took it upon himself to walk her home at the end of the day, even though it was out of his way.

Their first kiss came on a rather cold, grey day, under a mulberry tree – across the road from the house belonging to the old man, that nobody ever saw. It was just beginning to rain, and the couple were sheltering under the tree, branches heavy with hanging catkins, dripping down a light shower of perfumed droplets.

Jake's lips were warm and tender against the cold freshness of the air, his breath hot on her skin. Their kiss was a slow, sweet discovery; an unhurried pleasure. A moment that would become pivotal in Calista's life – referential, and revered. The time when she first began to feel the tug of real, pure love. It was a raw hunger, and a tumbling thrill. It was the taking of single, stark words and binding them together into flowing lines of poetry – poetry that finally made sense of the world. It was him, and her, locked together.

In love, was where she was always meant to be, Calista realised. With Jake.

•••————————————————————————•••

She took it for granted that Jake felt the same. All the signs were there. He would notice the little things: when she changed her hairstyle, or wore different earrings. He was always kind, and complimentary, even when she was having a bad hair day. And he jumped at the chance of spending time with her.

So when she asked for extra lessons, he was more than happy to oblige, immediately arranging a time and place. And he taught her with infinite patience and skill. To say he was a computer whizz, was an understatement. He programmed in Fortran, Visual C++, Perl, in fact every computer language there was. He created applications, developed code, and designed plug-ins. He was able to fix stubborn hardware problems, and upgrade computers by adding RAM, and replacing graphics cards. His head was so full of code and computer ideas, that sometimes on the train, engrossed with scribbling inside that dog-eared notebook of his, he often missed his stop, realising his mistake too late, and then having to get the train back – only to miss the stop again.

Infected by his passion, Calista soaked up everything he taught her. The heady mix of first love and programming syntax was potent to say the least. And she revelled in it.

Calista soon realised why, in the past, she had held back from keeping a steady boyfriend. It was because those boys never really piqued her interest, had nothing much to tell her. They talked only about what *they* wanted, and were obsessed with the physical, the material. But with Jake, she had begun to fall for his mind. His was a profound, brooding intelligence that thrilled her. And in turn, it sparked within her an equal and opposite reaction – an eagerness to learn, and a hunger for the thing that interested *him* so much. Computers.

This was a transformation for Calista – who was beginning to understand the latent power of assimilating knowledge, and then putting it to good use. Learning, and loving it. The beautiful ditsy blonde was emerging from her chrysalis...

•••————————————————————•••

Calista often thought that Jake was too good to be true. She wondered, how it could be that a boy so intelligent, so refined, could fall for someone as dumb as her? Exhilarating weeks with him turned to months, and then years, but in the end she discovered, to her dismay, that perhaps those tiny nagging doubts, those grains of insecurity, were justified: it couldn't last. It was in early May, two years after they had first met, that Jake suggested they stop seeing each other for a while, and go on a short break, to concentrate on study and revision for their impending final-year exams. 'And you need to swot up on your spelling, Cal – it's insane,' he told her with an affectionate squeeze of her hand. Months of trying to decipher her texts, emails, and messages, left him almost dizzy. She nodded deftly in agreement, though more worried about how she would survive for weeks without seeing him.

It was going to be difficult to be apart, inseparable as they were, but they both knew it was for the best. Reluctantly they stayed away from each other. And Calista studied and revised hard in that period, in the same way that she had studied hard for her GCSEs; her teachers then had warned her, as they did now, that if she didn't get the necessary grades, she'd have to retake the exams – and that was the last thing she wanted. So she worked hard, despite suffering from Jake withdrawal symptoms, counting the days, hours, minutes that separated them. Straining at the leash.

She sat through her exams, applied herself to each question, mentally checked her spelling, and double-checking each answer, just like Jake had taught her.

But as soon as time was up on the final exam, she grabbed her bag and ran out of the room, phoning him right there in the corridor. He didn't answer. Again and again she tried texting, emailing, and calling. But by the evening, she counted 21 attempts at contacting him that day, but not once did he respond. He didn't open when she repeatedly knocked on the door of his student digs. Nobody knew anything of his whereabouts, and she wandered through the school corridors, peaking into classrooms, checking with teachers, leaving note after note in his letterbox, and streams of voicemails.

She even got the caretaker to open his room with the master key, worried that he had slipped and knocked himself out. But his rooms were empty, and immaculate as usual – and she found nothing untoward. His slippers were still lined up neatly next to the door, clothes still hung in the wardrobe, toothbrush and razor by the sink.

Calista felt numb, sick, and lost. Her mind a daze. Everything was out of kilter.

The one thing that kept her from going completely insane was the fact that she discovered his laptop wedged at the back of his locker, behind a rolled-up sweater (they had memorised each other's padlock digits, just in case). She held the battered laptop to her chest, eyes glistening with tears, now knowing that something was deeply wrong, because he would never leave his computer.

When she brought it home, she sat it on her lap and stared at it for how long she couldn't tell. Then, taking a deep breath, she opened it slowly. The black screen stared back at her, as her finger hovered over the power button. When she turned it on, it whirred and clicked and bleeped, and the screen lit up – opening to a blank background, where a pixelated green cursor blinked feebly next to the words, 'Enter password'.

Calista thought for a minute, and then typed in Jake's year of birth. Rejected. His surname. Rejected. His favourite colour. Rejected. And then it dawned on her, and her heart skipped a beat as she typed one more word: 'Califragilistic', his nickname for her. And she was in. Black gave way to a brightly-lit desktop, with, at the top right-hand corner, a graphic of one of Calista's selfies, beaming. Around it he had drawn a love-heart. Calista stared at it, her heart melting, and she knew for sure now. He *did* love her...

And then she spotted another photo, it looked like an old one, in the bottom left-hand corner. It was of a pretty girl, perhaps 19, with black curls framing an oval, delicate jawline. Around her neck hung a fine necklace – camera-flare glinting from its blue gemstone. The girl's eyes were the same as Jake's, and from this Calista realised instantly that he had a sister. The likeness was unmistakeable.

But why had he never mentioned her? Not even in passing...

Baffled, Calista dried damp eyes with her sleeve. She was more determined now to find out why Jake had disappeared as suddenly and silently as text deleted from the screen. Perhaps she might even uncover something about this mysterious sister.

Calista began typing into the computer a string of commands, at first hesitant, unsure, then becoming faster and more determined. Yes, she was going to unlock all his emails, documents, and files, even the deleted ones, in order to search for clues as to where he had gone.

Things just didn't add up. She knew now that he loved her, just as she loved him, and he would never have disappeared without letting her know. Something was very, very wrong.

But as she dug around, she realised that there was much more to Jake than he let on. The laptop was full of reams of code, technical notes, half-finished computer programs, and pages and pages of indecipherable jargon-like notes. And his internet history made no sense to her. In the end she decided to follow his tracks, hacking into the servers that he himself had hacked into – though she took the utmost precaution, using an overlay network to hide her IP, deleting log files, modifying registries, and disabling audit.

By six that morning, Calista had already hacked into four servers, but was still none the wiser as to why Jake would be snooping around there. There was a courier company, a social networking site, a who's who directory, and the CCTV security files of an old people's home.

There was one last hack to try, and she noted with interest that it was a government database, which would no doubt have the highest security. Slurping down more coffee, she typed in its IP address, and waited for connection. When she found herself at the digital gateway, Calista typed a flurry of code to get through each level of encryption, like a girl possessed. The security was the highest, but she had learnt well over the years she'd been with Jake, and was able to breeze through it to get to the internal file structure. She located an unshadowed password back-up file buried deep within a directory, and while the passwords were one-way encrypted, she ran one of Jake's programs, a password-cracking app, to randomly try word/number forms as access keys, based on existing data. Two hours later the software beeped a triumphant match, and she suddenly woke up from a pandemonium of dreams – shaking the sleepiness away. Quickly Calista ran the Telnet program to log in – and she eventually discovered what Jake himself had accessed: files and files of medical data and personnel records. She copied them straight away onto her hard drive, then exited the server swiftly.

Suddenly, there was a pop of light from the screen, and a flashing red box appeared with red writing:

'YOU ARE IN DANGER. RUN! RUN BEFORE THEY COME FOR YOU. NOW!!'

Calista shook her head and rubbed her eyes in disbelief – sure that she was dreaming. She yawned spontaneously, and, in a daze, she slipped off the bed to get herself a coffee. When she got to the kitchenette, she doused her face with water, and then filled the kettle, and switched it on.

Strangely, Calista found herself waking up, slumped over the table – its glass surface cold against her cheek, and she shivered involuntarily. She touched the kettle with the back of her hand to gauge how long she had been out. It was barely warm.

Suddenly there was a faint knock on the door. It was not Jake's usual jaunty knock, yet Calista still flew to the door, hoping upon hope that it was him.

A woman in her mid to late twenties stood there.

Calista looked at her, deflated.

The woman chewed mechanically on gum. 'Calista Matheson?' she asked. 'I'm from the school, from the Student Laison department. Your teacher, Miss Juniper, sent me to have a word.'

Something didn't seem right to Calista; the way she said the word 'laison' felt wrong. But the woman, after quickly glancing along both ends of the hall, was already barging her way inside.

Speechless, Calista meekly followed her in, and re-took her position on the bed. The laptop was still open, and she saw again the warning message flashing bright red. Calista froze. Quickly, she pushed it closed, and then turned to face the strange woman, gulping down her anxiety. She mustered a smile, whilst desperately thinking of what she could say. 'Um, is Miss Juniper okay? She's been missing a lot of her geography lessons recently.' In reality, Miss Juniper rarely missed a day of school, and actually taught art.

The woman looked at her. 'Er, yeah. She's alright. She's, er, she's getting better.' But when the stranger saw Calista stiffen ever so slightly, she realised her mistake. She hadn't expected this dumb blonde to be so clever. Instinctively the woman dipped her hand inside her messenger bag. 'Don't move,' she said, menacingly.

The woman turned back to the door, twisted the mortice lock shut, and walked over to the desk at the foot of the bed. She began pulling out items from her bag and placing them on the desk: two bottles, a plastic syringe, a white rag, and a rather rusty old knife – all laid out neatly, like a nurse prepping instruments.

'You worked out I'm not from the school, didn't you,' said the woman, flashing a brief smile. Her teeth were stained yellow from nicotine. Quite casually she took the rag and doused it in chloroform. 'Now, as I see it, there're two ways we can do this. One, you can do as I tell you, and you won't feel a thing. That'd be better, and less stressful, for both of us. And two, you could make this very hard for me. But it's only gonna get really – and I mean *really* – messy. Oh, and it'll hurt... a lot.' She peered over at Calista, half expecting her to start screaming.

But the girl was frozen to the spot, wide eyes looking from the objects on the table, to the woman.

'Good,' said the stranger. 'Good choice.' She drew closer, moving her hand to Calista's face.

In reflex, Calista immediately grappled with her, trying to push her away – but it was too late – she had clamped the cloth over her mouth and nose. It reeked of sweet cotton candy. One, two minutes passed, and Calista's eyes rolled back, and she slumped into the woman's arms, limp.

The woman lowered her to the bed, and went back to the desk.

But the chloroform hadn't worked properly, and, to her horror, Calista found that she was still conscious – though her eyes were shut, and her thoughts were syrupy and slow. Her head pounding from the drugs, her body paralysed.

Yet, somehow, a hairline crack of light appeared between her eyelids, and she saw the woman picking something up from the desk. Outside, faraway sirens resounded, a dog barked in the distance, and a car horn beeped.

All at once nauseous, dazed, and sleepy, she prayed. *Please*, over and over again. *Not like this, not now...*

But then through the dull fog, she realised that the sirens were becoming very loud, and the woman stopped in her tracks. She hurriedly gathered her belongings, then ran to the door, unlocked it, and let herself out in a rush – the door left open behind her, and footsteps reverberating in the hall.

The sirens were deafening now. A screeching of tires. Car doors opening. The thunder of more footsteps on stairs. Urgent shouting. Uniformed policemen surging in.

'Miss!' a voice said close to her ear, 'Are you alright?'

More footsteps. A firm hand shaking her shoulder. The laptop disconnected and its power cord rolled up.

'We're taking you somewhere safe, young lady. Hang on there!'

But then a furious and agitated grey mist appeared. It billowed and darkened and swelled, so that it completely enveloped her – and she passed out.

# 3  THE BOY WHO KNEW

While Milly Bythaway knew everything there was to know about anything, and Calista Matheson had learnt the workings of a computer like the back of her hand – Tai Jones just... knew.

He couldn't explain it, and couldn't describe it – it was just something he could do. Most children get noisier and chattier as they age, but Tai instead grew quieter – silently absorbing the feelings, moods, thoughts of others. Not even realising that he was unique, and that he had such an amazing gift. It was not always a good thing though. He saw light in people, but he also saw their darkness – ugly, unfiltered thoughts, that made him shiver. Yet, Tai took everything in his stride; like finding a fly in your drink – he would notice it, pick it out, and move on.

That was his life.

And he could only accept it. He had to accept it when, as a chubby two-year-old toddler, every hug and every kiss from his father made him feel queasy, though he barely understood why. He just shivered, and looked up at the man he adored. His father was right there, yet somehow not there – like a shadow. And then one day he understood why, when his mother began sobbing hysterically, and repeatedly pushing toddler Tai away – all he could do was retreat to a corner, distraught, crying, hiccoughing, and knowing that his shadow father had finally disappeared for good. He had never really been there in the first place.

When Tai became a teenager, it wasn't worth his while remembering the names of the string of men visiting his mother – they barely registered on his radar. They just came and went as indiscernibly as seasons slipping one after the other silently. Yet even by then, his mother remained an enigma, and Tai regarded her with quiet attentiveness. She spoke her mind, so that he knew exactly where he stood – and most of the time she was fierce, and to be feared. But there were moments, though rare, when he realised that his mother was not quite as ferocious as she seemed. She loved him. He was certain of it. Until the day she made him sit on the rickety chair in the hall, and that's when he began to doubt...

He remembered that day well. Remembered the broken rattan scratching his butt, and the chair legs squeaking as he shifted awkwardly.

She threw a doubled-up carrier bag on the floor, and stooped to tamp down clothes into it. They were just *her* clothes. And she started explaining that her father was sick, so she had to go visit him, and leave Tai alone.

'I'll just be gone for a lickle while, chil',' she told him, curls of a thick Jamaican accent in her voice. 'So don't be messin' up the place!'

14-year-old Tai looked at her. She was solid, not like his father had been.

The first night his mother left him alone in the flat, Tai lay in his bed in the darkness, terrified. (His mother had a strict lights out after nine policy, and he dared not disobey, even when she was gone.) All the boy could do was pull the bedcover right over his head, and hope upon hope that sleep came soon to relieve him. But it only came in fits and spasms; it was the longest night of his life.

When at last dawn broke, he leapt out of bed and flung the curtains open, relieved to see the first glimmers of morning sun. He ran from room to room, only to find that she was still absent...

He comforted himself by going through the familiar motions of getting ready for school, pretending that his mother was right there – morning hair wrapped in a brown stocking, as she sipped tea from the chipped porcelain cup in between sucking on a Dunhill with hollowed cheeks. He imagined her firing out orders from the corner seat, as was her custom.

'Mek haste, boy! Yer gonna be late.'

'Tie yer shoelaces *proper* now.'

'What! Y'leavin' so much chaka chaka – go tidy!!'

He even imagined the stinging clip she gave him round the earhole when something went wrong. He found himself longing for the sharp pain of that slap.

Later that day, on returning from school, he opened the front door, smug from remembering to bring the key. He let himself into the flat, like a grown-up. But again, when he went searching through the small flat, his heart sank once more to find that she had not returned. He even looked at the ashes in the Bob Marley ashtray, like a seer, but they were cold, their pattern unchanged.

He sat back on her chair, miserable, wondering when he would see his mother again, and terrified by the prospect of spending another night alone...

Still, he could not cry.

Pretty soon, at night, he started leaving the lights on.

Routines at school and home continued for days and days. The leftover patties, plantains, and goat curry in the fridge, and tins of corned beef and pigeon peas in the cupboard eventually ran out. But, his mother had often sent him to fetch the benefit money from the post office, so it was natural for him to go and withdraw it just like before. Two lots of benefit to collect, only this time, it was his to do with as he pleased. A whole £196 and 48 wonderful pence. As he walked home, the money burnt in his fist inside his pocket. But he soon squandered it on lemonade and junk food wolfed down so fast it made him burp, and toys that he had never even dared ask for before. He even splurged on the fruit machines in the local arcade – they cheerily gobbled all his money, while his spirits sank. He had no idea that he should use some of that money to pay the rent.

And so, after several months of being alone, one day Tai came home from school to find a thick iron door clamped over the entrance to his flat. There was an official looking note stuck to the wrought iron – it used hard-to-understand language that he could barely understand, words like 'non-payment', 'rent arrears', and 'bailiff'. But it was enough to make him queasy and sick. He stood there for some time, just staring at it – slowly realising that he was never going to get back in. Never going to see the warming familiarity of his home. And with his mother's ID left inside, he was never going to be able to claim the benefit money anymore.

He turned round, and went back down the stairs.

The tattered rucksack on his back suddenly feeling like the weight of the world.

•••————————————————————•••

The first night spent outside turned out to be quite the adventure. He imagined he was a contestant on a jungle game show, needing to find shelter and bedding, water and food. Except, as he lay on a bench – an overgrown broom brush arching over him – the novelty soon faded as he shivered uncontrollably from the cold. His hands, held up toward a waning moon, looked almost blue.

He didn't want to give up school, because it was the one familiar thing still left. But he knew that the teachers would notice his unkempt hair, blackened nails, and the dirt on his clothes.

He was properly homeless now.

But Tai soon learnt to master homelessness.

If you knew where to look, there were rich pickings to be had from the streets of London – to schedule. On Wednesday mornings, at the corner of the marketplace, discarded crates, brimming with bruised fruit and limp vegetables, were left out for food waste collection. And the night before the bin men came, on Fridays, there were rows of left-out rubbish bags – which Tai jostled between his hands to ascertain contents. On Sunday evenings, the local cafés threw out expired meats, cheeses, and salads, before the fresh new delivery came early Monday morning.

It was impossible for him to starve.

He also learnt how to scout out the best places to spend his nights, no longer having to sleep out in the open, wet and shivering from cold. Just recently he had found an abandoned warehouse in an industrial estate on the outskirts of town. As soon as he walked inside, he knew that it was for him. There was even running water, a bathroom with a working toilet, and a small sheltered backyard, not over-looked, so that he could put together a fire to cook on. Afterwards, he would shovel the glowing coals into a battered pan, cover it with a mismatched lid, and set it next to where he slept – savouring the luxury of warmth.

But over the months, even though he followed his mother's mantra of strict cleanliness, the dirt on his skin somehow defied scrubbing. And he wore eclectic, mismatched clothes – obtained from donation bags outside charity shops, clearance skips, and unsuspecting washing lines. His hair grew into natural dreadlocks, nearly reaching his shoulders – and he often caught his reflection, in a window or a shopfront, wondering at the gaunt, straggly Rastafarian that stopped to stare back at him...

And so he became nocturnal, spending his days indoors, while at night-time he could freely wander the streets in peace and quiet, foraging for anything that took his fancy. An old rusty skillet for the fire, a colourfully decorated cigar box, a needle, a fork with bent tines, chipped plates, and old mugs. And when the sun appeared low on the horizon, casting out a sleepy net of light, Tai would immediately retreat to the abandoned warehouse to sleep. He slept well mostly, but on the rare occasions he couldn't, he would while away the time in an empty daze.

There was an office on the far side of the yard which bore a sign outside in impressive gold swirly lettering. 'CAA, Classical Artist Agency'. They often played music – belting out great orchestral pieces, or simple, haunting arias. He would lie in his makeshift bed, head propped up, endlessly listening, absorbing, dozing... Some pieces were loud and stirring and made his ears burst. And some were comical – a jaunty, tripping cadence, with instruments twanging against the clumsy beat of drums or timpani, often brought a smile to his face.

Some pieces, especially those with piano or violin, were threaded with a melancholy leitmotif that made him think of his mother, made him sad. Even the pauses – silence loaded with the promise of what might come – ached his hollow heart. That music spoke to him. It told him about life, its hardships, and the many disappointments there would be. And the boy had no choice but to roll on his side, bow his head, and listen respectfully.

At times like these, he sometimes slipped inexorably into depression. And those were dark, dark days. He would lie in bed for ages, half listening to music, half sleeping, wading through the mire of self-pity. Wondering what there was to live for... His head hurt from thinking so much. And from dwelling on childhood memories.

One memory, when he was six, came to him now. His 'why' phase. Constantly asking questions, always seeking answers.

'Why's the sky blue, Ma?'

'Why's psghetti so long y'have to suck it through your teef?'

'Why's there a man on the moon for?'

'Why'd the dinosaurs disappear?'

One particular question came to him out of the blue. 'Why'd you fall for Dadda, Ma?' he asked, without knowing from where the thought came.

But she always said the same thing. 'Because me was young and stupid. And too bone idle to do anything else but go with that no good excuse of a father of yours!' She spat this out, even though Tai was barely six. 'And look where it got me,' she said, eyeing the boy. 'Lumbered with a chil', and he, nowhere to be found. No money, no support. Me jus' left with chobble!'

Little Tai took all this in quietly, but just couldn't stop himself from asking one more question. 'So why'd you born me, Ma?'

His mother scowled at him, her patience wearing thin. 'You weren't planned, boy. Ya just... 'appened.'

But he only looked at his mother, observing how vexed she was. Always vexed. 'Did you have me just so's you could make Dadda stay?' he asked innocently, as calmly as if he were asking why bread was sliced.

His mother sucked her teeth long and hard at him, and stared daggers. 'Yuh cyaan shut dat mout up, chil'...' she said, accent thickening. And then turning away, she dropped her head, and breathed deeply until she had calmed. In time, she faced him again, serene, like water returning to mirror smoothness after a splash. 'Nonsense, chil'. I didn't have yuh to just mek him stay,' she said.

Somehow, Tai always knew when she lied.

But despite everything, the boy managed to find a way through the depression, and was able, eventually, to push himself out of bed. He knew that, whether he liked it or not, suffering was bound up with life. And trying to stop it was like trying to stop high tide from coming in.

But he never lost sight of the good, or at least the prospect of good. And that kept him sane.

Recently, he had made a discovery that cheered him a little – it came on Sunday and Thursday evenings. Tai prepared in advance for it, by hiding behind the wheelie bins at the side of the house of the old man that no-one ever saw. While he waited, the boy would pick some lavender and rub it between his hands, breathing it in with closed eyes. Then, just as it was turning dark, like clockwork the front door opened. And in the waning light, Tai could make out the man's shadowy form, as he bent down and clattered something on the outside doorstep. The door closed as quickly as it had opened. Tai counted to 30, wondering vaguely why the house was always dark, even at night-time – and then he crept to the front door, like a stealthy cat creeping upon its prey. As always, a scratched enamel bowl was left out with a hunk of glistening steak. Quick as a flash, he grabbed the meat and bolted.

Tai always waited till he got back to the warehouse before he tore into the meat. It was almost too good to be true, cooked to tender perfection, and still warm. Its succulent red juices ran down his chin as he ate.

And there was another welcome event. It came while he was lying back on his makeshift bed, savouring the sensation of a full belly. His ears pricked up suddenly, and he noticed movement near the door. Straining, he caught the edge of an approaching shadow...

A fat cat appeared, striped honey-beige and grey, and Tai breathed a sigh of relief.

It wandered casually into the warehouse, seemingly without a care in the world. Tai watched the cat stop, then turn to sit with its back to him. It sniffed the air delicately, as if it were too regal, too good for such a run-down place. It got up, stretched lazily, and drew closer.

Hesitantly, Tai extended his arm, and the cat sniffed his fingers with keen interest, and began licking them – its tongue was warm and rough. Realising that it was drawn to the smell of meat, Tai pulled out the remainder of the steak from a plastic bag, flattened the bag on the floor, and tore the meat into smaller pieces. The cat sprang forward, and began rubbing itself against Tai's ankle, purring loudly. Then it sniffed the morsels, before hungrily gulping down every last piece.

Day after day the cat returned, and Tai began to enjoy companionship after such a long time of being alone. He settled upon calling it 'Cat' because he had never been any good with names. And he didn't know that the cat had labelled its new friend something akin to 'Big Heart'.

Tai retrieved a tea chest from the alley behind the removal company, and he lined it with an old cushion, placing it on its side at the foot of his bed. Cat eyed him, eyed the box, and hesitantly moved nearer. Satisfied there was no bad scent, it began kneading the cushion by rote. Slowly, Tai extended a hand and stroked the cat, scratched its chin, and rubbed behind its ears. They soon became best friends. Though Cat didn't really do much – it just slept, went out to the toilet, ate food, and then slept some more.

Tai was grateful for the supply of steak which the mysterious old man put out twice a week without fail, likely imagining he was feeding the foxes. Cat didn't really eat anything unless it had steak in it; it had such a voracious appetite. No sooner had he given it a meal, than Cat seemed to cry for more.

More and more it stayed most of the day in its box, only going out whenever nature called, mewling raspily to announce its departure. Pretty soon, Cat meowed so much for food that Tai had no choice but to save the entire steak for it – and Cat just seemed to grow bigger and rounder every day.

At night when it was really cold, Tai constructed a makeshift tent from old dust sheets, propped up with a long wooden pole leant against the wall, fanned out, and pinned down with pillows. A small lidded pan wrapped in a towel was filled with glowing embers to heat the bed-tent, and without fail Cat would creep into the warmth, and stretch out. It sometimes rested its head on Tai's arm, staring up affectionately at Big Heart, its tail flicking gently from side to side. Tai always looked deep into Cat's gold-flecked eyes. They were large and round, encircled with paint strokes of white. He always knew Cat's moods, sometimes in good spirits, mostly dispassionate, at times wistful, invariably sad – so similar to his own.

He grew to love that cat.

Tai realised that he had forgotten what affection was; his mother had never really been affectionate to him. In fact, all he ever got from her was a string of chores and a barrage of threats - 'Chobble me an me a guh bax yuh', 'Lef me nuh', 'I'm noh have noh broughtupsy', or 'Yu dam lagga head!'

Yet he always knew she loved him from the food she made, spending hours preparing it. How he missed her cooking! She set before him tasty dishes of rice and peas, or ackee and saltfish, curried goat, crispy fried plantains, and soft dumplings the size of his fist. They always sat down together at mealtimes, and it was the only time the boy ever saw his mother smile. As he ate, Tai would admire her exquisite fine-boned beauty, ebony eyes, and hair that was like silky-black corn fibres.

●●●────────────────────────────────●●●

When the days became shorter, and it turned so cold that mornings were frosted with white, and the evenings cloaked in fog, Tai and Cat would both lie stretched out, dozing in that bed-tent. Cat mostly thought about food, while Tai, on the other hand, occupied himself listening to the starlings that nested under the eaves of the abandoned warehouse on the other side of the wall – chattering and squeaking and prattling in their hundreds up there. And in the warehouse behind the far wall, he listened to the foxes that had set up their den.

But then, something odd happened. For a couple of steak days, as Tai crouched in the shadows, he watched the old man go through the motions of leaving out the meat. But recently, each time Tai crept up to retrieve it, the bowl was empty. Puzzled, he wondered whether the man was going insane. But after a whole week of no steak, and Cat driving him crazy with its constant mewling for food, Tai decided he needed to find out what was going on. So the next Thursday, he crept out to the house, and hid in the usual spot behind the wheelie bins. This time, when the man left the food, instead of counting to 30, Tai dared to crawl out immediately after the door closed. He kept to the shadows, hunched down on all fours, and – agile as a leopard – slinked over to the porch. And there it was: a juicy steak glistening in the bowl. He swiped it up in the blink of an eye, and ran like the wind. When he got to a nearby alley, he stopped for breath and tucked the food into a plastic bag, put it inside his jacket, and zipped up.

That's when he heard the low growling.

He looked up to find a large, scrawny Doberman in front of him, teeth bared, legs bent firmly on the ground, ready to pounce. Tai looked at the creature's fierce eyes, and knew that the dog could rip him to pieces in minutes. He had no choice but to slowly reverse the zip, take the steak out, and throw it to the ground. The dog pounced on it and began devouring the meat straight away – intermittently looking up at the boy. It was ravenous.

Quietly, Tai backed further and further away.

When he rounded the corner, Tai turned to walk back home. But then he stopped, sensing something behind. It was the dog – following him. Half turned, Tai stared at the dog, and the dog stared at him.

He was stuck. With the dog following him, he couldn't go back to the warehouse, because it would put Cat at risk. So he made the decision to spend the night in the abandoned building in the park a few blocks away. It was dark by the time he reached it, and when he stepped inside the windowless shelter, the stench of urine made him gag. But the dog was just outside – and so he closed the door, pulled his jacket up over his nose, and settled on the ground in the centre.

And even though Tai worried that Cat had nothing to eat, and would feel abandoned – just as his own mother had abandoned him – sleep came surprisingly quickly.

Early the next morning, just as dawn was breaking, Tai roused, tired and lightheaded from a night of constant waking, and tossing and turning. He scrambled to his feet, and the stench of urine hit him once again – and he vomited. He went out, spitting onto the ground, and walked in a trance back to the warehouse.

When he arrived, he heard Cat meowing even before he got to the door – he could tell from the pitch that something was wrong. Tai stopped in his tracks, his skin bristling. And that's when he heard feet padding behind him. He knew it was the dog. Quickly he bolted through the door, slammed it shut, and then ran to search for Cat – knowing that it was just a matter of minutes before the dog found its way in through one of the broken windows. He had to get to Cat first.

But the Cat's box was displaced, as if there had been a fight or a struggle. A pool of red viscous liquid glistened next to it, with a trail of paw prints and clumps of fluff leading off. Tai followed the trail into the next room, his heart pounding in his chest. And there was Cat, lying still on the floor – a mess of blood and matted fur. Tai dropped to the ground, stricken. Cat's eyes shifted toward him, its side heaving with scattered breaths – and Tai reached for it, immediately sensing Cat's jumbled emotions of relief and joy, sorrow and resignation.

Cat's head was angled awkwardly, so that it watched the boy from upside down. And now that his Big Heart had returned, Cat could finally let go... Its eyes slid slowly closed, and it exhaled its last breath.

Tai groaned. At the same time, he knew that the dog had got in through the window, and when he looked up, it would be there in the doorway, staring right at him.

Tai stood up to confront it, but there was a sudden throb in his head, and everything around him swirled into a white storm. He swayed on uncertain feet, his eyes rolled back, and he felt himself keel over – collapsing on the floor next to Cat. A prickling sensation rippled across his body, and then light faded to black.

When he came to, Tai realised that he could not move. His face was cold, wet, and numb, partially submerged in a puddle. He was lying on the floor, his body twisted, with nothing but shadows in his field of vision. His ears funnelled and echoed every sound – the dry rasp of his breath, the steady drip drip drip of water, and the starlings prattling and shuffling in the roof next-door.

He heard the echo of his mother's voice shouting at him, and the roar of a hundred voices – schoolmates and teachers – all taunting him.

From above, he heard death hover over him like a circling vulture, hungry for carrion. Waiting to swoop down to pick him to pieces.

Tai drifted in and out of consciousness, not knowing what was real and what was dreamt. Unsure if time was still flowing, or had come to a stop. Not knowing whether he was dead or alive.

He was all at once damp and hot, cold and parched, and just as he began sinking into oblivion, he was brought back by the sensation of movement, a wet nose nudging, the stench of breath, and the moist lick of a tongue on his cheek. There was a tickle of fur against his skin, and the gentle rise and fall of a creature's warm torso. A streak of black-brown, and a shiny eye close to his.

He curled up like a foetus in a warm, downy womb, and he dreamt of milky liquid trickling drop by drop down his throat – dribbling from the side of his mouth.

His dreams dredged up a litany of forgotten memories that sparkled with crystal clarity. They flickered in his mind, as his eyelids twitched, and his head thrashed from side to side.

And here, seeping into his dreams came the memory of a river walk, not long ago. Sneakers crunching in the gravel beside silvered water that lapped and winked in the moonlight. There was a backdrop of silhouetted angular roofs, etched against a velvet sky. But as Tai walked under an old bridge that arched above him, his feet kicked into something soft but heavy on the ground. And he froze. He looked down, but was unable to see through the shadows pooling around his vision like black blood – yet Tai already knew what lay at his feet. It was a man, sprawled on the ground, near-dead. He quickly stooped down and felt with his hands: a head of short, unkempt hair, the smooth skin and bristly chin of a young man, and slumped, narrow shoulders.

Suddenly, the man grabbed him, and Tai jumped.

But then he heard a long, low exhalation. Felt his muscles spasm then relax for the last time.

Tai dropped his head, and held the man's hand; at least he didn't have to die alone. And in the moment that skin touched skin, Tai began to understand the man's arid, desert-like grief – from losing the love of his life. A grief that left him so barren, so dry, that he couldn't bear to go on. Tai closed his eyes. And it surprised him to see a blue-grey image of the man's last fading memory: the upper corner of a woman's face, the silky eyelashes of a deep-set eye, a high cheekbone, and a spray of flowing hair. The blue of the fleeting image intensified into a burst – just as the man's grief exploded into both wretchedness and oblivion. Tai's mind exploded with a bright flash of the man's thoughts and emotions, memories and sensations – they flared out like a million sparks of a firework, eventually fizzing and fading into nothingness.

Tai stumbled back, and sat, stunned, on the ground next to the dead man. There was an acrid bitterness in his mouth, and he spat it out into the river. It was as if he had tasted death itself, and it sickened him.

•••————————————————————•••

As Tai lay in the puddle on the ground of the warehouse, time and the world impacted inside his thrashing head. He did not understand if hours or months, seconds or years, had passed, as he muttered wildly and shivered with fever.

But then, like an epiphany, a sliver of light cracked open, and he found himself lying on the floor, aware. The boy's eyelids slowly flickered, and for a long time, he stared at the window ahead of him, watching the last glimmers of fading light. Every muscle ached, and the slightest movement made his head throb.

And then he remembered. His mother. The man slumped dead beneath the iron bridge. The dog.

And Cat.

He groaned, and pushed himself up feebly. He saw that Cat's body was gone – the bloody marks on the floor had dulled to brown, faded now against the dirt. Tai struggled to get up, and he walked on shaky feet back to the main room. He stumbled on the crate, pushing it. And that's when he heard the cacophony of mewling – tiny voices protesting at being rudely disturbed. Tai rubbed his eyes, and crouched down to peer inside. There was a mass of fur. Kittens! They spilled out of the box, eyes glued shut.

But Tai's skin began to prickle, and he stopped, sensing a new presence. The dog had returned. As the boy turned slowly round, it dawned on him that the dog must have looked after the kittens after Cat's death.

The dog glanced at Tai as he padded past him to go to the crate. It sniffed the kittens, licked one of them clean, and nose-nudged them gently back into a tidy pile. Tai watched in astonishment as the dog settled down on the floor next to them and rolled onto her side to reveal neat rows of pink teats glistening with milk. The kittens followed their noses, and scrambled blindly over each other to reach the dog, and drink from her.

Tai sat back and looked at them in silence. He watched as a hazy contentedness – wafting up like amber smoke – emanated from the kittens as they suckled. From the dog, Tai saw the same colours, only much stronger, but with edges tinged with the purple sadness of loss. Tai shuffled closer, and stroked the dog in wonder. And he realised then that the dog had somehow lost its own puppies and, on stumbling across Cat's kittens, found comfort in mothering them. He understood now that Cat had died after giving birth, and also knew that the dog had buried her, just as, not long ago, she had buried her own stillborn puppies – one by one. Heavy-hearted, and whimpering, as she did so.

Tai let out a deep sigh, as he pushed himself onto unsteady feet, and staggered to the bathroom. He was parched, and had to clean himself up. Needed to eat. He had a family now, and they too needed looking after.

J.Y. Sam

# THE WHITE

*'I was blown away by being able to colour. Then I started to draw... bringing a blank white canvas to life was fascinating.'*

James De La Vega

# 4 ACUZIO

Acuzio and his master did not speak the same language; his master's speech was foreign and complex, and full of varying and strange intonations. Yet somehow they understood each other perfectly well.

He had learnt a few words from his master's vocabulary, and also some gesturing signs and signals – and in this way, Acuzio was happy that they shared a special way of communicating with each other. Now that he thought about it, he did not know how he had come to learn these words, just that from as far back as he could remember, from infancy perhaps, he had begun to understand – and he learnt quickly, eagerly.

True, it was a rudimentary communication, and at times a little askew, nevertheless it was a language that was theirs alone. It made their relationship special. And obeying his master, and doing it well, brought deep satisfaction, euphoria even.

Yes, he loved his master, and was fiercely faithful to him. And his master loved him, he knew.

And so he had a good life, was treated and fed well, and at break times was allowed to roam freely, soaring around the vast gardens, marking, and sniffing, and discovering new things to his heart's content. Life could not be better, although (and he did not understand this completely – it only manifested itself as a barely-there dullness in his chest), he could not shake the sense that there was something missing...

But today was a day out of the ordinary.

New humans appeared, bringing with them curious smells, sounds of excitement, and agitation. Of course, as soon as he sensed the humans intrude on his territory, he began to bark their arrival to his master – but as usual, his master hushed him, and so Acuzio immediately sat on the floor in front of him, silent and alert. *Will he say the command to lead, will he ask to fetch, or put something away?* His eager eyes remained fixed on his master.

Two male humans entered the room carrying something long and limp between them. When they placed it on the sofa, and Acuzio sniffed it, he realised that it was another human, a female. Her head was framed by a flow of hair the colour of sun.

His master was distracted, busy talking to the newcomers, so Acuzio ventured to lick her hand, as it drooped from the edge of the sofa. Sniffing it more deeply, he sensed that there was a chemical smell about her, a smell that he could not identify. It alarmed him. And so he licked her again, hoping that the healing properties of his wet tongue would soothe her even as she slept.

He watched as his master eventually shuffled over to the female, unaided, and stooped to feel for her arm. He followed it down and placed two fingers on the inside of her wrist, listening for signs of life – though if Acuzio were able, he would have told his master that the girl was alive, only sleeping. His master turned to talk to the other males for some time, his voice urgent and low, gesturing wildly with his hands. And Acuzio knew that his master was anxious, worried, and that something new and out-of-the ordinary was unfolding.

When the two males left, his master shuffled over to the small shiny ringing box, again by himself. Except it did not ring, he only picked up the bone-shaped part, and held it to his ear, talking some more, again in that low, serious tone. When he put the thing back down, he sat for a long while, listening, or perhaps waiting, maybe thinking.

At last his master called him. 'Acuzio.'

Acuzio padded over, and sat at his feet.

His master pointed over to the female, saying, 'Guard her, Acuzio.'

Immediately he knew the meaning and importance of that single command: he was to stay with the female, and watch over her, make sure that she did not escape, and also protect her from any danger. He swelled with the dignity of such an important task, and resolutely turned and positioned himself by the female's hand, nudging it gently to see if she was yet awake.

His master turned to leave the room, and Acuzio's large ears detected exactly where he went within the house. He followed his footsteps as his master hurried up the stairs, to the first floor, and then entered the sleeping room. There were hurried banging noises for some time, and then it became silent. Meanwhile, Acuzio sat obediently. Glancing occasionally at the female, and waiting.

When his master eventually returned, Acuzio could see from the turning of the shadows that he had not taken long. The old man was panting heavily, and was dressed to go out, with his shiny shoes and hat. Acuzio knew what this meant, and he began whining in anticipation. He waited for his master to say the command, to take him through the gardens to the lake of Avernus, and the underground cavern deep within the dank belly of the earth.

But instead, his master shook the female to wake her; she was heavy with sleep and would not rouse. Acuzio stood up on his back legs, and scraped urgent paws onto the girl's arm. Making small jumps, he reached to lick her face, and then barked at her.

At last she murmured and grimaced, as he continued slobbering her with licks, her arms rising over her head.

Acuzio watched expectantly as the female awoke at last.

## 5 THE LAKE OF AVERNUS

Calista became conscious of the sensation of wet slathering all over her face and arms. She was being set upon by a huge animal, and when she braved opening her eyes (first one, and then the other) she saw an exquisitely beautiful husky, with one paw on her arm, its pink tongue lolling out from the side of its mouth. The dog was a magnificent creature, with a rich blue-grey-white fur, and piercing cerulean eyes.

But Calista sensed that they were not alone. Someone was standing at the end of the sofa, by her feet. She sat up to see who it was, her head throbbing as she moved.

It was an old man. And his eyes were so dim that, though he was looking right at her, they were blank. And she realised he was blind.

Then she remembered. The warning message on her computer. The scary woman. The chloroform! The knife!! Instead of a scream, only a pathetic gurgle came – her throat burnt from the harsh chloroform. Hands clutching at her throat.

The old man stepped forward, holding out a hand. 'Please, don't be afraid,' he said. His voice was soothing – like a grandfather with a child. 'You're safe here, at least for the time-being,' he said.

The dog barked at her, digging into her arm with his paws.

'Heel, Acuzio! Heel,' said the old man, and the dog sat down, panting with excitement, looking eagerly from his master to the girl.

The old man shuffled to the table, where there was a jug of water – he poured some into a glass and brought it back to her.

But she looked at him with suspicion, and gulped. 'How... how can I trust you?' she asked, hoarse.

The man blinked, took a drink of the water, then offered her the glass again.

She took it, and drunk the whole glass, while the old man sat on a nearby chair.

Calista looked around. 'W-where am I? Why's everything so dark?' she asked. She could see from the window that it was daytime, but inside, it seemed like night – everything in the room was in varying shades of black and grey, even the ceiling. She stared out of the window again – something looked familiar. And then she recognised the mulberry tree, where she and Jake had taken their first kiss...

'You... you're the old man who lives here.'

47

But he ignored her, instead speaking with urgency. 'I'm afraid we have to leave.'

While he said this, Calista noticed Jake's laptop on a large oak table, the power cable wrapped around it. 'D-do you know where Jake is?' she asked suddenly.

The old man hesitated.

'Jake Winters. My boyfriend,' she said impatiently. 'He disappeared a few days ago – and no-one knows where he is. I've been trying to find him...'

The old man suddenly sat up, and turned his head slightly, his expression hardening into a glare. 'Did you hear that?'

'Hear what?'

He held up his hand – and listened hard. When he turned back to face Calista, he looked anxious. 'Please, you must trust me,' he said. It was more an urgent demand than a question, and he held out his hand to her.

Calista looked from the window to the man, wondering what he could hear that she could not. She softened. 'I... I think you saved my life,' she said simply, and took his hand.

'Yes, you could say that. I... I'm sorry that you got caught up in all of this. I will explain as much as I can. Later. But for now, we must leave. Please hurry!'

Quickly, Calista snatched up Jake's laptop, just before the tug of his hand pulled her across the room.

Calling Acuzio to follow, and without a walking stick, without any assistance, the blind old man turned on his heels and led Calista out through the door into the corridor, as easily as if he could see. He passed through the hallway, also in dark décor, then turned away from the large front door, walking in long strides towards the back of the house.

'How d'you know where to go?' Calista breathed, as she half trotted, half ran behind him. 'You're blind right? But your dog's not leading you.' She wondered whether he was only partially blind.

'I'm completely blind,' he said, as if reading her thoughts – and with his free hand he tapped his ear, where a neat transparent hearing aid was embedded. 'It's wirelessly computer-linked, feeding audio instructions directly into my ear. Like satnav. Though I've lived here long enough to find my own way about.'

Calista was being led through the kitchen, and then they burst out of the back door into the garden. After the black interior, her eyes had to adjust to the bright burst of green landscape and blue sky. Suddenly, the old man stopped and tilted his head slightly, the colour draining from his face. 'Do you hear that? They're right outside...'

But still, Calista could hear nothing.

'They've broken into the house!' he said, grim.

Indeed, the dog, who had been silently trailing behind them, turned toward the house, its tail pointed straight up, alert. He growled, wrinkled his nose, and grimaced to reveal a flash of white teeth. His entire body was rigid, hackles raised, ready to attack.

'B-but how could they know I'm here?! Why would they be after me?'

The old man did not answer, and tugged her urgently behind him, down several steps into a garden so vast as to be more of a field, bordered with bushes and trees. A wide shingle path, dividing the neatly trimmed grass, led to a small lake over which curved a bridge that had sweeping arches and closed spandrels. It was beautiful – but there was no time for admiration. They hurriedly followed the path, ran onto the bridge, and the old man stopped on the far edge, just before the verge of grass.

Quickly, he ripped off his cravat, knelt down, and held it out. The dog snapped it up, an end trailing on the ground. '

'Give me something of yours,' said the old man, urgent and breathless. 'A scarf, a belt – anything with your scent.'

Puzzled, Calista pulled the cloth belt out of her trousers, and placed it in his hand. But the dog became distracted by something inside the house.

'Acuzio!' said the old man through clenched teeth. 'Take, Acuzio. Take!' The dog heeled to attention, snapped up the belt, and looked up keenly at his master.

The man fell to his knees and patted the ground for the verge of grass intersecting the bridge decking, and, to Calista's surprise, he pulled up a mossed and muddy hatch door in the ground. When she peered into it over his shoulder, she expected to see the glimmer of lapping water, but instead there was a deep hole that went far beyond the level of water, disappearing into darkness. A wooden ladder clung to its side.

Without any airs, the old man scrambled down onto the ladder, murmuring something about having to go first – if he should slip, at least he wouldn't take her with him.

Calista tucked her shirt into her trousers, slipped the laptop inside, then clambered down after him. But before her head disappeared inside the shaft, she noticed the dog's ears suddenly prick up, and he turned towards the house. Calista followed his line of sight, and saw in the distance the garden door being flung open. A man ran out, followed by someone who Calista recognised immediately – it was the woman who came for her. In her hand glinted a dull flash of something in the sunlight – a knife, and Calista shuddered. Quickly, she darted down into the shaft, her hands shaking as she groped for the cover.

The old man called out to the dog in a loud whisper. 'Run to the south exit, Acuzio. Then drop. Go!!' The hiss of his voice echoed in the long narrow hole.

Calista began to slide the cover back into place, and just before the circle of light disappeared above her, she saw Acuzio jump over it, as if he were flying.

•••————————————————————•••

Back at the house, the two figures that burst out into the garden frantically looked around for their targets, cursing. They had vanished into thin air (the curve of the bridge having obscured them from sight). The man shouted to something behind him, something inside the house, and out jumped two huge German Shepherds that looked ready to tear to shreds anything crossing their path.

The man raised his hand pointing out to the field, and both dogs shot out like bullets toward the bridge.

# 6 THE DNA SCULPTOR

'Stay very, very still, and don't make a sound!' hissed the old man. Both of them hung onto the ladder for dear life. Its rungs were rough, and a splinter dug into Calista's hands – she bit her lip to stop herself from squealing.

Overhead they heard dogs barking menacingly, followed by a loud rumble of running footsteps.

Excruciating seconds passed slowly, as the noises faded into the distance. Calista heaved a sigh of relief. The water outside lapped gently against the metal walls.

Still the old man waited until he was 100% certain the intruders were completely gone, until there was complete silence. Then he spoke out into the air, 'Lights, on.' A dim light filled the shaft instantly. 'I think we're safe now, but I'm afraid we have another 20 metres or so until we get to the bottom – so please be careful and take your time.'

'It's freezing,' Calista said – plumes of white breath curling into the air. 'What's this? A bunker?'

'Of sorts,' said the old man, his clanking steps reverberating. 'It's a place I call Avernus – an underground safehouse.'

They finally reached the bottom, and the old man blew on his hands for warmth, then brushed himself down. He pulled out a short white rod from his pocket, flicked it into a full-length walking stick, and said, 'Follow me.' He tapped it against the right wall for guidance, and walked effortlessly along, his earpiece having lost connection.

As she walked, Calista hugged the laptop within her shirt. They travelled about 120 metres along a labyrinth of corridors – the old man knowing exactly where to go without hesitation. 'Stay close, and don't stray,' he said. 'If you get lost you might never find your way out...' Eventually they reached a circular iron door that looked like a bank vault – it was the full height of the passageway, studded with bolts around its circumference, with a large metal hand-wheel in the centre. Calista tried to turn the wheel, but it wouldn't budge. 'It's completely stuck,' she panted from effort. 'We'll never get through that!'

Instead of answering her, he used his stick to feel for the right-angled intersection of the far wall, then moved along it for 12 further steps. He collapsed his stick and folded it into four, slipping it inside his sleeve, and then fingered the wall for a particular section of wall. When he pressed it, a concealed flap sprung back, revealing a steel input pad with 10 keys, each having differing patterns of raised dots. He pressed buttons in rapid sequence, and then turned to his right.

To Calista's surprise, a rectangular section of the stone wall indented to reveal a hidden door – it swung slowly inward, creaking stiffly, and letting out a fizz of warm air. 'The circular door is a ruse,' explained the old man. 'Behind it there is nothing but solid earth.'

They walked inside, and when Calista's eyes adjusted to the light, she gasped. It was a large room filled to brimming with row upon row of stacked shelves of equipment, and separated only by the concrete path on which they walked. 'W-what's all this?' she asked, eyeing the objects nervously.

'Ah, yes. A collection of machinery and equipment etc that I've accumulated over the years. But I'll explain later. Please hurry...' Withdrawing his walking stick again, he tapped his way along the path to reach the north-east corner, where there was another door that the old man opened from a keypad.

Inside was a computer room of sorts, that echoed the disarray of the previous one. There was a large and somewhat dusty old screen on the wall overhead, and various computer hardware scattered randomly around – all connected by a mess of wires that were like arterial veins feeding the room with thrumming energy. The other half of the room was a kitchen-cum-sitting area.

He made his way to an antique desk of burr walnut, covered in worn black leather. He sat down and let out a deep sigh, his back hunched, shoulders slumped, and combing a weary hand through his hair.

Calista gravitated to the chair at the kitchen table. She took the opportunity to really look at the man. At first glance he was rather unastonishing – of medium height and build, and dressed in a simple cotton sweater and herringbone trousers. On his feet were well-worn black brogues, though polished to shining. She guessed that he was in his 70s – and his skin was pale and mottled, delicate as rice-paper, and crowned by a shock of thick silver-black hair. He had deep worry lines etched over his brow, and crows-feet at the corner of his eyes – eyes that were so dark they were like black deserts.

He sat up, and said, 'Computer on.' The screen came to life and resumed the window last used. It showed the same flashing red dialog box that had appeared on Jake's laptop, but this time it read: 'Alert! Ingenious database compromised. Unauthorised file access.'

Calista eyes widened, and she turned from the screen to the old man. 'I-it was you who sent the warning to my computer,' she said feebly.

'Yes.'

'But,' she struggled to understand. 'How did you know to warn me?'

'It's... a long story.'

Calista harrumphed. 'Try me!'

'You must understand that the less you know about all of this, the better. It could put you in grave danger.'

She crossed her arms. 'People have just tried to kill me! So I don't think it can get any worse than that.'

The old man remained silent for some time.

Calista softened. 'Please,' she said. 'I need to know.'

The old man slumped back in his chair, mumbling, 'I'm going to regret this...'

Calista waited.

'The reason I knew to warn you was... because I have a vested interest in the government server you hacked today. You see, years ago, I had a kind of digital 'bug' placed at its ethernet gateway, to alert me of any incoming or outgoing movement in the data stream. It's a special kind of software, called MITM.'

Calista nodded. 'Yes, a Man In The Middle proxy's used to monitor and intercept traffic flow.'

'That's right. A few days ago the MITM software alerted me of someone repeatedly trying to break in – it was your friend, Jake Winters. And so I... kept an eye on him. Only to discover that, shortly after, he went missing. And despite using all my resources to locate him, nobody – including my police friends, and MI5 contacts – nobody knew where he was. This is why, when the same server was hacked into today, from the same IP address, it set alarm bells ringing. At first I thought it was Jake again, but after hacking into the laptop's cameras, I soon discovered, from my computer's audio description, that it was someone different... you. And that's when I sent the message, because I knew that you too were in danger.'

Calista thought about this for a while. 'In danger from who?'

'The truth is, I don't know...'

'Is it the government?'

'No, no. I have friends quite high-up in the government, and it's definitely not them.'

'Wait. So whoever discovered me hacking into the system, and sent that nasty woman, probably sent someone for Jake too!' Calista suddenly felt sick. 'That explains why he disappeared without a word – because they were after him. He only had time to hide his computer in his locker before he left. He must be on the run...' She refused to even think about the other possibility.

'Yes, it appears that way. But Jake Winters only *tried* to hack into the server – he never managed to get past the security on the system... But you did, despite the mainframe having several tiers of super-security.'

Calista thought for a moment. 'Look hard enough and you can usually find a flaw in the system, a crack in the code.'

'There was a flaw?' said the old man, incredulous.

'Yep. It took a while, because I was tired, working on Jake's computer all night. Anyway, I was able to tackle each level of security separately yet simultaneously – in effect, putting each encryption on hold until I solved them one by one. I then fit them all together again, like a jigsaw puzzle. So I got there in the end.'

The Professor was impressed. 'That is quite remarkable, young lady. Quite remarkable... May I ask to whom I am talking?'

'Calista Matheson,' she said, swallowing a yawn.

'Calista Matheson,' the old man repeated to himself thoughtfully. 'It is indeed a pleasure to meet you, even in these circumstances. My name is...' and here he faltered. He seemed at a loss, undecided. But then he said, 'My name is Professor Harald Wolff.' He pronounced his surname the German way, 'Volf'.

Calista thought of something. 'But why on earth was Jake trying to hack into those government files?'

'I... think it was because he had a... personal connection with the information he was trying to uncover. Someone close to him was connected to it.'

Calista remembered the photograph of the girl on Jake's laptop.

The old man quickly continued. 'It's understandable that you have a lot of questions, and you're anxious to find your friend. But I can tell you straight away that I don't have all the answers. I don't know who sent the woman that drugged you – and I'm guessing they followed the police car that brought you to my house... But I can start with what I do know. I...'

and here he paused for a while, his eyes darting from one point to another, as if he was unsure of himself. 'I just want to make quite sure first of all that, if I tell you, you accept the consequences this knowledge brings. If you agree, then I will go on.' He paused. 'Do you?...'

Calista did not hesitate. She wanted – no, needed – to understand the whole picture, in order to find Jake. 'Yes, I understand. I'm okay with it.'

The Professor swivelled his chair around so that he faced Calista directly, and then he began one of the most amazing stories that Calista ever heard. 'It all started about 17 years ago, when there was a very different government to the one we have today, with a different Prime Minister and cabinet. The thrust of their agenda and policies was geared toward development and progression – and so they put together a top-secret project within their scientific research division, and asked me to lead a pioneering new programme.' He shook his head. 'I say "ask" – but really I had no choice. You see, as a genetic scientist I was studying, researching, and writing medical papers on DNA and the effects of gene therapy in disease control. My research was exciting, and ground-breaking, because our experiments showed that we could replace faulty sections of DNA with healthy ones, thus helping to eradicate certain diseases. This germline therapy, as it is called, was performed on the eggs, sperm, and fertilized embryos of animals. Of course, the next step was human testing...

'Anyway, this government division was so secretive that it didn't even have a name. It was just known colloquially as B860, because that was the postbox assigned for receiving its mail... So, B860 commissioned me to work on a project in partnership with another scientist, the renowned Dr Axel Kendra – famous for his work on mapping the human genome. He is the most eminent genomics expert in the world. The doyen of genetics. So, you can imagine, to be asked to work with Dr Kendra was an unbelievable privilege. I could not refuse. Literally. And we were relocated to London–'

Calista interrupted. 'We?'

The Professor realised his mistake. 'Yes,' he said, his voice faltering. 'My family... my wife, and my son.'

Unsettled, Calista knew now that this story was going to have a bad ending.

The Professor continued, clearing his throat. 'They... they called the programme "Project Ingenious". And it was top, top secret. You see,

Dr Kendra, after years of mapping genes – stumbled upon an amazing discovery. He had identified the gene for intelligence, or genius.'

Calista's eyes widened. 'A genius gene?'

'Yes, exactly... Well, actually not just one gene, but a group of genes that work in conjunction with each other to produce heightened intelligence. Dr Kendra wrote many papers on this. One of them reported an experiment with mice embryos that had been created with this genius gene. When the mice had grown into adults, they were put in a special maze with doors that each triggered different musical notes when passed through. In time, the mice learnt that by going through the correct  sequence of doors, each door would trigger a note which successively made up the melody from the first bar of Beethoven's **_Für Elise_**. By learning the right sequence, the mice could get to their prize – a nugget of cheese – and, of course, the full rendition of Beethoven's wonderful score. Amazing I know, but completely true, and tested and re-tested by independent scientists. Ordinary mice could not understand the maze even after lengthy periods of time, but the ones engineered with the genius gene had no problems working out the correct sequence of doors within hours.'

Calista noticed the old man gently tap several fingers on his lap, as if playing the piano.

He continued. 'This is why the government became very interested in his work. You see, they wanted to breed _humans_ with the genius gene. They wanted to produce child prodigies.'

'But... why?'

The old man raised an eyebrow. 'Why? Because these prodigies would then grow up to be the most intelligent minds on the planet – scientists, engineers, strategists, inventors. The goal was that they would produce the best weapons, develop military defence systems, make super-computers, create the perfect body armour. In order that our country become the most powerful in the world. And this is where I came in. You see, Dr Kendra had identified the genius genes, and then B860 wanted me to... splice them into the DNA of human embryos – my area of specialisation.'

'Splice?' Calista asked.

'Yes. You could say I had to embed, or sculpt these genes into human DNA. Myself, and a small team of other expert medical staff. We all worked together, laboured for many, many months, until – at last – we perfected a technique to graft the genius gene into the DNA of an embryo in vivo. It was quite... amazing! We had developed the highest, and most intelligent, genetically engineered life form. Our first baby! That was a Eureka moment to the power of 10 I can tell you. We called him, very simply, Alpha. He was just... perfect.'

The Professor's eyes shone as he relived that incredible moment, but then he came back down to earth. 'Unfortunately, the pressure was on to produce more of such babies – extremely *intense* pressure. But, somehow, the next one wasn't as... forthcoming. It was as if the gods were against us; we kept getting failure after failure. And because of that, a heated dispute arose.' A weariness was developing in the old man's voice. 'The project got to the stage where certain... ethical issues were raised. We realised that it was somehow a fluke that our first baby was born with relative ease. A stroke of luck, even. You see, subsequent foetuses were either non-viable, or were miscarried, or came out... severely deformed. It was indescribably tragic. And we went from euphoria to utter despair. When I explained all this to the heads of B860, and told them that the project was unsustainable, they completely dismissed my concerns, instead ordering us to continue work, irrespective of the danger to, and complete disregard for, human life.'

The old man shook his head. 'But, after much agonising, and sleepless nights, I decided I just could not continue. Finally, I told them that I was going to leave... But they were not the type of people who take no for an answer. They intimated threats toward me, and my family... And so there was nothing I could do but continue. Reluctantly.' The old man swallowed.

'And so, against our will, we were forced to go on. After those first frustrating years, we somehow managed to get back on track, and were able to try several different techniques which invariably worked – eventually. In the end, and after three further torturous years, we had managed to produce seven...' he said, with a strange mixture of both triumph and despair. 'Seven prodigies. Seven perfect little babies. It took us five years in total – which was, believe me, interminably long. All the while, Dr Kendra and I, and the other staff in the laboratory, secretly plotted and planned our 'exit route' from the breeding nightmare – because that is what it had become. A factory, a human cattle farm. So we had no choice but to take decisive action.

'We planned, and waited for the right moment... And then, one night, we stole away the babies. We just had to leave everything – the laboratories, our homes, our belongings. Everything. You see, Axel, Dr Kendra, had friends in very high places, and they "arranged" a fire to be started at the laboratories, a convenient diversion, so that it would at first appear as if we had died in a tragic accident. No-one was hurt of course. But it had to be done, and we were able to get far enough away to make a new start. It gave us a new lease of life. And the babies and their parents (whose identities were anyway secret) were relocated, in the hope that they could begin to lead ordinary lives.

'Axel and I had agreed that we would each "watch over" a group of the children and their families – committing their new identities and their whereabouts to memory. Dr Kendra looked after four, while I cared for three. I was not to know anything about his children, and he did not know about mine. It was safer that way.

'So we took on new identities. Which is why I hesitated when giving you my name earlier. You see, my new identity is Johan Hindemith, but my real name is, as I told you, Harald Wolff.'

Calista took a few moments to absorb the full enormity of this amazing story, still sluggish from lack of sleep. 'A secret project to breed genius children...' she said thoughtfully to herself. And then to the Professor, 'But, there's one thing I still don't understand. How does Jake fit into all of this?' She was already guessing that it was something to do with his sister.

'I can't be sure of course, because it was many, many years ago – but I think Jake Winters' sister was somehow part of the project, either as a surrogate mother, or as an egg donor. As I said, there were hundreds who went in and out of the clinic. I'm told her name was Kara, and yes, I do vaguely remember a "Kara" in the programme. You see, she's been missing all this time, and Jake has never stopped searching for her... Like I said, nobody died in the fire. We were very careful about that. But all the records were burnt, and we made sure that there were no back-ups off-site. So I honestly don't know what happened to her. She's still missing after all these years...'

'Poor Jake!' cried Calista.

The Professor was at a loss. 'I wish I knew what had happened to her – if anything, to put him out of his misery, give him and his family closure. But unfortunately, because of all Jake's digging around, he's brought a lot of unwanted attention to himself – and the project. In fact, that's how he came to be on my radar.'

Here the Professor heaved a deep sigh and lapsed into silence for some time. Then he said, 'So that's my story...'

He had not realised that Calista was weeping – from a mixture of exhaustion, desperation for Jake and his sister, as well as the Professor's own sad story.

When the Professor heard her faint snuffling, he walked over, and held out a tentative, awkward hand to pat her shoulder. Calista immediately threw her arms around him, sobbing into his sweater. It smelled of mothballs.

The Professor hesitated, but then returned her embrace. 'There, there,' he murmured, listening to her sobs.

But then the silence was interrupted by the sound of click-click-clicking from behind. Paw nails against the cement floor.

Calista withdrew, and looked up to find Acuzio standing there, wet and panting. He had swum through the lake of Avernus on his way back, to throw off any scent that could be followed, and he was exhausted – still, the dog managed to muster the energy to weakly lick his master's outstretched hand.

The Professor fell to his knees to feel the dog's body all over, and was relieved to find no damage. The old man gave him a hug, not caring about the wet.

'Good dog, Acuzio. Good dog!'

•••————————————————————•••

Acuzio did not understand exactly why the master put his arms around him, squeezing him so hard that he could hardly breathe. He was not alarmed, for by now he understood it was a strange but harmless thing that humans did. Perhaps, he wondered, as he sat for quite a while being squashed by his master's affection, that this was the human equivalent to licks and tail-wagging. Still, he bore it happily, tired as he was, in the satisfying knowledge that he had carried out his master's command of exiting his territory, and dropping those things he'd been given far, far away.

Yes, he was very content indeed to be safe in Avernus in the arms of his dear Master.

J.Y. Sam

# 7 SECRETS

Penny Thompson was a keeper of secrets.

She counted them out meticulously, locking them away in her memory so that she would never forget. But hers were not the everyday secrets that normal people have – a child whispering gossip into a friend's ear, or the secret affair of a lonely housewife, or a pensioner's insatiable need to steal. No, her secrets masked the purest and most unadulterated evil... The type that could consume into blackness the very essence of life itself.

And she came in the guise of a benign, ordinary-looking woman, making her secret even more deadly.

She was a typist for a conveyancing solicitor, and every day performed her work to a sufficiently run-of-the-mill level, speaking with a small, nasal voice, and forcing fleeting disingenuous smiles onto her face when required. She was reliable at opening the office at 9am every day, and locking up at exactly 5pm, effecting a perfectly acceptable goodbye, but inwardly glad to see the back of everyone.

But this time, when the staff left their shared office space, instead of locking up and leaving as she usually did, she carried her weekend bag into the ladies', locked the door, and took off her grey polyester suit and white pumps. She replaced them with leggings, ankle boots, and a cropped leather jacket. Scraping her mousy hair back, she pulled on a thick, honey-brown wig, then put on make-up that her work colleagues never once saw on her pasty face: crudely applied eyeshadow, blusher, and cinnamon lipstick. The last thing to come out of the holdall was an old messenger bag, within which she checked for a bottle of chloroform, a phial of clear liquid, a rag, an old towel, and several packets of syringes clinically sealed within crisp white foil.

Extracting her mobile phone, she swapped out the SIM and turned it back on, whereupon two double-beeps instantly announced that text messages had been received. As she read the first message, her small beady eyes creased. Unusually, she had been given multiple jobs, and all of them to be done that night...

The second message gave the details of the hits: the first was a homeless boy who lived in an old disused warehouse on an industrial estate, the second was an accountant and his daughter.

She checked the time, then looked up the addresses in her offline streetmap app – of course she had already turned off cellular data, wi-fi, and GPS, so as not to be traceable. She scraped together all her stuff and threw it into the weekend bag, taking one last look around before unbolting the door to leave.

When Penny Thompson – looking very unlike herself – walked out of the workspace building, she bumped straight into her boss, who was returning to the office because he had forgotten some files. He looked her straight in the eye, and apologised profusely, without one hint of recognition. When he walked away, he surreptitiously checked his back pocket; his wallet was still there.

Not in a million years would he have guessed the dark, secret life of his quiet little administrator.

# 8 AN EVENING LIKE ANY OTHER

For once, Milly Bythaway and her father, Brian, were sitting down together, eating a TV dinner. He had finished work early, and so treated his daughter by making dinner himself – though burnt egg on burnt toast didn't turn out to be quite the treat he wanted... Unusually for a father and teenage daughter, they had exactly the same taste in programmes.

The BBC regional news was on. *'...recent inquiry from the Rail Accident Investigation Branch, on the train crash seven months ago in west London when two trains collided into each other at speed, killing both drivers instantly – leaving 26 passengers dead, and many in critical condition...'*

Milly shook her head at the news so close to home, whilst at the same time trying to pick out burnt bits from her food.

'Oh, I almost forgot to say, Pigeon,' her father remarked. 'Someone from the Inland Revenue's coming over at five.'

'Here?' asked Milly.

'Yes. I know, it's odd. They've never asked to meet me at home before. Very strange.' He glanced at his watch which showed the wrong time. He tapped it loudly, but there was no hope.

'It's 4.29, Dad,' said Milly, after pressing the guide on the TV to check.

'I'd better get a move on then,' said Brian, getting up to clear away the dinner things.

Milly went upstairs to her father's little office as she usually did after dinner, to continue her homework. She had already finished writing lengthy and brilliant documents, stored in a 'Homework A' folder – but then, with a sinking heart, she copied them to a second folder, 'Homework B', where she began vandalising them with bad structuring, inconsistent layout, spelling mistakes, and general errors. Dumbing her work down.

The doorbell rang downstairs, and Milly immediately remembered the 5pm Inland Revenue appointment her father had mentioned.

She glanced at the computer clock, it was 4.44pm, and she could only assume that the rep was early.

After a few minutes of editing, she suddenly realised that it was very quiet. She stopped to listen. But there was only silence. She pushed her chair and got up, but to her astonishment, felt a gloved hand clamp over her mouth from behind! Another hand grasped both her wrists. She was unable to cry out, could not struggle free – a vice-like force was holding her. There came a jarring prick in her arm, and several seconds passed, before her body went limp, and she fell back into the arms of her captor.

•••————————————————•••

It was about 10 in the evening, and Tai had left Dog and the kittens alone in the warehouse while he went out foraging for food.

He was out of sorts, because it was steak day, and the never-seen old man hadn't left out anything at all, hadn't even come to the door, although Tai had waited almost an hour crouching at the side of the house. His limbs were aching and prickling with pins and needles – but there was nothing to do but give up and search elsewhere.

He managed to find a couple of out-of-date sandwiches in the local supermarket bins, and then turned to go back home.

When he arrived at the warehouse, Dog and the kittens were nowhere to be found. Tai wasn't alarmed, because in the safety of night, Dog often went on short walks around the deserted back streets of the industrial estate, with a line of the six kittens padding faithfully behind her, lit only by the glow of the moon. If anyone could see them, it was quite a sight. The kittens were still small at just six weeks old, and they always made sure not to stray far from Dog, who led the way – she looked back every now and again to check that her 'pack' was nearby. But the little creatures were distracted easily, pouncing on each other, sometimes chasing after a tumbling leaf or discarded rubbish, and swiping at moths. So it wasn't an easy job.

They were of varying colours and markings – one was powdery ginger, another grey with fine black stripes, yet another was black with white socks, and another had fur the colour of treacle. And despite Dog's milk drying up after the death of her puppies, the sucking reflex of the newfound kittens had stimulated the production of milk again – so the little animals were wanting for nothing.

At the warehouse, Tai lounged on his bed to eat a sandwich as he waited for their return. But then, a strange prickling sensation crept down his neck, travelling along his spine. He sat up, sensing danger.

Out of nowhere came the soft sound of a muffled explosion, followed by a smooth whoosh. A sudden stabbing pain pierced his side. He could feel the point of a needle piercing between his ribs, and then a cold sensation of wet sticky blood trickling out, onto his fingers. He fell backwards onto the ground, and he lay helpless, unable to move, staring up at the broken ceiling.

Consciousness slipped slowly away, as he watched through gaping roof-holes pinprick stars high up, glistening against a purple sky. He thought of his mother and Dog and the kittens and Cat, as the stars began dropping to the earth like molten bullets, gradually fading away.

# 9  THE MAN WITH NO NAME

It was strange shopping in the dead of night, in a completely empty superstore. Outside, through large glass panes, Calista could see that the street and carpark were just as deserted as inside.

She stifled a yawn – earlier, she had passed out on the couch in the Professor's computer room, succumbing to several hours of much-needed sleep, before the Professor woke her rather excitedly. 'We have guests!' he announced, practically bursting with the news. 'And I need to get supplies.'

'I'm coming too,' said Calista, not wanting to be left alone.

And so here they were, in Madeley's superstore, shopping in the middle of the night.

For the first time in Calista's life, she was able to shop without needing to count her pennies. She was in her element! And the precariously-packed trolley she heaved through the aisles was filled to bursting. Apart from food, she had included clothing, shoes, make-up, hair-straighteners, and enough pot noodles to last for weeks...

She heard the shuffling of feet, and poked her head around the mountain of goods, to find the Professor led by the startlingly beautiful Acuzio. The dog wagged his tail at her, and Calista stroked his head, whereupon he licked her hand in return.

'Did you get the Earl Grey?' asked Professor Wolff casually, as if they had always gone shopping together. It was a surreal experience for Calista, after everything – the attempt on her life, finding herself in Avernus, hearing the Professor's incredible story, as well as discovering the link to Jake's sister. But retail therapy was giving her life. 'Um, yeah,' she said, sheepishly glancing at her massive trolley haul. 'With a few other bits and bobs too...'

When they finished, they exited without paying – taking the store-room door, wheeling through the warehouse, and then leaving via a backdoor that opened directly onto the carpark.

'Tell me again why we're able to take all this stuff,' asked Calista.

'I own the chain...' the Professor replied, a little confused, because he'd already told her.

Calista smiled to herself. Hearing it again made her happy. Very happy. Having struggled with very little money for most of her life, it was incredibly liberating to just be able to get whatever she liked.

In the parking lot, a chunky steel grey FX4 taxi cab was the only car waiting, and as they drew closer, the engine fired up and the lights turned on. The car's upgraded Rolls Royce engine purred softly.

The driver's door opened, and a large middle-aged man struggled awkwardly out of the driver's seat. He was pale with mousy hair, and had no outstanding features. He said nothing, and the Professor began gesturing with his hands – sign language. The driver nodded as he watched, and he then did a double-take at Calista's overloaded trolley, commandeered it, and wheeled it to the boot. Meanwhile they got into the back seats, and waited for the driver to return.

The large man moved slowly, and deliberately, so that it seemed an age before he got back into the driver's seat – yet when he fired up the engine, he drove at lightning speed, manoeuvring the car with smooth, Formula 1 style precision.

Calista quickly clicked in her seatbelt, and held on for dear life. 'He's fast! And deaf?...' she asked.

'Yes, he's both deaf and mute,' the Professor explained. 'And also has no family. You see, in my line of work, I must stay incognito – which makes him the ideal person to work for me, because he would never, and indeed cannot, tell a soul about me...'

'Can't hear *or* speak? That's tough...' she said, warming to him. 'What's his name?'

'Well, the thing is... he doesn't have a name.'

Calista blinked, incredulous. 'Wait, back up. He has no name?! How's that possible? Everyone's got a name.'

'He was given a name by a foster carer, but he didn't like it, and refuses to use it. So I just refer to him as the Chauffeur.'

Calista fell into silence.

'He has a story, though,' said the Professor. 'A sad one. Which I'll tell you sometime...'

Calista wanted to hear it now, but decided against asking. They remained silent for the rest of the journey, and after about 15 minutes found themselves turning into the industrial estate – entering on the east side, where there were two rows of double-height garages. They drew up to the penultimate garage on the right, and its door whooshed slowly open. They drove in, and the door reversed back down, swallowing them up inside. The car stopped on a circular galvanised steel surface, and the Chauffeur switched off the car engine.

Calista wondered why nobody was getting out, but, to her surprise, the sound of whirring machinery signalled the circular floor beneath them dropping slowly down. As they descended, Calista watched in amazement as great black walls slid gracefully up around them, until they reached the lower level, and the steel platform clunked smoothly into place.

The Professor let himself out, and Calista followed, while the Chauffeur unpacked the goods into another trolley.

The two walked ahead, through yet another maze of passageways. They arrived at a secure gateway similar to the one they had gone through from the bridge entrance, but instead of the junk room, it led to a long passageway. The Professor motioned for her to follow him left, down another corridor. Calista counted five doors on each side, and she peered into the first one. It was a shadowy room, that had an almost clinical feel to it, containing a small sofa, side table, a single bed, and a desk and chair, all in the same dark décor. She realised that these were the bedrooms. 'Is this for me?' she asked.

The Professor nodded, and she entered, while he waited by the door. 'You might as well get some rest,' he said. 'The guests... they had to be given mild tranquillisers to calm them, and to bring them in safely without hindrance. So they're sleeping now.'

'Who... who are they?'

The Professor's eyes lit up. 'I'm pleased to say we found two of the children from Project Ingenious.'

Calista gasped. 'Really? That's wonderful! But why bring them in now?'

'Well, I've been thinking about doing it for some time now. You see, my people found one of them recently, after he'd gone missing a few months ago. And then – just a few days ago – one of the children had been snatched from her house. And so, after Jake's disappearance, and what happened to you, I felt certain that all the children were in grave danger – that's why we decided to bring them into safety.'

'One of them was snatched?!' said Calista, eyes wide.

'Yes – Jemima Jenkins,' he said, looking away briefly, upset. 'She was the last of the seven we produced. The youngest... She's been missing for two days now, with no sign of her whereabouts. My people are looking for her as we speak...' He sighed. 'But at least we have two of the children here. Safe and sound!'

Calista wondered what these super-intelligent children might look like – she imagined pallid, scrawny children, with high foreheads, and large mesmerising eyes...

The Professor interrupted her thoughts. 'We'll meet them in time. But we should first get some rest ourselves. It's unlikely they'll wake before morning.'

'Sure thing, Prof,' said Calista, realising how exhausted she was.

'In the meantime, please, make yourself comfortable, and let me know if there's anything you need.'

Just then, the Chauffeur appeared behind the Professor with Calista's trolley of shopping, panting from exertion. Calista jumped up, beamed at the man in gratitude, and wheeled the trolley of goodies into her room. 'I've got everything I need, thanks,' she said. She rummaged round to extract the Professor's Earl Grey tea and a few other items. 'These are yours,' she said, and piled them in the Chauffeur's arms. She yawned fitfully - so tired, she was certain she'd fall asleep straight away.

The Professor bid her goodnight, and promptly left with the Chauffeur.

But unlike Calista, he knew he wouldn't be able to sleep.

He made his way to the computer room, and sat down in front of the screen. He mumbled for it to switch on, and the black screen lit up – the leaden tones of a robotic voice welcomed the Professor to 'The Workstation'. Through a combination of voice commands, and hand gestures, the old man was able to fully control the computer.

He sighed deeply, before opening a programme that he had been working on for many months – it was to help him search for the man that had worked with him in Project Ingenious. He had not seen Dr Axel Kendra in 12 years. Like him, he would have taken on a new identity, a new name, which meant there was no trace of the man on the worldwide web. Still, he never stopped searching. He desperately needed him now, needed to locate his children, in order to bring them into safety.

That is, if they were still alive.

# 10  BITTER

Dog had returned from her nightly walk with the kittens, blissfully unaware that Tai had been captured and taken.

As she neared the warehouse, she picked up on foreign smells all around, and she quickly became agitated, running from one place to the other, sniffing scents she did not recognise. Urgently she raced around the entire building, even sniffing the ground outside, but found no-one. The kittens – tired after their long walk – were mewling to be fed, and so she resigned and went back inside to them.

A growling stomach reminded Dog that she too was hungry, and seeing the sandwich abandoned on the floor in the cellophane, she ripped it open with her teeth, and both she and the kittens devoured it. When it was finished, she lay down and let them drink her milk, while she yawned, and promptly fell asleep. The kittens sucked with their eyes closed, paws kneading softly against her fur – and it wasn't long before they too were drifting off.

Outside the night had turned still and black – and above, the moon floated milky white behind gossamer clouds. Still the boy had not returned.

Dog suddenly awoke, panting from thirst, her tongue lolling at the side of her mouth – she was always thirsty suckling the little ones. She got up, and the kittens tumbled into a heap, while she went out to the next room for a drink from the water bowl. When she returned, she picked up the kittens by the scruff of their necks, one by one, placing them inside the tea-chest. But she saw that the stripy kitten lay unusually still. It had always been the smallest, and the weakest, and often fell behind on their walks – uninterested in playing like the others. It just lay there, mewling weakly.

Dog nudged it gently several times, but it did not move. Then she licked it, again and again, her actions becoming increasingly urgent even as the kitten became more lethargic. But in time, even her cries petered out. Eventually her head dropped, and she stopped moving.

Dog got up and began yelping at it – the other kittens jarred awake by the noise, and meowing in protest. But the stripy one still did not move, did not make a sound.

Dog watched it keenly, waiting, her large eyes locked onto the little creature. Hoping upon hope. But it was taking too long, and in the end, she knew. She knew that nothing could be done...

Dog paced around, whining and fretting and crying – eventually returning to the little kitten, and lying down next to it. She rested her nose against the stripy one's belly, breathing in its scent, locking in the memory of her smell. As she inhaled and exhaled, the kitten's fur moved up and back, up and back, caught in Dog's bereft breath.

That awful aching feeling, once again, cracked deep within her. It rose up, through her bursting heart, up into the back of her throat. She sat up, threw her head back, and let out a howl, so loud, that it penetrated deep into the night.

She dropped her head for breath, then threw it back again, letting out howl after agonising howl, over and over.

*Not again*, she thought with every breath she drew. *Not again*, she howled.

•••————————————————————•••

Pensioner, Livia Sandler lived on the south-west border of the industrial estate, in a 1920s ground-floor maisonette – which she hated. There wasn't much of a view. Her front garden looked out onto the grey office blocks and warehouses of the industrial estate. On the meagre inheritance from her parents, this was all she could afford – and for this, she repeatedly cursed her lot in life. She was a bitter woman, coming from a family that had, since childhood, cocooned her in a web of blame and recrimination. Not much, if anything, had gone right in their lives – and as such this gave her the right, she thought mulishly, of taking out her discontent on anyone and anything that crossed her path.

Her entire life was consumed by looking for things to complain about.

She cursed the rain when she wanted sun, and then, when there was sun, she swore at it for being too hot. She spat at cats as they pooped on her grass, and shouted at dog-owners for letting their 'nasty animals' mark her gate. She grumbled at lazy postmen for being late and missing days, and she forever cursed her dead mother for moving to a maisonette that was right on the border of a great big ugly industrial estate – the worst view in the world.

And so, when Livia Sandler was abruptly awoken at an unearthly hour of the night, by the constant howling of some crazed animal on the estate, she bore it for no more than 10 minutes, before swearing under her breath and calling the police.

Then she moaned that they took exactly 43 minutes to come – and, when they arrived, made sure to make the best use of the opportunity to grumble and complain.

The policemen were only too glad to get away from this disagreeable old woman, and they quickly left to drive around the industrial estate, now and then stopping the engines to listen. The loud howling eventually led them to a derelict warehouse. Inside, the darkness was almost palpable, and their pocket torches barely penetrated the syrupy blackness – and yet they found the source of the noise quickly. It was a Doberman whining pathetically against one of the walls, neck bent downward as if it bore an invisible load. It blinked in the light, glassy eyes bewildered and confused. To their surprise, the policemen managed to grab the dog with little resistance. They looped a rope around its neck, and led it to the back seat of the car.

Dog could only whimper in despair and stare helplessly out of the window as she was driven away.

•••————————————————————•••

Inside the warehouse, hidden in the shadows, were the litter of kittens – one of them lay motionless and silent, surrounded by fidgety siblings. Its small body growing colder and colder.

# 11  THE STUFF OF DREAMS

Just weeks ago, the night before her first AS Level exam, Calista was desperately trying to get to sleep. There was nothing for it but to phone Jake. 'Sing to me,' she pleaded, and rolled over, restless.

Jake had been expecting her call – before every exam period, nerves always got the better of her. And so he propped his mobile on the desk, pulled out his guitar, and sang her favourite song – Ella Fitzgerald's ***Dream a Little Dream of Me***. Calista didn't mind that he hummed now and then whenever he forgot the words. She just lay in bed, curled on her side, the phone pressed against her ear.

It was the only song her grandfather had learnt to sing off by heart; he had memorised it specially for her. For when her parents had left her home alone while they went out pubbing and binge-drinking, which was often. She would phone her Gramps, and he always came over to sing her to sleep, even though he was tone deaf and out-of-tune. It didn't matter. The song was reminiscent of a sense of belonging, and assured love.

So as Jake sang to the melancholy strum of his guitar, Calista felt that both her grandfather, and Jake, were close to her – so close. And it wasn't long before, caught up in the hazy solace of it, she at last drifted off.

But as Calista slept deep in the heart of Avernus, she dreamt that, this time, she was singing to Jake, down a coiling telephone line that disappeared far into the distance. Her voice was silky smooth, rivalling even Ella's – yet it was heavy with the ache of not knowing where Jake was, what had become of him...

Dreaming now in impressionistic paint-strokes of blue, she became a voyeur, spying on young lovers – herself and Jake – as they sheltered together under a mulberry tree. Its branches heavy with hanging catkins that scattered perfumed droplets. High above, the sky was a brooding indigo canopy. There came a flash-change of canvas, and the deep underground cavern of Avernus quivered and unfolded, morphing into a giant monster, its dark, ragged mouth yawning, wider and wider. It swallowed her whole, and, curled in a tight ball, she tumbled helplessly into its huge belly. And in her dream, Calista looked down at herself – exactly as she slept now, curled on her side, arms tightly hugging knees to chest. Another change of focus, a brush-stroke sweeping across to the room next to hers. And there she saw a lone, sleeping child. It stirred, and turned, revealing pitted, undead skin, and an unnaturally high forehead. Across it, a single messy gash, stitched together with zigzag sutures oozing and dripping both grey matter and blood...

---

Calista woke with a start, and gasped. Beads of perspiration glistening on flushed skin. She found that her pillow was damp with tears.

She sat up, panting, and dried her cheek with a sleeve. The room was dim and empty – and it seemed like night. She stared at the door, remembering: the Professor bidding goodnight, tapping his way out, the bolt clunking into place.

Doubt suddenly gripped her.

She slipped out of bed, and padded across to the door in bare feet – the floor surprisingly warm. Thankfully it was unlocked; her faith restored in the Professor.

She poked her head out into the corridor and looked up and down, wondering momentarily if she was still dreaming – it had seemed so real. She pinched herself a couple of times, and satisfied, walked out into the passageway and across to the next door. After unclicking the lock, the handle smoothly gave way, and the door swung silently open. Inside, a dim night lamp went on automatically.

And there, in the bed, was the form of a slight girl, lying with her back towards her – just like her dream.

Calista's heart thudded as she tiptoed closer. The girl snuffled and turned to her other side, and Calista froze, but the girl was still fast asleep. She was relieved to see that she had a perfectly proportioned head with porcelain skin – no gash, and no stitches, across her forehead. She drew closer, drawn by the girl's intense expression, even in sleep – wisps of dark hair tumbling out from under a knitted hat. She looked so... normal. Calista heaved a deep sigh, and quietly left the room, closing the door behind her.

The Professor's voice from behind startled her. 'Calista?' he whispered.

Calista jumped and turned. 'I... was just checking she's alright,' she said, trying not to sound startled.

'And? How is she?'

'She's good. Fast asleep.'

The Professor popped open the glass face of his wristwatch, and fingered the position of its hands. 'It's 3.30...'

Calista shrugged. 'Oops. Didn't realise the time. Sorry.' She made to go back to her room, but as she passed, she gave the old man a peck on his cheek, as naturally as if she were kissing her grandfather. She noticed dimly his red-rimmed eyes, and that he was still dressed. He hadn't even gone to bed.

The Professor waited, listening, as Calista went into her room – he turned to lock the door, and then shuffled off. Back in the computer room, he lay down on the couch and covered himself with a blanket. In the background, the Workstation emitted a light, soporific hum as it continued executing the search program. He lay back and closed his eyes, sleep tugging him. As he drifted off, a glimmer of a wry smile flashed briefly across his face; it had been a while since someone had given him a goodnight kiss.

●●●────────────────────●●●

The next morning, Calista and the Professor were sitting opposite each other in a brightly-lit kitchen-cum-dining room, with slick granite worktops, stainless steel fittings – a refreshing change from the dark interiors of the other rooms. The Chauffeur, who was preparing their food, looked somewhat ridiculous in a stripy blue apron and chef's hat. The Professor had earlier asked him to prepare them a fruit salad with their cooked breakfast, and freshly squeezed Murcia orange juice.

As they waited, Calista watched as the Professor fingered the objects on their table to gauge positioning and distance – then, with deftness, he poured a teapot of steaming tea into their china cups. Not a drop was spilled.

She watched him warily; it was strange being able to examine someone so closely, without the embarrassment of being seen doing it. The old man's hair was still slightly damp, combed back neatly in thick silver-black waves. He looked well for his years, but his eyes were crazed with fine red veins and underlined with grey shadows, testament that he had little sleep. Sometimes his gaze seemed to fall on her, and Calista smiled reflexively. But then his eyes flit away without recognition, zigzagging downwards.

The Chauffeur approached and placed bowls of perfectly diced fruit in front of them – a fragrant aroma of melon, kiwi, peach, and apple. But before he left, Calista grabbed his arm with both hands, and looked up at him. The Chauffeur started, a thick gravelly sound coming from his throat. He looked with alarm from the Professor to the girl.

'Chauffeur!!' Calista said excitedly. 'I want... to find... a name for you!' She spoke unnecessarily loud and slow.

The large man watched her lips, thought about this, and then tapped the Professor's shoulder. Whereupon the old man held out his hands, and the Chauffeur signed directly onto them – a series of light touches, strokes, and gestures. The Professor nodded, and turned back towards Calista. 'I'm afraid he doesn't like the idea. He says that names are merely labels – unnecessary. He told me simply, 'I am me, and you are you. That is enough.''

Calista frowned, and turned to address the Chauffeur directly. 'No, no! You... are your name,' she mouthed. 'It tells people... who you are. Sets you apart.' She tapped her chest. 'See, my name... is Calista... Matheson,' she said. 'I *want* to give you... a name. I'm good... with names!' she exclaimed, and then thought for a moment. Actually, she thought for quite some time, but no names sprung to mind. Except for 'Jake'. And she suddenly felt deflated.

By this time, the Chauffeur had become impatient, shook his head at her, and left to prepare the next course.

Calista sighed, and began picking at the fruit dejectedly.

The Professor sensed that something was wrong. 'Is... everything okay, Calista?'

Calista stabbed a piece of melon and popped it into her mouth, though she wasn't hungry. She chewed mechanically and swallowed. 'No, it's not, Professor,' she said miserably. 'I need something to do. I... I'm going crazy not knowing where Jake is. I need a distraction. If I don't keep busy, I'm gonna go mad.' She stabbed a piece of apple, and peach, and kiwi. But then dropped the loaded fork on the plate with a clatter.

'I'm sorry,' said the old man. He thought for a moment. 'As it happens, I do have some work for you. I'll show you after breakfast. But first, please, you must eat and drink. Then we will work in the computer room together. We should look properly through Jake's computer, for clues.'

Calista remembered. 'And that stuff I downloaded as well.'

'The files from the government server?' He shook his head. 'I'm afraid you won't find much there. You see, I've already looked into them. They are old files, pre Project Ingenious – only targeting potential candidates from the medical and scientific communities. Believe me, I've checked and double-checked. You see, I have a good and close... contact in Downing Street, whom I trust. He is very sympathetic toward our plight, and is willing to help in any way possible. You can of course look through the files and see for yourself if you want.'

Calista sighed again. 'Okay...'

'But don't give up hope! We might yet find clues that will tell us what might have... where Jake may...' The Professor had to choose his words carefully, he didn't want her to think the worst. Not yet.

'Where he might have gone?' volunteered Calista.

'Yes, exactly.'

There came a faint, repetitive beeping sound – and Calista looked around, puzzled.

'It's me,' said the Professor, resting a finger on the receiver in his ear. He listened for several seconds, and then looked up at her, his eyes bright. 'Motion sensors,' he said. 'They've detected that one of our guests has awoken. It's the boy! We'd better go, now.'

The Professor scraped back the chair, and Calista jumped up and followed him. He was already hurrying out of the door and through the dizzying twists and turns of the corridors. As they walked Calista asked, 'Just had a thought, Prof. What about the boy's family? Won't they be wondering where he is?'

The Professor shook his head, without slowing. 'We looked carefully into his family. His father left when he was just two years old, so he lived alone with his mother. And then we discovered that they were evicted from their flat several months ago – they actually lived just a short distance from here. We searched everywhere for them, but they had just vanished. And then, one of my people suddenly thought of searching amongst the homeless, and thankfully we soon heard reports of a homeless boy living on this very industrial estate. Can you imagine! I sent my men to fetch him, but I'm afraid we had to use a tranquilliser dart on him because of his... special abilities. But up to now we still haven't found his mother.'

They reached the bedroom corridor from the south end, and stopped at a door halfway along, on the opposite side to Calista's room.

When they entered, they saw Tai pulling himself up, groggy – his long dreadlocks swinging as he moved. Ruddy and chocolate-skinned, he had striking features on a high-cheekboned face that shone like an oil painting – at its centre, doleful, paper-white eyes. Those eyes locked on Calista, and she smiled reassuringly to put him at ease.

He managed to sit up, and began rubbing the back of his neck, his eyes darting from her to the Professor.

The Professor hung around the door while Calista ventured further in. 'Hey there,' she said gently, not wanting to startle him.

The boy watched her. He already sensed that they were not there to harm him, only help. And when he looked over at the old man in the doorway – silhouetted against the corridor lighting – there was a feeling of familiarity that he could not place.

Calista reached the bed, and perched slowly at the end of it. 'Hi,' she said, waving a hand in an arc. 'My name's Calista Matheson. But everyone calls me Cal.'

For the first time in months, the boy opened his mouth to speak. 'I... I'm Tai,' he said, with a soft Caribbean lilt. His voice was in the process of breaking, a little hoarse, but not yet as deep as a man's. He stared at the girl. It had been so long since he'd had human interaction, that he forgot it was rude to stare. Calista didn't mind – with her looks, she was used to it. She held his gaze in return.

The Professor drew closer, and as he did, a spark of recognition came to the boy. From the old man's form, his gait, the slight curve of his back, he realised it was the man who left out meat for the foxes. And he realised something else – he was blind.

Calista introduced him. 'This is Professor Wolff. Harry.'

But the boy was looking away, distracted by something in the corridor. He thought it was Dog, but then saw with disappointment that it was a much larger husky, with light grey fur, and piercing blue eyes.

Noticing his interest, Calista introduced him too. 'That's Acuzio. Acuzio, come say hello.' The dog willingly came closer and hopped up on the side of the bed, his tail wagging. Tai stroked him, saying, 'I have a dog too...'

'Uh, we didn't know,' said the Professor. 'Didn't realise you had a dog. But please don't worry, Tai – we'll find him for you, and bring him here.'

Tai made to get out of bed, but a sharp pain flared in his side, and he winced.

'I-I'm so sorry,' said the Professor. 'We had to bring you in very... suddenly. I can only apologise profusely. But we needed to ensure you were brought in safely, and that you didn't run away. You see, there are some very dangerous people out there, who... who...' He didn't want to alarm the boy, but Calista jumped in.

'One of them came after me – and she had a knife! I think she wanted to kill me! Thankfully the Professor called the police, and they came just in the nick of time. The woman got away though...'

Tai looked from her to the Professor. 'Why would they want to hurt us?'

'We're not sure,' said the Professor. 'But my people are working on finding out. At least you're safe now. So please, rest,' said the Professor, reaching out a hand. 'I'll make some calls, and we'll bring your dog here. I promise you, this is for the best.'

Tai took his hand. It was light and dappled with age spots, the skin giving way easily under his fingers. The boy looked up at the glow of light surrounding the old man – it was diaphanous and white. And he understood now that he was telling the truth, and was genuinely concerned for him. Tai acquiesced, and sat back.

Calista smiled kindly at the boy. 'Everything's gonna be okay,' she said, and then she thought of something. 'Stay here – I'm gonna make you a pot noodle,' she said, as if pot noodles were the solution to all woes. But before she left, she said, 'I know this is all new to you, and it must be hard for you to trust us. But even though I've only just met the Prof myself, I know that he's a good man. And he'll help you.'

But Tai could only look at her. He already knew that, very well.

•••————————————•••

Milly Bythaway woke up from a long night's sleep feeling unusually light-headed. And then she remembered – and her head suddenly exploded with alarm, frustration, helplessness, fear.

Her father, who was lying on the couch on the other side of the room, jumped up and went to her. 'Milly!' he said. 'Thank goodness. How're you feeling?'

His embrace calmed her a little. 'I-I think I'm okay.'

Brian stopped to look her over; she seemed fine physically. 'Thank goodness! That's a relief. I'm okay too, I think.' He perched on the bed. 'But we're locked in...'

'What happened? Where are we?' she asked, anxiously looking around.

'When someone rang our doorbell yesterday, I thought it was the lady from the Inland Revenue. But after opening the door, there was a man dressed all in black, with a mask – a mask! I tried calling out to warn you, but he'd clamped a hand over my mouth and injected me with something.' He rubbed his arm. It still hurt.

Milly realised she had a sore arm too.

'But, look at this.' He stepped back and waved toward the table. 'Look at what they left out for us.' There was a tray filled with a neatly arranged breakfast – two small packets of chocolate rice crispies, a jug of milk, fresh strawberries, and a little bowl of dipping chocolate.

'That's mad!' said Milly. 'How could they know?'

'I've been asking myself the same thing,' said Brian. 'All your favourite breakfast things, since you were little... Apart from your mother, the only people who knew exactly what you liked were–'

At that moment they heard footsteps in the corridor outside. Father and daughter glanced at each other, anxious, and Brian quickly looked around to see what he could grab. But there was no time, the door was already unbolting – and he could only stand protectively in front of his daughter.

The door opened, and an old man walked in – by his side was a large dog who looked at them with excited curiosity.

Brian recognised the Professor immediately, but then saw that his eyes were staring blankly into the middle distance.

'Professor?!'

'Brian, Melody!' he said. 'I'm sorry for all the cloak and dagger, but...'

'I can't believe it!' said Brian in wonder, relaxing. 'It's been years.'

'Yes, 12 years,' said the Professor, though it seemed much, much longer.

'But... what happened to you?' Brian couldn't help asking.

'Please don't be taken aback by my... condition. After we separated, there was in an accident, a fire, and the smoke burnt my eyes. I lost my sight.'

Brian couldn't help giving him a hug, then stepped back to look at him – the man's eyes were darker, and deeper, his skin etched with worry lines.

'I heard about Savannah,' said the Professor, shaking his head. 'I'm really, really sorry.'

Brian looked away. 'I... can't quite get to grips with it, her death. It's been seven years now, but sometimes, momentarily, I forget...' He tapered off.

'Believe me, I understand,' said the Professor. He took a deep breath. 'But I need to explain why I brought you here.' He paused, deciding in the end to come right out with it. 'One of the children is missing,' he said.

Brian and Milly looked at each other, knowing exactly what he meant by 'the children'.

'She was the youngest child born to the project,' explained the Professor. 'She's 13 now. Back then, we called her Omega – Meg for short. She's been missing for several days now, and we're extremely worried. Also, someone came after a young lady called Calista, very recently – I believe with no good intention. And we think both incidents are linked. In fact, I'm sure of it... Thankfully Calista managed to get away, and she's here too. So that's why we had to bring both of you into safety – as soon as possible.'

Brian nodded. 'I understand.' He looked around. 'But, where are we exactly?'

'It's an underground shelter I call Avernus. Named after the Italian Lago d'Averno, or Lake of Avernus – we're underneath a small lake you see.'

Milly, who had remained silent all this time, could not help chiming in. 'Yes I've read about Lago d'Averno, it's in the Campania region of Italy, in the south – owned by the Famiglia Cardillo.'

They both turned toward her, the Professor was delighted to hear both the girl's voice, how it had matured, as well as her encyclopaedic knowledge.

'Young Melody,' said the Professor, his voice softening. He stepped closer. 'I don't suppose you remember me?'

Milly looked at him. 'Yes, I do,' she said. 'Sort of.'

'Ah, that is because you were only three years old the last time we saw each other – which must seem like a lifetime to you, I'm sure.' He turned toward Brian. 'I suppose we should explain – may I ask how much you've already told her?'

This piqued Milly's interest considerably, and she swung her legs out of the bed, and sat up.

But instead of replying to the Professor, Brian looked at his daughter. 'You know, Milly, I've deliberately told you very little about your past, for your own good. To protect you.'

Milly nodded, 'Yes, I know, Dad.'

Sitting next to her, Brian took her hand. 'You're so clever, Milly, so intelligent – far wiser than anyone else your age. I know it's been hard for you, and I know you have lots of questions. I was going to tell you the whole story, and was working myself up to it. So, given what's happened...'

Milly gulped. Her throat dry.

Brian gathered his thoughts, his eyes glazing over as his mind turned back two decades. But then, unexpectedly, he smiled. 'Marrying your mother was the best day of my life,' he said with a tinge of sadness. 'She was beautiful, a dream come true, and everything I'd ever wanted in a partner. But, she needed more... She wanted a baby. And after nearly two long years of trying so many, many times, and spending thousands of pounds at fertility clinics, it seemed hopeless. And she soon sank into depression. I told her not to give up, but of course that's easy to say... Those months of struggling to come to terms with childlessness were miserable for her. I told her we could foster, or adopt, and that there were plenty of children who needed a home – but it wasn't for her. She needed her own child.

'Then, one day, she came home, all excited. She told me that after her last visit to the fertility clinic, signing release forms I think, she went to sit in the park for a bit. She told me that, in the park, a woman approached her on the bench. The woman explained that she'd seen her leave the clinic upset – and that she might be able to help. "Upset" was the word I think she used, but I knew that your mother must have been so much more than that. She must have been devastated. Anyway, the woman said she worked for such-and-such department of the government, and that they were recruiting for a special programme – a project – needing young women of a certain age, in peak health, to produce a... a special kind of baby. Your mother told her the fertility clinic had already tried everything, and nothing worked, but the woman explained that they could work around that by using a surrogate – they just needed donors to help produce a healthy test-tube embryo, to implant. Or something like that.

'The draw was that their technology was far more advanced than normal fertility clinics, which apparently were years behind theirs. We'd already looked at going down the surrogacy route, but we just couldn't afford it. And so, of course, when your mother heard about being part of this special project, she jumped at the chance.' Here, Brian looked up at the Professor. 'Maybe you should take over from here, Prof.'

'Yes, yes, of course,' said the Professor, and cleared his throat. 'The project, Project Ingenious, was set up by the government for a particular reason, which was explained clearly to your parents before they took part. It was a top-secret project – which is why they had to sign non-disclosure contracts, and why everything had to be kept under wraps. You see, the government's aim was to produce designer babies, so to speak, with particular genes grafted into their DNA that would give heightened intelligence. Child prodigies,' he said, 'for want of a better word.'

Milly felt strange. Suddenly everything was beginning to fall into place and make sense. For years she'd been overwhelmingly frustrated – both with wondering why she was so different from her peers, and also why she needed to stay below the radar – the pretence had been exhausting.

But now she was finally getting answers and explanations as to who she was. What she was. And it exhilarated her. It marked the starting point of something new and different – and, at last, it gave her the permission she yearned for, to be who she really was.

'Milly are you okay?' asked Brian.

She nodded, choked. 'Yes, sorry – I'm fine. Just a lot to take in.' She took several deep breaths, composing herself. 'I'm okay.'

Milly's father was quiet, introspective. The recounting of the story brought back a flood of memories and emotions. Particularly the moment when that precious tiny baby had been placed in Savannah's arms, and mother and child stared at each other for the first time, both in wonder – love at first sight. He was always going to be second after that. But he didn't mind. The miracle, their baby, made up for everything.

Milly looked at him. 'Don't get all mushy, Dad,' she said, reading him like a book.

He swiped at his eyes. 'What're you talking about! I'm fine.'

Milly squeezed his hand, but then a thought occurred to her. 'How many babies came out of the project, Professor?' she asked, her heart skipping a beat.

'There were seven in total,' he told her.

Milly could barely contain her excitement. 'A-are they here?' she asked tentatively. 'I mean, apart from the one missing...'

The Professor's heart sank. If only they were. 'No, not all. But we did manage to locate one other, and he was brought in last night too. Young Tai Jones.'

Milly's heart raced. This was the icing on the cake. She thought of L.M. Montgomery's *Anne of Green Gables*, and the eponymous protagonist's words. She knew them off by heart. *'Kindred spirits are not so scarce as I used to think. It's splendid to find out there are so many of them in the world. There's magic in recognising a kindred spirit...'* Tears welled up.

The Professor guessed what the girl was thinking, and a twinkle appeared in his eyes. 'Follow me,' he said, beaming. He tapped his way out into the corridor.

•••————————————————————•••

Calista and Tai were in one of the reading rooms – a quiet and cosy den, with several shelves of books, and a large inglenook fireplace. They sat on two well-worn armchairs on either side of the hearth. Tai had a tray of food and drink by his side, and they were chatting quietly in front of the warming fire.

They turned to find the Professor with two new people, an older man, and a girl. They were clearly father and daughter. When the girl with the hat came close, she did an unexpected thing. She threw her arms around Tai, and crushed the air out of his lungs in a long, hard hug. The scratchy yarn of her hat tickled his nose, but Tai didn't mind. He immediately relaxed, and put his arms around her.

Here was someone like him, he sensed. A kindred spirit.

For the rest of the day, the Professor and Calista fussed over Milly and Tai, making sure they were comfortable and had everything they needed. The Chauffeur cooked them a delicious lunch, and in the afternoon, the Professor showed his new guests around the main parts of Avernus – the dining room, the kitchen, the lounge rooms. The rest they could explore for themselves, though he warned them not to go beyond the doors with keypads, where there was a network of labyrinthine corridors. If they did, he told them in earnest, they could get lost and not be found for days...

'What's this room?' asked Milly, spying a large door down one corridor.

'Ah!' said the Professor, happy to explain. 'How could I forget. I call it the BC – the Bibliotheca Christian. Named after my son.'

Knowing that his son was dead, Calista glanced at the old man, but he seemed fine.

'A library!' gasped Milly. She thought of her own meagre book collection at home, precious though it was, the books had been read and re-read to death, and were practically falling apart.

The Professor pushed open the door, and they entered.

When Milly walked in, her hands flew to her mouth, and she could barely suppress a squeal of delight as she looked around in awe. The room was vast, octagonal, and about two stories high – with each wall containing row upon row of books, right up to the ceiling, their many colours glowing rich and warm. Narrow wooden landings were constructed at first-story level, hugging the walls, and criss-crossed with rolling ladders here and there. There were a variety of cosy armchairs, and tables, lamps and cushions, scattered haphazardly around.

'*Such stuff as dreams are made on,*' whispered Milly between her fingers, quoting Shakespeare's *Prospero*.

The Professor opened his arms. 'My little collection,' he said wryly. There must have been hundreds of thousands of books. 'A mixture of contemporary, antique, and even some rare first editions. You're welcome to borrow as many as you want. Er, except for the rare ones.'

Milly couldn't help herself – she just laughed out loud. It was literary heaven.

'Hmm, I imagine this'll keep you busy for a bit,' smiled Brian.

# 12 OSTRICH

When the Chauffeur was a teenager, cruel schoolmates used to call him 'retard', 'flid' or 'spazzy' – all of which he hated because, first of all, mentally, he was very capable, and secondly, his mother certainly never took thalidomide. Lastly, he was by no means incompetent, or uncoordinated, and had never had cerebral palsy.

He just couldn't hear or speak.

Also, he wasn't an invalid – and, as a person, he certainly needed no validation of his self-worth. Of that he was wholly confident. In fact, those kids' jeers and taunts and cruel choice of words were entirely invalid in themselves. Had he been able to tell them this, he would have.

Unlike most, the Chauffeur didn't mind being called disabled, or at a stretch, handicapped, because that was what he was. There was no going around it. And it amused him that people danced around the political correctness of such terms when talking to, or referring to him. But the Chauffeur had long ago come to terms with his limitations, and he had in fact embraced them. They were part of him now, and made him the person he was. And while he understood that not hearing and speaking was a disadvantage in many respects, in others, the silence, and the complete lack of audible interference, gave his life a quality of supreme tranquillity.

His entire world was peaceful, and serene.

He knew of deaf people rejecting hearing implants for that very reason. The world was too noisy for them. It confused them. And anyway, they weren't broken, so why should they be fixed?

But he was also far more than just a chauffeur – he was a cook, a handyman, a tailor, a decorator, a cleaner, a gardener, a mechanic, and best of all, he was – in *his* mind at least – a Formula 1 race driver, as soon as he got behind the wheel of the FX4.

And now, with the sudden appearance of newcomers to Avernus, he was, reluctantly, also learning to become a friend.

In fact, Pretty Blonde just wouldn't leave him alone. If she wasn't asking where to find things, or did they have any cake, and where were the teabags again – she was popping up in unexpected places, and offering more name suggestions. All of which he rejected outright.

Even now, she was in his kitchen, helping herself to the carrot batons he was chopping, patting him on the arm, and then gesturing wildly, and mouthing a string of unintelligible words in a slightly demented way. He sighed and stopped to try and read her lips, but she spoke so fast that all he caught was 'do something', 'boredom', 'help you'.

He had a lot to prepare, given the number of people there were to cook for – so, gruffly (though he was secretly pleased), he gave her a knife, passed her a garlic bulb, and made a chopping motion with his hand.

Calista nodded, and set about the work with great intensity, her tongue sticking out from the side of her mouth. But she sliced the cloves with the skin still on – and the Chauffeur shook his head, and showed her how to do it. Then he got on with the rest of the preparation. When he next glanced at her, he realised that she was still chatting away – though with her face turned away from him. He sighed, and just nodded thoughtfully whenever she looked at him, while he got on with his work.

After the Chauffeur had completed preparations, he found that Calista was on just her third piece of garlic – and so he grabbed his paring knife and did the rest himself. Calista gave him an emphatic thumbs up, and the Chauffeur just nodded and smiled.

Despite the hindrance, lunch was ready at exactly 1pm, with the table laid for five, and guests already arriving. But Pretty Blonde kept shaking a stern finger, pointing to him and then the dinner table, and making an eating motion with both hands. The Chauffeur shook his head again (he seemed to be doing that a lot with this girl) – he and the Professor had grown accustomed to eating alone, never together.

But to his horror the girl was already laying out a sixth place setting, grabbing his arm and forcing him to sit, while she ran round and started serving everyone. He was slightly irked. Least of all because there was no finesse to her silver service, if it could even be called that. She slopped food into plates, from both left and right, splashing onto his once spotless tablecloth – he cringed and gritted his teeth, which Calista mistook for a smile of approval, and she cheerily beamed back at him.

The Professor signed to the Chauffeur, saying that it was about time they sat together for meals.

Calista made sure to sit next to him – and he ate for the most part without interaction, though he was pleased to see everyone eating with gusto. At the end of the meal, he looked up to find that they were all staring at Calista, and he caught her telling them that they had *both* cooked lunch together. The Chauffeur restrained himself; chopping up three garlic cloves hardly constituted cooking! But when he saw that everyone was clapping for them, he couldn't help but smile back at them, and blush.

Pretty Blonde was turning out to be quite a whirlwind.

The Chauffeur, who was utterly pragmatic, had initially borne her frivolity with quiet tedium – but now, however much he wanted to deny it, he found that he was warming to her.

———————————

After lunch, the Professor beckoned Tai into a quiet room. In it was a large cardboard box, and to its side, a smaller one the size of a shoebox. Tai fell to his knees and pulled out the kittens, who were mewling with panic. But their mother wasn't there. The Professor explained that she was nowhere to be found in or around the warehouse, but they were still searching. Then he pointed to the smaller box. 'They found this as well... I'm so sorry, Tai.'

Tai opened the box and dropped his head.

Continuing, the Professor explained, 'She was like that when they got there. There was nothing they could do...'

Tai could tell that the kitten had died naturally – and knew very well that it was nature's unfathomable way. He spent several quiet moments holding the box, staring at its body. In time, the Professor told him that there was a remote place in his garden next to the lake where it could be buried. And so Tai left the kittens in the charge of the others, as he went with the Chauffeur to bury it.

He carried the box with a heavy heart.

People were abandoning him, and animals were dying. And he wondered what he was doing so wrong to be punished like this.

———————————

Later that afternoon, Calista and the Professor were in the computer room, looking at Jake's computer, when the phone rang. The Professor touched his earpiece. 'Hello?' The old man listened on the phone for some time, before touching the earpiece again to close the call. He sat down suddenly grim, and turned to Calista. 'There's been a development,' he said. 'My people have been keeping an eye on Tai and Milly's homes since we brought them in. A necessary precaution given Jemima's disappearance and your attempted abduction. We've discovered that, not long after they were extracted, a woman visited each of their homes. The description they gave me matches the appearance of the woman that visited you...'

Calista's heart quickened. 'Oh no! She was out to get them too...'

The old man could hardly believe it. 'Yes it seems so... But I don't understand. How did she know who they were, and where to find them?' The Professor was the only one who knew their true identities, and he had never given the information to anyone else. Ever. Yet someone, somehow, knew where to find them. 'It makes no sense, no sense at all!' He was completely thrown. 'For years I've deliberately kept below the radar,' he muttered, almost to himself. 'Changed my name. Kept out of sight. And lived a completely different life – all to ensure that the children were kept safe, and were forgotten. But... what could I have missed?' He turned toward Calista. 'What have I overlooked? Perhaps I was being overly simplistic. Perhaps I was just sticking my head in the sand...' The Professor held his head in his hands.

Calista was at a loss for words, she sat next to the old man and touched his arm.

He sat up, suddenly feeling tired. 'Funny expression that, isn't it?' he said softly. 'Burying one's head in the sand. People laugh at the ostrich for doing this in the face of danger – but, you see, parent ostriches bury their eggs in the sand, and turn them several times a day for incubation. The perception therefore is that they're burying their heads, when they're really caring for their young...'

'So you're not burying your head in the sand, Prof,' said Calista. 'You're looking out for the children. In a way, you're their guardian.'

'Thank you, Calista. But... I'm obviously not doing a good job.'

Calista thought for a moment. 'Okay. Someone's actively coming after the children – but, what if we reverse it? What if *we* actively go after this woman, locate her, and find out who's really behind all this? You said your people found this out by monitoring their homes – but what if we hack into street CCTV to find out where *she* came from?...'

The Professor nodded thoughtfully. 'Yes, yes.'

'We need to find that woman,' Calista said, determined. 'I'm sure she was caught on street CCTV near their homes – and we can use images of her as a key.' She was beginning to hatch a plan. 'Actually, Prof, since Jake's disappearance, I've been wanting to write the code for a progam that can sharpen and enhance images to gain facial biometrics. Then, encoding another program to reverse-search CCTV servers for those exact biometrics – which would then combine sitings on a map, sequenced by date and time. That way, we'd be able to literally track that person's course, at any given time.'

The Professor sat up, both impressed by her thinking, and infected by her enthusiasm. 'You can do that?'

'Absolutely. But... I need a really powerful, really fast computer. And lots of coffee.'

'That can definitely be arranged!' He stood up, enthused. 'I don't think the Workstation will hack it, pardon the pun! But leave this with me. I need to make some calls.' He hurried away, his mind buzzing with possibilities.

## 13  BACK TO SCHOOL

The next morning, the three teenagers buzzed with the excitement of waking in Avernus. Milly rushed her morning wash, and threw on her clothes, itching to get to the BC. Calista, as was her custom, lingered in the bathroom, washing, moisturising, blow-drying, and preening herself with all the makeup and toiletries from the Professor's superstore. She emerged beautifully 'au naturel', though it had taken her hours to achieve. Tai, out of habit, had slept on a duvet on the floor, instead of the bed, and found himself waking to a living duvet of kittens draped over him. He carefully put each one on the floor, before sitting up and rubbing his eyes.

Somehow all three teenagers managed to arrive in the kitchen diner at exactly the same time, enticed by the smell of a delicious cooked breakfast. The Professor was already there, drinking freshly percolated coffee – and several minutes later Brian arrived. They chatted excitedly and helped themselves to the buffet that was laid out, and joined the Professor at his table. The Chauffeur brought the Professor his food, for which the old man touched fingertips to his chin and moved his hand outward – thanking him.

'This is quite an amazing place,' said Brian, looking around.

'I like to think so,' said the Professor. 'More importantly, it's safe and secure. I... actually built it with the children in mind, in case the day came when... when you would need to be brought together again. Your safety is of course paramount,' said the Professor seriously. 'And so I would ask that you cease all contact with the outside world – friends, relatives, colleagues, anybody at all. Because it could compromise our security.'

They all looked at each other.

'I know it's a tall ask,' he said. 'You also can't do any kind of online networking while you're here' – Calista gasped; social media was her life. The Professor continued. 'I can't emphasise how important it is to stay under the radar.'

'Yes,' said Brian. 'I agree. That makes sense.' He looked at each of the children. 'It's for our own good.'

'Oh, and Brian,' said the Professor. 'Since you can no longer work, in order to stay here with Melody – I'm sure we'll be able to find a way to explain your absence to your clients. Perhaps mentioning something like medical leave, or a sabbatical.'

Brian nodded. 'That can definitely be arranged.'

'And, if you don't mind,' said the Professor, 'we can organise the paying off of your bank mortgage, so you don't need to worry about that side of things.'

Brian couldn't believe it. 'I... I don't mind at all. In fact, that would be wonderful!' His eyes began to well up, and Milly squeezed his arm. They both knew he was behind with payments, and the bank had been threatening him every month with repossession. Lately it had been getting harder and harder to make ends meet – juggling with impossible decisions between repairing roof leaks and structural damage, fixing the boiler, or paying the mortgage. And just when he thought he was getting on top of things, a tap would start dripping, or drains got blocked, or windows broken – and they either had to live with it or try and fix it themselves. But crudely sellotaped plastic sheeting over cracked windows could only last so long... Yet, in one fell swoop the Professor had solved all his problems. 'Th-thank you, Professor!' was all Brian managed to say, overcome.

'You're welcome! It's the least I can do,' smiled the Professor. He turned to address the teenagers. 'And for Tai, Milly, and Calista – I would like to arrange a special programme of education, here in Avernus.'

Calista groaned inwardly, Tai was impassive, and Milly looked as if she was about to burst with excitement.

'It will be an education tailored to each of your needs,' explained the Professor. 'Provided by a very special group of people. So, after breakfast, I'd like to take you to the classroom to meet them over Zoom. But first, please eat up. You can ask the Chauffeur for anything you like, anything at all.'

•••————————————————•••

After breakfast, the Professor fingered his watch, and then led everyone through more corridors, and yet another room. Inside they found a huge octagonal space, similar to the BC, but with walls of jagged, unhewn stone. Fixed to each wall was a massive sheet of crystal-clear bevelled glass – three metres high by five metres wide.

'I'm arranging for some special study desks and chairs to be made and brought in,' said the Professor, waving an arm to the centre of the room. 'Calista, you are a perfect example of *natural* genius – your exceptional computer skills are testament to that. Whilst Milly, Tai, you both have the most advanced genetically engineered minds on the planet. So I've taken the liberty of enlisting some of the most learned and renowned educators and lecturers in the world – made up of doctors, professors, and academics, taken from the best universities. They've all agreed to take sabbaticals from their current work, to come and teach you.'

The Professor lifted his hands into the air, and drew them apart, as if opening imaginary curtains. As he did this, each glass pane lit up with white light, and they all turned to watch them come to life, one by one.

'Please look at the screens around us. I would like to introduce you first of all to Dr Ben Bartholomew, Professor of Computer Science, at Oxford University.' The Professor lifted a hand, and the first screen flickered and displaying the giant face of a bearded, spectacled man, beaming at them. Calista waved at him enthusiastically, and Dr Bartholomew waved back, blushing.

The Professor lifted his hand again, and on the second screen appeared a rather serious, hawk-faced woman. 'This is Dr Samantha Milo, Head of Physical and Theoretical Chemistry, Cambridge University.' And in this way, the Professor introduced 10 learned professors from the faculties of the most prestigious universities, covering Mathematics, Physical and Life Sciences, Medical Sciences, Arts and Humanities, Engineering, Languages and Linguistics, as well as, unusually, the Head of Classical and Contemporary Dance from the Rambert Dance Company. There was even Sensei Aoki from the Kyokushin Karate Dojo, Tokyo. Their giant faces were spread out on the screens – some waiting patiently, others fidgeting and coughing, and one of them – Sensei Aoki – was struggling to keep awake, with his head bobbing up and down.

Calista turned around slowly, waving to each one cheerily.

Milly lifted her hand stiffly, a little shy. 'Will they teach us via these video links, Professor?' asked Milly, awed by the whole array.

'No, no. They'll be coming here, in person – some of them arriving as early as tomorrow. Planes, trains, and cars have all been commandeered to get them here.' He coughed, and then spoke out loudly to the screens. 'Thank you! Thanks for Zooming in.' And then lifting his hands and drawing the curtains closed, the screens faded to clear glass again.

The Professor turned back to the children. 'Now, while they're preparing your curriculum, and if you don't mind – I'm eager to find out each of your Intelligence Quotients.' The Professor lifted his hand into the air again, and the screens lit up again with puzzle diagrams, multiple choice questions, pictograms, and mathematical equations. It was bewildering, and Tai could only look at the screens in confusion.

Another raised hand, and the screens once again faded to be replaced by an old black and white photo of a boy barely out of nappies. The child was writing a long intricate equation on a chalk board. The Professor explained. 'The highest recorded IQ score was 230, which belongs to Korean physicist, Kim Ung-Yong. This photo shows him starting life as a child prodigy. He learnt to read several languages at six months old, and a couple of years later was able to learn entire languages in about a month. Seven months later he learned the concepts of differential calculus, and then started writing poetry and painting works of art. A marvellous case of natural genius. Of course, at your tender ages, I don't expect you to reach that IQ level just yet, but...'

'But why bother with all of this, Professor?' said Calista. Apart from computer sciences, she was a reluctant student. 'If they're already geniuses,' she waved her hand toward Tai and Milly, 'then surely they don't need all this extra stuff.'

'How can I explain...' mumbled the Professor. He turned toward her. 'I believe that genius is a mixture of both nature and nurture. Nature – as in your natural abilities, or in Tai and Milly's cases, the genes they were crafted with. Which is then complimented by a rich learning environment that *nurtures* intellect and thinking ability. So, this classroom will be the nurturing process, which will harness and build on your abilities. In the end, I must admit to hoping, actually *expecting*, your own IQs to surpass that of Mr Kim's.'

Calista gulped. 'No pressure then...'

The Professor smiled. 'No, I don't want you to feel any pressure. But I do really want you to be onboard with this... I want it to be a natural, organic learning environment, that goes at your own pace. We will also be giving you a carefully planned diet, because I believe very much that we are what we eat. So we'll be including a lot of foods that stimulate good brain activity – such as nuts and leafy green vegetables for vitamin e. Broccoli for vitamin k, and for enhancing cognitive function and brainpower. Oily fish for omega 3. Tomatoes for lycopene – etc etc. And there will also be a gentle but daily exercise regime. So as you can see, it's a complete and somewhat holistic programme that will bring you all to your intellectual and physical optimum!'

Milly, who had been silent for most of the time, was stunned. This was everything she had always longed for, and more – her eyes brimmed with tears. Tai put a reassuring arm around her.

'So, if you're up to it, we can do some preliminary IQ tests now,' said the Professor. 'It will only take an hour or so.'

Tai and Calista looked at each other, and shrugged. Milly piped up, 'Yes please!'

•••————————————————••

Later that day, the Professor took Calista aside, and sat her down with a tablet on her lap. 'Take a look at that, young lady,' he said.

She picked up the iPad and scrolled through the document. 'All my school reports!' She didn't even bother asking how he had managed to get them; she knew he had his connections. 'But why are you showing me these, Prof? What have they got to do with anything?' She wasn't proud of those old reports.

The Professor rubbed the light silvery stubble on his chin. 'You'll see I've charted your test results over your entire lifetime.'

Calista fidgeted awkwardly.

The Professor sensed her unease. 'Hear me out. In primary school, you were always at the bottom of the class – but then, look at the results over the last few years. Your grades have shot right up. Do you see? I... I've never seen such a steep learning curve. It's quite extraordinary.'

Calista looked up from the chart, and thought for a while. 'When I was little,' she said eventually, 'my mum always used to tell me how dumb I was, and the only thing I had going for me was my looks.' She smiled weakly. 'Parents can be so cruel can't they? Anyway, I believed her. Believed what she kept telling me – so I suppose it was like one of them... self-fulfilling prophecies. You see, if my own mother was telling me how rubbish I was, it must be true! So I didn't bother much with school. I only really worked a bit harder than usual for my GCSE years cos I didn't want the bother of having to retake exams. And now I think about it, I don't even know why I started college. I just went along with the crowd. And Jake was the only reason I took Computer Sciences...' She smiled sadly.

The Professor was amused by the paradoxical mix of extraordinary genius with unashamed superficiality. Eventually he said, 'You've been putting yourself down all these years, Calista. Because I can see from the reports that when you've tried, even putting in minimal effort, you've done really well academically. Your own perception of yourself stopped you from seeing how truly brilliant you really are...' He thought about the years of denigration her mother put her through, and asked, 'I wonder what made her treat you like that? Your mother.'

Calista thought about it. 'It was to do with my grandad Ben – or Gramps as I used to call him. Mum's dad. You see, me and him had a special relationship, even better than he had with his own daughter. I think it was because she was such a rebel, and me, being his only grandkid who adored him, made him spoil me rotten. Yeah, I think mum was jealous of that.' Calista shrugged. 'He always stood up for me,' Calista's smile faded, and she sighed. 'H-he's gone now... And he left everything to me. It wasn't much, just a few valuables, some of grandma's jewellery, some savings. But, the funny thing was...' She paused. 'Gramps wasn't great on paperwork. He just scribbled me a letter saying he'd left this and that to me. But there was no *actual* will. Then, the letter vanished mysteriously, and my parents kicked me out. Just like that.' Calista struggled to compose herself. She had thought she was over it by now, but her tears belied that notion. 'Can you imagine. My own mum and dad...'

The Professor shook his head, staring into the distance. His respect for Calista was growing – she had single-handedly put herself through college, got student digs, and managed to provide herself with food and clothing all these years, which was no small feat.

Unexpectedly Calista broke out in a smile, like sun breaking through dark clouds, and somehow the Professor heard it in her voice. 'Then Jake came along,' she said. The look on her face was bitter-sweet. 'I was in awe of him, wanted to find out why he loved computers so much. And when I did, it was infectious. Jake taught me how to build computers, programme them, control them, manipulate them. It was thrilling and empowering! For the first time in my life I started learning, I mean, *really* learning. And it was like... like something inside me woke up. And as I was falling head-over-heels for him, at the same time, I was developing another love, another passion. For computers.' She looked at her hands – her perfectly manicured hands – as if they held that knowledge.

'You obviously had the ability all along, my dear,' the Professor said softly. 'And Jake was just the catalyst... Your GCSE and AS results prove that – did you see what they were?'

Calista looked down at the tablet and scrolled through. Eyes widening as she discovered a perfect line of A* grades, hardly believing it.

The Professor continued. 'Also, Jake wasn't able to hack into the government's Project Ingenious files – but you were.'

Calista would have swelled if she hadn't just heard Jake's name. It brought her back down to earth. She looked at the Professor – the silvery stubble on his chin, his tired, black eyes – and even though they weren't really alike, he reminded her of her Gramps. He had that same caring nature, always encouraging her. She sighed. She missed Jake desperately.

Guessing how she was feeling, the Professor said, 'I'm expecting some deliveries tomorrow. Once they arrive, we'll be able to get your computer built, and you can start coding the program to find Jake.'

That was exactly what she wanted to hear. 'Really?' she breathed. 'That's good, Prof,' she said. 'That's really good!'

# 14 NOT SO COY KOI

Calista didn't waste any time. She immediately started writing the code for her program on the Workstation, though its processing power was wholly insufficient and grindingly slow – and she realised that both hardware and software hadn't been upgraded or updated in several years. But for Jake, she made a start.

Meanwhile, Tai, Milly, and Brian were left to explore for the rest of the day. But the more they wandered around Avernus, the more they discovered. Unexpected corridors, features, nooks, and yet more rooms, all unfolded, like a Japanese puzzle box, seemingly out of nowhere. The Professor made sure to point out that every corridor and public room within Avernus had sensors, microphones, and speakers – so that at any time they could ask the Workstation for directions, and the computer would guide them with verbal instructions. It was a smart building, though they discovered that some of the Workstation's hilarious replies were not so smart.

One of the more stunning finds was the swimming room. It was directly beneath the small lake at the end of the Professor's vast garden – so that the huge glass slab at the bottom of the lake, made of high-tensile acrylic, two metres thick, formed the transparent ceiling above the pool. At the far end of the room was a waterfall that cascaded down an entire wall, appearing as if the water was falling directly from the lake above. The shape of the room mirrored the BC and the classroom, with eight hewn stone walls springing from the floorspace, encircling the central octagonal pool. Lush, tumbling Areca palms were dotted around, giving the place a balmy, tropical ambience.

It was breath-taking, and they immediately arranged to convene there every day for a morning swim. In fact, so drawn were Tai and Milly to the water, that they couldn't resist returning dressed in t-shirt and shorts as makeshift swimming costumes.

They swam together now, on their backs, side by side – though Tai was quiet.

'You okay?' asked Milly, looking across at him.

Tai glanced at her in between arm strokes. 'It's Dog,' he said. 'They still can't find her. And the kittens are lost without her.'

Milly sensed that nothing she said would make him feel better, and so they lapsed into silence, their arms swinging backwards in synchronisation, mesmerised by their upside-down perspective of the lake above. They watched dappled water sparkle softly between great swathes of hard-soil, stones, and algae. Murky colours quivered and rippled, punctuated by clumps of starwort and waterweed swaying hypnotically in the undercurrent. Shafts of golden light speared the water. And koi flitted here and there in smooth shoals, swooping majestically in unison, sometimes slowing to nibble plants, and then swooping off again – their citrine scales flashing in the light.

The teenagers were rendered speechless at the beauty of it all as they paddled along. In time, they flipped onto their bellies, and raced – though undeniably Tai was the fastest. He swam like a fish, slicing through the water with minimal effort. After an hour, they decided on one more, final lap. Tai's eyes were half closed as they swam together, absorbing the steady rhythm of their breathing, water tinkling like tiny bells in his ears. Around the room bounced the hollow echoes of their movements.

But then Milly stopped, noticing something odd in the lake above. She told Tai to keep swimming around, while she swam to the side to sit perched on the edge of the pool – looking from Tai to the lake above, and back again. She had to rub her eyes and look again – she could hardly believe it. The fish were swimming at the same speed and pattern as he was, going round and round directly above him. Milly held her breath as she watched, and then she shouted out to Tai to stop swimming, and he obeyed, though somewhat bewildered. Then she told him to swim in the other direction.

Puzzled, Tai did as he was told, and then turned round to face Milly, bobbing up and down in the water. 'What is it?' he sang out, the lilt in his voice reverberating.

Milly looked back up at the koi, and saw that they had stopped too. 'The fish,' she breathed in awe. Then louder, 'They're following you!'

Tai looked up. There was a mass of them, all pointed in Tai's direction. Tai scissor-kicked himself onto his back, and swam off in random directions, and the fish chased him. When he looked over at Milly, she had disappeared, and he looked around for her.

Before long, Milly ran back in, with both Calista and the Professor in tow – she was excitedly telling Calista to watch the fish above as she once again barked out instructions to Tai.

Calista watched the fish follow Tai, stunned. 'Amazing!' she said, turning to the Professor. 'The fish. They're copying Tai's every move.

When he stops, they stop. When he goes in another direction, they do too.'

They experimented by swapping Tai with Milly, and she swam around while Tai sat at the edge of the pool. But the fish instead floated, stationary, directly above Tai's head.

'It looks like they're staring right at Tai, Prof!' said Calista.

The Professor shook his head, mystified. 'That's impossible. You see, the glass roof is one-way. Which means we can see them, but they can't see us. So the fish, the koi, see only a darkened mirror – their own reflections.'

'So then, how?' asked Calista, scratching her head.

'They must be sensing Tai,' Milly explained. 'Sensing his presence somehow. I guess like... iron filings aligning to a magnetic field. The fish are pointing themselves in his direction.'

The Professor thought about this, then tapped his way to a lounger. He sat down, mumbling to himself about Dr Kendra isolating certain gene sets, inserting them into embryo DNA – and it was entirely possible that a special, unique mix of genes for *feelings* was heightened and amplified in the DNA given to Tai, giving him a higher sense of awareness, thoughts, emotions. So heightened that the fish were drawn to him.

Calista, confused by his ramblings, looked at Milly. 'What's he talking about?' she asked.

The old man rubbed his chin. 'Basically, over the years, with each subsequent baby in Project Ingenious, we learnt more and more, and continually changed our techniques in order to try to improve and hone the somatic gene engineering process on stem cells.' The Professor was half mumbling to himself, half talking to them. 'Dr Kendra was still deciphering hundreds of genes that account for variances of intelligence – in fact, he found that there was a vast menu of intelligence traits within human DNA. So he had to cherry-pick a unique mixture of genes for every fertilised egg... However, each was given an extra copy of a 'learning' gene that produced the NR2B brain chemical, the common denominator for them all. But then various *additional* genetic enhancements were included to augment their abilities, in essence giving each respective child a unique blend of genes. And the particular gene set given to Tai, must have "overdosed" so to speak on awareness and emotion, feeling and cognisance. In this way he somehow ended up with abnormally high levels of sensitivity, feelings, perception... Amplifying and heightening his senses... with animals... and fish. That must be it, I think. Tai shares with the fish a kind of common wavelength, which makes them, in turn, sensitive to him.' He turned toward the others.

Tai, none the wiser, watched a magenta glow of suppressed excitement ripple around the old man. He then looked up again at the mixed shoal of fish, their black eyes bulging. Gazing, and lost in thought, he was like an awestruck child in an aquarium.

That evening after dinner, the three teenagers congregated around a hearty fire crackling in the den – their knees almost touching as they talked. They were comparing bits of the Professor's story that each of them knew separately, piecing them together to form a patchy whole. After that, they took turns listening to each other's stories. Milly explained how she had always thirsted for knowledge, and studied every book she could lay her hands on. Calista reminisced about Jake, and recounted the humorous story of pinching his textbook from the cafeteria, only to be found red-handed. She looked at Tai, not letting on that she knew about his mother from the Professor, and said, 'Your turn, Tai... if you want to?'

Tai looked down at the kitten on his lap and stroked it. 'My mother left seven months ago,' he said quietly. The girls glanced at each other.

'I'm so sorry, Tai,' said Milly. Realising how lost she would be without her father. 'Do you know where she is?'

'No,' he said. 'I...' he looked down at the kitten. 'I think she's dead.'

The girls were stunned into silence.

'She told me she was gonna visit Grampa, who was ill. And I haven't seen her since.'

'She... she might not be dead, Tai,' said Milly. 'There might be a reason why she never came back. Maybe she had an accident, or, or...'

'I just know,' said Tai firmly, looking up at her. He touched his chest with a balled fist. 'I can't feel her here, anymore,' he said. 'Before, I always knew how she was. Happy, sad, angry. I felt everything she felt. But now, there's nothing. Like she doesn't exist. Like she's dead.'

There was silence, and the girls dared not break it. Though he was reluctant, it was an inevitability that he would tell his story. It needed to be told. And so he recounted it with short, clipped, sentences – as if reading from a child's story book. His voice small and almost inconsequential. He told them of a father who had abandoned him, a mother who was nowhere to be found, he described homelessness, solitude, scavenging for food, clothes, and shelter, the death of Cat, his fever, the kittens and Dog. All the while he focused on the kitten on his lap, as if it were his reference. The other kittens, who had gone off to explore the room, were making their way back to Tai, climbing onto his lap and tucking themselves around the kitten. A purring heap of fur. They too were motherless.

Milly and Calista listened quietly, eyes glistening in the dancing firelight. Even the Chauffeur, who had come in with a tray of hot chocolate, stopped to read the boy's lips and caught the tail-end of his story. Struck by the rawness of it, he couldn't help but sit down, joining the others.

The kittens looked feeble, and were growing weaker without their mother. Even though attempts had been made to feed them, the little animals just sniffed the food, or tasted it, but then turned away. They were only interested in searching for Dog.

'Without their mother, they're going to die,' Tai said softly. He didn't tell them that he too felt the same. That he was lost without his mother, and felt hardly able to go on.

# 15 JASMINE

It was day three of Milly and Brian, Calista and Tai going underground – and there had been a delay in the arrival of the tutors and professors from across the world due to an ash cloud erupting from an Icelandic volcano, halting all plane travel to and from the UK. It was therefore decided to delay their specialised tuition by a week.

That morning after breakfast, the Professor motioned for the others to follow him into yet another undiscovered room. It was even larger than the rooms before, empty on one side, and on the other, it was filled with neat rows of cardboard boxes of varying sizes, laid out like bookshelves in a library.

Calista gasped, and then ran up and down each row of boxes, eyes wide in disbelief, like a child let loose in a sweet shop. She intermittently stopped to read some of the labelling. Cabinets, processors, graphics cards, racks, motherboards, fans, cables, and the latest high-resolution screens.

After a while, she returned to the Professor, out of breath. 'With all these components, we have the potential to build clusters of, at a guess, several hundred processors, which could achieve a combined peak performance of eight petaflops. *Eight*! That's about half the power of the IBM Sequoia supercomputer in California. That's mad!!' she exclaimed, placing her hand on her head. 'Of course I'd need to perfect the water-cooling system, to make sure nothing gets throttled...'

A smile crept across the Professor's face as he heard her chattering excitedly. 'May I suggest that – because time is passing, and we need this computer ASAP to run your programme – you start off with building the computer to just a few PETAflops initially? Just to get it up and running. Afterwards, you can expand its capacity, and add more servers, as and when time permits.'

'Yes. Yes of course,' said Calista. 'If I were to build it to just one or two PETAflops, it would definitely take less time, and...'

'About that,' interrupted the Professor – he held a finger to his earpiece, and then spoke away from her. 'Hello? Hello. Please, can you make your way in now.' He turned back to Calista, 'About that, I've already called in some extra manpower to help you build the computer, for what I'm calling the Spiderweb project, because, with this as the central hub, it'll connect every public camera server in the country, much like the connecting strands of a web.'

'Extra manpower?' said Calista.

She was answered by a throng of approaching footsteps, and they turned to find the door opening, and about 40 men of varying ages streamed in, all in grey overalls, carrying tool-bags, and with communicators attached to their upper chest. They lined up in front of them, and waited.

The Professor turned and addressed them all. 'Ah gentlemen, welcome to our project. Young Calista Matheson, over here, will be your project manager.' Calista waved, feeling rather out of her depth. The Professor continued. 'They've all signed confidentiality agreements, like the teachers, and have already been given basic instructions about everything being stored in order, as per the inventory you should already have. The deadline was yesterday, I'm afraid – which means we need this completed as a matter of great urgency. I therefore need you to pull out all the stops to get this computer built. And there is no room, or time, for error.' He turned back to Calista. 'Now Calista, these gentlemen are all experienced computer engineers, who are the best. They'll be able to work mostly by themselves, but you will of course need to oversee everything. Are you okay with this?'

Calista had never built a super-computer before, let alone project-managed anything. She took a deep breath, saying, 'Umm... yeah sure.'

Milly stepped forward. 'Count me in,' she said. This was exactly the kind of thing she loved getting her teeth into – a challenge, learning new skills, an important goal.

Brian stepped next to his daughter. 'Me too. I don't know much about this sort of thing, but I can at least help with heavy lifting.'

Calista beamed. 'Well then, no time like the present.' She rolled up her sleeves, took the tablet handed to her by the Professor, and went over to the engineers.

•••——————————————•••

There was much to discuss – and it took them several hours just to look over the inventory, work out an action plan, and who would do what, with an estimated timeframe. The architecture was agreed upon, and they chalked out the general setup of the supercomputer on the floor. Then Calista divided the engineers into teams, with each team having a leader, in charge of working on different sections of the computer – placing cabinet racks, physically installing the servers, setting up network switches above each chassis, and setting aside input devices.

The engineers had already checked out Avernus' electrical ring, and determined the appropriate wattage required for the power distribution unit – which would also be hooked up to the back-up generator in case of power failure. Then there was the cabling and networking, and they set up a private ethernet network to connect all the nodes within a cluster – designating a master node that could also act as a server over the network. Finally, they would have to ensure every component (especially the power supplies) worked properly before moving on to the next; a single faulty part could bring down the entire system.

It was generally agreed to use Linux as the operating system, because it was open-source and therefore easily modified to their needs, and it helped that it was already compatible with most of the hardware – Calista could write drivers for everything else, given a day or so.

The teams worked all day, and most of the night, with catering being brought in by the Chauffeur. He had also set up a side table of refreshments that was constantly topped up. They took it in turns to take breaks during the day, and power naps through the night. And both Milly and Brian hovered around to see where they could be useful – with Milly watching, listening, and learning from the engineers, and eventually mucking in with setting up the hardware, and laying out and plugging in cabling.

•••————————————————————————•••

The only ones that came to the dining room for dinner that evening were the Professor and Tai, and so they sat in mostly silence punctuated by polite conversation as they ate – though Tai didn't have much of an appetite with the kittens still listless.

The Professor got a call, and he put down his cutlery to answer. Listening for a few minutes, the old man quickly turned toward Tai to get his attention, and when he closed the call he smiled. 'Good news, Tai! They've found your dog.' He was relieved to be bringing good news. 'My friend is dropping her off at the house as we speak. We'd better go and meet him.'

Tai's fork clattered on his plate as he stood up, a mixture of relief and excitement on his face. He ran over to the box in the corner that held the kittens, picked it up, and followed the Professor.

'Is... is she alright?' asked Tai hesitantly, as they walked at speed through the corridors.

'I don't know... I think so.'

The trek seemed like an age to Tai, who could barely contain himself. They eventually burst outside into the cool night air, and walked along several roads through the industrial estate, then out into the residential streets until they reached the front door of the Professor's immaculate house.

Inside, in the lounge, an elderly policeman was already waiting. He shook the Professor's hand, and they began talking to each other. Dog was lying behind the armchair on the carpet, her eyes glazed over with listlessness – but as soon as she saw Tai enter the room, she leapt up and bounded across to him. Tai gently set down the box on the floor, knelt on one knee, and Dog jumped into his arms, licking his face, whining, and wagging her tail so hard it whipped the air. Tai laughed out loud as they toppled onto the floor together, disturbing the box. A cacophony of meowing ensued, and, realising that it contained the kittens, Dog practically jumped onto it. It fell on its side, and the kittens spilled out, crying with excitement. She quickly licked every single one of them – eventually lying down on her side to let them suckle. The past two days had been agonisingly painful, not only from their separation, but also because of the build-up of milk.

The police officer couldn't help staring at them. 'Would you look at that!' he said – he had never seen a dog nurse kittens before.

'I'm told she lost her own puppies,' the Professor explained. 'And so the dog took care of the orphaned kittens. Nature has an enduring way of righting itself, don't you think.'

Tai sat cross-legged on the floor next to Dog, stroking her. He found with relief that she was well, and had not been injured. Quietly he watched the undulating waves of amber contentedness radiate from the animals as they suckled – it was as mesmerising as glowing embers.

Nobody had noticed that, in the shadowy corner of the room, sat Acuzio. He watched Dog and the kittens silently at first. Observing these new intruders that were invading his territory. Very soon a raw anger began to well up in him, and his lips parted to emit a snarl, and then a low growl – his body itching to chase them away. He had disliked the kittens from the start, and now they were bringing a rival dog into his home. It angered him. And something would need to be done about it.

But Acuzio glanced across at his old master, who himself was staring at the creatures. He was not objecting. In fact, it looked like he was happy they were there.

And so, retreating quietly underneath the table, Acuzio held back – it would have to wait for another day.

•••————————————————————•••

Back in the computer room, there was a beehive of activity. With the help of the engineers it was going to be just a matter of days before the computer was completed. Though they were by now all red-eyed, pale, and pumped high with caffeine. Calista was a relentless taskmaster, staggering shifts so that the work was constant and ongoing, with just enough rest – only a few hours each – to keep them going. At last, late at night, they had completed the final set of tests with success, and they cheered and congratulated each other, patting themselves on the back for a job well done.

The next morning, the Professor and Brian, Milly and Tai, wandered into the computer room first thing to check on progress. They were greeted by an unexpected quiet. Just a low electric thrum emanating from row upon row of shiny, two-metre high steel boxes, and the sound of clicking on a keyboard.

Three large curved crystal screens were arranged end to end in a semi-circle, covering three of the eight walls – and in the centre was a large oval control desk with tiered shelves, and three clear perspex wireless keyboards. Hunched over one of the keyboards was Calista – who, upon seeing them, waved them in. Her hair was a mess, her skin tinged grey, with dark circles under her eyes. 'It's finished!' she said, with barely the energy to convey her excitement. She stifled a yawn, rubbed her eyes, and waved toward the servers. 'I'm getting speed readings of... two thousand trillion floating point operations per second.'

Brian leaned towards Tai. 'I think that means it's really, really fast.'

Calista cleared her throat, and then spoke into the air, 'Hello, Jasmine,' she said in a tone that was almost motherly.

The blank centre screen pulsed with light, and a warm, silky voice replied, 'Good morning, Calista.' She sounded almost omnipresent.

The Professor smiled. 'Lovely!' he said, smiling. 'Much nicer than the rather robotic-sounding Workstation.'

'Nicked her voice from an unsuspecting AI communications centre,' Calista said, winking. 'All for a good cause!'

Tapping closer, the Professor asked, 'And how's the program coming along?'

'Just spent the last few hours on the finishing touches,' she said, and then, turning back to the keyboard, started typing furiously. 'Just. A couple. More minutes...' she said, distracted.

They waited until she made the final triumphant keystrokes, turning round to face them. 'All done! I've also copied over the Workstation's voice recognition files, Professor. So why don't you go ahead. Say the word.'

He didn't need to be asked twice. He stepped forward and cleared his throat. 'Ahem. Good morning, Jasmine.'

'Good morning, Professor,' the AI replied effortlessly.

'Go ahead and execute program Spiderweb,' he commanded.

'Please identify who you would like to search for.'

'Jake Winters,' said Calista at the same time as the Professor said, 'Jemima Jenkins.'

Calista looked at the Professor, then back at the screen. '*Both* Jake Winters, and Jemima Jenkins.'

The computer whirred to life, and Jasmine's voice echoed around the room, 'Running program Spiderweb. Results expected in...'

Everybody held their breath; the old Workstation would have taken weeks.

'...26 seconds. 25, 24, 23...'

Calista couldn't help clapping her hands. 'You beauty!' she said.

Meanwhile, Brian whispered to Milly, asking, 'What exactly is this Spiderweb search thingy again?'

Milly dared not take her eyes off the screen. 'It's a computer program that connects every live CCTV server, and searches for images based on facial recognition, physical build, stance, gait. It sifts through all the databases for matches. That's practically every live CCTV server around the world – and then it connects the dots, putting everything in time order on a map, which will help us trace their movements.'

'...Nine, eight, seven...' Jasmine continued counting in the background.

'And who are they searching for?' whispered Brian again to Milly.

'Well, first there's Calista's boyfriend, Jake, and then Jemima Jenkins, the girl who went missing several days ago...'

'Zero,' announced Jasmine coolly. 'Displaying results onscreen.'

A long, scrolling table appeared onscreen. 'Possible matches for Jake Winters – 33,447. Possible matches for Jemima Jenkins – 28,258...' The table contained results for each person by country, which Jasmine started reading out loud...

'Oh...' moaned Calista, collapsing back into her chair, deflated. All their efforts were stymied in one fell swoop, and her fatigue turned into despair. The results were so numerous as to be inconclusive.

The Professor, disappointed too, shuffled closer and placed a hand on Calista's shoulder. 'I think it's time you got some rest, my dear. And when we've all got clear heads, we can reconvene, and decide what to do,' he said softly. Calista nodded weakly, got up, and left the room in pained silence.

The others stood around for a few seconds looking at each other, and then followed Calista out the door.

Automatically the screens blanked out, the light surrounding the keyboard dimmed, and the room darkened.

···───────────────────···

Just after one in the afternoon, sensors detected movement in the computer room, and the light automatically switched on. Calista padded in, in leggings and an oversized sweatshirt, with a bottle of water in one hand, and a cup of strong espresso in the other. Wedged under one arm was a packet of crisps. She yawned fitfully. She had slept for the rest of the morning, and the Chauffeur woke her with a pot noodle garnished with spring onions, seasoned seaweed, and a smattering of bonito flakes – the best instant noodles she had ever tasted.

Calista placed everything carefully on the glass desk. 'Hello, Jasmine,' she said, rubbing the sleep from her eyes.

'Good afternoon, Calista,' said Jasmine, her voice warm and smooth. The three displays powered up automatically, as well as the lights around the crystal keyboards. Start-up was instantaneous, with the desktop – spread across the three screens – appearing as a stunning macro photograph of penitent bell flowers bowing low, vibrantly white, and doused in gem-like orbs of dew. The images made her feel like she had been transported to the countryside.

Calista slurped some coffee. 'Display results of program Spiderweb,' she commanded, and the same tabulated data from earlier appeared. 'Thanks, Jas,' mumbled Calista.

Jasmine's powerful microphones dotted around the room were still able to pick up what she said. 'You're welcome, Calista.'

Calista's eyes scanned across the results for Jake, spilling onto the three screens. There were 33,447 instances of recorded CCTV footage worldwide that contained someone matching Jake's biometric details. 'Now, filter the Jake Winters results to footage recorded in the last... 10 days, and within 10 miles of his home address, and display in map format.'

Instantaneously, a London map appeared, spread across the three screens, with various red dots scattered around. 'Adjust dot results: red for the most recent sitings, through to grey for older sitings.' The dots immediately changed colour, and Calista squinted as she examined the results for several minutes. 'Now zoom into section A3 by C4, Jas. I want to see the most recent sitings, close up.' The map enlarged a cluster of dark red spots. Calista studied the results for some time. She was beginning to see a pattern: the route to and from college, his bedsit, the shops he went to regularly, the library, the internet café. But there was one lone line of dark-red dots, miles away from the clusters of others. Here, she used the crystal mouse to zoom into its location. It was in a road labelled 'Praed Street'. Calista stood up and walked over to the middle screen, puzzled. She knew this was unusually far from Jake's regular haunts, and she racked her brains but could not remember him mentioning anything out of town.

'Jasmine, on screen 1, display search results relating to and around this road... here.' She tapped her index finger on the touch-sensitive glass, where Praed Street was. 'Beginning with the most recent, in date-descending order, please.'

A Google web search appeared on the far-left screen, with, at the very top, a news story headlined: '13-year-old girl missing from family home in West London'. When Calista reached across to tap on the link, it displayed an article about Jemima Jenkins. Calista's jaw dropped – this was the missing Ingenious girl the Professor had been searching for. 'On screen 3, show me the CCTV footage for Praed Street,' she said, feeling both excited and nauseous at the same time.

Calista tapped impatient fingers on folded arms, even though it took just seconds. A large grainy image appeared on the third screen, in black and white. The aspect was from a high perspective, like a camera perhaps perched on a street lamp, and at the bottom right-hand corner of the image was a time and date stamp. Calista blinked at it, hardly believing what she saw. It was the same night that Jemima Jenkins had been taken, on 5 May. The time was 10.53 pm. 'Play footage,' Calista told Jasmine, and she stepped back and watched as the video showed the dark figure of someone walk along the road and across the screen, looking around nervously. He disappeared out of view in a matter of seconds. Calista's heart skipped a beat. 'Replay footage from the start.' And she watched the video again. There was no clear shot of his face, mostly the top of his head. But Calista knew it was Jake.

Her heart began pounding against her ribcage. After a while, she said, 'Jasmine, check if there are any other cameras further along the road... in any direction.'

'This is the only CCTV camera in Praed Street,' she stated.

'Okay...' said Calista, thinking. 'Just continue playing footage from this camera, at four times speed.'

'That is impossible, Calista,' said Jasmine coolly.

Calista frowned. 'Why not?'

'Video from 11.38pm to 3.38am does not exist. Would you like me to play footage from 3.39am onwards?'

Calista sat back down on the chair, tapping her fingers on the desk. 'That can't be – these are 24-hour cameras. Please double-check, Jasmine. It's very important.'

'I have already checked the server 254 times, Calista.'

'Check server log files.'

There was a momentary pause. 'I have now checked the server log files. The activity for the same time period has been deleted. The disk service information for that video has been deleted. The sector of disk space for that file has already been overwritten. There are no backup copies on the server. There are no backup copies in linked cloud storage.'

Calista blinked with disbelief, and started talking to herself. 'So a whole chunk of video footage is missing – but why? Why would there be a four-hour outage at such a crucial point?!'

'No data,' came Jasmine's curt reply.

'Are there any other CCTV camera outages in the immediate area at the same time?' She thought that perhaps there might have been a local electricity power failure.

Jasmine was quiet for several seconds as she gathered information.

'Negative. All CCTV cameras within a five-mile radius of Praed Street have continuous streams of footage for that date and time period.'

Calista gulped down the rest of her coffee. 'So only this particular camera has this mysterious power outage...' she muttered to herself, perplexed.

'Affirmative,' said Jasmine.

'Okay. Locate the case file for Jemima Jenkins from police databases.'

'Your request requires cloaked hack of high security servers, Calista. Please confirm permission.'

'Yes, yes, confirmed,' said Calista, antsy. 'Oh, and call the Professor – ask him to come here right away. It's urgent.'

'Executing cloaked hack into Metropolitan Police central servers, and I have also requested Professor Wolff's presence,' said Jasmine. In contrast to Calista's increasingly alarmed tone, Jasmine's voice was perfectly calm.

The Professor, who had been having an after-lunch siesta, arrived in the computer room dazed, with messy hair.

'Thanks for coming, Professor,' said Calista, without even looking up, busy speed-reading the police report on the screen. 'Just a sec.' She pushed a perspex chair toward him with her foot. The Professor sat down.

She finally turned to the old man and began explaining in an excited flurry everything she had discovered.

When he heard that Jake was in the street where Jemima Jenkins lived, and on the same night she disappeared, he suddenly became alert. 'Are... are you sure about the dates, the road?'

'Yes. Triple-checked. And what's more, the police file on Jemima Jenkins shows that the babysitter – a night nanny – turned up at around 12.30 am to look after her, and the parents left at around 1.10 am to catch a train for a business trip. The police themselves checked the CCTV camera, and noted the unusual fact that CCTV footage had been wiped, which they put down to a technology glitch. So there's no way of getting a positive ID of this mysterious babysitter. Interestingly, the company who usually supplies their babysitters – Safe Haven Inc – say that they have no records whatsoever of supplying anybody to the Jenkins household that evening, there's no record of the parents' email to them, and nothing booked into the system, even though the parents swear blind that they exchanged emails with Safe Haven. And even the email exchange on the parents' own computer has disappeared!'

'Somebody deliberately hacked in and permanently deleted everything to do with the babysitter,' said the Professor. 'I suspect the same people who deleted the CCTV footage as well.'

'I agree. It also looks like they spoofed Safe Haven's email account, and sent messages to Jemima's parents masquerading as that company.'

The Professor thought for a moment. 'Did you say the CCTV footage was wiped *after* your friend Jake was caught on camera?'

'Yes, it was,' she said firmly.

The Professor turned towards her. 'Okay. That's good news then.'

'In what way?'

'You see, whoever took Jemima Jenkins went to an awful lot of trouble to cover their tracks, including hacking into the CCTV mainframe and wiping critical data, so that nothing could lead back to them. If Jake had anything to do with Jemima's abduction, he would have also deleted the incriminating footage of himself. I think the fact that the footage of him was left, exonerates him from anything criminal.'

'Yeah, it makes sense,' said Calista, thinking about it. 'So... the question is, why was he there, that night, in the first place?!'

'It's too much of a coincidence. But definitely linked to Project Ingenious.'

Calista suddenly thought of something. 'Jasmine, run a check on all CCTV cameras throughout the UK, and search for similar CCTV outages of four-hour duration, or thereabouts. Display results in table format.'

'Performing check,' said Jasmine. When done, the computer read out the tabulated results, and the Professor listened intently, while Calista studied the onscreen table for several minutes. She stood up. 'No way!' she said. 'Look, Prof.' She pointed to the screen – in her excitement forgetting he couldn't look at all. 'There were similar CCTV outages on the same night that you brought in Tai and Milly, and then, before that, the night that woman turned up at my home.' She gulped. 'Th-that awful woman...'

'They're all linked!' said the Professor. 'So whoever sent that woman to you, and then Tai and Milly, was, first of all, sent to Jemima.' The Professor thought for a moment. 'I'm going to make a call,' he said, getting up. 'I'd like you to sit down with a sketch artist, Calista, to produce a composite image of the woman as you remember her. If we can identify her, it could help us identify who's behind this whole thing. Which in turn might also lead to Jake and Jemima...' He got up and said, 'Good work,

Calista,' before striding away, already touching his earpiece to make a call.

Calista was left alone, and she sat quietly for several minutes, suddenly emotional, and very shaky.

'Would you like to turn up the heating, Calista?' asked Jasmine, her room sensors having detected that she was shaking.

Calista shook her head, overwhelmed. 'N-no, Jasmine. I'm not cold,' she said, wiping her eyes. She tried to compose herself, and took several gulps of water, eventually saying, 'Jasmine, pull up the previous CCTV footage in Praed Street.'

'Footage playing,' Jasmine announced.

Calista slumped into a chair, and stared at the screen, heart aching as she watched over and over again the shadowy video of her boyfriend's last sighting.

## 16  GRANDMA NINJA

Over the next days, Calista asked the Professor on an almost hourly basis whether his people had discovered anything new about Jake. But always the Professor shook his head regretfully, said no, or just patted her arm gently. And as the week progressed, her questioning decreased by degrees, so that by the end of it she lapsed into a dejected silence.

When the ash cloud dissipated, the scholars – who had all signed non-disclosure agreements to keep the details of their new work, and the location of Avernus secure – started pouring into London, from all over the world. There was an excited buzz in the air. Calista, Milly, and Tai were set to work with a rigorous eight-hour educational programme, daily; while Milly revelled in the academia, Calista and Tai struggled, despite applying themselves doubly hard.

Yet there were some things that were bothering Milly. At the next opportunity she asked the Professor: 'Tell me again why we're learning performing arts? And martial arts?' She much preferred challenging mental exercises – languages, theorems, relativity, equations, statistics, even philosophy.

The Professor took a few seconds before answering. 'I'll try to explain... As a whole, Milly, we're all made up of a finely interconnected balance between mind and body, working harmoniously together. Upset the mind, and this has a direct effect on the body, a psychosomatic effect. Equally, upsetting the body affects the mind, and can even cause depression, despondency, irritation. So I believe very much that intellect and intelligence are only capable of reaching optimum levels when the body itself is in optimum condition.'

'So you mean, physical excellence equals mental excellence.'

'Exactly!' smiled the Professor.

Still, Milly found it hard to enjoy anything in which she did not excel. 'But... I've got two left feet, Professor,' she admitted. 'I can't dance, at all. Or fight.'

'I hear you. But is it that you don't *want* to, rather than you can't?...'

Milly thought about this and shrugged. 'Maybe.'

'And how have you been getting on with Sensei Aoki?' asked the Professor.

'He's good. He's a good teacher, but... it's just not my thing. I'd prefer to sit out, really. I'd rather read.'

The Professor, being a gentle soul, hardly liked to push anyone when they were clearly resisting. But on this he was adamant. 'Perhaps we can make a compromise. How about this: let's say you don't have to *participate* in the lessons – but would you at least keep listening to them, sitting on one side? The Sensei is excellent at what he does, and I'm positive that it'll be enriching to see him teach his art.'

'Well... okay,' said Milly. 'I can live with that.'

'Good, good,' he said. And then thought of something. 'Do you remember Aesop's fable, 'The Hart and the Hunter'?'

'Yes, of course,' she said. When she was little, Aesop's fables were her favourite stories, and even with the mind of a child, she often pondered on the moral lessons. Like most things she read, she could recite them word for word:

*The Hart was once drinking from a pool and admiring the noble figure he made there. 'Ah,' said he, 'where can you see such noble horns as these, with such antlers! I wish I had legs more worthy to bear such a noble crown; it is a pity they are so slim and slight.'*

*At that moment a Hunter approached and sent an arrow whistling after him. Away bounded the Hart, and soon, by the aid of his nimble legs, was nearly out of sight of the Hunter; but not noticing where he was going, he passed under some trees with branches growing low down in which his antlers were caught, so that the Hunter had time to come up. 'Alas!' cried the Hart. 'Alas!'*

'And the moral?' asked the Professor.

Milly knew this by rote. 'Not to despise that which could in the end turn out to be very useful.' It was clear he was telling her not to despise the dance and martial arts lessons. She thought of something. 'Are we in danger, Professor? Is that why we're hiding, and learning martial arts?'

The Professor stopped. He did not want to scare the girl unnecessarily, yet she needed to be warned. 'I... I can't say for sure. We still don't know what happened to Jemima. But I just want us – all of us – to be cautious, that's all. Please don't worry, nothing can harm us down here. And when we do go outside, we'll remain incognito...'

Milly thought about this. She was happy, at least, to hear they would emerge from Avernus at some point. But also worried about the danger that Jemima's disappearance intimated. She hated not knowing, hated being at a disadvantage – and she began to understand the Professor's vigilance and protectiveness. A Latin proverb came to mind – one she read in an encyclopaedia somewhere: 'Praemonitus, praemunitus'. She agreed, to be forewarned was most definitely to be forearmed. She thought about this for quite some time.

•••————————————————•••

During those first days of their educational programme, lessons were held mostly in the custom-built classroom that had eight crystal screens. And in time they did indeed venture outside, stiffly trying to look inconspicuous – with some wearing glasses, others caps, and Calista having great fun experimenting with changing her appearance. They went on field trips to the theatre, museums, art galleries, and places of interest – bringing to life everything they were learning in the classroom. Each of them had their own tablet with lesson sheets and exercises to be completed, which, when done, were automatically sent to tutors for assessment.

Brian was in his element, both accompanying the teenagers to museums and art galleries, but also with being able to take things easy, and indulging in a little of the high life. He swam in the pool, or lounged next to it. He took long leisurely walks – his phone pre-loaded with podcasts, audiobooks, and musical theatre tracks, humming to himself as he went. And curling up with a good book, sipping fine wine, with cheese and crackers, was one of his favourite things in the world.

One afternoon Brian made his way to the computer room, balancing a tray of tea things, and hoping to watch a 4K movie – which, on the huge screens with surround sound, was thrillingly immersive. But as he entered the door, the Professor was already there speaking to someone on the screen; they were just ending, and the screen went to a blank desktop.

'Sorry,' said Brian, awkwardly. 'Didn't mean to interrupt you, Professor.'

'Did... did you hear what I was talking about?' he asked.

'Not really. You were just finishing when I came.'

The Professor nodded, relieved. 'You brought tea?' he asked, hopeful.

Brian looked at his tray, dithering, but then capitulated. 'Sure, yes,' he smiled. He laid out the tea things on the desk next to his hand. 'Be careful, it's hot.'

'Thank you. I hope you understand, Brian. I have to be cautious when talking to the agents.'

'Agents? You have secret agents?' He asked, suddenly interested.

The Professor smiled. 'Not quite the James Bond style agent I'm sure you're imagining...' He patted the cup for the handle, blew it, and took several sips. 'But yes, they help with intelligence, protection, operations, and even a little espionage.'

Brian was fascinated. 'So... are there many of them?' He ventured, wondering if he was over-stepping.

'There are 50.'

'Here, in London?' he asked, feeling braver.

'12 of them are based in London, and the other 38 are in locations all over the world. They are everyday people, some of them having normal "day" jobs. There's even a grandmother who works in a local bakery. Each had at one time or other worked for government agencies before I enlisted them. Five of them, for example, are located around this very industrial estate, for our protection, albeit blending in with the locals. Our very own Sensei Aoki having trained them in the martial arts.'

'That's amazing,' exclaimed Brian. 'So they're ninjas! And there's even a grandmother – a grandma ninja!' He smiled. 'How wonderful.'

The Professor laughed. 'Well, ninjutsu is *one* of the arts Sensei Aoki teaches, and one of the agents *is* of the older generation, but that's all. I suppose you could say they are hybrids – a cross between traditional ninjas, and the more modern secret agent, with varying remits. Many of them specialise in intelligence, and are – as we speak – sifting through the matches thrown up by the Spiderweb program.'

'And?'

'And not much to go on yet, I'm afraid. Out of the 28,000 matches for Jemima Jenkins, it's taken almost a week to eliminate around 2,000 of them from our investigations.'

Brian, as an accountant, was good with figures. 'That's only about, say, 7%. So it'll take another... 13 weeks or so to complete.'

They both fell silent; progress was slow.

'Of course,' offered the Professor, 'it's entirely possible that the *next* match could be positive...'

'True,' agreed Brian, not wanting to dampen optimism. 'We could get lucky.'

The Professor drank some more. 'Good tea,' he said, and then remembered something. 'Do you remember the lady sitting at the table next to yours in the Science Museum café?'

Brian thought for some time. 'Vaguely... actually, no. Not really.'

'That's good!' the Professor smiled. '*She* was the one you've quaintly dubbed "Grandma Ninja".'

Brian was astonished. 'Damn,' he said, annoyed with himself. 'No, I can't remember!'

'I'm not surprised. She's one of my best, and obviously did well to blend in, incognito. In fact, this particular lady has a unique skill: Taijutsu, which is open-handed self-defence, without weapons. Also she has a heightened, almost ferocious, will to protect those within her care – which you can imagine makes her an extremely dangerous adversary...'

Brian whistled in admiration.

When Brian later saw his daughter, who was with Tai and Calista, he told them about the agents living around the industrial estate, as well as Grandma Ninja, and they all marvelled at this.

The three teenagers soon began hatching a plot. The next time they were on a field trip, they would be extra vigilant to try and identify the agents.

•••————————————————————•••

As time passed, and lessons continued, Tai discovered a love for music, especially classical music.

He remembered well those long, lonely days by himself in the warehouse, listening to concert music blaring from the nearby office, and the haunting arias that were all too ethereal as they drifted through the dusty warehouse, like lost souls.

Tai was enthralled by every aspect of his music lessons and devoured the accompanying text books – spending more and more time listening to classical music whenever he could through his AirPods. In one lesson, he had been given a ream of blank music sheets, but instead of copying out music as he should have done, he found himself putting down the notes to the melody forming in his head. It started as a simple yet evocative phrase. And then he thought of his mother, his father, the death of Cat, and the full force of those emotions seemed to possess him – he scribbled out note after furious note. Before long he was harmonising rhythms, adding chords, changing tempo, playing with texture. His repeating leitmotif interwoven between a melancholic first movement, rousing to an appassionato fervour in the second, in the third, crescendoing con fuoco, and then – at last – releasing him in the fourth to the light, enchanted strokes of a thought-provoking coda.

He learnt to play the piano to bring his music to life. Inelegantly at first – his own over-eagerness pushing him too fast. But then his music teacher, a white-haired retired concert pianist, told him: step back, take your time, allow the music to distil within you – in your mind, your soul – so that it soaks into you, becomes part of you. Tai had to close his eyes to do this, thinking, absorbing, feeling. And then he played. His fine, delicate fingers, holding captive each note until released, with beguiling strokes, onto the piano.

His music teacher could hardly believe Tai's progress had he not witnessed it himself. The man was so astounded that, despite the non-disclosure agreement he had signed, he could not help but call a close conductor friend, urging him to listen over the phone to 'this remarkable young man' playing Chopin's ***Prelude in E Minor***. At the other end of the line, the Maestro listened respectfully to Tai's recital, and when it was concluded, he remarked that he did indeed play well – almost, but not quite, to the level of his own assistant conductor, whom he had been mentoring for several years. When Tai's teacher told him that the boy was just 14 years old and had only started learning to read music and play the piano weeks ago, the Maestro silently questioned his friend's sanity. 'My dear, Hartmut,' he responded, shaking his head down the phone. 'I am no fool. Your student's freshness of expression, the immaculacy of phrasing, and the autumnal warmth of sound – this can only come from many, many years of study!' The Maestro put down the phone, rolling his eyes. He had never before taken his friend for a merry Andrew.

•••———————————————•••

The Professor had never been so busy, and he soon realised the need to delegate – reluctantly relinquishing ongoing Spiderweb work to his agents. And so he turned his attention now to Milly, Tai, and Calista. He regarded them with keen interest, fascinated by the difference between natural and engineered genius. He too was having an education.

He first began working with Tai, wanting to understand the exact nature of the boy's extraordinary ability with a variety of animals. They started with goldfish in a tank, and the Professor soon discovered that, although the fish were drawn to the boy, that was as far as his interaction with them went. The fish just crowded to the side of the tank closest to Tai, like magnets.

When the Professor asked Tai to feed them, the boy did so hesitantly, fearful that they would bite. And they did – rapaciously, like piranhas on a feeding frenzy. 'Ouch!' Tai yelped, jumping away. He raised his hand to inspect it, and pink water dribbled down his arm. 'I'm bleeding...'

The Professor, who had been standing next to him, was surprised. 'That's odd. Goldfish aren't aggressive. They really only peck and nibble, Tai. Are you sure it was the fish? Maybe you caught your finger on something – a splinter perhaps?'

Tai wrapped a tissue round the cut, and wedged his hand under an armpit. 'No. They attacked me.'

The Professor thought about this. 'Could it be that they're sensing some kind of uneasiness from you, and responding to that. Tell me, Tai, how do you feel when you look at them?'

Tai frowned. 'I don't know. I don't think they like me.'

'It's possible they're sensing your fear, and somehow absorbing that – hence the biting.'

'May...be...' said Tai, uncertain.

The Professor paused for thought. He felt for the edge of the tank and dipped his fingers below the water level. The fish were slippery and cold, and he gazed into the middle distance, waiting for a reaction.

Tai looked at the Professor, and then looked at the fish. The fish, in turn, watched Tai. But they did not bite the Professor once.

•••——————————————————•••

When the Professor held progress meetings with the teachers, they could only gush with praise for their students. They told the Professor that never had they lectured students with such deep levels of concentration, who soaked up everything they were taught and produced polished homework that was easily on a par with, or even better than, their best university graduates.

'Especially young Bythaway,' said Dr Higginson, who taught Humanities, 'she's in a league of her own.' He was referring to Milly, and his eyes shone with appreciation. 'Last week we read the fifth canto of Byron's "Don Johnny" in class, and this week we had a discussion on its humorous paradoxes – closed-book, I might add. I quoted from memory the first few stanzas as a reference: *"When amatory poets sing their loves, in liquid lines mellisonantly bland, and pair their rhymes as Venus bridles her doves, they little think what mischief is in hand..."* Whereupon young

Bythaway immediately shot her hand up saying that the actual expression Byron used was "*mellifluously* bland".' Dr Higginson clapped his hands together, clutching them to his chest.

'And?' asked the Professor, intrigued.

'Of course, I had to look up the text there and then, and my goodness she was right! After a whole week, she still remembered the entire canto, which is made up of 159 verses.' The doctor shook his head in wonder. 'It's quite extraordinary, Harry, don't you think?'

The Professor absorbed this quietly, belying the pride that swelled inside him. 'Very good,' was all he said, nodding. 'Very good.'

 An evening was organised by their Art lecturer to watch Antonio Pappano conduct Verdi's **_La Traviata_** at the Royal Opera House. Dressed to the nines, the teenagers walked through the plaza entrance and stopped, hushed with awe, to soak in the sleek lines of creamy marble and striated walnut panelling – blank sheets that beckoned them to the main attraction, the music. Trailing behind the Professor, the Chauffeur, and Brian, the three teenagers whispered and nudged each other conspiratorially, plotting how they could discover the agents. Calista scanned the crowds with narrowed eyes, whilst Tai honed in on the rainbow colours seeping above them, and concentrating on how they made him feel. Milly instead observed the detail of people's faces and expressions, mentally memorising and labelling each one – and there were hundreds.

They soon became swept up in the mass of people making their way to the main hall, one and all hushing as they entered the darkened, wine-red interior, gleaming with lustrous golds. They had front stall seats, with the Chauffeur sitting at the end of a row, and waving to the interpreter who stood by the stage; they were regulars and knew each other well. By the time they found their seats, Milly had, by a process of elimination, narrowed down seven possible agents.

But the orchestra was already warming up, lights dimming, and there was a round of applause. The conductor bowed, turned, and, with baton in hand, he coaxed out the violins into a thin stream of a single note – the beginning of the score.

The Chauffeur sat forward, a glimmer of excitement on his face as he glanced from interpreter, to performers, to musicians. He gripped the seat in front, absorbing vibrations through the wood, soaking up the flow, tempo, intensity – and the pounding rhythm of their dance, through his feet. He watched the performers in gaudy, sweeping costumes, above him. The spectacle of the opera animated him, and he swayed or clapped his hands to his chest, enchanted.

Calista smiled – watching the Chauffeur was almost as entertaining as watching the performers.

In time, the curtains descended for the first interval, and Milly hurried away rather quickly, for a toilet break she told them. By the time she returned, she whispered excitedly to Calista and Tai. 'I know who one of the agents is! *My* agent, I think. Don't look – but it's the white-haired elderly woman, two rows back on our right, wearing a grey jacket.' Of course, they one and all looked back, craning their necks to see. A sweet old lady was sitting there, fanning herself with a programme, and peering over wire-framed reading glasses into the crowds.

Calista turned back to Milly. 'I don't believe it!' she said. 'She looks too cute to be an agent.'

'But that's just what the Prof told Dad – they're trained to blend in.' Milly was sure of it. 'Believe me, she's an agent.' She was itching to look back to take another peek at her own personal guardian angel. 'Cute as a button, isn't she?' And then she had a thought. 'Hey, it'd be nice if we could thank her somehow?'

But Calista shook her head. 'Not a good idea, Mills. If their cover is blown, they're on the scrapheap...'

Disappointed, Milly reached for her flask to pour herself some tea, but then stopped. 'I have an idea,' she said, eyes lighting up. 'But you need to do exactly what I say.' They huddled together, heads touching like rugby players at a scrum. In time they parted, looking knowingly at each other, and Milly suddenly stood up and shuffled along the row of seats to exit. A few seconds later, Calista made her way out in the opposite direction, then Tai got up and went off somewhere else.

Quietly, the old lady rushed off after Milly.

Outside in the hallway, Tai stood waiting, counting to 100 in his head as Milly had instructed. All around him a kaleidoscope of people milled, some stood chatting with drinks in their hand, others queued for ice-cream. He turned around and abruptly bumped into someone, apologising. It was the white-haired old lady! But she had already turned away from him before he finished speaking, disappearing instantly into the crowds.

Tai watched the smoky trail floating in her wake. Dusky shades of brown melancholy peppered with dots, like a cloud of gnats. And fleeting though their interaction was, Tai was beginning to understand her. Understood that her brother had died, and her mind was speckled by a million thoughts of remorse, and what-ifs. He saw too the brownish tinge of regret, streaked by a dark-grey impotence and powerlessness, as she watched him die a slow, painful death.

Tai closed his eyes and breathed in all her colours.

When the white-haired old lady returned to the hall, she found that Milly was safely installed in her seat, and she heaved a sigh of relief. Scooting along the row to get to her seat, she was surprised to find, tucked into it, a small silver thermos flask with a piece of paper wrapped around it. She uncurled the note, and read:

*'Hello. And thanks ever so much for looking out for us – really appreciate it. Here is a nice flask of tea for you!*

*Hugs and kisses, Milly & co.*

*P.S. This is just between us – we won't tell anyone. ;)*

*And now, this note will self-destruct in five seconds... Only joking!!'*

The old woman glanced at the backs of the teenagers further down. They were sitting altogether, suspiciously still and upright, watching the stage.

Grandma Ninja smiled to herself, and poured herself some tea.

By the end of the performance, nearly two hours later, the teenagers were flagging, especially after a full day of lessons. Milly yawned and pulled the rucksack onto her back. As they left, she looked for Grandma Ninja amongst the crowds, hoping for a knowing glance between them, or a nod, a smile. But she was nowhere to be found, and Milly left with a pang of disappointment.

•••———————————————•••

Back in Avernus, in her bedroom, Milly dropped the rucksack onto the floor, and was surprised to hear a hollow clunk from inside. She quickly rummaged through the bag to find her flask magically returned, empty, and wiped dry. A tip of paper was sticking out from the cup, and Milly quickly unscrewed it to find her note. On the back there were perfect lines of beautiful handwriting:

*'Thanks for the tea – was just what I needed. And yes, silence is golden! Hugs from me too. P.S. Please don't disappear like that again!'*

Milly fell back on the bed. Despite her exhaustion, she couldn't help grinning to herself.

# 17 PATTERNS

The growing kittens seemed to be healthy and thriving, with clean fur and bright eyes – always mischievous and playful. Olly, with his fine black stripes, thought himself a tiger, though he was rather small and easily scared. Whereas Pasha just lived to eat and sleep. Black Max, with his white socks, was far too refined for his silly siblings. Missy Mop and Treacle on the other hand, were inseparable, in between getting on each other's nerves.

Being cared for by a mother from a different species had an interesting effect. The kittens thought they were dogs, taking their nightly walks with her and Tai in front. During the day they played fetch, wriggling little bottoms in excited anticipation as they waited for Tai to throw the ball – and then scrabbling over each other in the race to get it. They would return to Tai's feet, drop the ball on the floor, and wait expectantly. And when Tai whistled for Dog, the kittens came bounding up with excitement. Yet, at the same time, they were still very much cats – and did things on their own terms, when they decided. They might allow someone to pet them if they cared for it, didn't always like to be picked up, threw themselves on the floor in someone's path when they were feeling neglected, and completely ignored the humans when it suited them.

Still, they and their mother had settled well into Avernus – though Dog was not entirely comfortable imposing on the alpha's territory as they were. The alpha purposefully kept away, not even coming over to sniff them out of curiosity. For the first few days after she arrived, Dog often wondered whether her babies might be in danger from him, so she hovered around the kittens constantly, as any protective mother would – and when he was around, she positioned herself between them and the alpha, just in case. Though she never looked him in the eye, to avoid confrontation. Dog was a gentle soul, and intended no malice – and she was sure the alpha would sense that of her. Up to now at least, the alpha had not made a move, except when he emerged from the shadows from time to time, snarling, frightening the little ones, before walking stiffly away. The kittens would immediately run yowling to their mother. But

Dog knew it was just a show of bravado.

Acuzio on the other hand barely knew what to think. So much had changed, new humans, new animals, strange smells – it was bewildering. And though he did not want to show it, he craved attention from his old master. But the man was always distracted and busy, and just patted him on the head as he passed.

Acuzio found it irritating that food was given to the other animals at the same time as his, and in the same corner of the feeding room. His bowl was rightly the biggest, being the alpha, and so far the other dog and those annoying little beasts knew never to touch it. Acuzio could not deign to eat with those creatures – after all, they were not a pack. So he would saunter up and eat his food first, taking his time, and glancing round now and again to ensure the other animals held back. Sometimes he even snarled at them if they strayed too close. It wasn't until after he licked the bowl clean, took a long drink of water, cleaned himself, and stretched, did he finally saunter off. From the corner of his eye he saw that the others pounced on their food almost as soon as he left the room.

But then, one day, after the large voiceless one had put their food bowls on the floor, unusually, he also commanded Acuzio to follow him elsewhere to do some chores. As they left the room together, Acuzio turned to the kittens and growled at them in warning – don't touch his food!

By chance, Dog was also called away by Tai, leaving the kittens to stare hungrily at the bowls. They held back from eating, but now and again raised moist noses to the air to sniff the meaty aroma. But Pasha – the fattest kitten, who had large round eyes like saucers, and stripy marmalade fur – had fallen asleep on a chair, and she eventually awoke, to find that the alpha was not there. Presuming that he had already eaten, she jumped down and bounced over to the food, wondering why the others weren't eating. She was so hungry she almost inhaled the meat, not realising that the bowl was the alpha's... The other kittens could only meow loudly, glancing nervously at the door, not quite believing Pasha's foolishness.

When Acuzio returned to find the offending little runt eating *his* food, he was furious, and barked hysterically. The kitten jumped with fright, her fur standing on end, her tail puffing out – and a manic chase ensued as she darted between chairs and tables, yowling for her life. The noise was tremendous, and dishes, cutlery, cups and glasses smashed to the floor as the animals dashed around.

Acuzio lunged and snapped hold of the kitten's tail. He was just about to swing her round, when a streak flashed at him like black lightning. To his shock, he found himself pinned to the floor, hot breath filling his nostrils, powerful jaws clamped around his neck. He stayed stock still, knowing that the slightest movement would trigger a hairspring reflex, sinking teeth into him, going for the kill. His chest heaved with breathlessness. Helpless white eyes strained to see.

It was Dog.

A stampede of footsteps thundered into the kitchen.

Tai was the first to arrive to see Dog pinning Acuzio to the ground. Even though Acuzio was stronger, Dog was fuelled by a mother's fierce instinct to protect her young – an indomitable force. Tai immediately threw himself on Dog and wrenched her off. 'Away, Dog!!' he shouted.

Released, Acuzio sprung to his feet and shook himself. There were no wounds, except to his pride – and, with his head low, he slunk off to take shelter behind the Chauffeur.

Pasha had been thrown sideways across the room, skidding across the floor, and thudding to a stop against the wall. She was still.

Tai picked her up and cradled her in his arms. Dog went over and scratched at his leg, whining, and so Tai bent down and she licked the kitten vigorously. At last Pasha stirred, opened her eyes, and meowed feebly – much to everyone's relief. Tai sensed that life and energy ebbed through her body unimpeded. 'She's okay,' breathed Tai, suddenly feeling drained.

'Thank goodness,' breathed Calista. 'Thought she was a goner for a minute there...'

'Me too. But she's fine,' Tai said weakly, wondering why he was so exhausted.

Content that her kitten was unharmed, Dog stole a glance at Acuzio, and sniffed the air delicately – there was a faint whiff of blood. She padded cautiously over to the alpha, sniffed the scratches on his flank, and gently licked them clean. Acuzio dared not move, did not know what to do – helplessly he looked from Dog to the others.

When Dog was done, she nudged Acuzio's shoulder with the top of her head – a sign of affection, a peace offering – and then returned to Tai and her kitten. She scratched the boy's leg with a paw, so Tai gently placed Pasha on the floor, and Dog picked her up by the scruff of her neck – disappearing into the corridor, promptly followed by the kittens.

Tai went over and knelt beside Acuzio, stroking him. 'Good boy, Acuzio,' he whispered. 'Good dog.'

•••—————————————————————————•••

The next morning, the three teenagers were wearing goggles, masks, and white lab coats, and were surrounded by Bunsen burners, tripods, beakers, and flasks bubbling with jewel-coloured liquids that vaporised into white smoke. Milly pushed her beanie back on her head, and massaged her temples – she had been nursing a low, throbbing headache all morning. When she glanced up, she noticed Calista staring at the doorway, and she turned to glimpse the tail end of a shadow. 'Who was that?' asked Milly.

'The Professor,' Calista replied, still staring at the door. She immediately put her hand up, and asked to be excused for a toilet break. Milly quickly requested the same, and followed her out. But Calista went straight past the toilet, to the computer room, not caring that Milly was following her. 'Jasmine,' said Calista as she stopped in front of the desk. 'Where's the Professor going?'

Unusually, there were a few seconds of silence before the computer answered. 'That is classified information, Calista.'

Calista huffed with annoyance. 'Please pull up the last files the Professor was working on.'

'That too is classified. Can I help you with anything else?'

Calista ignored her and sat in the chair, pulled herself toward the keyboard, and started typing.

Milly drew closer. 'What's going on?'

'I'm finding out why the Professor's being so secretive, making stuff classified...' She trailed off as she concentrated on breaking through the Professor's security – she had originally programmed the supercomputer in a way that pre-empted this very situation, and had given herself backdoor access to all files. After several minutes the files were unlocked, and she looked up at the screen, expectant. An image appeared – a hand-drawn composite picture, that was clearly a police sketch. Calista instantly recognising her. 'It's the composite sketch of the description I gave,' she said. 'The person that attacked me...' She pushed her chair back, as if distancing herself.

'They must have a lead,' Milly looked from Calista to the screen.

She nodded, stopping herself from saying too much. Instead, she turned back to the screen to scroll through the other documents, speed-reading. She stopped at a driver's licence. 'Penny Thompson...' she read. An unremarkable yet unsettling name. 'And there's an address!' Calista quickly AirDropped the file to her phone. There were also employment documents showing that she worked full-time at a conveyancing firm. She looked at the time, and quickly got up. 'She must be working now, so I'm going to check out her home,' she said. 'Break in if I can. There might be something that can tell us where Jake is...'

Just then, Brian came into the room with his earphones plugged in, humming to *Les Misérables*. He stopped when he saw the images onscreen, and pulled out the earphones. 'What's going on?...' he asked.

Calista turned to Brian. 'Jasmine's found that person who attacked me, Penny Thompson, and the Prof's rushed off somewhere. So I'm gonna break into her home to see if she has anything on Jake.' She looked at him, half expecting to be challenged, adding, 'And there ain't nothing you can do to stop me!'

Brian blinked, absorbing the rush of information, his expression turning to one of incredulity. 'You can't be serious. That's crazy – and dangerous! I'm sure the Professor's gone to investigate with his agents, so you should leave it to them.'

Silence.

Brian turned to his daughter. 'Milly. Please tell me you're not part of this!'

She had no intention of going, initially, but thought about it now. She looked at Calista, saw the determined glower on her face, and realised there was no way she was going to be talked out of it. And she couldn't let her go alone. Milly closed her eyes momentarily. The low throb in her head was turning into a migraine – it sizzled through her nerves.

'Milly, I forbid you to have anything to do with this–'

'You can't stop us!' she blurted out, defiantly.

Brian looked at his daughter, not believing her tone of voice.

Colour rose up in Milly's cheeks – red blotches on pale skin. 'It's better than doing nothing! So... so I'm going with Calista, whether you like it or not!' She took deep breaths to calm herself, surprised at her own defiance.

Over the past weeks, Milly was beginning to embrace how brilliant she was – the teachers told her this at every opportunity, marked her work with glowing praise, gushed at her exceptional talent. She was no longer on the same level as everybody else. It was undeniable. She was far, far superior. And the knowledge of it was percolating into her consciousness, drip by drip – fermenting quietly into latent arrogance and pride.

Who was he to tell her what to do?!

She took Calista's hand, pulling her toward the door. 'You can't stop us,' she told him, before barging past.

Brian hung back, calling out to her. 'Milly? I... don't understand...' he said, confused, upset, mortified. But they had already gone.

Further down the corridor, Calista pulled her hand away. 'Milly, are you okay?' she said, concerned. 'What just happened?'

She turned toward her, her eyes damp. 'I... I don't know. My head... it really hurts,' she said, smarting from the pain.

'You need to lie down for a bit,' said Calista, hooking an arm into hers, and gently leading Milly to her room. She sat her down on the bed. 'Stay here. I'll get some painkillers.'

Returning in record time, and huffing from breathlessness, she carried a packet of Panadol in one hand, and a bottle of water in the other. Tai was with her.

When they entered, the room was dark, and they left the door half open to let in some light. Calista fed her two tablets, and gave her the water.

Milly lay back against the pillow, turning away from the light.

'I don't know what just happened back there,' said Calista hesitantly. 'But... you should stay, Mills. You're not well, and if anything happened to you, I'd never be able to forgive myself. And besides, your dad would probably kill me.' She nodded to Tai. 'Besides, I roped Tai in, and he's bringing Dog. So they'll look out for me...'

'No!' said Milly abruptly, immediately regretting raising her voice, and smarting from the pain. 'Please,' she whispered. 'Give me... half an hour. Painkillers'll kick in... by then.'

Calista and Tai glanced at each other. 'Look, we'll get ready, and come back in about half an hour. If you're better by then, then fine. But if not...'

'I'll be okay,' Milly insisted.

Calista looked doubtful.

Ever late, Calista returned after 45 minutes, her hair pulled back in a ponytail, dressed in a black jacket, leggings, and trainers. And to her surprise, Milly was already up, putting things into a plastic carrier bag.

'You're okay?' asked Calista.

'Yes, much better,' Milly said, distracted. 'Where's Tai, and Dog?' She bent down to lace up her boots, put on a rather scruffy bomber jacket, and wedged on her beanie.

'They're meeting us at the lift... What're you packing?' she asked, peeking into the plastic bag.

'Stuff we might need,' Milly said, without explaining. 'Did you bring anything?'

'Of course – no self-respecting girl goes anywhere without her lipstick and mascara,' Calista replied, patting her bag, completely missing the point.

'Okay... Um, how're we getting there?'

Calista looked at her, blank.

15 minutes later, Tai, Milly, Calista, and Dog were sitting on the 64 bus, in silence. After half an hour, they changed to get the E6 bus, and after that, took the underground. In all, they travelled for well over an hour, and it seemed like an age. Unfortunately for Milly it was the quiet part of the day, and with the train compartment practically empty, it left her alone with her thoughts. Her headache had disappeared, and she was beginning to feel like herself again. But she couldn't stop thinking about her father, and her tantrum, hardly understanding what had come over her. She cried silently.

Tai pulled out a packet of tissues from his pocket, and handed her one. Milly took it without a word and wiped her eyes.

When they got off the train, there was a short walk to reach the council estate where Penny Thompson lived. It was a deceptively quiet area, consisting of four rows of high-rise towers, that loomed incongruously into the sky. From afar, it appeared neat and pristine, but as they walked through, they saw peeling paintwork, soiled pavements, graffitied walls, and litter scattered everywhere. The loud thud of techno beats blared from someone's open window. From another, a woman shouted at a screeching child.

They stopped outside the entrance to one of the blocks. 'Okay. Well, this is it,' said Calista looking up at the rows of balconies. 'She lives at number 78.'

They piled into an elevator, holding their noses from the stench of urine as the lift heaved and lurched slowly upwards. At last it stopped on the tenth floor, and they burst out, gulping in fresh air.

'Phew!' Calista breathed. 'What a stink!'

Milly looked down the corridor. 'So, what's the plan?' she asked.

Calista nodded knowingly at her. 'The plan is.........' she said, desperately searching for an idea.

Milly just stared at her. 'There is no plan, is there?'

'Well, she should be at work right now. But... erm... maybe we should knock on the door first, and pretend to be them Johanna's Witnesses. Just in case.'

'You mean Jehovah's Witnesses,' said Milly.

'Yeah, them,' Calista replied. 'And then, if she doesn't reply, we can break in.'

'But what if she's really there, but just doesn't answer?'

Tai glanced at Dog, who was standing bright-eyed at his side. 'Dog can tell whether there's anybody inside.'

Calista smiled. 'Great. So if she's not there, we'll definitely break in. But if she's there, we'll have to stake out the place, until she leaves.'

They agreed, and made their way down the corridor. Strip-lighting hummed above their heads, laced in fine layers of cobweb. One of them crackled and flickered, plunging them into momentary darkness, playing havoc with their nerves.

At last they neared the door marked '78' – a plain blue door, exactly like the others. Calista and Milly held back, while Tai and Dog crept up to the door silently. Tai held up a finger in front of Dog's face, getting her attention, and then pointed to the door and cupped a hand to his ear. Dog sniffed the door first, and then stood sideways against the uPVC, and listened for some time. Eventually she turned to Tai without a sound, and sat down. It was empty.

He signalled thumbs up to the girls, and they went over.

Calista began rolling up her sleeves. 'Right, step back,' she whispered.

Milly looked at her. 'What're you doing?'

'I'm going to kick the door in. I've seen it done a hundred times in police shows.'

'The neighbours will call the police!' said Milly. 'Hold on a minute.'

She examined the lock and started rummaging through her carrier bag, producing a set of long thin curved metal picks, and a flat-headed screwdriver. She slid the screwdriver tip into the keyhole and turned it round clockwise, and then anti-clockwise, exerting pressure. At the same time, she pushed a pick inside, and felt for the lock pins. It took her several goes before hearing the satisfying click of each pin fall into position. 'Bingo,' she whispered, smiling. 'Amazing what you can learn on YouTube...'

Calista lifted an eyebrow. 'And where did you get all that from?' she asked, nodding to the picks and screwdriver.

'The junk room in Avernus...' Milly said, 'It's packed with all sorts of interesting equipment. I think the Professor's a bit of a hoarder...' She rustled through the carrier bag again, and produced a rolling pin and a small fire poker, and handed them out to Tai and Calista. For herself, she took out a long screwdriver and held it solidly in her hand. 'Just in case!' she said.

She pushed open the door, and Tai stepped in first with Dog, the girls following cautiously behind.

It was dark, all the curtains closed – the air seemed charged with electricity, making their skin prickle. They crept through a narrow corridor about four metres long. It led to three doors at the end, and Tai pointed at the first two doors to the girls, and then reached for the handle of the third. Silently they each opened a door, at the same time holding up their makeshift weapons.

Tai found himself inside a bedroom, Calista in a kitchen, and Milly was in the sitting room. They looked around with trepidation, and, to their great relief, found that the flat was empty.

They regrouped in the sitting room, astonished to find a mix of both luxury and cheap gaud. There was a large yellow sofa, with a thick purple and green rug at its foot. A mix of both modern and classical artwork hung on orange patterned wallpaper.

'It's a council flat, but this woman's got money,' Milly said.

'And awful taste,' added Calista, looking around in disgust.

Milly produced latex gloves from her Tesco bag, handed them out, then stretched a pair onto her hands. 'While we're looking around, we should make sure that everything's left exactly as it is. Or she'll suspect...'

'Agreed,' said Calista. 'And we're looking for anything about Jake Winters, Jemima Jenkins, and whoever this woman takes orders from.'

Tai told Dog to wait by the front door and keep guard, while they busied themselves searching. They did so methodically, replacing rugs, drawers, items, exactly as they had found them.

Calista also sat in front of the laptop, taking the USB stick Milly handed her, and plugging it in to download anything that was of interest.

After a few minutes, Tai called out from the bedroom, and the girls went in to find a room that was not much bigger than the double bed and wardrobe it contained. Tai was kneeling on the floor in front of the wardrobe, pulling out a hold-all bag, which he placed gently on the bed. He unzipped it and the girls crowded round to see. He pulled out a wig, clothes, a make-up bag, high heel shoes, and finally a dark grey messenger bag.

Calista instantly recognised them and shuddered. 'That's what she was wearing when... when she tried to...' She couldn't finish.

Milly rummaged through the messenger bag and pulled out a bottle of chloroform, surgical gloves, masking tape, and crisp white packages of injection needles. Forensic examiners would have needed to photograph everything, but Milly had already memorised every single item. They made sure to return everything carefully.

They kept searching, but Calista was becoming more and more exasperated; they'd uncovered nothing about Jake.

Milly looked around one last time. 'What about out there?' she asked, motioning toward the balcony door. They peered through the glass.

'Looks empty,' said Calista.

Milly opened the door, stepped outside, and looked around. The balcony could barely hold two people, its railing plastered with bird droppings that Milly veered away from. There was a large empty wire-framed bird cage hanging in one corner, and a black plastic bin tucked under it. Opening the bin, it was filled with birdseed, and Milly dug around in case anything was hidden inside.

Tai stepped out onto the balcony, and – out of nowhere – four pigeons descended, landing on Tai's shoulders and head. Milly and Calista jumped, but Tai instinctively stood stock still and extended his arms. The pigeons cooed and twitched, heads twisting round to watch Tai with beady black eyes. Sharp claws dug into his arm, scratching his skin. The pigeon on his head began pecking at his hair, making Tai panic. He shook his arms and body, so that the birds swooped away in a mass of feathers and flapping wings.

'Whoah!!' cried Calista, watching the pigeons fly off. 'What just happened?'

Tai shook himself down, and they stepped inside. He rubbed his arms. 'They scratched me up,' he said, rolling back his sleeves. His arms were covered in red welts.

'Ouch,' Calista flinched.

Tai closed his eyes – both from the pain, and also to remember. 'They each have mates,' he said, opening his eyes. 'But their mates are far away.' His Caribbean lilt rose and fell like a melody.

Milly thought about this. 'They must be homing pigeons.' She gestured to the birdcage. 'They must've escaped, and are flying back to their mates.'

Calista looked over her shoulder, antsy. 'Guys. Can we discuss this later, before a certain someone gets back?' She shot a nervous glance towards the corridor.

They went back in, packed up their things after a final look around, and then started to leave. Calista glanced at the awful artwork on the walls. 'Those things are clapped!'

Milly glanced at one of them, a portrait. 'Hang on a minute.' She rummaged through her bag again, and then drew closer to the painting. It was the portrait of a girl with a misshapen head, one eye high up on the forehead, and another, much lower, resting on a cheek. The mouth was so far to one side that it nearly touched her ear. 'It's in the likeness of Picasso's "Dora Maar",' said Milly. 'But cruder, uglier.' She studied the painting carefully. The only pleasant thing about it was the muted background of a country house and garden, painted in the impressionist style.

'Look,' said Milly. 'It's telling a story. The subject – a young girl, perhaps 10 or 11 years old – looks troubled, her eyebrows are furrowed, mouth turning downward. Her jewellery, clothes, hair are all perfect – not a wisp out of place, as if she's been forced into a mould, propriety drummed into her. But the girl's expression shows that something doesn't sit well... I'm guessing Penny Thompson saw something of herself in this painting.' Milly reached up and dislodged the frame from its hook. 'But, you're right, Cal,' she said, scrunching her nose. 'It's really ugly.' She sat down on the sofa, pulled out a pen-knife, and stuck it neatly through the hard impasto oil paint, in the middle of the eye. Milly next produced what looked like a large black washer with a small dome of glass in the middle, lined it up with the hole at the back of the canvas, and taped it down with masking tape.

'A bug?' asked Calista, fascinated.

Milly turned the picture round and checked her handiwork. 'Yep. It's a camera, as well as a microphone.' She hung it back on the wall.

Calista inspected it carefully. 'Hang on a minute,' she said. She extracted her mascara and touched up the paint around the iris, so that the tear was practically indiscernible. 'There,' she said pleased with herself. 'Now, can we go?!' she begged.

They at last stepped out of the front door with Dog, closing the door quietly behind them. They could not bear to take the elevator again, and practically flew down the stairs – arriving on the ground, gasping, dizzy, and relieved.

Their journey back to Avernus on public transport was made in complete silence. It was slowly dawning on Milly just how easily things could have gone wrong – their only protection being a rolling pin, a poker, and a dog, who was, at that moment, affectionately licking Tai's ankle.

The three were completely unaware that as their train slowed to a halt at a junction, waiting for a signal change, another train hurtled in the opposite direction on the tracks next to theirs. Inside sat Penny Thompson, staring blankly out of the window, and chewing gum.

••• ————————————————————— •••

When Penny Thompson arrived at her small flat on the tenth floor, she paused just inside the front door, sensing that something was wrong. She sniffed the air curiously, small eyes narrowing; there was a smell she could not identify. An animal smell. Quietly she looked through the flat, checking each room. But there was no-one, and she shook her head as if doubting her sanity. She went out to the balcony to feed the birds, but found that they had escaped – all but one. It had flown back inside the cage, and was hungrily pecking at leftover seeds. She tutted, locked the cage door, and threw in a fistful of seeds. When she went back inside, she noticed the abstract portrait of the girl on the wall next to the sofa. It seemed... different. She stared at it, trying to work out what was wrong – in the end reaching out to straighten the sides until it was perfectly level. Satisfied, she went off to the kitchen to microwave her dinner.

••• ————————————————————— •••

Back in Avernus, when Calista, Tai, and Milly returned, the Professor descended on them like a swooping owl – furious. The dark frown on his face scared them. 'What were you thinking?!' he said, through gritted teeth.

As he ranted at them, Calista stared into space, her eyes welling with tears, Tai looked straight ahead, while Milly stared intensely at her feet. They dared not say a word, knowing that the Professor was justified, knowing they hadn't thought it through.

The Professor turned away from them too quickly, and he stumbled on a chair. He reached out a hand to steady himself, and Calista saw that he was shaking. She tried to help him, but he pushed her away. They could only leave, unable to speak, overcome with emotion.

As they walked past his room, Brian sat quietly, listening to their footsteps outside – relieved that they had returned unharmed. But he did not emerge to greet his daughter.

••• —————————————————————— •••

That evening, when everyone's nerves had calmed, Milly sought out the Professor. She found him sitting in the den in his armchair, next to a roaring fire. He was swirling a snifter glass of brandy around, stopping to sip now and again, then swirling some more. It was as if the continuous movement oiled his thinking.

As Milly entered the room in bare feet, the old man was just beginning to nod off, the glass tipping in his hand, when he heard her. He gripped the glass firmly. 'Who's there?' he said, his head turning from side to side.

'I-it's me. Milly,' she said hesitantly, drawing nearer.

Grunting away the sleep, the Professor sat up.

'I... I wanted tell you,' she said, her voice cracking. 'I'm really sorry!' She threw her arms around him – and the Professor was surprised to find himself in a bear hug. He eventually melted, and hugged her back.

When Milly let go, she sat on the floor near his feet. 'I just... I just didn't think.' Her voice sounded small and weak. 'You told me before that I have one of the most intelligent minds on the planet. But still, I realise now, how stupid I am. How impetuous.'

The Professor breathed deeply. 'I suppose, at the end of the day, you're still growing. And, like the rest of us, you're bound to make mistakes too.'

They lapsed into silence for a while.

The Professor put his glass on the side-table, reached down and felt for a log, then threw it into the fire. The wood hissed and popped, and the flames crackled.

He turned toward her; his eyes cast downward. 'How long have you been having headaches?' he asked. 'Your chemistry teacher – he noticed that you kept rubbing your forehead in class today. And then the Chauffeur told me Calista asked for painkillers for you,' he explained.

Milly pulled her knees up and linked her arms around them. 'I've had headaches for as long as I can remember,' she said. Then quickly, 'Not every day. Just every few days or so. When it's a bad one, I... I can't think, can't function. I just need to get to bed,' she said candidly. 'But most of the time I get by. Painkillers help. But...' Milly shifted awkwardly, hot tears stinging her eyes. 'I... I had an argument with my dad today. I'd been battling a headache all morning, and it just made me really ratty. I don't know why...'

The Professor stiffened. 'I-I'm sorry to hear that, Milly, and sorry about your headaches. Please come to me whenever they return. I know a doctor, a good friend. He can prescribe something to help. I also want to arrange a thorough medical examination, just to be safe.'

Milly wiped her eyes with her sleeve. 'Okay. Thanks.'

'But for now, I think perhaps you should go and find your father,' he said softly. 'Don't you?'

'Yes...' said Milly, sighing. 'You're right.' She got up and left.

The Professor listened to her go, feeling himself tense up with the knowledge that she was starting to have headaches too... He felt for the glass on the table, needing the anaesthetising effects of the alcohol.

He took a gulp of the sweet amber liquid. Its warming notes of vanilla, cigar box, and earthy black truffle, slipped smoothly down his throat.

Slowly, he swirled the brandy glass round and round in his hand.

# 18 TO CATCH A KILLER

The next morning, the Professor rushed into the computer room unusually early, just after six. He stopped to listen to who was there, and heard the dull clunk of a mug on glass.

'Prof!' said Calista, swallowing. She was sitting at the desk.

'I got your urgent message,' his voice was hoarse.

'I've been watching the live feed from Penny Thompson's flat. And about five minutes ago, she was contacted.'

'Contacted?' repeated the Professor, drawing closer.

Calista clicked through the video player onscreen to find the exact point in the timeline. 'Yes, at... 5.58. One of the carrier pigeons returned, and Penny Thompson took something that was tied to its leg. I saw her put it in a mobile phone.'

'A SIM card,' said the Professor.

'Exactly. As soon as she put it in the phone, it beeped with a text message. Then she quickly disappeared into her bedroom. I think she's getting ready to go out.'

The Professor stiffened. 'Just 10 minutes ago?'

'Yes.'

Immediately the Professor sprang into action, and commanded Jasmine to call in agents V1, V2, and V3 – to be ready outside with the helicopter - ASAP. 'And Calista, tell Jasmine the coordinates and description of this woman. Also, relay suitable stills from the video footage, so that the agents can identify her. The best face and body shots possible. We must intercept her...'

Calista started tapping furiously on the keyboard. 'I'm on it.'

Just then Milly entered the room, holding a mug of steaming tea and an iced bun.

'Milly!' said Calista. 'Your timing's terrible – you missed all the action.'

She couldn't believe it. 'What?! I just went out for five minutes! What happened?'

'You were gone for 10 minutes, actually.' Calista rewound the footage, for Milly to see, at the same time explaining that the Professor was calling in three of the agents, hoping to catch Penny Thompson before she hurt anyone.

In the background the Professor was talking urgently through his earpiece – and as soon as he had finished, Milly ran up to him, both nervous and excited. 'Will... will you let us go with them, Professor?'

Calista's jaw dropped open, hardly believing what she was asking so soon after they'd been blasted for going to Penny Thompson's house.

Surprised for the same reason, the Professor's immediate reaction was absolutely not! But even though he could not see, he imagined her eyes now. Wide and expectant. And he understood that Milly and her brilliant mind, the mind that he helped create, would never be satisfied with just sitting by the side-lines. Learning had to be supplemented with actions, and one without the other was like theorising but never experimenting. As a scientist, he understood this very well. He remembered his son, and the over-protectiveness he had for him – and his dear wife's wise words came to him now. *'You're going to have to let go gradually, mein Schatz. He's a growing boy. He needs to discover things for himself. He knows you love him, but you can't protect him every second of every day.'*

The Professor sighed, regretting what he was about to say even before he said it. 'You'll be a liability, Milly – not just to yourselves, but to the agents as well.' He paused. 'But... if you promise to stay inside the helicopter, and just watch what happens via their bodycam links, I'll let you accompany them. Okay?'

Milly nodded excitedly. 'We promise, Professor. Don't we, Cal?'

But the Professor heard only the rush of footsteps as they ran out. 'We promise!' shouted Calista from the corridor.

•••————————————————————•••

Tai was unceremoniously pulled out of bed, while Calista barked out orders in barely intelligible cockney, saying that she'll explain later – although Tai hardly ever needed explanations.

Later, all three of them, and Dog, were piling into the elevator that would take them up to the garage. When they stepped outside into the cold morning, they were confronted by almighty gusts of wind, and the deafening thak-thak-thak of the rotating blades of a Gazelle helicopter. It had landed in the empty parking lot – its grey and beige camouflaged body at odds with the bright orange paint on the nose and undercarriage.

The door clunked open, and Grandma Ninja jumped out, looking very different from the frail old lady at the opera house. She was wearing a black bodysuit, with her fine white hair scraped back in a small ponytail. Her posture was strong and poised as she motioned for them to come over.

They stooped down, ran towards her, and she waved them inside, thudding the door closed.

The engine noise was even more deafening, and Grandma Ninja handed out noise-cancelling headsets to each of them. They put them on, and positioned the microphones to the side of their mouths. Milly couldn't help smiling. 'I'm so happy to meet you!' And threw her arms around the old lady in a bear hug.

'Pleased to meet you too, Milly,' she said, hugging her back. 'I'm agent V3.' She had a light, refined way of speaking. But there was no time to chat, and she pulled away and motioned to the four seats. 'Calista and Tai, you'll sit out here with me, and, um, your dog as well. Milly, you'll have to go into the cockpit with agents V1 and V2.'

Milly realised she'd hit the jackpot, and she turned round just as the cockpit door opened. A tall, middle-aged man, with a shiny bald head came out, and motioned for Milly to enter. There was a small side seat just behind the two pilot seats, and he gruffly belted Milly into it, clearly not amused that children were joining their mission.

The chief pilot turned round and waved cheerily at her. 'Ignore him,' he told Milly. 'That's V1, and as you can see, he's not a morning person!' he grinned. He was the youngest of the agents, Milly guessed in his thirties, and was delicately handsome, with dark clipped hair. 'I'm V2, by the way. Make sure your seatbelt's fastened at all times during flight, okay? Hold on, we're clear to take off.'

There was a sudden roar of the engines, and the entire helicopter began to vibrate as rotor blades increased speed and built up centrifugal momentum. As the helicopter lifted from the ground, the motion of weightlessness nauseated them, and Milly grasped her seat – her eyes fixed onto V2 as he expertly handled the controls.

'How long?' asked V1, still grumpy.

'ETA 11 minutes.'

They hurtled upwards and flew over the grey industrial estate, a wide blue sky opening up in front of them.

In the back, Calista grabbed Tai's hand on one side, and Dog tucked her head under his arm on the other, whimpering. With every manoeuvre of the helicopter, Calista tensed. She dry-heaved several times, mumbling miserably, 'Good job I didn't eat breakfast.'

Those 11 minutes seemed like an age – but they at last heard the roar of engines change pitch as they made a slow descent, and the helicopter skids came to rest on hard ground. The engines died down, and the teenagers peered out of the small windows, recognising the cuboid blocks of flats but from a higher perspective. They were on the roof.

Agents V1 and V2 immediately unstrapped themselves, and went out to join V3, where they swapped their headsets for earpieces, tested their comms equipment, and then turned round to the teenagers, who had all unbuckled themselves.

'The Prof told us you'll be staying inside – locked in,' said V3.

'That's right,' said Calista, slightly green.

'Just make sure not to touch anything!' V1 said forcefully.

'We're going to bring in the target, so just wait here, and sit tight,' said the kinder V2.

All three teenagers nodded.

V1 turned to address the other agents. 'The target Penny Thompson is to be brought in alive,' he said, looking at both of the others. 'I repeat alive.'

The teenagers glanced at each other. The possibility of harming anyone had never even crossed their mind – a stark reminder that the agents were deadly assassins, trained to kill. When they turned around, the agents had already put on their black ninja masks, opened the door, and were jumping out – the door slammed closed behind them with a thwump.

'Well, we're locked in,' said Calista. Ignoring V1's no touching rule, she immediately began looking around – rummaging through drawers, boxes, cabinets. She found two laptops in drawers under the seats, together with a mass of equipment and cabling. She took a minute to look it all over, then began hooking everything up – finally switching it on. It came to life with beeps and flashes and whirring.

She took a few minutes to check out the operating system and software. 'Right,' said Calista. 'This first laptop's satellite-linked to Jasmine,' she said. 'And the second shows the live feed from their bodycams.' She nodded over to the drawer, to a box filled with bodycams and earpieces.

Tai and Milly gravitated around her, and together they watched the video: the agents were running noiselessly down the stairs, the sound of their light, even breathing, amplified through the speakers.

They reached Penny Thompson's flat quickly, and gathered at the side of the familiar front door. V1 held up three fingers, counting down, and then kicked in the door with a single blow so that it burst open. The agents quickly ran inside, silently checking each room, until they had searched the entire flat in just seconds. It was completely empty, and they regrouped in the corridor. Just as they turned to leave, the Professor's urgent voice came over the agents' comms. He had been listening to Brian describing their movements from Avernus. 'The target's been spotted on street CCTV!' he told them, after the Chauffeur himself had pinpointed her with his keen eyesight. 'She's walking up Henshaw Street in a north-westerly direction. I'm sending the coordinates to your handsets now.'

A map appeared on the second laptop, marked with a bright yellow dot onscreen – the last siting of their target, Penny Thompson. It was just a few roads away from the tower block.

'Agents,' said the Professor, breathless from the intensity. 'Split up and intercept the target from three different directions. We should be able to get a GPS fix on her mobile phone in just a few minutes – Jasmine is working on it as we speak. But for now, I'm relaying to your handsets the different routes each of you must take. The aim is to surround and close in on the target, lessening her chance of escape.'

The agents held up a ten-hand signal in front of their bodycam, confirming their understanding – and they ran out silently, descending the same stairs that the teenagers had taken yesterday. They went round and round for 10 floors, until they reached the ground – and then ran off in separate directions, sprinting like gazelles.

The teenagers huddled round both laptops, watching avidly, and glancing from one screen to the other – the first showing a map with a single solid yellow dot, as well as three blinking blue dots that represented the real-time positions of the agents. They ran along streets, overtaking astonished passers-by, jumped over walls, sped through side roads and passages, circumnavigated obstacles – all without faltering, without let-up.

With bated breath the teenagers watched as the blue dots surrounded and moved closer and closer to the yellow marker.

The Professor's voice came through the speakers again. 'We've got a GPS lock on the target's mobile!' On the other screen, the yellow dot suddenly moved from Henshaw Street to County Road, which was just under a mile away, and perpendicular to the north end of Henshaw Street. It changed colour from solid yellow to blinking green.

Minutes passed, and the blue dots were rapidly closing in on the green, and they suddenly heard agent V3's voice breathe into her microphone. 'I have a visual! Repeat, I have a visual of the target!'

Next came V2's voice. 'I have a visual too.'

After a few seconds, V1 confirmed, 'I've got a visual as well.'

Milly drew closer to the screens, looking from one to the other. She frowned. From V3's camera, they could clearly see a distant view of the target, and the petite figure of a woman with shoulder-length hair. Quickly she turned to Calista. 'Can you convert the map to a satellite view?'

Calista adjusted settings, and in a few seconds it was changed to a birds-eye aerial view. They saw that the dots were very close to a park, as shown by a large stretch of green.

'Now zoom into the target,' said Milly, looking worried.

Calista pinched on the mousepad, and the view of the camera magnified onto Henshaw Street. Milly examined the shot carefully, and she suddenly sat up, feeling sick. She grappled with one of the communicators in the box, plugged it into her ear, and spoke out loud. 'Th-this is Milly. Agents – are you 100% certain you have a visual on the target? I'm looking at the map, which shows there are obstructions where Henshaw Street meets County Road. That would make it impossible for all of you to be seeing the same target.'

They responded simultaneously that they each definitely had a visual. Milly was confused.

And then, inexplicably, the agents' dots onscreen suddenly moved off in different directions: V1 began heading off in a north-westerly direction, V2 went northwards, and V3 was just turning eastward into a secluded alleyway, closing in on the green dot.

'What's happening!' came the Professor's voice. 'Agents V1, V2. You are both moving away from the target - why are you going off in different directions?!'

'Negative,' said V2. 'Eyes still on target, and I'm now closing in.'

Milly's brain whirred, sweat glowing on her face. She watched the three bodycam perspectives of the agents, each clearly showing the back of Penny Thompson looming ever closer, even though they were in completely different locations. The woman looked exactly the same – same height, same hair, same clothes.

Milly shook her head. 'No, no, no... Something's very wrong.' And finally she realised, and shouted out: 'You must be marking *different* targets! It has to be a trap! Get away from her!! Abort mission. I repeat, abort mission!!'

But it was too late. V3 had already reached her target, and was extending a hand to grab the woman's arm. They could only watch helplessly, as the target turned round to face the bodycam, and Calista's mouth dropped. 'Th-that's not her,' she said. Then louder: 'That's not Penny Thompson.'

The impersonator immediately produced a knife from inside her jacket, and slashed at V3 like a crazed animal. With lightning reactions, V3 jumped back, avoiding by millimetres the cut of the blade.

Calista and Milly screamed.

They glanced nervously from one video to the other; the same was happening to agents V1 and V2 – somebody, who was not Penny Thompson, turned round and attacked them.

V3 fought back. Her movements were fast and agile as she dodged each assault in the ways Sensei Aoki had taught. The imposter woman screeched and lunged and growled at her, yet V3 remained perfectly silent, blocking, dodging, striking, kicking, and swirling around – smooth and precise. But she was knocked to the ground, and the girls squealed as they watched the glint of the knife plunge down toward the camera. V3 quickly rolled away and sprung up, like a coiled cobra. The two circled each other slowly, deliberating their next move, the imposter's face contorted into an expression of pure savagery.

And then, out of nowhere, three other opponents appeared, joining with the imposter, and surrounding V3.

'No!' gasped Milly, feeling her stomach churn, eyes fixed on the screen. The attackers threw themselves at V3, and the picture descended into swirling black motion that made it impossible to see. There was just the awful, sickening sound of blow after blow – bone crunching, flesh tearing, punches pounding.

Milly burst into tears, and Calista yelled with frustration. There was nothing they could do...

There suddenly came a loud thwack and the view from V3's bodycam became very still. She was lying on the ground, the sound of her chesty breathing was light and scattered. She swayed, tried to move, tried getting up. And then one of the attackers approached and began kicking her, again and again. The camera splattered with red, eventually crunching broken. And the screen turned black.

V1 and V2 were still fighting valiantly, but they too became outnumbered by attackers. It was turning into a bloodbath, unbearable to watch.

Milly sobbed as she watched with horror, crumpling onto the floor. Soon each of their screens became dark too.

Tai picked himself up from the floor – he was both mortified and seething with anger. His hands balled into fists. 'I have to help them,' he said.

'How?' said Calista, red-faced. 'What can we do? We're locked in!' She scrambled to her feet. 'And even if we get out, by the time we make it over to them on foot, it'll be too late.'

Milly's heart thundered in her chest, not quite believing what she was about to say, what she was about to do. 'Strap in,' she said, glowering. She turned to face them.

Tai and Calista looked at her with disbelief. 'You can't be serious...' said Calista.

'There's no time!' Milly barked. 'I can get us there in a few minutes. I can work out how to open the door. But we have to leave now!'

Calista began freaking out. 'Have you ever flown a helicopter before?!!'

'No,' said Milly, quietly. 'You just have to trust me.'

Calista glared at her. She had seen Milly excel in the classroom, her brilliant mind, her intelligence, clear to everyone. But was it enough to put their lives in her hands? To go along with this crazy, spur of the moment thing? Still, against her better judgement, and in a daze, Calista found herself gravitating into the seat, and feeling for the seatbelt. Tai followed.

Without a word, Milly disappeared into the cockpit.

Calista closed her eyes, her body rigid, and she felt for Tai's hand. They gripped onto each for dear life. The next thing they heard was the engine starting – first choking and spluttering, and then roaring. Her stomach lurched as the helicopter jerked upwards, stalled, and then suddenly heaved up again and sideways, frighteningly fast. Dog cried.

Calista's eyes squeezed firmly shut.

•••————————————————•••

In the cockpit, Milly was a small figure amidst the high walls of equipment and machinery and rows of buttons and switches and lights. She inched forward just to be able to reach the controls, her mind bringing back the exact movements she had seen V2 go through.

She clutched the twist-grip throttle of the collective with her left hand – a stick similar to the handbrake of a car – and pulled it upwards. The rotor blades above her sparked to life, and she felt their power pull on the weight of the helicopter. The blades built up speed, turning and turning, until the helicopter lifted inches into the air. Her feet reached for the two pedals, and rested on them. Had she blinked at that moment when watching V2, she would have missed him pressing the right pedal by a fraction as they lifted off – a small but critical step. She mimicked this now, feeling the satisfactory balancing out of the torque effect, lifting them higher into the air. Milly's memory churned through everything she had observed V2 do, every arm movement, every finger-flick of switches, the rise and fall of his knees – mimicking it all herself.

They whooshed up and sideways with a jerk. Right off the top of the building. Gulping, she looked out the window – they were suspended in thin air, with nothing beneath them but a 100-metre drop.

Milly's heart pounded. She had not factored in the 'feel' of the weight of the controls, the amount of pressure needing to be applied to each, and the solidness and 'give' of the machinery.

Doubt gripped her, and in that moment the helicopter lurched in a series of jolts that threw her forward – and she panicked. The helicopter veered round in a circular motion, and suddenly began freefall, straight down the west face of the tower block.

The ground sped up towards them at a frightening speed – in a matter of seconds it would all be over.

There was a muffled scream from behind.

Air blew upwards, making her ears pop.

And Milly's mother whispered in her ear. 'You can do it, Milly. I believe in you.'

Milly gritted her teeth, re-gripped the controls, and repositioned her feet. Quickly, she wrenched back on the cyclic, pitching the nose up, levelling the machine into a landing flare. She added power to the engine by raising the collective, maintaining altitude and rotor thrust. At last, the helicopter submitted to her control, so that the iron beast stopped – hovering just a few metres from the ground.

Sweat dripped from her as she dared to look out, trembling. A sea of grass billowed beneath them in frenzied waves.

Milly sobbed with relief, caught her breath, and then manoeuvred the helicopter into an anticlockwise turn with increasing, but shaky, confidence. 'Love you, Mum,' she whispered. And they whooshed upwards again, into the sky.

Below, the ground shrunk and faded, miniaturising to Lilliputian proportions.

Milly watched the controls, adjusted direction, and checked navigation, flying in silence. Before long, verdant parkland came into view, and then the familiar buildings that she had seen from the aerial map rushed closer. She began to descend, hovering just above the narrow strip of alleyway that V3 had entered to approach the target. From the air, the alleyway – a dark crack between two tall building blocks – looked impossibly thin, and, in her head, Milly made quick mental calculations. But there were unknown variables, and it was anyone's guess as to the diameter of the rotor blades, and so she had no choice but to estimate. There might be just a metre's allowance beyond the rotor blades. Maybe less. But there was no room for error.

Milly manoeuvred round to make her approach. She kept her eyes on the spot where she planned to land, close to the end of the alleyway. Slowly she lowered the helicopter, holding her hands as steady as she could. The helicopter inched downward. Her feet pushed pedals, maintaining the rotor disc flat with the cyclic – glancing nervously at the ground, and keeping her eyes on the surrounding walls.

But she didn't see that clinging to the building walls were a mass of crane flies. They were thrown up by the turbulence, and whooshed helplessly into the air in a dark cloud. Thrown, Milly lost control just before touchdown, and they crashed into the ground, the helicopter skids buckling underneath them like tin cans. Sparks flew out in all directions from the instrument panel, and the frame of the helicopter shuddered to a halt.

Milly was thrown sideways across the console, scratching her arm and bumping her head. But she quickly recovered, unbuckled herself, and ran to the back to find Calista, Tai, and Dog already standing, looking hugely relieved. The door had been thrown open, and was hanging ajar.

'Let's get out, quick!'

Tai ran across to the helicopter door and climbed down first.

Standing on solid ground was blissful, but the alleyway was far too quiet for their liking, apart from the hiss of smoke rising from the helicopter.

They ran further down, but there was no-one to be found. Dog suddenly picked up a scent, and began whining. They followed her to a bank of leaves brushed up against the wall, and she began digging frantically – revealing a blackened hand. Milly gasped and fell to the ground, brushing away leaves to reveal V3 lying there, covered in blood, her face swollen and puffy.

Her eyes flickered open, just a crack – the whites bright against the red and the dirt. She looked up painfully at Milly.

'Don't move,' whispered Milly, tearful. 'Please, keep still.' She looked her over to assess the damage, but there was so much blood, her body twisted at awkward angles, she didn't know where to start.

V3's lips quivered, trying to speak.

'Please,' Milly begged, '*please* save your energy... hold on...'

And that's when they heard the skid of a car's wheels at the entrance of the alleyway. The teenagers turned round, hoping upon hope that it was the Professor with help. It was a black car they did not recognise. Doors flung open in quick succession, and out climbed five thugs – with dishevelled and dirty clothing, messy hair, and blackened hands wrapped in knuckle-dusters. The teenagers instantly recognised them as the agents' attackers. Terrified, Calista looked round for an escape route. But there was none.

Milly started fumbling with something inside her jacket, but her hands trembled so much that she nearly dropped it. The thugs were almost upon them by the time she pulled out a yellow plastic water pistol, and held it in front of her, shaking uncontrollably. 'D-don't come any closer, or I'll shoot,' she said.

The men stopped, hardly believing their eyes, and burst into laughter – pointing at the little girl with her water pistol.

Frantically Milly fiddled with the rubber cap on the gun's nozzle, and then squinted one eye as she lined up the front with the rear sight, aiming at the closest thug. 'I'm warning you!' she shouted. 'Don't come any closer!!'

But one of the men had had enough, and he rushed forward. Milly instantly squeezed back on the trigger, releasing a stream of liquid that doused the man's entire face. Quickly she aimed at the next man, and shot the remaining fluid onto his face as well.

The first man stopped in his tracks, and reeled back in mock surprise, pretending to be hurt. Then he wiped the liquid from his eyes, blinked, and decided enough was enough. He reached out to grab Milly, who managed to dodge to one side. In her head, counting, 'Four, three, two...'

All of a sudden, the man stopped in his tracks, let out a pathetic gurgle, and collapsed on the ground with a thud. The second man followed suit. Their bodies convulsing, eyes bulging, as they writhed and squirmed on the ground until, finally, they went limp.

While the three other thugs watched in stunned silence – Tai looked across at Dog, who was hiding behind some bins against the wall. He got her attention, and silently held a flattened hand to his leg, then his arm, and flicked it outwards in a pointed finger to the three remaining men.

Like a bullet, a streak of black fur launched toward the thugs, and Dog jumped up onto one of the men, sinking her teeth into his right arm, and shaking it violently. He bellowed in pain. But Dog had already released and was tearing into the man's leg so quickly he barely had time to react. He sunk to the ground, screaming with pain.

The fourth thug grabbed a discarded broom stick that was propped against the bins, and swung it at Dog with such force, that she was thrown back against the wall, whimpering.

Infuriated at the attack on Dog, Calista ran up to the man screaming like a banshee. Quickly, Tai sped toward him as well, outrunning Calista, and launched himself at the man, with a flying Geri kick, exactly as Sensei Aoki had taught him. He followed this with an Oi Zuki punch, balancing out his weight with the left hand and his other foot. A flurry of Uchi punches followed, as his feet danced in a flow of rapid Kata movements. Each limb moving like a machine, feet sliding with precision.

The thug was spinning out of consciousness, and just as he began swaying in a dazed stupor, his eyes locked on Tai's hand as it coiled into the shape of a snake. Tai flattened his feet into the ground, and compressed abdominal muscles, releasing the flow of power from his spine into the last whip of the snake as his hand struck out at his opponent's head – knocking him to the ground. Quickly Calista sat on him, pinning him down.

Meanwhile, Milly had dropped her spent plastic gun, and found herself face to face with the fifth and last remaining thug. She had never participated in Sensei Aoki's lessons, remaining a passive spectator – shunning any kind of violence. The man was huge compared to her, and as he rushed at her, she screamed. He grabbed her neck in a garrotting stranglehold, and such was his strength that she was lifted clear from the ground.

Milly gurgled helplessly, her eyes bulging, arms flailing.

And then – out of nowhere – a single leaf tumbled from the sky. Flitting and rolling softly downward. She noticed it only in the fringes of her consciousness, the shine of its waxy surface gleaming in the light as it passed close to her head. Ominously, the sky darkened, and an immense black cloud slid down. The gloom somehow flapped and vibrated – quivering and shape-shifting into a tighter, compact mass, as it engulfed the thug strangling Milly. It seethed around him. And he screamed in horror, letting go of her. She stumbled back, clutching at her throat, watching the incredible spectacle, unsure of what she was seeing.

The man tried frantically to bat away the blackness that covered him – throwing himself against walls, and rolling on the ground. The dark cloud seemed to be like thousands of small fluttering things flying into his face, and mouth, and ears.

When Tai and Calista finished with the other thugs, they turned to watch with amazement as the man was consumed by darkness, rolling around, crazed and hysterical – eventually knocking himself out against the wall. Unconscious now, the mass settled onto him and the wall, becoming still. Covering them like a blanket of fine black snow.

Just then, two ambulances came screeching up, and stopped behind the thugs' car. The back doors of the first one opened, and several ninja agents ran out – one of them jumped into the black car, and drove off at speed, while the others scooped up the four unconscious thugs and piled them into the back of the ambulance. When they saw that the fifth was completely covered by a dark mass, they ventured cautiously closer, and the blackness burst off of him, fluttering and settling on the wall. They picked him up and took him away.

From the second ambulance, two paramedics poured out with a stretcher, and ran over to V3, where they gently pulled her onto the fabric, and ran off with her, past the astonished teenagers without a word. Both ambulances drove off within seconds of their arrival – leaving the teenagers standing alone, watching them disappear.

Finally, there was a flash of silver, and the FX4 pulled up, just as wailing police sirens resounded in the near distance. The Chauffeur's window slid down, and he motioned frantically for the teenagers to get in. They ran over as fast as their legs would take them.

The Chauffeur revved up and pulled away with a great screeching of tires. Milly turned to look out of the back window at the ambulance disappearing down the road. A line of police cars came rushing up, and halted at the entrance to the alley. Milly's eyes glistened with tears, and she wiped bloody hands on her trousers – hoping upon hope that V3 would be okay.

The stick-like creature started out life as a tiny dot – one of thousands of eggs laid in water-logged soil. The warmth of spring signalled her hatching, and then the race for survival began. She did not know it, but only a fraction of her kind survived predation by beetles, spiders, dragonflies, and birds – she was the lowest link in the food chain, and her chances were slim.

But she managed to grow into a writhing brown worm, with sharp mandibles, instinctively shredding her way through algae, diatoms, and bacteria to fuel tremendous growth. It seemed she existed only to eat, soon progressing to roots and leaves. In time, as a fully-grown leatherjacket, she rested by the surface of the soil – as if conserving every energy for her big metamorphosis. Then, at last, she pupated and emerged, leggy and stick-like, her delicate transparent wings glistening in the sun, antennae quivering with life.

She now had just one purpose, to mate, and have her eggs fertilised; it was easy enough, as clambering males were already swarming around her. And now she just needed to search for a safe place to deposit her eggs.

She flew in straight lines, with certainty and purpose. But a strong gust of wind blew her off-course, and she found herself trapped in a spider's web. Frustratingly, the more she struggled, the more she became glued to the silk. It bound her like molten steel. Remaining helpless for many revolutions of light and dark, she dangled silently, aware of precious time passing, and heavy with eggs that she yearned to lay.

And then a miracle happened. A giant thing appeared – so large that it blocked the light, and her domed eyes could not make out the full extent of it. She was strangely drawn to this hot, thunderous, breathing thing, though she could not understand why.

And suddenly the crane fly found that she was free, and being lifted up to the sky, whereupon a strong gust swept her up into the air – her wings glistering like slices of diamond, as she flew off into the vast blue.

At last! That very day, she found a good stretch of waterlogged soil and laid her precious eggs, one by one – pushing her ovipositor deep within the darkest crevice she could find. Her purpose fulfilled, the crane fly could rest now. Yet, inexplicably, an unusual urge rose within her, to return to the giant thing that had freed her from the spider's web. And so the hapless crane fly retraced her path and found a way to rest with the giant – clinging to her, or hovering nearby.

But then, one day, her wings quivered nervously as her giant was suddenly thrown this way and that – and the little crane fly sensed danger, and hurt, and fear. She flew up into the air, and, to her surprise, merged with a swarm of more of her kind. They joined her, and together descended as a dark, shifting mass, crowding around that dangerous thing, and completely engulfing it. When at last the threatening giant lay still, the crane fly settled on his face, resting from the battle. Around her, she saw many others of her kind dismembered, or crushed, or lying dead, but the vast majority were alive. Her large compound eyes smarted from exhaustion. And then she saw the other giant, *her* giant, running off, away from her. But the crane fly had no energy to follow. And anyway, the life within her was beginning to ebb and wane. She resigned to it. The circle of life was complete – and as she watched her giant disappear, leaving her forever, there was an overwhelming satisfaction that her purpose had been accomplished.

She somehow sensed that after this final rest, there would be nothing.

# 19  DEATH AND LIFE

There should have been dark skies, storms, lightning, and thunder, to fit the mood – but instead it was bright and clear, and birds sung gaily. The small group stood, sombre, around a neat rectangular hole dug deep into the churchyard soil. A gnarled yew tree spread long branches over the mourners, offering dappled shade from the sun.

Professor Wolff stared into nothingness. His eyes were somehow even darker than before.

The three teenagers stood in a numb, silent line – with Tai flanked by Calista on one side, and Milly on the other. Calista and Tai seemed mesmerised by the stark blackness of the pit before them – a gaping mouth that would soon devour its prey. But Milly hung her head, barely able to look.

Her expression was pained beyond words. Her young mind churning through dizzying emotions: shock, grief, numbness – but most of all, guilt. She thought she had been clever, hiding the camera in Penny Thompson's flat. But instead, it had been discovered, and was used to trick them, draw them out, and corner them into a trap...

The cortege of pallbearers marched forward, heads bowed, weighted by the coffin on their shoulders. Their shiny black shoes advancing step by step toward the beckoning grave. When they reached it, they strained and grappled – lowering the casket into the ground. It disappeared from view, and Milly finally broke down and sobbed.

•••——————————————————•••

As they drove back to Avernus in the FX4, Calista slipped her arm into the crook of the Professor's. 'V1 had no-one?' she asked. It was only the four of them at the funeral, beside the pallbearers.

The Professor's eyes drifted downward. 'It is the way of the ninja, Calista. They have chosen to remain unattached in order to fulfil their responsibilities. A lonely life, but the safest.'

Calista had guessed that was what the Professor would say – but still, it was doubly saddening to think that V1 had been buried without any loved ones to mourn him. No public recognition, no-one to acknowledge his extraordinary courage. His tombstone marked 'unknown'. There was just a silent burial, a covering with soil. In the end, a macabre disappearing trick – here one minute, gone the next.

'Is... that why you never re-married, Prof?' Calista asked hesitantly.

The Professor did not answer immediately, but then he murmured, 'Maybe.'

After a long pause, he continued. 'When you are blessed with the perfect wife, and the perfect son, it's hard to find anyone... anything that even compares. And besides, having such a blessing even once in a lifetime, is a miracle. One cannot be greedy, and expect it twice. Anyway, I suppose my situation is much like the agents'. It's safer for everyone this way.'

•••——————————————————•••

Back in Avernus, V3 lay still and unconscious in one of the numerous underground rooms.

Bandages covered most of her body, and the part of her face that was not covered was unrecognisable from congealed gashes, and bruises flowering purple and yellow. The Professor stood beside her, as the doctor talked through the prognosis. 'It's a waiting game, Harry,' he said as he scribbled something on a tablet. He returned the pen to his jacket pocket. 'And a miracle that she's still alive. There are multiple stab wounds and lacerations to the chest and abdomen, broken ribs, with contusions around the upper arms. She has a nasal fracture, and severe intercranial injuries. Their intent was not only to kill, but to inflict as much pain as possible. It was savage, Harry. Savage. Which is why we've induced a coma, to lessen swelling of the brain and relieve pressure – in the hope that it will reduce the possibility of brain damage. But, as I said, it's a waiting game, and only time will tell.'

The Professor slowly nodded his understanding. 'Thank you, Dan,' he said. The doctor placed a hand on the Professor's shoulder, before leaving the room.

Alone now, the Professor hesitantly reached out to feel for V3's hand, squeezing it gently. In time, he traced the line of her arm upward, lightly brushing her jaw with the back of his fingers, and then resting them on her cheek. With eyes closed, the Professor flinched as his fingers glided across the contours of V3's face, the hard cast around her nose, the dried scabs, and the swelling of her skull beneath thick bandages. His hand began shaking uncontrollably, and he snatched it back, holding it still with the other.

He had known V3 as strong, intelligent, and skilled – but there was just the husk of her lying before him now. Someone else in her place. A persona non grata.

Unable to bear it any longer, the Professor turned and left the room, crossing with the nurse who was entering, her shoes squeaking on the cold, hard floor.

For the ensuing days, Avernus was like a ghost town, drained of life and colour. The teenagers passed each other silently, went back to their rooms, picked at their food for lack of appetite, hardly concentrating on their studies – it was all they could do to keep their minds distracted.

Where once there had been optimism, camaraderie, and a playful desire to learn and grow and discover together – they had one and all become miserable and disconsolate.

The teenagers did not know it, but in a secret location, the captured thugs had been secured and individually interrogated by senior agents. The rogues' eyes betrayed nothing, their silence resolute. Even after hours and days of utterly exhausting questioning – shoulders hunched, eyes dark with determination, white bandages seeping – they did not budge.

At the same time, another group of agents were going over Penny Thompson's flat with a fine-tooth comb. Now that she had been found out, she would either be on the run or in hiding, and was unlikely to ever return. When one of the agents went out onto the balcony there was a pungent smell of bird mess, but no sign of a single pigeon.

On the table in the sitting room, the small camera device that Milly had planted was left, forgotten, still attached to the masking tape.

•••————————————•••

Milly's head was stuck cruelly on repeat.

And though she tried hard, she could not emerge from it – remembering and replaying with crystal clear clarity every second of every minute of those hapless events. Postulating how she might have changed things, what she could have done better...

There was a hesitant knock on the door, and Tai popped his head in, holding a small plate with a croissant. Milly looked at the pastry, looked at Tai, and turned away saying nothing. She shifted awkwardly.

Tai dared to enter without being asked, and placed the croissant on her bedside table, sitting next to her on the bed. His hip touched her foot, and he quietly absorbed her guilt, anger, self-loathing. And pain.

'Can I get you some painkillers?' Tai asked softly, like a child.

Milly shot him a look that was an obvious no. The pain was her punishment, and she welcomed the sharpness of it, tearing through her skull, ripping her nerves to shreds. She needed to feel every iota of it.

Tai sat quietly as Milly's heady emotions seeped deep into him. Slowly, his shoulders hunched, his body curled inwards, as he absorbed everything she was feeling.

In his mind's eye came a memory of his mother, sitting in the kitchen, chopping vegetables. The weight of the world on her shoulders. He was a small boy then – sitting next to her, nibbling on a carrot stick – and he saw how, every now and again, she glanced momentarily at the blade, and wondered at how easy it would be to kill herself. End it all.

Involuntarily, Tai's mind threw him back even further, to when he was a nursing baby, nestled in her arms, feeding from her. Sleepily, he would look up at his adored mother, one eye open, one eye closed. Taking in every detail of her downcast face – vaguely wondering why the milk tasted so sour.

His mother's indolence, the same loss of the will to live, was now in Milly – as if it had infected her, like a virus.

After a few minutes, Tai started, 'Your father...'

But the door was already creaking open, and Brian stepped in.

Tai got up, they exchanged places, and he left quietly.

Milly fell into her father's arms and broke down, sobbing. She buried herself into the one man that could make everything seem better even if the whole world were falling apart.

'There, there,' he said over and over, stopping now and then to kiss the crown of her head. 'There, there.'

'I... I'm sorry, Dad,' she sobbed. 'Really, really sorry! I don't know what came over me. I love you more than anything, and I just don't know why I acted like that...'

Brian hushed her. 'No need to explain, Milly. I knew you weren't yourself back then. All that matters right now is that I've got you back.'

After some time, Milly pulled away and swiped at her eyes with the back of her sleeve. 'I... miss mum,' she said, through juddered breaths.

'Me too,' he sighed. He held her hand. 'Been thinking about going back to the house – to get our family photos. The ones in the old biscuit tin under the stairs...' He had a sad look on his face. 'Not sure why, but I really want to see the one where she's wearing that purple bedgown, holding you as a tiny baby – just back home from the hospital. Her smile lit up the room. She was brimming with happiness. And that picture... the two of you were so beautiful together.' He squeezed her hand.

'I know the one.' Milly's eyes softened with the memory. 'Her bedgown was purple because it had a pattern of irises. They were her favourite flower. Mum's hair was scraped back in a messy ponytail, with a few strands over her left eye, and her cheeks were flushed pink. Baby me was half wrapped in a cream coloured blanket, that had little brown bunnies on it. She told me once that she'd bought it from Oxfam. And you can just about see in the photo that only half her nails were painted – she said that the first labour pain came when she was doing her nails, making her spill the bottle of varnish. The stain is still there on the carpet...' Her photographic memory was a double-edged sword; along with the memory, it dredged up the full, brutal force of her loss.

A curious expression came on Brian's face. 'That's funny...' he said, in wonder. 'The way you describe it... it's like I can see the photo right now, in my mind – clear as crystal.'

Milly smiled sadly and squeezed his hand.

••——————————————••

On her way to the computer room, Calista walked past the open door of the den, balancing a pot of instant noodles in one hand, and a tall glass of milk in the other. Behind her trailed the round marmalade kitten they had named Pasha, who was licking up milk that was sploshing behind her as she walked. Calista stopped – from the corner of her eye she'd noticed movement next to the open fire, so she backtracked, and peered into the room. To her horror, she saw Acuzio with one of the kittens in his mouth, and she almost screamed at him to put it down. But then she realised that he was in fact carrying it across to Dog, who was lying on her side, with her back to the fire. Little Max, gently held by the scruff of his neck in Acuzio's mouth, meowed in protest, until it was placed along with the other suckling kittens.

Calista went inside and watched with fascination as Acuzio then padded over to Pasha behind her, picked her up too, and deposited her at Dog's belly. He nudged her closer with his snout, and sat back on his haunches, content that the kittens had all been found. Both he and Calista watched the fat Pasha barge her way in and settle down to feed along with the others.

Tai appeared at the doorway with a bowl of water, and placed it on the floor close to Dog. She was sure to be thirsty afterward. He stood back, and Calista hooked her arm into his, resting her head on his shoulder. Silently they took in the heart-warming scene.

•••————————————————————•••

After their evening walk around the hauntingly beautiful moonlit lake and gardens, Dog and the kittens had become accustomed to returning to Avernus and sleeping with Tai in his room. The boy did not use the bed, but instead folded the duvet on the floor, and settled on top of it. Dog nestled at his side, with the kittens piling on top of him – their fluffy bellies warm against his skin. Tai's eyes soon bobbed as he drifted into sleep – but then a scratching noise at the door jolted him back. He pushed himself up onto his elbows and listened. It was the sound of claws against wood. Realising who it was, Tai got up to open the door, and, quite casually, Acuzio padded into the room, as if he had always come.

When Acuzio saw Dog, his tightly curled tail wagged cautiously, timidly. Dog looked at him, and heartily wagged her tail in return.

There was space on Tai's right side, and so Acuzio settled himself on the floor next to him. He looked at the kittens, and found himself licking one of them in reflex, before curling into himself, to sleep.

They were a pack now, and so it was only right that they all sleep together.

# 20 HOPE GARDENS

The Professor was alone in the computer room, talking out loud into the air. It was the first time since the death of V1 that he'd been able to sit down and work. 'Jasmine, remind me of the list of tasks you've been working on.'

On the middle screen, Jasmine displayed the Task Manager which showed a table of applications, processes, and services – and Jasmine proceeded to read these out to the Professor.

Calista walked in, catching the tail end of her description. 'Hang on a sec,' she interrupted. 'Repeat the top items you were working on, Jasmine. I see it took up a lot of your processing power.'

'I was analysing Jake Winters' netbook, Calista.'

Calista became alert. 'What did you find?'

'After checking historical logs of access to cloud storage servers on the Dark Web, I discovered hidden files. I was processing through passwords to unlock the files. I have tried 6,630,196,847 word and letter combinations, but without success.'

Calista blinked as she absorbed this. 'I take it there's no unshadowed password back-up file?'

'I have already checked, but there is none,' replied Jasmine.

'Jake kept files on the Dark Web?' asked the Professor, surprised. 'Do you have any idea why?'

They both knew that the World Wide Web was very much like an iceberg, where the visible part above water is comparable to the surface web of the internet, accessible to the general public through search engines. But that was just a small fraction of the whole. Below the surface, and invisible to the vast majority of people, was the Deep Web, where governments and large corporations kept files hidden from public view. And even further down was the Dark Web – used mostly to store illegal and criminal information, data, and images, saved on private servers that could be accessed only by very specific means.

Calista shook her head, struggling with gnawing doubt. 'I had no idea, Prof. But... let's not panic,' she said, trying to convince herself. 'Jake might've used the Dark Web to store important files.'

Calista started typing furiously. 'I'm locating a special browser to check it out,' she said, distracted. When the app downloaded, Calista unpacked it, and used the other screen to trace Jake's history. She identified in the Dark Web the server that he had repeatedly visited – it was a .onion domain, which meant that both provider and user would be difficult to trace. Calista fell silent for some time, typing fervently on the keyboard. At last she said, 'I've managed to locate the server, Prof.' She shook her head with frustration. 'But we've hit a brick wall,' she sighed – a password was needed, but every word she tried was failing. 'Just need a mo' to try and figure out a way to get in...'

The Professor raised an eyebrow. 'Considering you hacked into government servers, Calista, I hardly expect this to be a problem for you...'

Calista scratched her head. 'You would think. But Jake must've really wanted to keep these files secure for some reason.' Every password she entered was answered by a double-beep. Fail. Fail. Fail.

Minutes soon turned into hours, and an exasperated Calista marched out for a toilet break. After she washed and dried her hands, she noticed the dark circles under her eyes in the mirror. And then saw that her hair was a mess too. 'Great! Bags *and* bad hair, just to top off everything...' she muttered to herself with disgust. She stepped back from the mirror, and suddenly remembered how Jake always insisted she was beautiful, even when she knew she looked awful. That was one of the things she loved about him.

Suddenly, Calista stopped, thought for a minute, and then rushed out of the bathroom, calling out to Jasmine as she went. 'Jasmine, the Dark Web server where Jake's files are stored. Unusually, the sys admin gave it a proper name – can you tell me what it was?'

'The server was named "Poppins", Calista.'

'Poppins! That's what I thought,' she said excitedly. She burst into the computer room, whooshed past the Professor, and sat down next to him, commandeering a keyboard. She limbered up her fingers, muttering to herself, 'Right, let's see if I can remember how to spell it...'

In the password box, Calista slowly typed in a very long word indeed: 'supercalifragilisticexpialidocious' – then hit the enter button, and, suddenly, the complete file structure opened onscreen. She punched the air with exhilaration, beginning to understand now Jake's advice to improve her spelling. 'I love you, Jake!!' she exclaimed, glancing at the Professor and reeling off a barely comprehensible explanation – something about the server being called 'Poppins', which reminded her of the word 'supercalifragilisticexpialidocious', and her name 'Cali' was part of it, and they'd discovered that 'Cali' meant beautiful or lovely – and Jake always told her how beautiful she was, even on a bad hair day. 'Don't you see, Prof?' she breathed excitedly. 'It's like Jake's leaving a trail of breadcrumbs for me to find. He knew I'd come looking for him...'

She typed at the same time as she spoke, downloading all his files. Then she quickly exited. Jasmine's processing speed was so fast that it took just seconds to copy over whole terabytes of data. Calista began examining the contents. 'Okay,' she said. 'So far, looks like a lot of video files. Loads of them, over years. Let's see...' She chose a random file, and clicked on it. 'I'm playing one now.'

Calista watched as the video player displayed grainy images of a small bedroom – from the info stickers on the walls and window, and the pullcord next to the bed, it looked like a nursing home. The bed was perfectly made, though with clothes thrown over the end, and there were piles and piles of books, scattered on the floor, on a table, the window ledge, and shelves. Next to the end of the bed was a well-worn but smart brown leather suitcase, standing upright, with its handle extended fully. Calista described all this to the Professor, and just a few minutes into the video, an old man was wheeled into the room by a nurse in a stiff white uniform. She helped move him from the wheelchair to the bed – and when the woman turned, Calista saw that her lips were moving, but there was no sound.

'Looks like Jake encrypted the sound file as well,' she sighed, and then began typing again. 'I think I can get it back though...'

'Whatever's being said must be highly sensitive then,' said the Professor thoughtfully.

Calista glanced up at him as she typed. 'It's some old guy in a nursing home who looks like he's lost his marbles... so how sensitive can it be? But, hang on a mo... the encryption is pretty heavy stuff. Nearly there, and... I'm in.' She changed several settings and a tinny voice wafted from the loudspeakers:

'Okay, back home now,' said the nurse, catching her breath. (Calista increased the volume.) 'It's important you get your exercise – we don't want those muscles seizing up and wasting away now, do we? It was such a lovely walk, don't you think? We've been getting really good weather for this time of year – too good to waste sitting inside...'

As she talked, the old man looked straight ahead, morose, silent.

'Right, I'll just park you over here and get your bed ready. And if you like, you can watch some nice TV in a minute.' She began folding the clothes that were on the bed, slotting them into a drawer – but when she turned back she accidentally knocked a book onto the floor.

Suddenly, the man came to life. 'Don't. Touch! My!! Books!!!' he bellowed.

The nurse stopped in her tracks, and turned round slowly, eyebrows raised in surprise. She picked up the book and returned it to its pile.

The man continued, 'And don't touch the suitcase, either. I've a train to catch. Can't miss it. It's very, *very* important.'

The nurse backed away, a sassy look on her face. 'Okay, okay,' she said, holding up her hands. '*Somebody's* got their knickers in a twist! I won't touch your precious suitcase, or your books, Mr Laszlo – though I don't think you'll be going anywhere anytime soon...'

The old man harrumphed. 'I don't know why you keep calling me *Mr* Laszlo. I am a doctor, a specialist in human genomics.'

(The Professor suddenly sat up.)

The nurse continued. 'Of course you are... *Dr* Laszlo.'

Calista paused playback, and looked at the Professor. 'You know him, don't you?'

'Yes!' he said, feeling somewhat ambivalent. He had been searching for him for years, and somehow, Jake had already found him – or what was left of him and his once brilliant mind. It was Dr Axel Kendra, his Project Ingenious partner, but not quite as he'd hoped to find him.

Both Calista and the Professor spent the rest of the day listening to and watching the video files in descending date and time order, and they learnt a lot. They learnt that the sanatorium was called Hope Gardens, and that the doctor had been resident there for at least six years. His mind had long gone, and he often wandered from his bed, to the bathroom, to the locked door, picking up things and returning them, checking the suitcase, and spending ages lining up the piles of books. He mumbled to himself, and shouted out loud – mostly the ramblings of a demented mind, where nothing made sense. But at times, here and there, he mentioned things from Project Ingenious... And the Professor began to understand why Jake had encrypted the audio. He lapsed into silence.

It was ironic that their efforts to keep the children safe had ultimately turned out to have failed – Dr Kendra's dementia was the crack in the defence; the leak, his own insane ramblings. They had toiled for years in creating an excelling intelligence, a superior mind, but it was all being unravelled by the doctor losing his... And very quickly the Professor's exhilaration on finding Dr Kendra faded.

The Professor roused himself from his thoughts. 'Calista, you need to hack into the Hope Gardens internal server, and get me the details of his next of kin. Particularly the address. It appears he calls himself Dr Laszlo, so you need to look for a Mrs Laszlo.'

Calista nodded, got to work, and after several minutes she located the data. 'Got it! She calls herself Adrienn Laszlo – and there's her address.'

'Good. Send it to the Chauffeur's phone, please. And Jasmine, recall agent D2 – ASAP. She will accompany the Chauffeur to bring in Gaia... AKA Mrs Laszlo.'

But before they left, the Professor intercepted the Chauffeur. He took him to the side, and rather than rely on his lip-reading, the old man signed slowly and deliberately to him. The Chauffeur stood stock still, watching the Professor's signs intensely, sometimes interrupting with his own frantic gestures – his eyes gradually widening.

Then the Professor did something he never usually did – he put his arms around the Chauffeur, and gave him a long hug.

•••———————————————————•••

The old lady was slightly bothered to find someone knocking at her door in the middle of the afternoon. It was nap time, and so she was inclined not to answer it. But though she couldn't quite put her finger on why, something changed her mind. She opened the door to find a young woman dressed smartly in a grey pin-stripe skirt suit, with a heavy-set man partially obscured behind her.

'Hello, Mrs Laszlo,' said agent D2. She was very pretty, in her thirties, with long blonde hair tied back in a simple ponytail. D2 had an open, kind face, that you knew you could trust.

The old woman was immediately drawn to this personable young lady, but still, something puzzled her. 'I'm sorry – how do you know my name?'

The woman smiled politely, her eyes softening with candour. 'Professor Harald Wolff asked us to come. He would very much like to meet with you. He said it was important.'

The old woman was dumbfounded. 'Harry?' she said. 'Oh my! It's been at least... 15 years since...' But then she thought for a moment, eyes narrowing. 'How do I know he really sent you?'

D2 turned round to her colleague, and the Chauffeur stepped out from behind her, smiling nervously – overcome with emotion.

The old woman gasped. 'I-is it true?' she said. Stepping outside, she reached for the Chauffeur, gently cupping his face in her hands. She took a good look at him. 'It... it *is* you. My goodness! You're all grown up now.' With unabashed affection, the old woman embraced him so hard that he could barely breathe. At last she broke away, and ushered them inside. 'Come in, come in,' she said, wiping her eyes. 'I'll get my things, and you can take me to meet with Harry. We've all got a lot to catch up on.'

•••————————————————•••

When Mrs Gaia Kendra reached Avernus, she was shown to the den, where, sitting in his armchair, she immediately recognised the profile of the man that had worked so closely with her husband for many years, his face now lined with wrinkles, and silver streaks peppering his hair.

The Professor, having heard the shuffle of a walk he did not recognise, turned towards her as she entered the room. 'Hello, Gaia,' he said.

Gaia stopped in her tracks, her brows knitting together as she realised that he was blind. She rushed over and flung her arms around him, her cropped hair tumbling against his face. 'Harry! What happened to you?' she said, eventually pulling away. Her voice was deeper than the Professor remembered.

'Please, don't be alarmed. There was an accident... sometime after we left the project. A fire.'

Gaia gasped. 'A-and what about Chiara, Christian?' Please tell me they're alright...'

The Professor looked away. He'd had years to come to terms with his loss, but every time he had to mention it out loud, it was like a knife cutting right through him. 'The same fire... it killed them both.'

Gaia clamped a hand to her mouth, her eyes brimming, heart breaking – both for them and for the Professor. Eventually she took his hand and held it in hers, squeezing gently. They were damp with tears.

The Professor broke the silence. 'Gaia. I've been searching for you and Axel for quite some time – I was... surprised to discover him in a nursing home.'

Gaia noticed a half bottle of sherry on a side table, and she poured some for both of them, glugging the ruby red liquid into glasses. She sighed. 'Yes, it's true. Dear Xeli.' She placed a glass in the Professor's hand, and took her own glass, sitting back in the chair opposite – sipping on the warming liquid. 'He... deteriorated over the years. Slowly at first, so that it was hardly discernible. He started doing odd things, but I just put it down to stress and his ongoing work. In the end, he became... very difficult. I-I tried looking after him at home, but it just got harder and harder. Eventually, I had to come to terms with the psychiatrist's recommendation, and have him admitted to Hope Gardens. For both our sakes – and... to preserve my sanity!'

The Professor nodded. 'I understand.'

'It's incredibly hard watching someone you love – someone as brilliant as Xeli – slowly losing themselves. Yet you can't grieve, because they're still very much alive, still with you. Except, his mind... is just... gone.' Gaia sniffed, her eyes damp. 'Since the project, he was never quite the same anyway. Something broke him... Particularly after that night, when we all left. I-I think it was to do with one of the children from the project – but he never talked to me about it.

'Anyway, the night we all fled, we had a bit of a setback. Xeli fell ill, and wasn't well for some time. It took several months, almost a year, for him to recover. Then, as you know, we had to take on new names, and relocate. We lived in a nice house, and Xeli threw himself back into his work – the work he was doing *before* the project. I don't know if you know, but Xeli's father had been diagnosed with early onset dementia – I think he was just 47 or 48 at the time. As a teenager, Xeli was devastated. He and his father had been *so* close. But his father's mental decline happened very quickly – in the end, he was just a vegetable. Didn't even recognise his own family when they visited... So that's why Xeli decided to study medicine, and dedicate himself to finding a treatment for dementia.'

'Yes, I remember,' said the Professor. 'Before the project, I read one of his papers about genetically modifying the cells of Alzheimer sufferers, to produce a protein that prevents brain cell death, and in that way, stimulating cell function. With the possibility of potentially halting and reversing the disease.'

Gaia sighed. 'Can you believe that the very thing he was working against, overtook *him* in the end...'

The Professor stirred. 'About that... We need to get him out of that home, Gaia – you see, Hope Gardens uses CCTV in his room, which is recording everything he says, even details about the project, and the children.'

Gaia's eyes widened. 'Oh no!' She raised her hand to her chest in shock. 'I... I had no idea. I'm so sorry. If he were in his right mind, he would be mortified to hear this. But... I can't look after him by myself, Harry. I've already tried and...'

'Actually, I thought we could bring him here, to Avernus – of course with your permission. I have access to excellent medical staff who can take care of him.'

Gaia nodded, at first slowly, and then more firmly. 'Yes, that's a good idea. And of course you have my permission. I'll ask Hope Gardens to discharge him into your care, right away.'

'Thank you.' The Professor sat back, relieved.

Just then, the Chauffeur entered, clattering a silver tray with a bone china teapot, cups, and saucers.

Gaia stopped to look at him, how big he had grown. 'You've taken good care of him, Harry. For that, I'm eternally grateful.' When he had set the tray down, Gaia caught the Chauffeur's attention by touching his arm, and squeezing it affectionately. 'Will you join us?' she asked the Chauffeur.

The Chauffeur took her hand and kissed it lightly, but shook his head. Then he signed something to her, whereupon she nodded. 'I understand. So while you get our room ready, we'll go and bring Axel back. He'll be so pleased to see you. But you know, don't you, that... he's not quite the same as he was?'

The Chauffeur squeezed her hand, nodding kindly.

•••——————————————————•••

Mrs 'Adrienn Laszlo', aka Gaia Kendra, arrived at Hope Gardens with D2 and the Professor. When they had completed all discharging paperwork in the office, and finances were settled, the three went to Dr Kendra's small room. The low bed was covered by an avocado-green crocheted blanket, beige curtains were drawn at the windows, and almost every surface was covered by dusty piles of books, precariously balanced on top of each other. Amongst them stood a vintage brown suitcase, with rusted brass locks, and two thick straps holding it closed. But there was no sign of Dr Kendra. Suddenly, the toilet flushed from inside the en-suite bathroom, and out hobbled an old man, bent forward from spinal kyphosis.

Despite his wife and two others appearing in his room out of nowhere, the old man merely glanced at them, and carried on. He was used to seeing figments of his imagination. He sat on his bed next to the bedside table, and stooped closer to a vase of withered flowers. 'What was that?' he asked the flowers. The old man nodded meaningfully as he listened to them. 'Yes, I agree entirely,' he said, and then, with some difficulty, pulled his legs up onto the bed. He lay back against the pillows and closed his eyes. 'I definitely concur,' he muttered to himself.

The Professor dared to speak out to him. 'Axel?' he said softly, turning his head this way and that, straining to hear.

But the old man did not respond. He appeared to be sleeping – but then sat up all of a sudden, exclaiming urgently, 'The trees! They cut them down?!' He sucked in a stuttered breath, and indignant eyes swept across the room – as if the objects themselves were his audience. 'What was that? Cornflowers, you say? A field full of cornflowers? I... I can't imagine anything more... lovely,' he said in a hushed, awed tone.

Gnarled hands moved to his legs, and he dug his nails hard into his pyjamas, and then loosened them, again and again. 'All those people, buried... and the beautiful flowers...'

Sitting half in shadow, a chill ran down the Professor's spine as he listened to this monologue.

Gaia threw an apologetic glance at him and D2. 'Spouting nonsense as usual...' And then she walked over to her husband, 'Whatever are you wittering on about, Xeli!' she asked, rolling her eyes and sighing. Then she motioned to the Professor. 'Anyway, look. It's Harry, dear – he's back. Isn't it wonderful! And you'll be pleased to know that we're taking you away from here. We can stay together, in a special safe-place. Thanks to Harry.'

Meanwhile D2 picked up one of the books, and flicked through it – its leaves were old and dry, and crackled under her touch. 'What about all these books?' she asked. 'They look quite important.'

The Professor stopped. 'Why do you say that?'

'They're notes of some kind, all handwritten. Scientific notes.'

Gaia had begun taking out clothes from the drawers, but then stopped. 'Yes, they're *his* notes – what he was last working on, before he became ill. Nearly screamed the house down insisting that they be brought with him.'

The Professor was suddenly interested. 'Scientific notes, you say?'

D2 looked through a few of the books from separate piles, working them out, and then went to the pile that was nearest to the door. 'Actually, judging from the dates, they're in some kind of order. Here, this one looks like the first.' She opened it, and read out loud the handwritten text. 'Dr A.J. Kendra. A Cure for Dementia. Book 1.'

The Professor's skin prickled. There was no mention of hypotheses, or theories, or concepts. It was a cure.

D2 continued leafing through, and stopped at a page, to read out loud slowly what she found. 'The neurotransmitter, EphB2, was discovered to have a dampening effect on mice that had neurodegenerative disease. Later experimental tests showed that the mice had improved brain function when their levels of EphB2 were enhanced with drugs.'

She looked at the Professor thoughtfully, and then had an idea. She searched around the room, and then went over to the last pile, and carefully lifted it up to pick up the last book. She opened it, and read quietly for a few seconds, at last saying, 'It says here that he began testing on humans... In fact, his last test subject – Patient Q – was the first to have reacted positively to the treatment. Then... there was a subsequent observation period for several days afterwards – watching the subject eat, drink, read, take care of himself, etc – basically starting to behave normally.' She continued reading. 'It says that after a while, Patient Q began to vacillate between mental clarity and reversion to his previous state. In the end, gradual deterioration continued to the extent that, after some time, the dementia returned in its full and permanent state.'

The Professor paused to take in the enormity of this. 'My goodness. This is amazing! He found a cure for dementia, albeit temporary. Bringing Patient Q back to mental clarity. Well. I'm... that's just... phenomenal!' He thought for a moment. 'You see, dementia is a neurodegenerative disease, where the brain cells deteriorate to a point of no recovery. So the fact that he was able to stop progression, and turn this around, even for a short period, was a great achievement!' He was thrilled. 'We must definitely take all these notebooks with us. And handle them with great care. They're invaluable...'

●●——————————————————————●●

While they made their way back with a bewildered Dr Kendra in tow, Calista was sitting in the computer room, performing a cloaked hack into the Hope Gardens computer system, making sure that any CCTV footage of them in the building, and subsequently in the surrounding area, was deleted. She then spliced in a loop of pre-recorded footage to make up for the missing period, so as not arouse any suspicion.

By the time the Professor, Gaia, and Dr Kendra had returned to Avernus, Calista had quite literally made them disappear digitally from the Hope Gardens CCTV.

•••————————————————•••

Back in Avernus, two crates of Axel Kendra's notebooks had been placed in one of the many spare rooms, and Dr Dan Fargo, who had been caring for the comatose V3, was brought in to inspect them. The Professor knew that he would be the ideal candidate to replicate the medical research.

Dr Fargo sat looking through several of the books, in quiet wonder – his eyes lighting up. 'These are remarkable, Harry. And yes, yes of course I would be honoured to lead such a project.'

Just then Milly walked in, looking for the Professor. 'Oh there you are, Prof. And Dr Fargo, nice to see you.' She had gradually returned to her usual self, and was looking brighter. But she was puzzled. 'It's 6pm, isn't it?'

The Professor closed his eyes, remembering. 'That's right. Sorry, I completely forgot.' Ever since her headaches, the Professor had asked her to check in with him at 6pm daily, so that he could monitor how she was feeling, how her headaches were. Dr Fargo had also been consulted, to prescribe her a more appropriate type and strength of painkiller.

Milly piped up. 'Well, so far so good today,' she said. 'Nothing to report really.'

'I'm glad,' said the Professor. 'But you're sure now? Not even a twinge?'

'Not even a twinge,' she repeated, and then patted her pocket, which rattled from a small bottle of tablets. 'Thanks to Dr Fargo prescribing these new tablets.' She stopped to think. 'In fact, the last headache started at 2.53pm on Tuesday – so I haven't needed to take them for two days now.' She couldn't help notice the books in the crates, and drew closer. 'What're these?'

Dr Fargo glanced at the Professor. 'I'm not sure you should–'

'It's fine,' interrupted the Professor. 'In fact, it would be good to have your take on these Milly.'

Dr Fargo blinked. Any other doctor would have wondered why a learned Professor was asking a teenager for advice. He had been told they were prodigies, but were they able to understand work that had taken him decades to learn?

The Professor continued. 'You've met Dr Kendra and his wife – well, these books contain Dr Kendra's notes on his last project, before he deteriorated.'

Milly picked up one of the books. 'May I?'

'Yes,' said the Professor. 'Please do.'

Milly opened the book cover, and read, 'A Cure for Dementia.' She looked up at both the Professor and Dr Fargo, wide-eyed, hardly able to believe it. 'Is this true?'

The Professor responded. 'I hope so... That's what we're going to find out. Before Dr Kendra deteriorated, he was a brilliant scientist – you could say his work was trail-blazing in the field of genetic therapies. So I've commissioned Dr Fargo to continue Axel's work, maybe even improve on it. You see, he's the son of the late Professor who mentored me. Professor James Fargo taught me everything I know – he was a truly eminent scientist. And Dan here has written extensive papers and books on his father's work and research in the field of genetic therapies, so that's why he's the perfect person to work on Dr Kendra's cure.'

'That's awesome!' said Milly. And then turning to Dr Fargo, 'May I... may I observe as you work, Dr Fargo? I promise I won't get in your way.'

Dr Fargo glanced at the Professor, then said to her, 'I'm told you need to be stretched, and that you also have a photographic memory?'

Milly nodded fervently.

The doctor smiled at her enthusiasm. 'And I'm also told that you're quite a whizz at chemistry?'

The girl glanced blankly from the doctor to the Professor.

Dr Fargo explained. 'Your chemistry lecturer, Dr Milo, told me you concocted something during your lessons? Apparently you used it against some thugs?...'

Milly understood now. 'That's right. I've been researching powerful chemical compounds found naturally in living sources, such as plants, herbs, shrubs. For example, I was reading about the Piaroa tribesmen of Orinoco, in the Amazon. They make a concentration from the tar found in the bark of the curare tree, known as Strychnos toxifera – and use it to daub on arrow tips for hunting. This chemical compound has a very similar effect to neuromuscular-blocking drugs, which produces a kind of temporary paralysis. I mentioned to Dr Milo that, if we could harness this same naturally-occurring drug, and create just the right concentration, then, instead of stopping the heart, and killing, it could be used as a type of temporary paralysis agent. So Dr Milo and I have been experimenting on this in the lab, and came up with our own special formula. We tried it out with toy pistols at first, as a way of propelling it.' She turned to the Professor. 'After Jemima's disappearance, and our chat about sitting out of the Sensei's classes, I realised we might need some form of protection. That's why I came up with the paralysing formula, and the water pistols...'

'And I'm pleased you did!' said the Professor, proud of her initiative, her brilliance.

Dr Fargo was beginning to understand what the Professor had been trying to tell him about these quiet but exceptional children. He glanced from Milly to the Professor. 'Well then, if the Professor agrees, I would be honoured for you to observe, Milly, and maybe even help.'

The Professor said, 'I see no harm in your involvement, young lady.' And then to the doctor, 'And yes, I think this will be a good way to stretch her.'

The doctor motioned to the crates. 'There's no time like the present then. We should start by reading Dr Kendra's books. Your photographic memory, Milly, will be a useful point of reference.'

'And I've arranged for the medical and scientific equipment to be shipped in right away,' said the Professor. 'So your laboratory will be ready in just a matter of days – for an immediate start.'

'I'm sorry,' said the doctor. 'Is this urgent?'

'Yes,' replied the Professor firmly. 'I want to use Dr Kendra's own cure on himself. You see, his mind holds the identities and whereabouts of the remaining Project Ingenious children, and so I need to gain access to that information as soon as possible. I know. It's a longshot. But we have to try.'

The doctor thought about this. 'Yes, it is a longshot, Harry. I take it you'll be bypassing animal testing then?'

'You are correct.'

'That'd mean we'd need to scour sanatoriums for human test subjects,' said the doctor. 'And it'll take time to get consent from their next of kin...'

'I'm afraid we're bypassing human testing as well,' said the Professor. 'We need to try it directly on Dr Kendra himself...'

The doctor stared at the Professor, astonished. 'So... you've asked

Mrs Kendra for permission, and she fully understood the risks?'

'Yes of course,' said the Professor earnestly. 'I explained everything in great detail, and also answered all her questions as best I could. I told her it could go both ways. That it's possible it could make Axel's condition degenerate even more. She took time to think about it, but in the end, consented.'

Dr Fargo thought about all of this. He looked at the notebooks, and looked at Milly, as she stooped into a crate to pull more out. Apart from being pioneering, this was also turning out to be a very experimental science.

••——————————————————••

Meanwhile, Calista had Jasmine transcribe a script of the continuous ramblings of the hapless Dr Kendra while he was in the nursing home, which spanned many years – and she spot-checked them against watching excerpts of the video footage herself. She finally emerged one day from the computer room, bleary-eyed and pale, urgently seeking out the Professor. On finding him, she said, 'You're gonna want to listen to these, Prof.' She grabbed his hand, and placed the USB into it. 'You were right, Dr Kendra had been leaking details about the Project, the children, everything. I imagine that's how the bad guys got the information too, and targeted Milly and Tai.'

The Professor thought about this. 'That can't be right, Calista. Dr Kendra and I had made a pact, that he would submit to memory only four of the children's new identities and whereabouts, while I would memorise three. Milly, Tai, and Jemima. So he couldn't have known about my three, just as I don't know about his.'

Calista shook her head slowly. 'Then you've been duped, Prof.' She patted his hand. 'It's all there. Recorded. The old guy clearly blabs about Tai, Milly, and Jemima, mentioning them by name, their whereabouts, everything.'

The Professor absorbed this with a sinking heart. He had always thought of Dr Kendra as his good friend, one who he could rely on with even his life. But his entire understanding of his character, his integrity, was beginning to unravel.

Calista interrupted his thoughts. 'In fact, I'm guessing that's why Jake was in that street-cam footage, because he'd learnt about Jemima Jenkins' whereabouts from those tapes too, and probably wanted to talk to her. To see if she knew anything about his sister. So Jake might know something about Jemima's disappearance too... Anyway, listen to the files, Prof, and you'll see.'

The Professor thought about it. Yes, that did make sense.

Calista turned to leave, but then stopped. 'By the way, apart from the ones we know about, there was one other name Dr Kendra mentioned, in all his rantings and ravings – could it be another one of your genius children?...'

The Professor's heart skipped a beat.

Calista continued. 'Some Japanese sounding name. "May" something or other.'

On hearing this, the Professor was both excited and nauseous. 'There was indeed a *Chinese* baby born to the project. And if her full name, her new identity, can be identified from the tapes, as well as her location, then she is in danger too. We must try and get to her, before they do.'

'Okay. Let's go.' She took his hand, and they walked together down the corridor, as fast as they could.

As they went, the Professor asked, 'Do you remember if anything else was said about this girl, her whereabouts for instance?'

Calista wracked her brain. 'I remember some funny sounding Chinese place being mentioned. I got Jasmine to make a transcript of everything, so it'll be easy to search for that section of tape. I'll play it back for you.'

'Of course,' said the Professor, thoughtfully. 'No better place to hide a Chinese girl than in plain sight – within China, the most populous country in the world...'

•••————————————————————•••

In a few days' time, shiny new laboratories were being installed, and lab technicians sourced and recruited, while Milly and Dr Fargo had already begun working on Dr Kendra's notebooks, making their own digitised notes on his methods, procedures, and tests. At every waking moment, Milly had her head buried in books, or was reading scientific articles and case studies on her tablet, absorbing Dr Fargo's extensive published works, as well as his father's. She only needed to read something once, and was able to build up a medical knowledge that would have taken anyone else years of study.

She did not realise it, but her understanding had already reached BSc and MD levels. And Dr Fargo was amazed to find that, despite a beginning of asking numerous, if basic, questions, in no time at all her understanding had grown so rapidly, her knowledge so in-depth, that they were able to have meaningful scientific conversations together, bounce ideas off each other, and formulate hypotheses and a plan on how they could improve Dr Kendra's brilliant work.

The Professor too joined them for many hours, giving them insight and pointers from his expert knowledge of genetics. They started early in the morning, and finished late at night.

In time, they realised that Dr Kendra's research was two-fold. The first branch was based on halting the imbalanced build-up of proteins in the brain, which stopped the progression of degenerative disease. And the second branch involved a gene therapy which stimulated oligodendrocyte cells to produce myelin – a substance that repairs and rebuilds brain cells. Dr Kendra had tested this out on mice with prion disease, and not only was he able to stop the progression of brain cell deterioration, but there were also incredible improvements in their mental acuity. But just as the notebooks had documented, the mice gradually deteriorated, and returned to their former state. With the baton now passed to them, Dr Fargo, the Professor, and Milly applied their own expertise to refine and improve Dr Kendra's gene therapy.

And in time, after much frenzied work and sleepless nights, they eventually developed their own cure for dementia. It was distilled within a clear amber liquid that glistened like honey from glass ampoules, stacked in neat rows in a refrigerator. The fluid contained an adeno-associated virus which was loaded with their new gene therapy. And so, at long last, Dr Fargo sought out Gaia, and took her aside. 'It's time,' he told her.

The old woman nodded solemnly, mentally braced herself, and then went off to get her husband. She returned with a bewildered and disoriented Dr Kendra in tow – reluctantly pulled from bed and his afternoon nap.

The Professor approached her as they entered. 'Gaia, are you sure? Absolutely sure? If you change your mind, I'd understand...'

She squeezed his arm. 'I am. Quite sure.' She glanced at her dazed husband, who was clutching her hand. His eyes had been dim for such a long time, and she needed to see that glint of recognition again. She could not reconcile his being there, but not being there, and was certain he would have wanted his own cure. Too, she would have regretted it if she didn't at least try to bring him back to her.

The Professor was relieved to hear the firmness in her tone, the determined resolution.

The two laboratories were on one side of a consultation room, and on the other side was a bedroom with a hospital bed, two chairs, medical equipment, and stacks of supplies. A nurse stood waiting with Milly as Dr Kendra was led inside the bedroom and laid down. He nodded to the nurse, who was ready with a steel tray containing syringes, cotton wool, and two ampoules. She rolled up Dr Kendra's sleeve and sterilised the skin on his upper arm, filled the syringe, and gently sunk it into the old man's pale arm. She did this a second time, with the other ampoule, and it wasn't long before sleep overcame him, and he closed his eyes.

Dr Fargo turned towards the Professor and Milly. 'It's done,' he said, with a tired smile. And though they were brimming with anticipation, they knew that it was a waiting game now. How long, was anybody's guess. 'I suggest we all get some much-needed rest,' said Dr Fargo, himself exhausted. 'It's been a long few days...'

•••————————————————•••

On that first day of Axel Kendra being administered with the very treatment that he himself had formulated years ago, his wife Gaia pulled up a chair next to his bedside, settled down with a cup of tea, a book, and a blanket over her lap. Every now and again she stopped to turn the page and sip her tea – always keeping a watchful eye on her dormant husband. Hours passed with occasional visits from the nurse, or Dr Fargo, or the Professor, checking in to see if there was any change.

A full night passed and morning arrived with Dr Kendra still fast asleep, and everyone in Avernus in a limbo, unable to continue as normal until something – anything – happened.

On the second day, on Mrs Kendra's request, they placed a divan in her husband's room. She was intending to sleep there – unwilling to leave his side for anything more than bathroom visits. She had already finished the first book, and the Professor soon went to fetch her a second, one of his favourites from the BC, Victor Hugo's *Les Miserables*. She thanked him graciously, but raised an eyebrow on seeing the thickness of it – wondering how long he expected they wait...

On the third day, she woke to find her husband sitting up in bed staring at her. 'Xeli!' she breathed, both startled and uncertain. She sat up and blinked the sleep away.

'G-aia,' he said, uttering her name as if it were something he had just plucked from the air.

Tears welled in Gaia's eyes, not just because he hadn't spoken her name in seven years, but also because he recognised her. He reached for her hand, but she threw herself upon him, crushing the breath from him, hot tears spilling onto his neck.

Her husband opened his mouth to say something, but nothing came out.

When she pulled away, and realised he was struggling with speaking, she shook her head. 'What's wrong, Xeli?'

He was frightened, bewildered – and didn't know where he was, couldn't work out why his wife looked years older, didn't recognise his hands gnarled with arthritis. And now, all in a rush, came a mass of agitated people running into the room, talking loudly and swarming around him. He clamped his hands over his ears, drew his knees up, and tried to sink away from them, into the bed. His wife kept repeating, 'What's wrong?' over and over, her voice rising.

And then there came a tapping sound, and a man, an old man with a bow tie and tweed jacket – eyes that had a faraway look, flitting around, unanchored. Dr Kendra recognised him. And he opened his mouth again, surprised by the sound of his own gravelly voice. 'Ha-rry?'

The word had a kind of power to it because, on its utterance, everyone stopped and stared.

The Professor drew closer, and held out his hand to his friend. Dr Kendra took it in his, and the Professor smiled. 'Yes, Axel. It's me.' His black eyes shone like wet obsidian.

'Why... why can't he speak properly, Harry?' asked Gaia.

Dr Fargo, standing at the foot of the bed, told her, 'I think this is just a temporary disorientation, Mrs Kendra. You see, your husband's notes mentioned a similar thing in the mice that he experimented on – initially after treatment, they were in a kind of mute daze. But it didn't last long, just a few hours in their case, before they began vocalising again. You see, the gene therapy is still in the process of rebuilding and repairing damaged brain cells, allowing new synaptic connections – in effect, re-mapping the brain. Once he gets used to it though, maybe in a few hours, maybe days, we should see a marked improvement.'

'Ah,' said Mrs Kendra, heartened by this. 'That's good to know.' She perched on the edge of the bed and stroked her husband's arm affectionately. 'Did you hear that, Xeli? You'll be right as rain before long.'

Dr Kendra settled back in his bed, savouring his wife's comforting touch. To him, all those years in the mental asylum were just a bad dream. And this was the morning after – only everyone was much older than he remembered, even himself.

He sighed, laid back, and closed his eyes – concentrating on the soothing sensation of his wife's gentle strokes.

Later, at midday, while Dr Kendra slept, Gaia was able to join the Professor for lunch in the dining room – a simple but delicious pesto pasta with roasted tomatoes and asparagus. Gaia looked around as they ate. 'It's quite amazing this underground place, Harry – what do you call it again?...'

'Avernus,' he replied. 'There is a crater containing a lake in Italy, called Lago d'Averno. But I took the name from Virgil's epic poem, the Aeneid: *'Easy is the descent to Avernus, for the door to the underworld lies open both day and night. But to retrace your steps and return to the breezes above – that's the task, that's the toil'.'*

Gaia frowned slightly. 'The door to the underworld? Sounds gloomy. Is that why everything down here is painted black?'

The Professor's fork was nearly at his mouth, when he stopped, and put it down. 'Yes, I suppose it must look quite morbid...' He took a sip of wine, and clunked the glass softly back on the wooden table. 'When I became blind, oddly, all I could see – all I *can* see – is the colour white. It's a kind of milky haze.'

'So, you can't see anything at all? Not even outlines or shapes?'

'No. Nothing at all. And because I'm blinded by this "white noise", I keep hoping that, someday, should by some miracle my sight improve, the blackness will seep through the white. And then I'll know for sure that my vision is returning. It's simplistic, I know. Foolish even. But... you never know.'

Gaia said softly, 'Makes perfect sense, Harry. Only, I'm sorry that–'

'Please,' interrupted the Professor gently. 'I do not want pity.'

'I was only going to say that I'm sorry this has happened at all, Harry. I don't pity you – on the contrary, I admire your spirit, and the fact that you've improved yourself, and your circumstances, despite everything.' She paused. 'Another question – and please forgive me for such inquisitiveness. But tell me, why did you name this place after something so grim?'

The Professor tilted his head, his black eyes gravitating toward her. 'Well, a door can be both an entrance and an exit. And, in my mind, the allusion lies, not in Virgil's mention of the *descent* to Avernus, because he explained the descent was easy – but rather, it refers to the part about retracing your steps back up, to return to the breezes above. Finding your way back *from* Avernus, *that* is the hardest part. The task and the toil, as he put it. And indeed, that is my aim.' He stopped to think. 'After the project, and after my family were... taken from me – my journey's aim, you might say, is solely to return to the land of the living. To breathe in the freshness of air that is so... wanting.' He breathed deeply, as if imagining it now. 'Could I call this "life"? If I could come out of the living hell that I've been in since their death. If I could ascend to a place that has worth and meaning again. Then maybe...' The Professor faltered. 'I- I'm sorry for getting carried away. But... I hope that explanation makes my home appear less... grim. Less morbid.'

Gaia closed her eyes, trying not to cry, for him, and his loss, and for her husband. But she failed. Her voice cracked as she said, 'I do understand, Harry.' She squeezed his hand, and they returned quietly to their food. The Professor did not know it, but Gaia's tears fell silently as she finished her meal.

# THE BLACK

*'The process of delving into the black abyss is to
me the keenest form of fascination.'*

H P Lovecraft

# 21 PROBABILITY

That afternoon, much attention was paid to Dr Kendra, and the continuing of the gene therapy that they hoped was curing his dementia. The treatment seemed to have flicked an 'inverse' switch in him: previously, with his mind ravaged by dementia, he babbled a near-continual stream of nonsense – the ravings of a madman. But now that his mind was clearing, and his thoughts were returning to near normalcy, he seemed barely able to string two words together.

The Professor was discussing this with Dr Fargo, when Brian ran into the room excitedly.

'Professor, Professor! The news. Have you seen the news?!' he gasped in between breaths.

The Professor turned toward the frantic voice. 'Brian? What news?'

'An outbreak, some kind of virus, at Oxford University!' Brian stopped in front of the Professor. 'You need to watch it – now.'

The Professor immediately went with him to the computer room, where he said out loud, 'Jasmine, replay recent TV news.'

Brian turned to look at the screen as the familiar musical gong of the title sequence played. Deadly serious, the newsreader reported, 'Breaking news: one Oxford university student is now dead from a mysterious disease, and six more have been taken critically ill with the same symptoms.' The opening credits finished, to reveal a female newsreader, her eyes glued sternly to the camera.

'Robert Milligan, a first-year undergraduate at Oxford University died this morning after three days of headaches and vomiting which doctors have confirmed were due to a rapid-onset brain tumour. Fellow students report that previously he showed no signs of illness, and was known to be in good health, with no underlying illness. Doctors are puzzled as to how such a brain tumour could develop so suddenly. But in a startling turn of events, six more students have come down with the same symptoms, all of whom are studying the same subject as the deceased – Genetics.

'Head of the university's department of Physiology, Anatomy, and Genetics, Professor James Robins, in an interview with our reporter, told us earlier today that "it is impossible for cancer to be contagious – cancerous cells cannot infect another person".

'Experts are therefore baffled as to how students, who attended the same lectures as the deceased Robert Milligan, can all be displaying identical cancer symptoms. They are therefore working around the clock to come up with an effective treatment. Meanwhile, Oxford University is in lockdown as hundreds of staff and students are being held in quarantine for precautionary screening, despite Professor James Robins' advice that no contagion is involved. Our reporter talked this afternoon with cancer expert, Peter Davids.'

The television screen gave way to the face of a tired-looking man, with droopy basset-hound eyes, and cropped hair showing signs of balding. He was speaking to an interviewer just off-camera. 'It's nearly impossible to prove exactly what causes cancer in any individual because cancers can be due to a variety of factors, such as environmental pollutants, obesity, tobacco, radiation, as well as hereditary predisposition. But what we have here are seven different students, who attend the same genetics lectures, all diagnosed with the same tumour – of course this begs the question as to how. How could all these students develop exactly the same kind of cancer, and at the same time? Initial findings from an ongoing pathological autopsy of the deceased student seem to indicate that the cancer is of a type that has been extinct for many centuries. Yes, that's right, extinct. In antiquity many suffered from this type of cancer, but in modern times it's unheard of – until now.

'Ironically, these students study genetics, and it *may* be that genetics itself holds the key as to how this could be possible. You see, the human genome contains traces of ancient and extinct viral infections – called Endogenous Retroviruses. And traces of antibodies to these viruses still remain in human DNA, despite the diseases being extinct for hundreds of thousands of years. Now, some human ERVs have been implicated in certain motor neurone diseases, some autoimmune diseases, and cancers. My theory therefore – and I stress, this is only a theory – is that somehow, something may have triggered these ERVs to becoming active and harmful within each of these students, giving rise to the brain tumour. Obviously we are still at a loss as to *how* this could've happened, but this is one possible explanation as to how all seven students are suffering from the same cancer, at exactly the same time.'

The picture returned to the original newsreader who flicked to the next page on her tablet, and moved on to interviews with family members.

Brian turned to the Professor, astonished. 'Don't you think this whole thing is too close to home, Professor? Genetics, seven students...'

The Professor, deep in thought, rubbed his jaw. 'Uncomfortably so... I think I need to make a few urgent calls, if you don't mind...'

Brian nodded, saying as he turned to leave, 'Okay, well, let me know if you need anything.'

'Yes, thank you.'

The Professor waited for a moment as Brian's footsteps faded down the corridor, and was just about to ask Jasmine to make a call, when her voice came from the loudspeakers.

'You have a telephone call from Downing Street, Professor.'

Startled, the Professor straightened, took a deep breath, and told Jasmine to patch him through. There was only one person he knew that would call him from there. 'Prime Minister!' he said. 'I was just about to call you...'

'Ah, great minds!' boomed an authoritative voice.

The Professor personally knew the man before he recently became Prime Minister – the son of a close and trusted business partner. And being a good man, with the highest values and principles, the Professor had made the decision to divulge to him everything about Project Ingenious – especially since he needed an ally in the face of Jemima Jenkins' disappearance. It transpired that, after all, and to his great relief, the PM was wholly supportive, as well as flabbergasted that a previous administration, decades ago, could have been so brutal with their scientific experimentation programme.

The PM asked, 'You've seen the news, I presume?'

'Yes, I have.'

'Good. There's something quite important I have to tell you – but first, I have Dr Davids himself here. He can bring you up to speed.'

'Hello, Professor,' came another man's voice on the phone.

'Good to meet you, Dr Davids,' responded the Professor. 'I just heard your comments on the news. I have to say, this whole thing sounds horrific.'

'It is. On every level. Though I'm afraid I have more questions myself, than answers. You see, as I mentioned in the news report, it's a novel disease, and practically impossible for so many cases of the same cancer to be diagnosed all together – seven students afflicted at the same time, in the same place. This of course indicates a common causality. And secondly, most startling is the *type* of cancer – not only that it has been extinct for millennia, but also because it's a particularly vicious one that invades surrounding tissue like... well, like nothing I've ever seen in all my 43 years of oncology. The first signs of the disease were nails turning black, and falling off. Then lips and the sclera of the eyes also turned black. Having examined the body post-mortem recently, I saw the tumour myself... it's a kind of necrosis of the organs, degenerating everything it invades into a kind of inky black pulp, so that, like the brain and the eyes, everything just... liquifies.'

The Professor absorbed the horror of the doctor's words. 'Awful, just awful,' he breathed. 'Like you, I've never heard of anything like it. But you mentioned "a common causality", and in the television interview you also said that something "triggered" the disease in these students. Would it be outrageous to suppose therefore that – rather than this being a purely natural phenomenon – *someone* is actually behind these deaths, and orchestrated the whole thing?'

Dr Davids went quiet for a while. 'To be honest, it's impossible to tell at this early stage, and I do believe the police are investigating every avenue. But the jury's still out. We've been looking at environmental factors, the food they ate, the lecture hall, whether they did anything together at some stage, etc, etc. But as to your question... if there was somebody behind this – that person would have an exceptional scientific knowledge of diseases and genomics, beyond any science that we know today.'

'I understand, doctor.'

'What I mean is that it would be extraordinary, but also not impossible. To be honest, anything's possible at this stage...' He paused, his voice lowering, 'I can't help being very worried about the implications of your line of thinking, Professor. If you're right, that there's someone behind it, this could be disastrous – to the entire human race. You see, this retrovirus resides naturally inside the cells of well... probably within every single living human on the planet. And so, what's to say that – if there is indeed a person or an organisation behind this whole thing – what's to stop them from activating this cancer in the rest of the human population?' He paused. 'If someone were weaponising this disease, then that would be catastrophic for us all!'

They were silent for some time.

Eventually, the Professor said, 'It is therefore imperative for us to find out what caused this disease in the first place.' He cleared his throat. 'How are the students faring?'

'Not good,' said the doctor. 'In fact, their prognosis is very, very bad. At the moment they're all unconscious, because the tumour, having attacked the brain, has caused a kind of system shutdown.'

'And what about the other students, beside these seven?'

'No symptoms, thank goodness. They're clear.'

Eventually the Professor said, 'I should very much like to take a look at the forensic pathology report for the dead student's body...'

'Yes, indeed. I will send you everything we have.' There was a muffled sound, and then he said, 'I'm afraid I have to leave now. We're setting up a scientific council to explore this new disease further, and I have a meeting in ten minutes...'

'Of course,' said the Professor. 'Thank you for explaining.'

There came the sound of movement, and the man's footsteps retreating, and a door closing shut.

The Prime Minister's voice came back on the phone. 'I have to say, Professor, when I first heard of this, your connection with Project Ingenious immediately came to mind... and then... well, I think you had better sit down, Professor.'

The Professor felt for the chair and lowered himself into it, suddenly feeling very sick again.

The PM continued speaking, his voice grave. 'This is something we haven't told Dr Davids at all. And it basically answers your question, about a perpetrator... We've since been sent a very disturbing message *definitely* connecting you with all of this. I'm going to read it to you...' There was a rustle of paper. 'The message reads: *'Professor Wolff must hand himself over to me, together with the children, in exchange for a cure for the Oxford students. If they do not show, other members of the public will without hesitation be infected. The rendezvous will be at 12 noon tomorrow'*.

The Professor could not speak for several minutes.

Eventually the PM broke the silence. 'Professor?'

'I'm here.' His voice was weak, barely audible.

'Did you... did you understand the message?'

'Yes. I did.' He said, still trying to process everything.

'Now, we don't know whether it's a bluff. But until our intel says otherwise, we have to take it seriously. I can tell you that two more of the diseased students are going to die imminently, and I imagine the others will follow suit, unless by some miracle our scientific council find some kind of cure or treatment very soon. But that doesn't look likely. The cancer is too far gone...'

'So, I take it you want us to give ourselves over?'

The PM chose his words carefully. 'We have as yet no alternative, Professor.'

'And... does this person know that I have only two of the children? That there's no way of locating the others?'

'All I have is this message. Nothing else. I don't know what he – or she – knows, or thinks, or presumes. Your guess is as good as mine.'

The Professor closed his eyes – it was hard to think through the shock of everything. 'Do you have a line of communication with them? Can we talk to them?'

'I don't know. I'll have to ask my chief of security. Why, what did you have in mind?'

'They would have to take our word anyway that we have only two of the children. So... what if you tell them that we're unable to locate any of the children at all, tell them that they've all but disappeared? Or, what if we told them they died?' The Professor was thinking out loud, perhaps clutching at straws.

'There are a lot of "what ifs", Professor... and six lives hanging in the balance. Not to mention the possibility of further spreading of the disease,' the PM reminded him, grim. There was a muffled sound as he turned to talk to someone in the background, before speaking again to the Professor. 'I'm summoning my security aide, so we can see whether there's a way to contact the person who sent the message. But you're right. If we can at least open up a dialogue with them, we may be able to negotiate. We'll obviously do our best to avoid having to exchange you and the children, for the cure. Though it's certain to be a very, very difficult negotiation.'

'Yes, I understand.'

'They would need to make contact again in any case. The message said you should be handed over at 12 noon tomorrow, but we have no idea of the location. I'm guessing they'll let us know just before, for their own security.'

'Yes, that's likely.'

'Ah, here he is. Professor, I have Rory Sanderson here, chief of security – I'm putting you on loudspeaker. Right, Rory, tell me. Can we open up a dialogue with the person behind the message?'

The voice of a no-nonsense Scotsman came on the telephone. 'I'm afraid not, Prime Minister. The message came as a text from a burner mobile phone, and was recorded on your dedicated line as a voicemail. We've tried everything to gain intel on the number – tried triangulating the phone signal, return telephone call, text message. But the user has either switched off the phone, or blocked everything, or just destroyed the SIM. The SIM wasn't registered, and there's therefore no information on the user.'

'I see,' said the PM. 'So there's absolutely no way for us to communicate with them?'

'Correct. It's a one-way street, Sir. We can't contact or send anything back to the person who sent the message.'

'Hmm. Okay, thanks, Rory.' The loudspeaker was switched off. 'Well, Professor – that's put paid to that avenue.'

'Most unfortunate...' said the Professor, disappointed. Then he said suddenly and decisively, 'I can tell you now, Prime Minister, that I will *not* allow the children to be handed over. I won't put them in harm's way. The person behind this is obviously a psychopath, and will stop at nothing to get what he, or she, wants. They may have abducted Jemima Jenkins, maybe even killed her. And who knows what else...' The Professor thought of V1's death, and V3 lying in coma. 'Th-the way I'm feeling now is that I will hand myself over, and tell whoever is behind this that the children are dead, or impossible to trace... or anything that will put them off the scent of the children.'

'I see,' was all the Prime Minister said. And then eventually, 'I respect your decision, Professor. So... let's hope your plan works, and will be enough to receive the cure in return – if indeed a cure exists. Otherwise, the possible consequences... to the human race...' He paused. 'I hate to put it in such simple terms, but the maths of two children, against the possibility of widespread infection...' he trailed off.

'Yes, I understand,' said the Professor quietly. He thought about the mathematics. 'I... I need to go away and do some calculations, Prime Minister. I want to look at alternative scenarios and their probabilities. May I speak to you, say, first thing tomorrow morning? I have a feeling there'll be a lot more to discuss by then.'

'Yes of course. I'll be up at the crack of dawn, most likely in emergency COBRA meetings all morning, but I'll instruct my secretary to patch your call through directly to wherever I am.'

'Thank you.'

'Try to rest,' said the PM kindly, knowing the turmoil he must be in. 'Goodbye.'

The call was ended, and the Professor slumped against the cold glass of the desk – his own heart cold as ice.

In time, he stirred, pushed himself up on uncertain feet, and spoke out weakly. 'Jasmine, record my air notes into a document, entitled...' He paused. Only one thing came to mind, and he had neither the will nor the strength to think of anything else. 'Entitled, "Probability of the end of the world".'

'Document created,' said Jasmine pleasantly.

Her voice echoed in the Professor's mind. She didn't get it, he thought. For all her artificial intelligence, and super-powerful programming, she couldn't understand the gravity of the phrase.

The Professor raised his arms, like a conductor holding the attention of an orchestra. And then his hands started moving – drawing equations into the air with his fingertips – at first slow, and half-hearted, and then gradually increasing speed, so that his movements betrayed a pent-up fury, a ferocity that surprised even him. Anger and outrage poured out of him. For the project, his wife and son, Jemima, V1 and V3, the lost children, and now this horrible cancer – there seemed no end to the woes that surrounded him. It was as if he were plagued. As if Project Ingenious had opened up Pandora's box, releasing curse after curse. Brought forth by an evil he could not see, even if it were standing right in front of him...

The Professor threw everything he had into the maths – spelling out life and death in numbers and symbols and equations.

But he did not realise that Jasmine was displaying his probability equations on the three screens, in continuous lines that scrolled up as the space was filled.

He spent hours and hours considering pathway analyses, multiple events, conditions, exclusivity, distribution, and Gaussian curves – pulling into the equations one dead student, six critically ill, and an unknown variable. He factored in himself alone as the sacrificial lamb, and then, in a moment of weakness, also pondered the probability of Milly and Tai being handed over – but he immediately regretted it as soon as he'd completed the line, and quickly erased the two from the equation. He tweaked this variable, changed that figure, wrote in different components, added varying pathways, erased options – always back-tracking and checking his theories again and again, to reduce margins of error.

Both his mind and the screens were an explosion of symbols.

Eventually – arms aching, sweat pouring from his face – he at last came to the end. He hung his head, and mumbled, exhausted, 'Jasmine, calculate result.'

She immediately told him, '2.07' – and the number appeared in huge lettering onscreen. Bright white figures against a black background.

The Professor's legs buckled beneath him at the thought of it, and he stumbled back, just managing to stop himself from falling.

Finally, he murmured, 'Jasmine – save file in a hidden and secure location, with the following password.' He wrote this out in the air, as the screen simultaneously darkened to black.

'Document saved and secured, Professor.'

The old man stood there for some time, head bowed, eyes closed.

He did not hear the steps of someone hiding in the shadows creep silently away.

•••————————————————————•••

With the flurry of activity in Avernus, it was decided that there would be a brief hiatus in the teenagers' lessons of several days.

Calista still kept herself busy in the computer room, constantly searching for Jake. Milly had disappeared elsewhere in Avernus – and Tai concentrated on his music.

After experiencing the exceptional sound of the music at the Royal Opera House, Tai had become wholly dissatisfied with the sound of his grand piano in the relatively small music room. He therefore asked that his piano be moved to the BC, figuring that the larger space and shape of the room would vastly improve the acoustics and sound.

When at last he sat down at his piano in the BC, and began playing, he discovered that the greater height and expanse of the ceiling, combined with the almost circular walls packed entirely with row upon row of dampening books, made his music reverberate with a hauntingly beautiful sound.

And so he placed several sheets of music onto the rack, and pulled the piano stool to his preferred position. He sat there in his jeans, t-shirt, and sneakers, limbering up his fingers. Setting his hands on the keyboard – his left poised on an octave, his right on a triplet figuration – he began playing the first movement of Beethoven's 14th Sonata, *Quasi una Fantasia*. Gently he caressed the keys, teasing out the Adagio sostenuto, which was all at once introspective, sombre, and determined. It flowed and rippled  in a beautiful motif with the sense of something coming, the yearning for it even. An acknowledgment of calm before the storm. It soothed him, held him spellbound. And at last he reached the last contemplative chord in c-sharp minor, played twice, each fermata fading into perfect silence. When Tai removed his hands to his lap, he bowed his head in respect.

Just then, someone entered the room, and Tai opened his eyes to find himself back in the BC.

Milly walked in, surprised to find Tai and the piano there, and she hesitated – but then quickly walked past him, clutching books to her chest – waves of hair falling over her face.

'Hey,' Tai said, nodding to her. 'Hope you don't mind...'

'N-no, that's fine,' she said awkwardly, and scuttled over to a pile of large floor cushions scattered to the side.

Tai turned back to the piano, arranged his music sheets, and immersed himself in the second movement – a much lighter, blossoming allegretto, played with accents of piano and sforzando. But before long it came to an end, and it was time to tackle the third, most difficult, yet most important movement. He took a deep breath. He was still learning the piece, and, technically, it was undeniably hard. With trepidation, he released the music onto the keyboard, presto agitato, ravaging the keys as his hands flew up and down with dynamic energy, his head lowered with concentration, a sheen of sweat building on his forehead. The melody rolled and rumbled, like storm clouds brewing and gathering at speed – hurtling toward the inevitable. There should have been an epic and emphatic finality, but Tai found himself floundering, and with the first error came doubt, and then loss of confidence, until mistake followed mistake. In the end, it became almost unbearable. He wrenched his hands away, like pulling iron from an unyielding magnet, and quickly scraped back the piano stool. 'Aargh,' he growled in defeat, dropping his head. He remembered that Milly was there, and he turned round to find her sitting on the floor, hunched over drawn-up knees, crying.

'Milly?' he said, melting, and immediately went over to her. 'What's wrong?'

She wasn't able to look up, to respond, she was so overcome.

Tai sat next to her for a while, and in time, quite innocently, put a comforting arm around her. But when he closed his eyes, a world opened up in his mind. He saw Milly hiding in the shadows outside the computer room, listening to the Professor's telephone conversations with both Dr Davids and the Prime Minister. He felt her heart race, sensed her horror, and then resigned to the same futility and impotence she herself resigned to. Tai loosened his grip, and sat back, disturbed. Eventually he told her, 'I know, Milly. I know what you overheard.'

Milly wiped her eyes, and turned to him, puzzled. 'Y-you know? How?'

He took a deep breath. 'Sometimes... when I touch people, I... know things. Feel things. See colours of emotion. Just now, I saw you hiding in the corridor. Listening to the Professor.'

Stunned, Milly sat there for some time, grappling to absorb this, to understand. 'But... how is that possible?'

Tai just shrugged. 'I don't know. When it first happened, when I was little, I thought it was the same for everyone – it took me years to realise it was just me. I-I think something went wrong in those experiments, when they were... making me.'

Still in a state of shock, Milly examined his face. 'How does it feel?'

Tai shrugged again. 'Normal, I suppose.' He looked up, watched the glow that surrounded her– it was the colour of dusk. A rich, sad indigo. 'You're blue,' he said simply.

'Yes, I suppose I am,' said Milly in a daze, not understanding. Her mind felt like it was melting, floundering, exploding – all at the same time. Both with what Tai had just revealed about himself, as well as the Professor's equations for the end of the world. Tears filled her eyes again. 'I... can't...' She stopped, fighting to control her emotions. Battling to get to grips with such astounding revelations. Eventually she said quietly, 'There's not much time, is there?' But Tai didn't respond.

She leant into him, and he put his arm around her again. Somehow his touch made her feel better.

Tai watched in wonder as the blue haze that hung about her flowered into deep purple, and then rosy pink. It was beautiful.

•••———————————————————•••

Milly slept fitfully that night.

That number plagued her. It seemed small, insignificant, yet it wielded a terrible and dark power.

2.07.

Her head spun with it, even in her dreams. She thrashed, clawed the mattress, and muttered a monologue of fear. She saw the 2 as a crouching giant, unfolding and rising to its full height. The 0 was a void that sucked her into oblivion. The 7 – a vast cliff edge over which she tumbled to her death. And the point, that tiny point, was the worst of them all. It was a microbe that doubled, and quadrupled, multiplying exponentially until it engulfed the entire planet.

Yet somehow, at the break of dawn, when Milly opened her eyes on a pillow damp with sweat, she sat up and found that her thinking was surprisingly clear.

Her mind was made.

She threw back the cloying bedclothes, got up, and went to seek out Tai.

## 22 TRUSTING EVIL

The Professor requested that everyone meet him in the dining room that morning at 7 am, where the air was filled with the aroma of coffee and croissants. But nobody had the appetite. The Professor himself looked pale and exhausted, with dark circles under his eyes, hair combed messily, his bow tie angled slightly askew. He spoke to them in a monotone – explaining the call from the Prime Minister, the message that named him as a ransom for the cure, and his plan to give himself up at midday. He left out any mention of 'the children' in the message, and Milly and Tai glanced knowingly at each other. He was trying to protect them.

There were gasps of shock at these revelations, and nobody knew what to say. When they did eventually think of questions, it was too late – he had already excused himself, mumbling something about a meeting with the Prime Minister, and he was practically already out of the door.

Calista watched as he left, stunned with disbelief. She wanted to call out to him, tell him not to go – but found she could not. As the tears started to stream, she jumped to her feet as if to follow him, but she felt light-headed and dizzy, and her legs buckled beneath her. The floor suddenly whooshed toward her at breakneck speed, and the world disappeared in white swirls.

Everybody crowded around her collapsed body, fussing.

Oblivious, the Professor tapped quietly down the corridor, silent and alone.

•••————————————————————•••

The rest of that morning in Avernus was like a strange dream. It seemed that time was playing warped tricks on them – passing excruciatingly slowly as the seconds ticked closer to midday, and yet, before they knew it, it was already 11.45am.

Brian, Gaia, Dr Fargo, and the Chauffeur found solace in each other's company, having congregated in the dining room, watching the wall-mounted television, and talking in hushed tones.

The teenagers on the other hand appeared to need solitude. Calista, distraught by the Professor's leaving, was recovering from the shock in the den, with Brian hovering close-by, while Milly and Tai it seems had disappeared to their rooms. Or so everyone thought. Until the Chauffeur came rushing into the kitchen, beside himself, clattering a tray of untouched breakfast things on the table.

'What's wrong?' signed Gaia to him frantically.

The Chauffeur's hands were a flurry as he signed back to her that he was bringing Tai and Milly some brunch to their rooms, when he discovered that they were missing.

Brian listened quietly as Gaia interpreted. 'They... they're probably in the swimming pool,' he told them. 'They like to swim in the morning.' He called out to the air. 'Jasmine, tell me where Milly and Tai are right now.'

Jasmine's congenial voice replied, 'Milly and Tai left Avernus at 7.35 this morning, Brian.'

He could not believe that his daughter would leave without telling him. He asked Jasmine, 'D-did Milly and Tai leave together with the Professor?' He braced himself for the answer.

'No. The Professor left Avernus separately at 7.33 this morning.'

Brian stumbled back, crashing into a chair. 'They... they've followed the Professor!' he said, feeling sick.

•••————————————————•••

The blind old man, in his tweed jacket and bow tie, looked pathetic and feeble as he slowly tapped his way to London's Barrier Gardens Pier. Behind him were a barrage of police cars waiting at the visitors' centre, with Rory Sanderson, chief of security, standing at the head.

Powdery sunlight bleached the old man's figure as they watched him walk further and further away. Scattered strategically around were plain clothes policemen blending in, walking dogs, sitting on benches, or pretending to be tourists. Overhead was a helicopter hovering in the distance – and from rooftops, snipers were scouring the area through the telescope of their rifles.

The instructions sent to Downing Street at exactly 11.40 am detailed the rendezvous for the Professor and the children, and it was a feat for Sanderson to coordinate mobilising their forces in just 20 minutes. Yet, by some miracle they managed to cover everything, so that whoever was meeting the Professor would be followed either by helicopter, car, or on foot.

The simple directive that had been sent to the Prime Minister was that the Professor and the children should wait on the pier, alone, while the police were to hold back and stay at the visitors' centre until 'the package' was delivered.

The Professor reached a particular gangway close to where the barrier straddled the width of the Thames – it curled down like a giant grey caterpillar toward the water. Across the river, large, steel-clad shells shimmered like silver sentinels, their curved gates recessed in the open position. The Professor felt for the ridge of the gangway with his stick, and then stepped over it – disappearing inside the tunnel. The taps of his cane echoed dully as he made his way through it, until he emerged the other end. He found himself out in the open air again, balancing on the pontoon deck that gently swayed on the water. A light breeze and the warmth of the sun caressed his skin; seagulls squawked overhead. He tried to remember the last time he set foot on a boat – a distraction attempt to calm his nerves. But he couldn't remember, and it didn't work. Instead, he waited there, for two, five, ten minutes, the whiff of musty water filling his nostrils. He realised that he had not said goodbye to his friends and the children in Avernus, even though he always hated goodbyes.

And then he heard it.

A watery pop in the river just a few metres away from where he stood. Then another pop, and another, until there was a stream of gurgling bubbles. The Professor turned his head this way and that, trying to hear. There came a faint smell of diesel, and then a muffled mechanical noise which grew louder and louder, until it broke the surface of the river, sending a cascade of waves crashing against the deck. The Professor was flung to the decking, his stick thrown aside, and he rolled dangerously close to the edge of the pontoon before coming to a stop. He clung onto the decking for dear life as a small submarine – a midget, of the military kind – emerged from the water. Its conning tower and periscope rose up, and the full size of it – 11 metres in length, a two-metre beam, and a four-metre draft – rippled in the murky water.

The Professor was confused, unable to understand what was happening – when, all of a sudden, there came a clattering, rumbling sound from the gangway behind him, getting louder and louder. The vibrations rocked the pontoon even more, and the old man squeezed his eyes shut, bracing himself. He flinched when a hand touched his shoulder. But then another one gripped his arm, pulling him up. 'Professor!' came

Milly's voice.

And someone else. 'A submarine!' gasped Tai, staring at the vessel in astonishment.

Back on his feet, the old man pushed the teenagers away from him. 'No, you mustn't be here!! You have to go,' he shouted at them. 'Go now!!'

But it was both too late, as the submarine hatch door sprung open, and also useless, as Milly and Tai stayed put. Two men climbed out of the submarine and jumped onto the decking. They each grabbed one of the children and manhandled them roughly toward the hatch, barking out to the Professor, 'Follow us, and get in, old man!'

'He can't see!' shouted Milly at them, her cheeks burning red. 'He's blind!' She pushed the man away from her and turned to help the Professor – but she slipped and fell onto the pontoon with a yelp.

Tai pulled himself away and rushed to her, helping her up. 'Milly! Are you okay?'

Her jaw was throbbing with pain, and she fingered it gingerly, but nothing was broken. 'I-I'm fine.'

One of the men barked out to Tai, 'You! Bring the girl. We'll get the old man.' Then one by one, they disappeared into the hatch.

Finally, the submarine sank into the water and disappeared out of sight.

On the far corner of the pontoon, lay a small brown bottle of tablets that had fallen from Milly's pocket. A gentle wave sloshed over the edge, and pushed it into the river.

<hr />

By the time Rory Sanderson and his men reached the pontoon, breathless from running, there was no sign of the Professor, or the children. The submarine had already descended into the water and was well on its way, completely undetectable by their helicopters. He kicked the edge of the gangway with his boot in frustration. And he clenched his teeth as he pulled out his mobile and auto-dialled a number. 'I'm sorry, Sir,' he told the Prime Minister. 'The Professor and the two children were taken, but the package has not been dropped. I repeat, no package was received.'

The response was stunned silence, and then a grim, 'Understood.' And the call was ended.

Rory Sanderson balled his fists. He had guessed that this would happen. After all, you couldn't trust evil...

# THE RED

*'Red is the first colour of spring. It's the real colour of rebirth. Of beginning.'*

Ally Condie

# 23  BEAUTIFUL WISDOM

14-year-old Mei Hui often pondered the random elements in her life that had led, with almost irresistible compulsion, to her long streak of bad fortune. And she realised that they could be boiled down to four simple things: her plain and unremarkable looks, a fall on the way back from the water well, an ill-fated mahjong game, and her husband's lazy and drunken ways...

Awakening at 5 am every day, she had plenty of time to consider such things. She would put on her work garments in readiness for collecting the 'night soil' excrement from both the out-house and pig pen – and as she carried it to the fields on the bamboo pole pivoted against her shoulder, two sloshing buckets perfectly balanced on either end, she contemplated those very things. She trekked toward the first glimmers of morning light, gritting her teeth both from the weight of the night soil and from the cruel hand that fate had dealt her.

•••————————————————————•••

Her plain and unremarkable looks. This was the first unfortunate thing. Despite her mother being the beauty of the village, and her father, though not obviously handsome, having a pleasing ruddiness of the cheeks, large, honest eyes, and a good set of teeth – Mei Hui had the bad fortune of inheriting nothing from her mother, and from her father, only his rounded features and evenly-aligned teeth. Her parents' and grandparents' expectation of her eventually 'blossoming' with her mother's beauty was sustained with almost bated breath. Yet despite the promise being there, it remained unfulfilled, much to everyone's disappointment – except her own. There was no pale smooth skin, no delicate hands, and definitely no shapely, feminine physique. This was not good marriage material, and her maternal grandparents changed tack and worked her into the ground in punishment for not inheriting their lovely daughter's looks – and so she was set to working around the house, in the fields, and washing clothes in the river, in the knowledge that at least her ability to work hard increased her worth in another way.

A fall on the way back from the water well. Since she was nine, Mei Hui had been given the daily chore of collecting water from the nearest water source. Being both slight and a fledgling bird (not yet mastering the art of balancing a shoulder yoke loaded with heavy water buckets), made it a long and arduous task. She could only inch her way back by shuffling pigeon-steps the two li from the river to her family house which, being a poor family, was on the furthest outskirts of the village. Mei Hui always returned home vastly relieved, despite every muscle in her body aching – home being nothing more than four brick walls patched with corrugated iron sheeting, barely large enough to house their beds, a wood-burning stove, and crates for storage.

Her family had dubbed that particular day, Red Brick Day. The memory of it throbbed painfully in her mind. It was the day when a clay brick must have fallen from someone's cart, and lay hidden under thick ochre dust – she remembered kicking her foot against it, and losing her balance, the delayed pain hitting her as she thudded into the dirt. Water sloshed everywhere. Dazed, she eventually sat up and looked at that brick, the empty buckets, and her wet clothes. The smell of blood rose into her nostrils, the tang of it in her mouth. When she curled an explorative tongue along her teeth, she found with alarm that three were broken. She spat out the debris, and fought back tears. Then, without a word, she got up, re-attached the buckets to the bamboo pole, and turned to walk back to the well...

Her parents were livid when she returned without her front teeth. Country folk could not afford expensive dental care, and they were already in debt from the loan taken out to buy a replacement ox for ploughing. And this would cost them dearly for any bride price negotiations in the future, if indeed they could find a family willing to take her. That was the second unfortunate thing.

Mahjong. The third unfortunate thing was her paternal grandfather's weakness for gambling on mahjong. By now Mei Hui's parents had left the village, migrating to the nearest industrial town, many hundreds of miles away, to work in factories where the pay was much better than anything they could earn locally. Mei Hui was entrusted to the care of her grandparents, who had more or less given up on finding a husband for her, because most of the young men and women had migrated – leaving children behind to be cared for by other family members, or even just to fend for themselves. Her parents sent home money regularly – just over half their wages – and so her paternal grandfather took things easy, spending more and more time at the local teahouse, and indulging in gambling. Anything that moved could be bet upon, but worst of all was the addictive game of mahjong.

When he played, he had a strategy and a clear plan of attack, not just picking up tiles for the sake of it. His friends thought that the Thirteen Orphans hand was the most perfect one, but he did not agree. The Sacred Lamp of Nine Lotus hand was, in his mind, the easiest to complete – having both perfect harmony and brilliance. And so he usually gave priority to that, though being sly, there was nothing to stop him from changing tack at any time during the 16 rounds, if things weren't going his way. Realising that mahjong was half skill and half good fortune, the old man peppered his game with silent prayers to the gods. Occasionally they listened to him, and he won. But if he had the good sense to weigh up his total cumulative winnings against his losses, he would have realised that the gods in fact thought very little of him.

And so his debts grew greater and greater. And in time, he resorted to selling their prized black-and-white TV, the pig, and their one rather emaciated ox – until he realised that the only thing of any value he had left was Mei Hui. And so, after several months of harassment and increasingly aggressive threats from the local loan shark, for fear of his life he eventually decided to sell his granddaughter to pay off all his debts.

'What's her name?' demanded the prize-winner, after asking a hundred questions about her health and ability to cook and clean. When told, the man repeated it thoughtfully. 'Li Mei Hui? Hmm – that's a good name. But is she beautiful?'

The grandfather shifted his eyes sideways, and quickly looked back with a smile. 'Let's put it this way, her handwriting is breathtakingly good! But what matter are looks, when she works as hard as an ox. And she is very bright too – in fact, if she were a man, she would definitely become a successful and rich trader.'

And so it was agreed that Mei Hui would be handed over as payment for their winnings.

Mei Hui silently packed up her few belongings, and in the middle of the night, left with the strange couple who had won her. They lived in a faraway town, and Mei Hui walked, trailing behind them for what seemed like days and days – surprised by her own unceasing flow of tears as she followed, her head hung low, like newly-acquired livestock.

The shuffle of her purchasers' feet were ahead of her, just within sight – and in rhythm with their steps, her trembling lips mouthed the words to a familiar folk song:

*The eagle flies high in the sky*
*Pigeons flee the winter winds*
*Ice freezes the Yellow River in February*
*When I sing, my heart freezes too*
*Why is it that among human beings, a girl's life is the most pitiable?*
*Pity the girls, the poor girls*
*If I were a pigeon, I too would flee the winter winds of life.*

Her new owners, husband and wife, eventually reached a small brick house, and their raspy voices called to someone inside. Their son emerged, and they told him to begin arrangements for his marriage. They did not even check if the couple's birthdates matched.

The young man had only just got up from bed, though it was well into the afternoon, and he didn't even bother to bring them a drink of water. He took a long distasteful look at Mei Hui. 'Are you joking with me?! This thing is unsightly and toothless!!'

The parents had already come up with a counter-argument on their long journey back. 'We will pay you a good-sized dowry, on behalf of her absent parents. Will that do?'

He went off to get himself something alcoholic to drink, mumbling as he disappeared.

And so Mei Hui found herself betrothed to Longwei – a rather grand name meaning 'Dragon Greatness', though there was nothing magnificent or dragon-like in his pot belly, nose-picking, and constant scratching of his backside. He was older, having 23 years, and, to Mei Hui, the pigs she had raised at home were much better looking. Added to that, his parents had indulged him, and he was bone idle, never having done a full day's work in his life; whatever work his parents did manage to secure for him, he was usually kicked out by the afternoon for laziness, or for stealing, or for making lewd passes at the female workers.

For their wedding ceremony, none of the usual traditions were observed. There was no incense burned to appease the gods, no offerings made at the temple. They did not hire a hand-cart for the bride, or even bother with her red veil. Even the plain blue sky proffered no clouds to drench them in fortuitous rain – all of which did not augur well.

But by now, Longwei's parents realised that Mei Hui was a diamond in the rough – hard-working, respectful, and always polite. And so they handed over the dowry money to the girl, trusting, as her name suggested, that she would use it wisely; their son on the other hand, being a 'wine ghost', as they often referred to him, would have squandered it all in one night on gambling, women, and alcohol.

An uncle gifted the couple a small hut and some fallow land in the next village, and so after the marriage feast, Mei Hui and Longwei left for a place that was not much bigger, or better, than a chicken coop.

When the young man's parents watched them leave, disappearing into the distance, they sighed with relief that they were eventually rid of their woe-begotten son. But Mei Hui – then, at just over 12 years old – was thus burdened to cook, clean, wash, and bed, such a good-for-nothing man.

This was the fourth, and some would say the worst, of the unfortunate things in Mei Hui's life.

And thus did Mei Hui's young life unfold. If her story were a Xiqu, a traditional operatic play, the girl was completely powerless to the direction of the script, even though it was her own story. And while she should have been its main character, instead found herself in the background, waiting in the wings for her bit part. Her husband, Longwei, had become both the playwright and director of her life. And never having been taught any of the traditional decencies, he was always critical, rude, abusive, and lazy. And almost every day, when Mei Hui returned home from her work in the fields, he was in a drunken stupor lying on the warm kang and wasting all the precious wood in the fire so that there would be none left for the evening, when it was coldest. Yet, to Mei Hui, this was preferable to him being sober and conscious – because then, there was the revulsion of being set upon in the middle of the night. And even after that, as he slept, she had to endure his incessant breaking of wind, thunderous snoring, and flailing limbs.

Mei Hui found herself pregnant in their second year of marriage.

But the baby inside her was just over two months old before the physical strain of Mei Hui's chores and work in the fields caused unexpected bleeding. She could only clean up the bloods from the miscarriage in a dazed silence, gently wrapping the foetus – not much larger than a kidney bean – in her best scrap of material, grabbing a spade, and then walking out quietly to the bamboo forest. She dug a grave too deep for such a tiny thing, the soil riven, as she thrust the spade forcefully into the ground, again and again and again. Then, when the little cloth parcel was deposited and covered over, she stood – spent – looking up at the magnolia tree that marked it, memorising every detail, every branch, and the creamy petals of its flowers. Breathing in its delicate, lemony scent. She eventually dropped to her knees, sobbing – watering the grave with her tears. At last she got up and turned to leave, dragging the spade – chunk, chunk, chunk – behind her.

Later that day, she carried on with her work as usual, bearing in silence the sharp pains below her abdomen. They prodded her to remember this day forever.

She told nothing of this to her husband. He would not have cared less anyway. She only prepared a simple meal of sweet soup, to counteract the bitterness of death, braised pork with cloud ear fungus, and white rice.

For their two-month old daughter, Mei Hui laid out in the middle of the table a single magnolia blossom.

One good thing about her marital house was that it was in a propitious location: not far from the main road that led to the village centre, close to the communal well, and on the outskirts of a large plot of land. The lease had been fully paid off by the uncle, and still had several decades on it. And though it would need much weeding and tilling to get it going, it held rich, loamy soil that was fertile and well-watered thanks to the stream that ran along the furthest perimeter.

The first time she had arrived at their marital home, it was perhaps just as well that it was in the dark of night, because she would have been horrified to see the state of it. But, two days later, Mei Hui got to work, undeterred. She borrowed her neighbour's hand-cart and travelled to a nearby construction company just three li away; she had noticed their sign-post when they first arrived at the village. The company's buildings stood on a plot of land that was sectioned off for both storage holdings as well as dumping ground, the latter containing piles and piles of construction debris. She brought the site manager some home-made dumplings of pork and preserved vegetable, and a flask of good hand-picked tea, three-times brewed, politely requesting permission to sift through the dump for reclaimed building materials. It would help make space for more refuse, she reasoned with him. And the old manager found that he could not refuse such a beautifully thought-out request.

When Mei Hui scavenged for materials, mostly she found old bricks hugged by clumps of cement, which she hacked at with her hammer, so that they were clean and straight-edged by the time she piled them carefully into the cart. All in all, over the proceeding months, she counted 224 homemade dumplings, and 56 trips to the construction yard. Each time she struggled back home with a cart 10 times her weight, she found her husband either sleeping, or disappeared, most likely stumbling around the village, chasing after girls, and harassing people to give him wine or lager.

Workers from the construction company watched this dusty little girl at first with suspicion (in case she might steal from their stored supplies). But their distrust soon turned to admiration and amazement, as they watched her toil for months, hefting her cart to and fro, even in the rain. Some kind souls would help her during their lunch break for she was not much older than many of their daughters, and some, noting that she did not even stop to eat, would give her some of their food, or a cup of fresh tea, or some water. Mei Hui dared not refuse their gestures, gratefully lowering her eyes at their kindness, and bowing profusely to honour them. When they found out why she needed the bricks, they were quick to give advice on the best way to dig a foundation, and how to produce a strong and solid brick wall – also insisting she take their unsellable bags of cement that had split. She listened gratefully to all this information and memorised their instructions to the letter.

The digging of the trenches for the foundations of her house was the hardest part, because although the fields contained soft, malleable soil, their house was set on higher, drier, rocky ground. Her spade made slow progress as she dug. Her small hands, unused to such hacking, were blistering and bruising so that the only relief would be to bind them in rags. Her husband dozed in the shade of the rust-holed corrugated iron roof, while Mei Hui laboured until her hands were raw. She sat back in despair, looking at the extent of her two days of digging: a hole which was not much deeper than a chi, and only just long enough for a woman to lie down in. Her eyes swept over the expansive markings she had chalked out to widen the boundaries of their tiny home, and she stifled a choke in the back of her throat. The hole she had dug was small and shallow, but her despair seemed to open up like a bottomless chasm.

As a despondent Mei Hui lay against the incline of a large, flat boulder, staring up at the celestial blue of the sky, she fought back sudden waves of desolation. Lifting a tattered, bandaged hand to shade tear-filled eyes, she watched the silvery white clouds sweep majestically by. But then, suddenly aware of movement to the side, she sat up and looked round to find one of the villagers arriving carrying buckets of water on his shoulders. He was staring right at her and laughing his head off, at the same time beckoning with his hand to someone behind him.

Mei Hui blinked away the tears, and she realised that there was a small crowd of people in his wake, some carrying hoes, others spades. They were the elderly folk of the village, with mottled skin wrinkled as prunes, toothless grins, and wearing straw coolies or cotton caps. One of the men had a rather fat baby strapped to his back, its bare chunky thighs dangling on either side.

'You'll be there for an eternity, working by yourself!' laughed the man. He set to work dowsing water from his buckets to soften the dry earth, while the others cheerfully waved at her, then began hewing and digging at the ground behind him. The old folk were used to physical toil, and had the strength of people half their age.

Mei Hui was so astonished that she slipped from the boulder and fell into the dust.

The villagers laughed good-naturedly. 'That's it. You lie down and relax and leave the work to us,' joked one of the women.

Mei Hui got up unceremoniously, and rushed to fetch her pick – joining the line of them hacking away at the ground. They worked for hours and hours, taking it in turn to fetch water for everyone, with snacks of dried plums, and haw flakes.

Every now and again the man with the baby would respond to the chubby infant's movements and cues, and he would release it from the sling, hold it firmly at arm's length, and dangle it over the trench. The baby wore only a crudely-sewn hemp top, with its lower parts completely bare, and it would proceed to baptise the freshly-dug trench with a perfectly aimed line of pee. One time it was lowered down, the man held up its legs with his free hand, whereupon, after several grunts and red-faced straining, it produced neatly released stools. 'There you go, Mei Hui,' smiled the man, nodding his head in approval. 'Some little boulders to strengthen the foundations!'

The entire group laughed.

Mei Hui watched, amazed, as the old man rinsed the infant's bottom. 'Please tell me, Uncle,' asked Mei Hui respectfully, though he was not related to her. 'How do you know whether baby is going to pee or make a stool?'

'Ah, that's easy,' he smiled. 'When he needs to relieve himself, he grunts and kicks, like so.' The man began to imitate the baby's movements and noises, puffing out his cheeks and comically mimicking the child – much to the infant's wide-eyed pleasure. 'But when he needs to poo, he announces this by producing the most noxious farts I hope you never have the misfortune of smelling.'

Mei Hui laughed, clapping her hands to her chest.

Meanwhile, the baby looked up adoringly at his grandfather.

And so, the obliging old villagers and Mei Hui worked for several weeks, digging the trenches all around – mostly in quiet absorption, but every now and again bursting into chatter, jokes, and laughter, and at times singing in unison – hearty and motivating folksongs.

One of them remarked, 'These trenches cover more than just the foundations, Mei Hui. This central one is very deep. And what is this long one that trails out into the field over there? What are the plans?'

But Mei Hui was not inclined to answer, and she quickly deflected such questions by offering more tea, or snacks, or freshly steamed bao.

When the trenches were complete, they began mixing up the cement – one part cement, three parts sand, and six parts aggregate – and forming lines where they passed buckets to pour into the various sections. After disappearing for several weeks to allow the footings to cure, they returned with renewed vigour to start on Mei Hui's neat stack of salvaged bricks, using brick hods balanced carefully on their shoulders or head, and piling them up at strategic points around the site. There was only one old bricklayer amongst them, but several of them including the fast-learning Mei Hui were given a crash course – others mixed mortar, and still others cut the half bricks needed for staggering vertical joints.

All the while, the appreciation Mei Hui felt for their hard, unpaid labour made her heart burst. In her home village, the neighbours there had never shown any community spirit – they looked out only for their own interests, and all they ever offered her and her family was a constant stream of criticism.

When eventually Mei Hui was presented with the solid, strong, and white-washed walls to her new house, she looked at her dear, hard-working friends, and breathed, 'How can I ever repay you?!' Her eyes brimming with tears.

They were busy tidying and picking up their tools and belongings. 'Don't worry,' said the rather plump wife of the skinny water-bearer. She hurled a glob of spit into the bushes, and said, 'Do good, reap good,' citing the well-known proverb. She grinned kindly. 'So you see, sooner or later we'll get our reward!' She turned to go, stopped, and then turned back round. 'Maybe... in the spring, when the red-rump swallows return from their winter migration to roost, you can come and help plant the rice, or look after the children. After you've finished your house, mind – you need to get the roof on before the rains come.'

Her words echoed in Mei Hui's ears as she watched them shuffle back to their homes, and she took note.

She had already given much thought to the roof. She was not content to put the usual roof of corrugated metal onto her precious new home, topping the neatly-constructed walls with a beggar's crown of scrap iron. Instead, she set her heart upon beautiful jade-green clay tiles, a few of which she had already found at the builders' yard. But she would need to buy the rest, and they were expensive. So in her usual, prudent way, she made a deal with the construction company manager who had become her friend, to give her the tiles – on trust that she would repay him in instalments when she had the money. His basis of trust was the months of hard work that he saw her put into reclaiming bricks from his dump-yard; he had never seen anyone work as hard as this girl.

Again, Mei Hui called upon the tireless villagers to help her put up the roof timbers, fix the waterproof membrane, and tack down the tiles – this time, promising to work for them in return, either with house chores, washing their clothes in the stream, or baby-sitting their grandchildren. This was a happy arrangement, and before long, Mei Hui was rewarded with a handsome house that was like no other for many li around.

In time – with the money that her parents-in-law had given her – a new kang stove was added, and she devised a system of pipework from it that hugged the walls of connecting rooms in order to provide central heating – so important for the long, cold winters common to that region. She divided off two small washrooms, with a water-conserving system – precious water that would be used for the fields. But (puzzling to her lay-about husband) she left a large central room – almost a third of the entire house – unused.

Even the ramshackle old out-house was not overlooked by her resourcefulness. She insulated this by sandwiching dry straw between the repaired walls and an inner wood panelling, covered the roof with reclaimed tarpaulin, and replaced the commode with a newly-designed one that was more hygienic, easy to empty, and less smelly.

And the crowning glory to her land (something that the whole village admired) was the system of bamboo pipework and waterwheels that fed water from the stream at the edge of their land, first into a holding vat, and then through more pipes, several layers of steel mesh and tough gauze for filtration, and finally to hand-pumps right into the sink of their kitchen. Thoughtfully, she situated the holding vat in a strategic position so that other villagers could easily help themselves, thus lessening their load of work too.

••• ———————————————————————— •••

Yes, this very morning, Mei Hui reflected on her life so far, as she walked to the fields, in the haze of dawn, carrying buckets of slopping 'night soil' excrement. She covered her nose and mouth with a handkerchief tied at the back of her head, and then got to work with spreading the muck evenly around the soil. She hummed Chinese songs under her breath, her heart light with gratitude for the small blessings that had begun to trickle her way.

'Your lazy, rice-bucket husband should be doing that work, Mei Hui!' shouted out one of the villager women as she walked along the narrow dirt track, pulling a hand-cart behind her.

Mei Hui waved to her, her cheeks red with exertion. She pulled down her mouth cover. 'You know very well, Aunty Bo, that lao gong Longwei's bad back prevents him from doing any kind of labour.'

The old woman narrowed her eyes, her sun-wrinkled skin scrunching into a frown. But then she soon realised it was a joke, cackling. 'Really?! And I was Hua Mulan in a previous life...' She knew this honourable girl would never criticise her husband, even though there was plenty of reason to.

Mei Hui smiled to herself. She waved the old woman farewell, finished up washing the bucket, and made her way back home. As she walked along the path, she admired, with her wide, crescent eyes, the beauty of the building that was unlike any other in the village. Its smooth, straight, white-washed walls, and the vibrant jade-green tiles that made it both watertight and cool.

A young boy, no older than five, came skipping up the path to greet her. He had a thick head of glossy hair and ruddy cheeks, and in his hand he held a long stick. When he got close enough, she realised that he was singing completely out-of-tune:

> *'Little swallow, dressed so colourfully*
> *Who comes here every spring*
> *I asked her, 'Why do you come here?'*
> *She said, 'The spring here is the most beautiful'*
> *Little swallow, let me tell you*
> *It is more beautiful here this year*
> *We've built a large white house with a jade green roof*
> *And re-done the out-house*
> *Please live here forever.'*

His voice crescendoed to maximum volume, and he had – with childish artistic licence and a cheeky grin – changed the words in the last lines to fit their own circumstance.

Mei Hui waved at him frantically to stop singing. 'Hush now, An!!' she hissed. 'You're going to wake up Longwei, and you know how bad-tempered and grizzly he becomes when he doesn't get enough sleep. He might even come out and beat you.'

Little An stopped in his tracks, and turned to look behind, half expecting to see the man standing there glowering down at him. To his relief there was no-one, and An's feistiness returned. He balled up tiny hands into fists. 'Oh yeah?! Well then, I'll punch him again and again, and kick that stupid melon right up the–'

'An! Please control yourself. What a brave and mighty 'one chi' warrior you are – when he's not around!'

The boy looked at her and smiled – one chi was a third of a metre, and his height was more than double that, but he didn't mind her teasing. He threw his arms around her and gave her a hug. 'My Mei Hui!' he breathed, smiling up at her affectionately. And then drew back. 'Phew – you stink!' He pinched his nose with one hand and waved away the odour with the other.

'I've been spreading night soil, silly. Now, what have you been doing with that stick? Please tell me you haven't been poking the wild beehive hanging from the Longan tree.'

'No.'

Mei Hui watched his face carefully for any tell-tale signs, but satisfied herself. 'Good – you know that a particularly fierce type of bee colony lives there...'

'I know, I know.'

'You're up early. Are the others up too?'

He nodded enthusiastically, and trotted beside her as they went home. 'Yes!'

'Are they doing their chores?'

'Yes!'

'And have you done *your* chores?'

'Yes! Er... well, actually, no. I was just about to when I saw you coming.' He looked up at her with irresistible eyes.

'Come on then, let's do them together.'

The little boy did not beg off. He knew that he and his older sister were fortunate to be in Mei Hui's household, along with the other four – all children of parents who had migrated out of the villages to work in factories. But these children had no other family to take care of them, and Mei Hui, realising their disadvantage, and with a pure, kind heart, fitted out the large empty room in her house with three sets of bamboo bunk beds to accommodate them. Before long, the children's parents began to send her money for their expenses, together with a modest stipend for herself, gushing with gratitude. And as an unexpected though pleasant consequence, Mei Hui, her husband, and the children found that they could live in relative comfort, with even some money left over. She used this to pay off her loan to the manager of the building company, and even indulged in her first ever dental appointments, in town, to replace her missing teeth. The rest of the money was carefully set aside in savings.

An and Mei Hui entered the house to find the five other children, still sleepy-eyed, yawning, and in their bed clothes, sweeping the floor, tidying the beds, setting out the breakfast things, warming the water for washing themselves, and feeding the rabbits, pigs, chickens, cats, and pond fish. An ran over to pick up a small, wicker basket, grabbed Mei Hui's hand, and they went outside to collect warm eggs from the chicken coop.

'Waaa!' cried An appreciatively as he picked out six perfect eggs, glowing white.

Then, each of them took turns to wash in the two washrooms with jugs of lovely warm, fire-heated water (Mei Hui was very strict about cleanliness, making sure they were squeaky clean from the grime and dust of the countryside). She heated up the rice porridge, and for a special treat popped nine red bean dumplings into stacked bamboo steamers. The room was filled with the delicate and delicious fragrance, and the children – freshly dressed in their school clothes – slurped it all up heartily, each of them savouring the sticky sweetness of the bao.

The aroma had woken up Longwei, and he padded out of bed, scruffy-haired and whiskery, heading straight for the table and his food. He wolfed down his two red bean buns and rice congee, then stretched over to take the food from Mei Hui's plate – and greedily scoffed that too, snorting like a pig. The children glared indignantly at him, then glanced across at Mei Hui who discreetly shook her head at them, to keep quiet. But they already knew better. They cleared away their dishes without a word, and then busied themselves with preparing for school.

Each child filed out of the house, waving goodbye to Mei Hui, and walking straight past Longwei without a word. He was sitting outside, next to the perfumed trails of flowering jasmine, already puffing on his first smoke of the day.

Much later in the morning, Longwei washed and brushed his teeth, oiled back his coarse black hair, and dressed himself unusually neatly – placing a single jasmine flower in the button of his shirt pocket, and splashing copious amounts of cheap aftershave on his chin. From this, Mei Hui understood that he was going out to meet his mistress. It beggared belief that there was a woman out there in the village needy enough to fall for him, but Mei Hui wasn't complaining – in fact, she was rather grateful, for it meant that he would leave her alone that night, and she could sleep in peace.

•••————————————————————•••

When the children returned home from school that afternoon, dinner was already waiting for them – and they always ate up every scrap, including their vegetables, tidying up after themselves. Evenings were spent playing together – the boys particularly enjoyed collecting crickets, and comparing their qualities, strengths, and weaknesses, and discussing the merits of each male's trill song. Or they told each other stories, listened to the radio or the old hand-cranked phonograph that was donated by one of the better-off farmers in their village – their only two luxuries. And Mei Hui always ensured their homework was not only completed on time, but that they thoroughly understood it and presented it in their neatest writing – often having to explain things herself.

After a session with Jiao-jie, the girl looked curiously at Mei Hui, someone she had come to view as her 'older sister' being just two years senior. She tapped the page of equations laid out in front of them with a pencil, and asked, 'How come you know so much, Mei Hui, when you dropped out of school yourself?' Jiao-jie lived up to the meaning of her name, 'Pure and Lovely'. She was An's sister, and at 12 years old had been charged with looking after her younger brother when her parents first left to go out, forced to migrate to the factory town to make enough money to support them. Jiao-jie watched them leave without a word, and took on the responsibility of caring for her little brother, even though she herself needed caring for. Thankfully, Mei Hui had taken them in.

Mei Hui smiled and gently stroked back a loose strand of hair behind the pretty girl's ear. 'Everything I know is learnt from listening to the radio while I work at home,' she told her. 'Also, I've read every single text book you children have brought home from school, including your workbooks, and your English language books. I read them over and over again because... well, there's not exactly much else to read around here.'

Jiao-jie thought about this. 'But when I read my text books, I don't always understand what they're saying. Algebra, especially. How come you understand them so well without anyone explaining them to you?'

Mei Hui shrugged. 'I don't know why, but I just do. It helps that I can remember everything by heart – word for word.'

Jiao-jie's pretty eyes widened. 'Word for word! Really?!' she gasped.

Mei Hui laughed at her, and told her to open the geography textbook onto any page, and tell her the page number. Jiao-jie did so, and Mei Hui diverted her eyes and cited the first paragraph. The children gathered round and followed the text in Jiao-jie's book, cooing and gasping with amazement.

When she had finished, the children immediately rummaged through their school bags to extract their own various textbooks, and then asked her to recount certain paragraphs on certain pages. Little An even snuck up behind her and covered her eyes with his hands to make sure that she was not cheating. But Mei Hui rattled off the citations without even a sweat, smiling at their sounds of astonishment.

An released his hands, and Mei Hui rubbed her eyes to find him staring at her with his mouth open in astonishment. 'And what about those women who sing as if they've got stomach ache?' he asked. 'Do you know that by heart as well?'

Mei Hui looked puzzled.

'You know, that funny wailing song you keep listening to!' he said, waving an impatient hand.

'Ah – Leo Delibes' 'Sous le dôme épais'?' Despite the foreign words, they fell from her tongue with ease, as if she had spoken French all her life. Jiao-jie rushed across to retrieve the vinyl record, and carefully took it out from its paper sleeve. One of the older boys took off the cloth cover from the phonograph. 'Let's see if Mei Hui remembers all those strange words, sung by the women who desperately need to go to the toilet,' he sneered.

When the boy cranked the handle, the scratchy sound of Delibes' **_Flower Duet_** rose and filled the room. Every now and again the record jumped, but still, Mei Hui's heart soared when she heard the rising crescendo of the sopranos' voices. She sang along with them in French, her own vibrato locking in with the singers', so that she and they were in perfect unison.

> 'Sous le dôme épais
> Où le blanc jasmin
> À la rose s'assemble
> Sur la rive en fleurs,
> Riant au matin

*Viens, descendons ensemble.*

*Doucement glissons de son flot charmant*
*Suivons le courant fuyant*
*Dans l'onde frémissante*
*D'une main nonchalante*
*Viens, gagnons le bord,*
*Où la source dort et*
*L'oiseau, l'oiseau chante.*
*Sous le dôme épais*
*Où le blanc jasmin,*
*Ah! Descendons*
*Ensemble!'*

The children listened quietly, enthralled that she mimicked the song flawlessly, beautifully, her pitch perfect, her vibrato mesmeric. And when eventually the record came to an end, and the stylus clicked up from the turntable, there was a moment of complete silence – and then, one and all, they clapped and roared with appreciation. 'She is a Kouji master!' they shouted. 'She is a grey shrike bird!'

But before long, little An stopped and drew closer to her, puzzled. 'Mei Hui, Mei Hui! Why are you crying?' The song usually made her happy.

Mei Hui could not speak, and found that she was unable to stop her tears. Perhaps it was the music – its ability to transport her to another world, a place far, far away from the dusty farm that had swallowed up her childhood, her life. Or perhaps it was the sheer beauty of the singers' voices set free to soar high into the sky, like spring swifts. Even she did not know the reason for her tears, and the ache in her chest. She just shrugged, wiped her face with a sleeve, and quickly began tidying up their things. 'It is time for you to go to bed,' she told them, turning away.

•••————————————————————————•••

Longwei did not return home that night.

And so Mei Hui lay on the kang bed, staring up at the rafters, deep in thought – pondering over the music, and how it broke through the dam of her deepest feelings. There were so many questions it brought to mind that were impossible to answer. What motivated the songwriter to write such music? What did the words mean? Why did the singing affect her so deeply? How she longed to know the answers, the hidden meaning locked behind those mysterious words.

And she also longed to find out why her parents had not come looking for her, why there was no word from them, not even a letter.

And furthermore, what were those distant memories of times in a foreign country, a foreign place, that pained her like splintered shards. Memories of when she was a toddler, in a grey, shiny world that she could barely remember.

But there was nothing she could do. Except resign to the fact that, most likely, she would live out her entire life, grow old, and die in the dirt, without finding any answers to her questions – without knowing how to get back to the world that had forgotten her.

Mei Hui slept fitfully that night.

Yet she dreamt of only one thing.

She dreamt of a lotus flower that grew up out of the muddy waters, reaching for the sun, and then delicately opening its pink and white petals skyward. A single beetle emerged from within, and hovered across to the next blossom, pollinating it in the process. But where the rest of the vast lake should have been filled with myriad lotus blossoms, there were, unusually, only seven scattered flowers. Each of them clambering for the sun.

*** ———————————————————— ***

The next morning, Mei Hui sensed her depression and despair begin to lift, like bright skies after a storm. Exhausted from a night of tossing and turning, the pressing need of caring for the children, the fields, the housework, soon pulled her out of the haze.

The children realised that Mei Hui was back to normal when they smelt the pleasing aroma of wonton soup seasoned with ginger, sesame oil, and freshly picked scallions. They grinned at each other.

'Mei Hui's back!' said Jiao-jie with damp eyes.

The children had always borne Mei Hui's silent depressions with good-nature and forbearance – though they never could understand.

Little An rubbed his belly and licked his lips, 'Mm, I like it when Mei Hui's happy again. It's always very tasty...'

Later that afternoon, one of the village men came running to Mei Hui's house all in a flap, with water marks up to his knees. 'Mei Hui!' he shouted, gasping, and bending over to catch his breath. 'Come out... bad news... You must come... follow me, immediately!' She appeared at the door, surprised by the old man's sudden presence. But the villager did not have the heart to tell her what it was. Instead, he took her hand and pulled her gently, encouraging her to follow. They ran together along the lane that led to the stream, and, after about 15 minutes, they arrived at the man-made levee of the river, where the stream changed course and skirted the village. There, the water was shallow, at less than two chi deep. Mei Hui could see a group of about four or five other villagers crowding around the reeds, a couple of them bending low, and pulling at something heavy in the water. At first Mei Hui thought that one of their pigs had escaped from the pen. But as she drew closer, she saw the back of a man lying face down in the mud, and realised it was Longwei!

Her heart froze, and she splashed into the water to help him. But she soon realised it was too late. Her husband was already dead.

She took several steps back, toes curling in the soft mud.

The rippling water capturing sparkles of sunlight.

In a daze, she slapped away a mosquito buzzing around her ear.

Meanwhile, the villagers crowded around Longwei, and managed to flip him over and drag him out unceremoniously onto the dry bank. In so doing, the water washed some of the mud from his face, and they saw that his flesh was white and swollen – eyes popping like a fish. Mei Hui recoiled and turned away.

'He's obviously been there all night,' said one of the women, glancing sheepishly at the young girl. 'The water is less than two chi deep here. He must have passed out in drunkenness, and fallen face down.'

One of the men said, 'If he'd been sober he could have saved himself, pulled himself out.'

'But... what was he doing all the way out here, in the middle of nowhere?' asked another, puzzled.

A fourth villager scratched his head and stared at Longwei. 'Being drunk, maybe he got confused and couldn't find his way back.'

But they had to resign to the fact that it would be impossible to know the truth of what really happened. How could they discover it? The man was dead, and the place was so remote it was unlikely there were any observers.

For a reason that she did not understand, Mei Hui dared to wade closer.

But just then, at her feet, she saw a streak of silver-pink wriggling in the turbid water. A large bream flashed into view amongst the muddy reeds, and Mei Hui caught sight of its blood-shot eye looking directly at her. *I know what happened*, it told her. And then it flapped into a clear eddy, and swam away forever.

The village woman saw it too. 'If only that fish could talk!'

Mei Hui, with a strange look on her face, glanced at her.

The first villager who had run to fetch Mei Hui urged her to go home, there was nothing she could do, and they would take care of fetching a horse and cart to transport the body to the funeral parlour. Mei Hui nodded, still in a daze, thanked them weakly, and turned to trudge back. Her feet, numb and cold.

But as she walked, and her limbs began to warm, she realised that she was beginning to feel very light indeed. Like a beast of burden freed from its yoke.

When she told the news to the children in a hushed, awed tone, they just looked at each other, and at her, hardly knowing how they should react. Inside, they were happy to be rid of the good-for-nothing man, but for decency, they behaved respectfully, for life was precious.

And so, they hugged Mei Hui, and made her some soothing tea, urging her to change into dry, warm clothes before she caught a cold.

'Why are you all acting like this?' whispered little An to his sister. 'I'm happy that old fire-breath melon-head is gone for good!'

••• ———————————————————— •••

Mei Hui sent word to Longwei's parents, and over the next days, they put up notice banners around the village, and – though she was not superstitious – for the sake of propriety and for her parents-in-law, she set a small borrowed gong to the left of the main door, pinned coloured cloths to the children's sleeves, and dressed herself in white hemp-cloth. Mei Hui knew that, in public, she should wail with mourning for the prescribed amount of time to show honour to her dead husband – but this was one thing she could not bring herself to do, for neither she nor the villagers believed for a moment that he was deserving.

However, when her parents-in-law arrived, she submitted to the custom of preparing food for their son's shrine, and burning paper money, coloured gold and silver. It was believed that such burnt offerings would be 'transferred' to the deceased in the afterlife, so that, even in death, they would not be wanting.

Unsurprisingly, very few people attended the funeral, and nobody, not even the parents, hired professional mourners.

They simply stood around, ate the food, and tried to look solemn.

Little An noticed Mei Hui's damp eyes and miserable countenance. 'Why's she sad?' he asked.

Jiao-jie whispered to him. 'She's not sad. She's happy, dolt-head!'

An glanced from Mei Hui to Jiao-jie and frowned. 'But, she's crying.'

'She's not. She's *mourning*... She has to mourn for 100 days. It's the proper thing to do. It's tradition.'

An was none the wiser, in fact, he was thoroughly confused.

While Mei Hui was being surveyed by little An, she herself looked around at the few people attending the funeral, and nodded to them with gratitude for showing up. But there was one face she was surprised to see – a widow, in her 30s, who had lost her husband several years ago. Her eyes were sad and pretty – and tinged unusually with a touch of blue.

Later, at the wake organised by Longwei's parents, Mei Hui took it upon herself to offer rice wine to the guests. One of the older children carried a tray full of drinks by her side, and Mei Hui picked one up, and – balancing the cup on an open hand, held steady with the other – offered it to the blue-eyed woman.

The woman, who had been hovering around the house in the background, suddenly froze, finding herself face to face with Mei Hui, unsure of what to do. Trying, but failing, to hide her panicked expression, the woman bowed her head, lowering her eyes to the ground. Eventually, she straightened, and reached for the proffered cup, her fingers lightly touching Mei Hui's for a fraction of a second. But it was too much. And unable to bear it any longer, the woman turned away and rushed out of the house.

An electric shock jolted right through Mei Hui, from her hand right to her head, as she watched the woman disappear in stunned silence.

Longwei's mother descended immediately on Mei Hui. 'You're shaking,' she said, clutching her daughter-in-law's sun-burnt hand. 'You are upset from the death of your husband, my son...'

Mei Hui blinked at her mother-in-law, noticing her smooth fingers against the roughness of her own.

Mother-in-law continued speaking. 'You have paid for all the funeral costs, but don't worry about the expense of the ancestral tablet, Mei Hui. We will take care of it. You were clearly a good wife to Longwei, performing your duties well – and for this we are grateful. You have honoured us.'

Still shaken, Mei Hui withdrew her hand and bowed long and low. 'Thank you, popo, for your kind words and kind deeds. I...' But she could not find the words, distracted as she was. 'I-I'm sorry,' she said, and rushed off, retreating to the seclusion of her room.

It was dark inside, with the curtains drawn, and at last Mei Hui could dispense with the formalities and display of respect. She collapsed onto her bed, still trembling, and rolled herself into a ball. Her thoughts turned back to the moment when the blue-eyed woman took the cup of rice wine from her hands. The touch of her fingers on hers. The unexpected jolt of something... Recognition? Understanding?

And then, in her mind, an explosion of images flickered like stills from a projector. Amongst them, she latched onto one. A memory.

She closed her eyes and saw it now. As clear as day.

Longwei, preened and drunken, a single jasmine flower in the buttonhole of his shirt pocket.

He was staggering along a path, approaching a run-down house – late afternoon light bathed him in a honey glow, making him look almost handsome. In this memory, Mei Hui became the blue-eyed woman, and the blue-eyed woman became her. Standing at the door of her home, the blue-eyed woman threw her arms around him and kissed him, but then recoiled from the reek of alcohol and cheap aftershave. 'Please,' she begged. 'Please stop drinking so much, Longwei. You don't need to. You have me. You can stay here, and I'll look after you.'

Longwei stood in front of her, swaying drunkenly from side to side, and then laughed. 'Why would I want to stay with you?' he said, his words slurred. 'Look at this hovel, look at *you*... It's true what they say. "Men of 40 are a blooming flower, but women of 40 are dregs of beancurd".'

The woman laughed nervously. 'You... you don't mean that. Anyway, you know I'm not yet 37. Come in, come in. Look, I've made your favourite.'

Longwei pushed her inside, and only glanced scornfully at the food laid out on shiny green lotus leaves. Instead, he started looking around her hut. 'Where is it?' he demanded.

She backed away from him, uneasy. 'W-what do you mean?'

'Where is it?!' he shouted.

'I... I don't have it anymore. I told you. I sold it a long time ago.'

'Liar!' he screamed. And then tore through the woman's hut like a furious demon, shouting and demanding her to 'hand it over'.

Terrified, the woman stood away from him, refusing to speak.

In a rage, Longwei smashed to the floor the family photos of her dead husband that had hung with pride on the peeling walls, and rifled through all her belongings, searching everywhere.

All the while the woman was crying quietly.

Eventually, he pulled up the bed mattress, revealing a neat parcel of muslin, small enough to fit in the palm of a hand. He pounced upon it, released the mattress, and sat down opposite the woman. Unfolding the cloth revealed a bright green bracelet – a perfect circle of flawless jade that seemed to absorb light and glow even in the dimness of the hut. It was the most expensive type of jade which her husband had taken three whole years to save up for. A symbol of his deep love for his precious wife. A thing that she cherished with her life.

Longwei looked up at the blue-eyed woman, and Mei Hui saw her image reflected back in the sheen of his glazed eyes. Her mouth a gasping o, eyes brimming with tears.

And then the scene was suddenly rent in two as Mei Hui was hurled even further back in time, to the memory of the woman's husband giving her the bracelet. Their home was not the spartan hut she lived in now – it was a larger house, neat and tidy, and filled with shiny ornaments and nice furniture. Mei Hui smelt the ubiquitous presence of love all around; it hung in the air, like the pungent sweetness of incense. It was a love evident in her husband's face as he gazed at his dear wife from his sickbed. Reflected in his eyes was the woman herself – young, and beautiful, and broken-hearted that her husband was dying. Looking down, the jade bracelet felt cold as he slipped it over her lily-white hand, onto her wrist...

Yet another flash of light, and Mei Hui found herself back in the memory of Longwei's last night. Distraught, the blue-eyed woman watched as he thrust the bracelet into his pocket and staggered outside into the darkness, ignoring her entreaties to give it back. Not knowing what to do, she found herself tumbling after him, struggling to hold back her sobs, willing herself to calm down. All she could think of was her bracelet, and so she followed him wending his way along the pitted narrow roads of the village. One lone figure trailing behind another. Past rows and rows of bungalows and shanties in varying states of dilapidation.

They reached the square, and on the other side of it was a villa surrounded by a wall – standing out as neat and well-maintained. The front door was painted green, a colour that stood for health and prosperity – and Longwei threw himself on it, banging and banging for someone to open.

A rather small man appeared, who eyed the drunkard up and down distastefully. But when Longwei showed him the bracelet, the man immediately recognised the opportunity of an unexpected bargain. The dealer took the jade and fingered it, greed lighting up his face. Of course, he protested that the item was of poor quality and hardly worth his while – and so the two men haggled, finally settling on 800 yuan – a fraction of its real value as her husband had bought it for well over 2,000. Even then, that was a good price for such smooth and beautifully translucent Jadeite.

The blue-eyed woman was hiding behind the corner of the next building, her heart breaking into a million pieces as she watched her precious bracelet pass hands. Lost forever. She had no savings, and would never be able to raise the funds to buy it back.

Unbidden, her feet followed Longwei as he made his way to the village shop to buy a pack of four Tsingtao beers with his ill-gotten money. When he left a 50-yuan note, and didn't even wait to take the change, her skin prickled with anger. How dare he! How dare he take her precious bracelet, and even treat the money he had gained from it with so little respect!!

Yet still she followed him. With every step, her misery was compounding and transmuting into rage, as he staggered around, stopping to swill now and again, and singing raucously as he walked here and there, one aimless path after another. He drank and stumbled and drank, until he reached the edge of the village, marked by the intersection of stream and river. A dense growth of bushes gave way to the river bank, where a single pine-nut tree stood. It was tall and hunched, with a thick canopy of branches spreading across the stream, like a wizened old giant in a hat.

The blue-eyed woman watched Longwei's silhouette, smudged and inky against the silver backdrop of the river. He sat down on the ground at the base of the tree, resting against the crackled bark. When she dared to inch closer, she saw that he was crouching over the ground, digging with bare hands between the roots of the tree. Surely he could not be insane enough to dig for fu-ling! It was an edible fungus that had roots bearing a coconut-like husk – smashed open one could obtain its white, starchy innards. But if it was over-mature and concentrated, it contained a toxic chemical. Only the youngest, freshest fu-ling might be able to be eaten raw, but one had to cautiously chew it at the side of the mouth to first ascertain toxicity.

The woman covered her mouth with a hand as she watched Longwei's drunken stupidity. Watched him wolf down the starchy root and swig the last of his lager, throwing the empty bottle into the river. He lay back against the tree, as if settling down to sleep... but after a while, he suddenly sat up again, choking. Frantic hands clawed at his throat. His lips, mouth, and gullet burned so badly that he wanted to tear out his own flesh. He stumbled into the river, throwing himself in to drink its cooling water. But the poison and the swelling was already strangling him from the inside.

The blue-eyed woman broke free from the shadows and ran to him now, calling his name, throwing herself into the water to try and save him. But he was struggling and desperate and waterlogged, his thrashing body impossible to tame. He gasped for air, fought to breathe – a guttural gurgling coming from his throat.

In the end, he lay still, face down in the water. His last breaths floating in a froth of bubbles by his head.

And though she clenched her teeth and tried with all her might to heave him out, the woman was too small, and bound to fail. She fell to her knees, waist-deep in the water, and sobbed under the over-arching branches of the solitary pine. It was ironic that the evergreen pine – which symbolised longevity due to its ability to survive the harshest winters – was the very tree under which Longwei's life ended abruptly.

In time, the blue-eyed woman lifted her head and saw a speck of masticated fu-ling float out of the cadaver's bloated mouth, and – quick as a flash – a silver-pink bream swallowed it up with a gulp. But the fish spat it out immediately and wriggled in protest, trapped amongst the reeds.

Even a simple fish had proved wiser than Longwei, and the thought of such absurdity cast a shadow over the woman's damp face. She got up on uncertain feet, water dripping from her in rivulets. Found herself hovering out of the water, in a daze. In the dream-like glow of the moon, she walked back to her home, sobbing and miserable, desperate and inconsolable. She closed the door of the hut behind her, disappearing like a shadow merging with darkness.

Mei Hui watched this, tears flowing, heart breaking – not for her husband, but for this woman, who was now haunted once more by the ghost of loneliness.

And she watched as the blue-eyed woman turned and closed the door of her hut, dripping wet.

In the woman's mind lingered a single thought.

What was there left to live for?

•••————————————————————•••

After a long, unyielding winter, the sweet, warm smell of spring rose in the air, and Mei Hui's children were half playing in the warm afternoon sun, and half working – picking large, fuzzy peaches that were fragrantly ripe. They laughed as the sticky juices ran down their chins, because for the first time they were able to eat freely without Longwei scolding them for stealing 'his' fruit. Mei Hui was busy preparing the jars to preserve the surplus from their little spring crop: peaches, kumquats, pomelos, plums, and the date-like jujube. But then she heard a scream.

'Aaaaiieeeeee!!'

It was Zhu, the oldest boy, who was standing at the top of the ladder, immersed in the foliage of the peach tree. He had sprouted whiskers in adolescence, with a recently broken voice – yet he screamed like a girl.

'What is it?!' cried Mei Hui, afraid that he had been bitten by a stink bug. But when she craned her neck and shaded her eyes to see, she saw that he was looking far into the distance. He pointed to the object of his fear, and she turned to follow the line of direction.

'T-two ghosts,' he stammered. 'Two *white* ghosts over there! Can't you see? And they're heading this way!!' Quick as a flash he scrambled down the ladder, shouting at the children in warning. They one and all squealed with fear, disappearing into the house and shutting the door behind them.

Zhu opened it again and beckoned frantically for Mei Hui to get in too. Ignoring him, she walked inquisitively toward the foreigners, who by now were just at the edge of their holding. She wiped her hands on her work clothes as she went, squinting to see in the sun. They were indeed foreigners, but young ones – the first a man not much older than Zhu, and the other was an even younger girl with pale skin and hair the colour of bleached rape flowers. They walked closer, and Mei Hui saw that they were Westerners – both looking at her and smiling.

The boy spoke to her in what seemed like Mandarin, but the rise and fall of intonations did not match the words, which was confusing, giving all the wrong meanings. Still he chanted several memorised phrases as best he could – and to her surprise, she heard him say her name, Li Mei Hui. Dumbfounded, Mei Hui shook her head to show she did not understand. The boy misunderstood this, and disappointedly started to leave. But the yellow-haired girl held him back, and then stepped closer and spoke in near-perfect Mandarin, 'Are you sure you don't know young girl, whose name is Li Mei Hui?'

Mei Hui managed to control her surprise. 'Why do you ask?' she said cautiously.

The girl began to look excited, glancing at the young man, and then turning back to Mei Hui. 'Because...' she replied in Chinese, 'she is very special, and part of my family. We were together when children – I was just baby, and she was toddler. There were seven of us altogether.'

Mei Hui's face muscles twitched, and she struggled to control her pounding heart. 'Please tell,' Mei Hui said, her eyes sliding across to the boy and back again. 'How is it possible that a Chinese girl could be part of a Western family?'

The young girl grinned, bursting with barely controlled excitement. 'Might I be bold, make a suggestion?' she asked respectfully, even though they were of similar age.

'You may,' said Mei Hui.

The girl looked at her with a twinkle in her eyes. 'Could you give a drink of water, please? We've been searching for weeks. Then we can sit together, and I can explain everything, Mei Hui...'

Mei Hui blinked at her.

The girl continued. 'Surely you, whose name means "beautiful wisdom", appreciate it is wise thing to do...'

Mei Hui's jaw dropped in astonishment, and then quickly closed. Eventually, she ushered them both to follow her – but then she stopped, and turned back round to face them. 'Since you both know my name, and even its meaning, may I ask yours?'

'Yes of course,' smiled the girl, looking at her with large, mesmerising eyes. They were the colour of deep sea. 'My name is Jemima Jenkins, and I have nearly 14 years.' She motioned toward the young man. 'And this is my good friend, Jake Winters. He has 17 years, and only knows few words of Mandarin. And no, we're not related, and he's not my boyfriend!' she added, rolling her eyes as if she had been asked this absurd question a thousand times.

Mei Hui nodded and turned to open the door, but it was locked.

'Aaiiee!!' came Zhu's muffled scream from inside.

Mei Hui leaned into the door. 'It's only me, Zhu!' she called out. 'There's nothing to be afraid of.' She paused for a moment, and then said to him, 'Some of my family have come to visit, and we have a lot to talk about...'

## 24 THE YIN AND THE YANG

When the door was eventually opened, and they were let in, Mei Hui introduced the two visitors to the ashen-faced, goggle-eyed children, and asked one of them to make them tea, and the rest of them to go about their chores or do homework. Mei Hui then went outside with them, away from the keen ears of the children. They spoke in low, hushed tones, all afternoon.

Jemima Jenkins recounted her own knowledge of their beginning. That, many years ago, her mother and father had taken part in some kind of confidential government experiments, in England, the details of which were unclear to either of them. But all she knew, and all her parents explained to her, was that it gave them a very *special* child. They were sternly told not to speak of this to anyone, but it soon became apparent what the nature of their 'specialness' was, when she developed acute intellectual abilities, with a particular gift for numbers and mathematics. Jemima explained that when she looked at physical equations and formulae, it was like she could see the very structure of the world unfold in front of her, blossoming like a flower of numbers. The elegance of those equations revealed relationships between space, time, matter, and energy – a relativity that connected all of us together, and at the same time, merged us with the universe, she said. Her parents did well in keeping a low profile, and they took the decision to home-school her. At the same time, they nurtured her intellectual talents by encouraging her to write, and she eventually published a successful line of books under a pen name. She flourished as she grew, and all seemed well. That was, until one night several weeks ago, something 'bad' happened.

At this point, Jemima glanced away briefly, visibly shaken. Someone had tried to kill her, she told Mei Hui. She took a deep breath and continued. Thankfully, Jake had stepped in just in time to save her life. He'd climbed into her room from the back garden – through her bedroom window which, fortunately, had been left open. He immediately got her urgent medical help, and she recovered quickly.

Jake himself had been searching for his sister who disappeared many years ago, after she too had taken part in this secret scientific project – though exactly in what capacity, he did not know. Ever since, Jake has been trying to find out whatever he could about those special experiments – to help him find his sister. And he stumbled across some clues that led him to Jemima as being one of the children in the experiments. Anyway, to cut a long story short, she said, they both decided to act upon another clue that Jake had uncovered: the name of a second child born from the government project, Li Mei Hui... And so, the two of them set out to find her.

Mei Hui listened to this amazing story quietly. It had answered many questions, but also raised countless more. Yet the first thing Mei Hui asked was: 'Your parents... are they not worried about where you are?' She was sensitive to this, because she had written to her own parents many times at the address of the factory where they worked and boarded – but they never replied, never came looking for her.

'After we left the country safe, I contacted them,' said Jemima. 'We had to lay low, I did not want them to be in danger – after all, we still don't know who tried to kill me, or why... But when I explained everything, mummy was okay eventually, daddy too – they were relieved to know I'm alive and safe! Mummy cried though...'

'Why would someone want to kill you?' asked Mei Hui.

'I don't know,' said Jemima, her eyebrows slanting from bewilderment. 'I honestly don't know. Might be something to do with government project. That's all I can think.'

'If that is so, then am I in danger as well?'

Jemima's eyes widened, 'I hope not...' she said, but then quickly looked away, and Mei Hui's question was answered.

Mei Hui turned to look toward the house, and thought of the children. The sun was setting, casting long shadows – evening darkness drawing near. The children, who Mei Hui had taught to be self-sufficient, had already started making a simple dinner of steamed whipped egg with dried shrimps, spring vegetables, and rice – setting out portions on the table for Mei Hui and, a little tremulously, her 'white ghost' friends.

When the visitors went into the house to eat – aromas of scallion and dried shrimp suffusing the air with a delicious saltiness – Mei Hui watched as the visitors used their chopsticks with ease, picking out morsels of food, and scooping rice directly into their mouths from the bowl.

'How did you find me?' Mei Hui asked eventually, setting aside her half empty bowl.

Jemima polished off her rice. 'One of the clues Jake had was the name of province where you lived. But it was like finding a needle in a haystack, as we say in English! So Jake managed to... let's say "get into" the Chinese government's computers, and find names of a couple that fit the description, working in town.'

Mei Hui stopped. 'You... you found my parents?' she asked.

'Yes,' smiled Jemima. 'I forgot to tell you in all the excitement! They were in a town about 15 li away from the factory where they first registered. We discovered they'd been kicked out of first factory, and because they couldn't find local place that could take both, they decided to search further away, to stay together. They're both well, but really worried about you. They said paternal grandfather told them you'd run away with a boy, and didn't want to be found...'

Mei Hui caught her breath, eyes brimming. 'That sounds like something my paternal grandfather would say.' She smiled bitterly. 'Though it's not true.'

Jemima continued. 'I told them that if we found you, we'd let them know. Since then, we travelled from village to village, asking around. And then, when we started hearing stories of remarkable girl, looking after group of children in a beautiful green-roofed house, we started getting excited. As soon as I saw this house, the well-kept fields, the system of water pipes from stream – I just knew it was you. And for your parents, we can of course go see them... on the way to airport.'

Mei Hui was quietly thrilled at the thought of seeing her parents again. 'Yes, I would very much like to see them,' she said, managing to contain herself as she got up and started clearing the things. 'We should make arrangements to see them as soon as possible.' She stopped, and looked at them both. 'Perhaps tomorrow?'

Jemima was surprised to hear of such a sudden plan. 'When I said we were going back to airport...'

'I know. You want me to go with you,' interrupted Mei Hui, matter of fact. 'Back to your country.'

Jemima looked at her. 'Yes, we hoped so. But–'

'The children,' Mei Hui said, finishing her sentence again. She glanced across at Jiao-jie, who was huddled together with An, Zhu, and the others, furtively glancing across at them from time to time. Tears came to Mei Hui's eyes. 'I... I hope they will not be in danger, because of me.'

'I don't see how. We're so far away...' said Jemima, not very convincingly.

Sitting down again, Mei Hui said quietly, 'I cannot allow them to be in danger.'

'I understand,' said Jemima, getting upset herself. 'I... I'm sorry.'

Mei Hui touched her shoulder. 'You will stay here tonight, and rest. Meanwhile I need to hurry and make some arrangements.'

Jemima nodded. 'O-okay.'

•••————————————————————•••

That night, the two visitors were given makeshift beds – Jemima's on the floor in the guest bedroom next to Mei Hui's room, and Jake's was by the warm kang in the main room. He drifted off almost immediately. Mei Hui however, with so much to think about, was sure she would lie awake all night. She stared up at the ceiling, her mind buzzing and whirring, plotting and planning. Very soon, exhaustion overtook her, and consciousness slipped away as fluidly as water drips from the sheath-like leaves of the banana tree. Fast asleep, silence descended on the household, with only the chirruping call of crickets, courting outside in the brisk night air.

Jemima found it hard to sleep these days, since just weeks ago, that strange woman sitting on her bed had tried to kill her. Even when the girl eventually dozed off, she still awoke in fits and starts throughout the night – and each time she closed her eyes, she saw the macabre vision of that awful woman glaring down at her, night after hapless night. Those eyes were unforgettable. Empty, and soulless. A forehead creased with makeup. The faint smell of chewing gum. Hands, reaching for something she could not see. She often woke up crying out.

Mei Hui's eyes opened suddenly, and she sat bolt upright – but she did not know what woke her. She listened intently, conscious of the hairs on her neck standing on end, but detected no sound. Not even the chirp of nocturnal crickets. Complete silence, apart from her own scattered breaths. She crumpled back down onto the bed, and drew up the quilt, though not so far as to cover her ears. She closed her eyes.

Jemima's eyes sprung open, heart thudding like a drum against her chest when she saw the face of the killer sitting casually on the side of her bed. But... this dream was different. The woman had a pitted scar on her cheek, her hair was shorter – and there was a sickly, cloying stench of sweat.

The woman calmly pulled a knife from her messenger bag, and with her other hand, she pressed hard against Jemima's mouth so that her head sunk into the pillow. The girl's eyes widened, and she struggled to breathe, the room spinning. And yet the nightmare continued.

*If she died in her dreams, would she also die in real life?* The thought came to Jemima's mind as consciousness slipped away.

But then there was a wrenching feeling, followed by a loud thwack, and Jemima opened her eyes to find Mei Hui holding a trembling poker, her hands spattered red. At her feet, the woman lay on the floor.

Mei Hui looked around, frightened, as she wiped her hands on her pyjamas, then held a finger to pursed lips. She pulled Jemima from her bed, and together they crept into the corridor, then the main room, where they woke up Jake, motioning for him too to be silent. They followed her to the children's bedroom, which was right at the centre of the house.

Mei Hui turned to close the door and slipped a thick wooden bar into keep-plates, bolting it shut. She woke up the oldest child, telling him to be very quiet, and whispering instructions. He then tiptoed to the other beds, and stirred each child awake, passing on the message.

Mei Hui fell onto her knees on the floor beside a bunk bed, to pull open a trap door in the ground. She beckoned for the children to get in, and they all bustled down several steps into what appeared to be a low cellar, just high enough for them to stand upright – the head of the tallest, Zhu, grazing against the ceiling. The cellar was 12 chi wide, a bare space hemmed in by clay walls, with a small kang in one corner, next to which stood reed baskets filled with kindling and firewood, as well as a large metal trunk, secured with a padlock. Mei Hui glanced knowingly at Zhu, who nodded solemnly back at her, and he immediately set to making a fire in the kang. Mei Hui turned to Jemima and Jake, and whispered to them urgently. 'I heard the footsteps of at least nine others surrounding the house. Very soon they too will enter, and I will lock them in from the outside...'

'Lock them *in?!*' hissed Jemima.

'Please,' said Mei Hui. 'You must trust me. When I leave the cellar, lock the trapdoor from inside. You must do just as I say.'

Terrified, Jemima just stared at the girl who was even smaller than she. Eventually she nodded.

'Zhu knows what to do with the fire. Make sure he shuts the furnace door tightly after putting in the herbs.'

Jemima nodded again. One of the little children began to whimper, and Jemima realised that she was shaking too. 'I'm scared...' she told Jake, her voice childlike. Jake took her hand and squeezed it.

'You are safe down here,' said Mei Hui reassuringly.

When little An saw Mei Hui turn to leave, he let go of Jiao-jie and ran to her, throwing his arms around her, begging her not to go. Mei Hui turned to kiss the top of his head. 'I'll be back before you know it,' she told him, her voice tender. She pulled away, and climbed the steps.

They could only watch as she disappeared, and Jiao-jie closed the trapdoor after her, bolting it tight.

The first thing Mei Hui did when she was back in the bedroom was to stop and listen. The intruders were not trained in the ways of Ninpo, she could tell, because they walked clumsily on dry grass and sticks that heralded their coming. Their whispers audible in the still night air. They had surrounded the house on all sides, just a few metres outside, and a couple of them were already at the main door, paying no heed to the dull jangle of the bamboo wind chime as they passed.

Quickly she stooped down, and opened the air vent to a steel pipe that protruded from the floor, which was flush against the wall and ran straight to the ceiling into a chimney.

Mei Hui knew that timing was key, as she dragged one of the bed frames in front of the pipe and over the trap door, and then climbed the bunk bed to reach a hinged escape window in the roof. But she did not go out. She waited, and seconds ticked by as she listened to the noises they made: the intruders' footsteps creeping around the house, moving deeper into the building, until they were just on the other side of the door. She jumped when they rattled the door and started bashing it with a heavy, blunt object, again and again.

Quickly, Mei Hui pulled herself out of the escape window, and swivelled round to bolt it shut. She reached for the top of the chimney flue, and flipped closed a snugly fitting steel cover, and then nimbly climbed down from the roof to the far side of the house. All the while, their loud bashing sounds masked the sound of her movements. She checked that it was clear before jumping down a short distance onto the ground – and then ran as fast as she could back to the main door, slamming it shut, and bolting it from the outside with a lock.

Meanwhile in the cellar, Zhu retrieved a key from a hole near the ceiling, out of reach from the smaller children, and stooped down to open the fireproof container next to the baskets of wood. When he was sure that the fire was roaring, he put on thick leather gloves and heaped the contents on top of the flames – keeping it at arm's length. Jake moved closer to examine what was inside: harmless-looking dried flowers, wrinkled berries, and roots, all shrivelled and brown. After Zhu had carefully placed most of the contents into the kang, he quickly closed its door. And they one and all watched through the little glass window as smoke billowed out of hissing, popping, crackling herbs. Zhu waved them back, away from the stove, saying urgently, 'Dian qie, dian qie!' And they pressed themselves against the far wall. Jake's eyes followed the line of the steel pipe that exited the top of the stove, straight up into the ceiling – a kind of central heating system, that was now being used to fumigate the house with smoke.

They waited with trepidation, either looking at the fire, or staring up at the ceiling, picking out the noises and movements of the intruders as they made their way through the house, halting at the bedroom door. The children were petrified, and flinched with every sound.

The fire roared, smoke swelled, and billowed upwards.

Then came the loud crunch of breaking wood – the door of their bedroom.

Urgent footsteps padding all over their room.

And suddenly, there was panicked shouting, and hollering. Then choking sounds, and screams that became increasingly high-pitched.

In the cellar, the young children burst into fresh tears, some of them covering their ears, and burying their heads in the arms of the older ones.

Upstairs, the burly intruders found themselves surrounded by a silent smoke that crept all around. It was noxious and acrid, and they frantically batted it away, but to no avail. The grey smoke curled into their nostrils –

delivering its payload of tropane alkaloids, which quickly entered their nervous system. They began to stagger around. The psychoactive chemical seeping through the spinal cord, saturating the brain, and disrupting the neurotransmitter chemical, serotonin. Within minutes, glutamate receptors began to alter perception and responses. And that's when the hallucinations began.

They were of the worst kind.

Their deepest, darkest fears and imaginings made real, materialising as terrifying monsters right before their eyes.

Ear-piercing wails rent through the smouldering air.

Outside, Mei Hui hid in the shadows and listened, her blood turning cold. She sniffed the air. It smelled odd – like body odour – and she turned, only to find a brusque hand grabbing her shoulder. She stared up in shock at the two large men. And there came a whooshing sound, and the searing impact of a fist connecting with her jaw. She fell to the ground like a rag...

••••————————————————••••

The small, furry creatures were very, very angry, and had been for a long time.

Even though spring rains followed by several days of high temperatures brought abundant blossoms and flower syrup, a large colony had divided and settled nearby, which meant there was less nectar to go round. Their new neighbours were even queenless, which made the workers much more aggressive.

When the great circle of light in the sky disappeared into darkness, they still could not relax. They were justified, for a group of robber bees from the new colony suddenly appeared, out of nowhere, and the little creatures instantly released alarm pheromones into the air, which in turn triggered a defence signal, putting their entire colony on alert.

Workers burst out of the hive in a frenzied counter-attack, grappling the first wave of oncoming intruders mid-air, locking onto them, and spiralling down together to the ground. One by one, more workers piled on top of the intruders, becoming a seething ball-like mass. Eventually, the combined body heat alone was enough to kill each of the offenders. They knew well that their strength was in numbers, working together in unity, with one hive mind.

They sent more soldiers to guard the entrance of their hive – and though they were females, and physically the smallest of their group, with a life span of less than six weeks, these guards were at their peak of strength and energy. Ready even to die protecting their home.

But the young female soldiers sensed new and strange vibrations outside, which unnerved them. Their large, dark eyes stared out into the night, illuminated by the faint glow of moonlight. The air was suffused with a heady perfume from nearby Dragon Fruit flowers that peppered tumbling cacti, their petals unfurled into large white-yellow stars, which blossomed only at night.

Suddenly there was a thunderous, rhythmic pounding of the ground, which throbbed through the guards' tarsi. Boom! Boom! Boom!! Hairs bristled on their six legs, and delicate wings shivered with expectancy. Large, compound eyes, that allowed them to see in all directions in ultraviolet colour, strained to pick up the minutest variations in movement and light. Deep in their abdomen, their two stomachs felt a sickening stir; poised stingers quivering and tingling almost painfully.

Immediately the little soldiers delivered a high-frequency head-butt to their neighbours, who in turn passed on the same message, so that in a matter of seconds, the whole colony had been warned. The entire hive of bees braced themselves for the battle – all 60,000 of them.

•••———————————————•••

Mei Hui picked herself up from the ground, in her head she screamed, Run! She dived between the legs of one of the men, jumped up, and sped off. Like the roaring gales of the Dabancheng mountains, she hurtled into the night.

Mei Hui ran and ran, through the fields, and up a low incline, gasping for breath, cold air sucked into hot lungs. She saw the silhouette of the old Longan tree in the distance. Its trunk was flanked by wide and low branches, heavy with fruit clusters that shone like glass globes in the moonlight. As she ran, she stooped to pick up sticks from the ground without stopping – the first in one hand, and the second in the other. She kept going, like a sprinter in a two-baton relay race, until she reached – at last! – the old tree.

She hid behind it, gulping in air, her skin prickling with fear. The wait was unbearable. But then she heard the two thugs approaching, and she braced herself. When they were just a few metres away, quick as a flash, she reached up to the wild beehive that hung like immense misshapen fruit, and speared it from opposite sides with the sticks. Withdrawing them, they dripped with thick honey and wax, and she hurled them spear-like at the men's torsos. Running further away, she threw herself into the bushes for cover.

Instantly, a swarm of maddened bees responded to the attack on their hive. And like a brooding cloud, they rose up into the night – the drone of their anger was deafening. Sensitive chemoreceptors in their antennae homed in on the smell of their precious honey on the two men. And now, at last, they could attack, and they zoomed in for the kill, wings a blur. Just as they reached their target, they swivelled their rectum forward, and injected a hooked sting into the enemy as they landed. Wave after wave of bees. The men fell to the ground, rolling and screaming and desperately swiping at them.

After the sting, the bees wrenched their bodies away, tearing the venom sac and abdomen out of themselves. They could only fly off in staggered bursts, throbbing with pain – eventually spiralling to the ground in droves.

Mei Hui watched from afar with a thudding heart, saddened for the little creatures she had sacrificed.

Sobbing, she waited until the men lay perfectly still – then she rustled through the bushes, and once again sped off into the darkness.

She slowed only when the house came into view. But instead of running toward it, she turned right to skirt the perimeter of their holding, until she reached a large barn at the far western edge of the land. Tentatively she knocked a special signal on the door, and, after a few seconds, there came the sound of bolts unlocking – and the door was opened. Mei Hui went inside to find the children and the visitors sitting together in a corner – pale and shaken, though thankfully unharmed. They were relieved to see Mei Hui alive and in one piece, and on her beckoning, they got up and tumbled out into the night air. With wide eyes, they looked across at their house, dimly glowing in the night. It was quiet and still, belying the evil it held within.

Mei Hui urged Zhu to run to a neighbour's house which was a good 15 minutes away, keeping to the shadows. They had a working telephone, and he was to ask permission to call the police, giving him specific instructions to pass on. Zhu nodded solemnly, and ran off straight away.

When the police received the frantic call at the police station, with instructions to tell medics to bring hazard suits, they could not understand why. Until they went to the Longan tree on the hill and saw angry bees hovering around it in circles, with thousands more carpeting the ground. They were amazed to discover the semi-conscious men on the ground, their faces and every inch of exposed skin was swollen and dotted with countless red wheals. They were also amazed to find young Mei Hui's house in such disorder, filled with twitching bodies – and white ghosts at that. One of them stone cold dead with blood pooling around her head.

When at last the bodies were cleared from the house, the broken furniture taken outside, and the floor swept clean, Jemima and Mei Hui sat at the kitchen table, in a state of shock, quietly drinking tea. Jemima had a blanket around her shoulders, and the cup trembled in her hand as she drank.

'It is a tea peculiar to this region,' explained Mei Hui, a bruise throbbing on her jaw. 'And it is very rare. I pick the youngest tea leaves from the top of the plants – they are the freshest, purest leaves. And then I gently dry-fry them in the wok, to fix and seal in the taste. When they are steeped in water, it is said that the first infusion is not sweet, the second is still bitter, and the third infusion is the perfect and most desirable taste.'

Her rhythmic words and the hot tea were soothing Jemima's nerves, and at last she said, 'Th-thank you, Mei Hui. You saved my life.' She put down her cup. 'But, how did you know to come into my room when you did?'

'Something woke me,' she said. 'I think it was the crickets. They were silent – and that's when I knew something was wrong.'

'And... in basement, what were the herbs that Zhu burnt?'

'They are dried dian qie plants – which are very poisonous. Eating just a few berries can kill you, and I've heard stories of unsuspecting people dying because they did not know what they were eating. The root of the plant contains a toxic drug, which causes hallucinations of the worst kind. The reason why I keep it is because there has been a curse in China for many decades, of gangs blighting defenceless villages. They are on the prowl to steal away children, who are vulnerable because many of the parents, like mine, leave them behind, while they go to the big towns for work. Once stolen, the children are sold – as easily as one sells bak choi in the market. They are bought by families who want cheap slaves, or to add to their organised begging rings, or criminal gangs, or even sold into prostitution. Lately, there have been reports of gangs dealing with human organ trafficking. Demand is higher than supply, and gangs have now resorted to drugging unsuspecting ones, and performing crude operations to harvest what they can...' Mei Hui closed her eyes, upset. 'One boy of six years old from the Shanxi province had been playing in the streets, when a woman kidnapped and drugged him. Days later, he was found wandering the streets, screaming hysterically, his faced covered with blood. They had taken his eyes...'

Jemima went white as a sheet.

Mei Hui breathed deeply. 'So this is why I keep dian qie in the basement, and why I've built a secret escape tunnel to the barn.' Mei Hui turned and peered through the window. 'At least we are safe for now, with the police guarding outside. It is still early, and we should at least try to get a few hours' rest.'

'Yes,' said Jemima, her voice weak. She sighed. At least, with the woman dead, and the thugs locked away, she had a chance of getting some sleep.

····················································

But Mei Hui herself had only an hour's sleep before she rose again. Washing and dressing quickly, she fetched several packages, placed them in a hemp bag, and left the house to follow the path that would take her to the poorest huts in the village. To one in particular. She recognised the shoddy hovel immediately, which was part brick, part corrugated iron sheeting, and patched with nailed boards. She knocked, but no-one answered, though there were faint sounds inside. Mei Hui rested her head against the door, taking in the tangy smell of rusted iron. 'Please, would you kindly open the door,' she called out.

The movement inside stopped.

Mei Hui tried again. 'I have brought something for you... Something from your husband.' There was still only silence, until at last came the sound of shuffling feet, and a door bolt sliding back. The blue-eyed woman appeared through the suspicious crack. She was dishevelled, her skin sallow.

Seeing Mei Hui, the wife of her lover, she lowered her eyes and locked them on the ground at her feet. Finally, she said, 'Forgive me...'

'Please. There is nothing to forgive.'

Surprised, the woman looked up to find the girl smiling kindly. Mei Hui dug inside her bag and took out a small object wrapped in muslin, and held it out to her.

The woman took it gingerly – and immediately, from the weight and feel of it, knew exactly what it was. She burst into tears, clutching the parcel to her chest.

'I bought it back from the dealer a while ago, knowing what it meant to you. And I am only glad that such a beautiful jade bracelet can be returned to its rightful owner.'

'But... how did you know?' She looked at her, and wiped her eyes.

Mei Hui realised it would be hard to explain. 'It's... a long story.'

The woman was astonished at such kindness from a girl she had so blatantly wronged. 'I do not deserve this. But thank you! I... I am indebted to you. I wish there was some way I could repay–'

Mei Hui's eyes slid downward as she interrupted, 'Actually,' she said, looking up again. 'I have a favour to ask. A big favour. I will be going away, very soon, and I need someone to look after my children...'

The blue-eyed woman blinked at Mei Hui. *Her* children, she thought. She was just a child herself.

Mei Hui righted herself. 'That is, they are not my own children. I look after them. But they have become my family, and I love them dearly. I would wish for someone to look after them who has lots of love to give, a pure heart, and kindness in their soul.' She looked into the woman's eyes. 'And I sense that *you* have all those qualities.'

The blue-eyed woman felt tears well up. It had been a long time since someone spoke to her with such kindness. 'I do not know what to say. Except, I am willing to help you, and your children.'

Mei Hui beamed. 'Of course, it is a paying job, with a modest stipend,' Mei Hui explained. 'It is certain to be hard work, but there is enough money to hire labourers to help in the fields. And you must use the profits of course to care for the children, and the house. And if all goes well, I believe there will also be some left over for a small bonus for you.'

'I am happy with those conditions, and happy to help. But when will you be going?'

'That's the thing. I will be leaving very soon, in fact, tomorrow... So you would need to come today. I know it is short notice...'

The woman looked around the shack where she had lived in destitution for many years. It was plain and simple, and she had never really called it a home. She disappeared for a few seconds and returned, clutching a wodge of photos to her chest – of her husband, and her, when they were happy. She tucked them inside her jacket, along with the bracelet. 'I will come with you now,' she smiled, patting her chest. 'I have everything I need here.'

Mei Hui was very happy to hear this. 'Thank you!' she said, but then stopped. 'What is your name?'

'I am Yin,' said the woman, stepping out and shutting the door behind her.

The two walked together along the path. 'I am Mei Hui.'

And as they went, Mei Hui explained at great length the situation with the children, and what, in practical terms, she would need to do. But when they reached the intersection with the main road, Mei Hui said, 'I have a few more errands to run, so please go straight to the house. I hope you don't mind, but my children and the visitors will be expecting you.' She grinned cheekily, and turned to leave.

●●●————————————————————————————●●●

Mei Hui's next stop was the building company.

The manager welcomed her into his office immediately. 'Ah, Mei Hui. Come in, come in.' He was always happy to see her, even when she wasn't bearing gifts of home-made bao or baskets of fruit.

Mei Hui bowed low. 'I am very grateful that you can see me at such short notice, ya fu...' She used the respectful term of endearment for someone that was like a father, and the manager happily accepted this. '...But I need your help,' she said.

The manager looked at her quizzically. 'What is it? Are you in trouble?'

'No, no, not at all. You see, I must soon go away, and as you know I have six children that need taking care of...'

'But... I do not know how I can help you there. I don't have the skills to–'

'It is not that,' she interrupted. 'I have already found someone from the village – Yin – who is moving in and will look after them in a practical way. But I need someone who can be like an... uncle to them. Their parents have gone out, and they have no other family...'

The manager nodded slowly, beginning to understand.

Mei Hui took out the paper package stashed inside her bag. 'Life has been good to us,' she told him. 'There have been small blessings, and some good fortune, and so I was able to save a little money for them. I would like to entrust my money with you, ya fu. You have a good head for business, and might even be able to earn some interest. For the children, and for Yin.'

The manager looked at the package of money, and then at Mei Hui thoughtfully. Eventually he said, 'It is not "life", or "blessings", or "good fortune" that has dealt you this hand, Mei Hui.' He smiled at her kindly. 'Whatever good things you have are due solely to your own hard work and prudence. Of course, you know you can trust me to look after your money, so I will happily do as you ask. And though I cannot promise to make a great amount, I will definitely look for some good dependable business in which it can be invested, so that there is no risk, and you will gain some return. Enough to give the children a decent living, and perhaps a little extra for the odd present now and then. Of that, I give you my word.'

'Thank you,' said Mei Hui, smiling gratefully. 'I will ask Yin to stop by every month to collect a portion of the money, an allowance for her wages, as well as expenses for their needs.'

The manager lifted up his hand in objection. 'No – do not tell her to come all this way. It is a long walk, and she will be busy enough as it is looking after six children, and the land. No, I have a truck, and will drop by with my wife to deliver her the money every month. It will be a nice outing for us, and an excuse to see your beautiful house again.'

'Then you will honour my house with your presence,' smiled Mei Hui, and, forgetting propriety, she threw her arms around him and hugged him. 'Thank you!' she breathed – he smelled of warm sandalwood. He was a good man, she knew instinctively, and could be trusted with every yuan of her savings.

The manager, surprised by this unusual display of affection, softened and hugged her back.

Mei Hui wept quietly for her six children as they took it in turns to hug her, themselves crying profusely. Except for little An, who was the last to bid her farewell. His narrow eyes smouldered, and his bottom lip stuck out stubbornly, defiant arms folded across his chest.

'Don't be angry, An,' said Mei Hui softly. 'You must remember this,' she told him, and then pecked him so lightly on the cheek, it felt like the lightest touch of a feather. 'Whenever you feel the touch of something against your cheek, like this kiss, you should know that I love you, very, very much. And every time it happens, remember my promise that I will one day return to you.'

In an instant, An's anger melted, and he cupped his hand over his cheek. 'You promise?' he said, his lips quivering.

Mei Hui knelt down beside him and gave him five more kisses. 'That's how strong my promise is,' she said.

Little An threw his arms around her, and buried his face in her hair.

From that day on, whenever An felt the lightest sensation of something brushing his cheek – the delicate silk of a spider's web floating in the air, the tickly flap of moth wings, or the gentle billow of hot air – he counted each promise that would bring his beloved Mei Hui back to him.

---

Travelling to the airport was an exhaustingly long journey, and the ambivalence that Mei Hui felt toward her parents stewed into doubt and uncertainty. But as the taxi drew closer to their agreed meeting point, she scanned the street, unable to spot them. When they were just a few metres away, she saw them standing next to a lamp post looking impossibly thin and gaunt. Was it really them? When the taxi stopped, and Mei Hui climbed out, the couple threw themselves on her, sobbing with happiness. Mei Hui cried too, both from the emotion and because their bodies felt like skeletons within her arms. When they drew apart, they looked at their daughter, just as Mei Hui looked at them. Their eyes had sunk into their skulls, and their cheeks were hollow.

Her father took her hand, and kissed it. A sizzling sensation burnt through Mei Hui's skin, and her eyes widened as she saw a glimpse of her parents' lives: years of endless hard work, rising at 6.30 every morning to work 12-hour shifts, rationed food, five-minute toilet breaks – and sleeping on grubby mattresses on the floor, in vast communal boarding rooms that reeked of body odour, fermented cabbage, and stagnant water.

And suddenly, all of Mei Hui's misgivings dissolved.

They went to sit in a local teahouse, with Jake and Jemima in tow – and Mei Hui listened as her parents described all the money they had sent home to her grandparents for her education, all the presents they'd bought her, the letters they wrote.

But she had seen none of it. Mei Hui immediately knew where it had disappeared to – and she felt no compunction at telling them about grandfather's gambling addiction.

When Jemima Jenkins heard this, she suddenly scrambled through her rucksack, eventually pulling out a rather scruffy but thick brown envelope. 'I'd like your parents to have this...' she said. 'I've published a line of maths books for children under a pen-name – and they're doing well. That's what funded this trip. And this is the leftover cash, which is quite a lot because I didn't know how long we'd be, searching for you... Anyway, I'd really like to give it to your parents.'

Mei Hui took the envelope tentatively and peered inside, it crackled in her hand. 'Are you sure?' she said, hesitant.

Jake spoke up on Jemima's behalf. 'This is pocket money to her, Mei Hui. The girl's loaded,' he grinned.

Jemima elbowed him playfully. 'Yeah, about that, I noticed you didn't put up a fight when I paid for everything...'

Mei Hui couldn't believe it. She handed the packet to her parents. 'You... you won't need to work anymore. You can leave the factories!'

Her parents looked through the envelope, and their jaws dropped with shock at the wodge of notes. They thanked their benefactor profusely.

•••————————————————————•••

Mei Hui bore the plane journey with restrained silence, fearful of the roar of the engines and the fact that they were suspended many miles high in the sky with nothing beneath them. She tried to distract herself by watching film after film, turning on the subtitles to perfect her English at the same time. But after quietly absorbing five films, she just lay back in the chair, staring into space.

Jemima noticed her uneasiness. 'Don't worry, Mei Hui,' she said. 'The children will be fine. You've been through the worst, and it can only get better.' It was something her father always told her.

Mei Hui glanced at her. 'You are right, Jemima. We have seen the yin, and now there will be yang. A balancing.'

Jake – who was across the aisle from them, lying in a window seat – suddenly sat up after hearing the words yin and yang. 'What exactly is all this business with yin and yang?' he asked. 'What does it mean?'

Mei Hui understood what he had said in English, though she replied in Chinese. 'Yin and yang are the symbols for two opposing and complementary forces, that are both equal and opposite,' she said. Jemima immediately translated for Jake. Mei Hui continued, 'We cannot constrain yin virtues, but for simplicity, one might say that its qualities stand for all things dark, or passive, feminine, downward, cold, contracting, or weak. While yang is light, or active, masculine, upward, hot, expanding, or strong. And though they are opposing, one cannot exist without the other, which is why the symbol shows the seed of one ever present in the other. This is the way all things exist – in complete harmony and perfect balance. Once we accept this, we will understand the nature of life itself. Dark must have light to define it, cold is balanced out by heat, man cannot procreate without woman. Love can so easily turn to hate. Within a good heart lies the ability to do evil, and vice versa, someone evil can become good. And I believe that if we upset the perfect balance and harmony of nature, then things tend to go wrong.'

Jake thought about this. 'Then what do you think about Project Ingenious?' he asked eventually, his brows furrowing. 'Those scientists, who, for all intents and purposes, messed about with nature in order to make you super clever, for their own gain – haven't they tampered with what is natural? Is it good that they've done this? Or bad? Are they dark, or light?'

Just then, a voice came over the speakers announcing the imminent landing at Heathrow airport. They immediately buckled up and remained in silence as the plane began to descend.

But Jake's disturbing questions remained very much in their thoughts.

# 25  DIVINE WIND

As soon as the three stepped off the plane air-stairs onto the tarmac, there was a deafening screech of tyres, and they found themselves surrounded and blocked in by a swarm of police cars with flashing lights. Men with gun holsters and Kevlar vests jumped out, and Jemima and Mei Hui latched on to each other, bewildered, while Jake stood protectively in front of them.

Their names were shouted out by someone, and the three nodded, bewildered – whereupon they were bundled into a people-carrier, with a driver and policeman in the front, the teenagers in the middle, and two more policemen in the back. The line of police cars sped along the motorway, eventually reaching the A4 which took them straight into central London.

At last, the car turned into a heavily gated road, manned by five guards, and then pulled up outside an impressive line of grey brick buildings. A suspended lantern hung above a large black door, with two more guards standing on either side. Jake and Jemima recognised it instantly. It was surreal stepping out in front of 10 Downing Street.

They were ushered inside, flanked by four policemen, and told to wait in a lavish meeting room with a large red and green rug, ornate furnishings, and a huge mahogany table in the centre. It smelt of beeswax and lavender.

Jake stopped in his tracks when he saw who was waiting for them. 'Cal?!' he breathed in amazement.

Calista jumped up and ran over. 'Jake!' she cried, embracing him. 'It... it's really you!' When they eventually separated, she bombarded him. 'Are you okay? Where did you go?! Why didn't you let me know you were leaving? Why didn't you contact me?!'

Jake looked into her bewildered but beautiful eyes, and remembered how much he loved the girl. 'I'm sorry...' was all he could say.

Jemima, who was standing next to Mei Hui, turned aside and stuck out her tongue, making a nauseated faced. Mei Hui couldn't help but smile.

Calista looked at them, asking Jake, 'And who are they?'

Jemima corrected herself and smiled angelically. 'My name's Jemima Jenkins. And the reason that lug over there disappeared without a word, was because he saved my life, rescuing me from an evil night nanny, and we had to go on the run, and stay incommunicado, eventually winding up in China, searching all over the place for a missing girl, who turned out to be Mei Hui,' she said sweetly, drawing breath.

Calista glared at her.

Suddenly the door opened, and an imposing figure breezed in – a stout man with a head of thick ash-coloured hair. 'Ah, I see you've already met,' he said in a booming voice.

Jemima's eyes widened with awe, and unsure how she should greet him, bobbed in a curtsy. 'I-it's a privilege to meet you, Mr Prime Minister. I'm Jemima Jenkins.' She held out a tentative hand, and the Prime Minister shook it vigorously.

He flashed a brief smile. 'It's a pleasure to meet you too, Jemima. I only wish it could have been under better circumstances.' He turned to the young Chinese girl. 'And you must be Mei Hui,' he said, offering his hand.

Mei Hui shook it, and answered him in English. 'I'm very honoured, Mr Prime Minister.' Her pronunciation was flawless.

'You *can* speak English!' said Jake.

'I have been learning from the children's school books for years, and it helped to watch five subtitled films on the plane,' replied Mei Hui.

The PM beamed. 'Excellent! We can all speak English. Fantastic,' he said, making a mental note to cancel the interpreter.

A stiff-looking butler entered the room with a tray of tea, sandwiches, and cake, and set it on one end of the table. 'Please, tuck in,' said the Prime Minister, motioning for them to sit. 'You must be tired and hungry after your journey.'

The man poured the teas, as the Prime Minister sat beside them. 'I take it Cal's brought you up to speed on developments?'

Calista raised an eyebrow. 'They've only just arrived, Boz!' she said.

Jake spluttered on his tea, and Jemima handed him a napkin. 'Boz?!' he whispered, not believing her nickname for one of the most powerful men in England.

'Forgive me, Cali,' said the Prime Minister, and then settled back in his chair. 'I shall of course be glad to fill everyone in...' He started explaining about the sick Oxford Uni students – but then Calista immediately barged in, took over, and recounted events in a rather excitable and haphazard way. She told them that the students had been infected with a flesh-eating cancer, then there was a message sent to the PM asking for Professor Wolff and the children to be handed over in exchange for a cure. The Prof wanted to go alone, but Tai and Milly sneaked out to join him – two days ago. And they were taken into a submarine by an evil so-and-so, who then double-crossed everyone because no cure was given. So it was all for nothing!

'Um, yes, thank you, Cali,' said the Prime Minister, silently noting never to ask Calista to recount anything, ever. He turned to Jemima and Mei Hui. 'Now, I understand that both of you are Project Ingenious children.'

Jemima nodded, 'Yes, we are.'

The PM continued. 'Well, I must say it's a great privilege to meet you both,' he beamed. 'Though I have to admit that I knew nothing about this most unusual project until Professor Wolff contacted me, just after Jemima's disappearance. There are no official records of any significance about it – so whoever implemented it obviously wanted the whole thing kept very quiet. I'm only sorry that you've had to go into hiding. That must have been distressing... But I absolutely want to rectify that by supporting you as best we can.'

Mei Hui and Jemima were very pleased to hear this.

Jake looked like he was bursting, and jumped in to say, 'I'm sorry, Mr Prime Minister – but I just need to find out something...' he turned to Calista. 'So, Cal, this Professor that you mentioned – he worked on Project Ingenious?!'

'That's right,' she said. 'Professor Harald Wolff.'

'And how are you connected in all of this?' he asked, confounded.

'Well, actually *he* found *me*. Basically, when you disappeared, I searched your laptop for clues, to try and find out what'd happened to you, where you'd gone. One of the things I did was to retrace your hacks – including the government server.' She winked at the PM and smiled unapologetically. 'Turns out it was a bit of a honey trap, because the Prof had been monitoring the server gateway himself. And that's how he found me. He took me in, looked after me. And we've become friends... really good friends.' She caught a choke in her throat. 'H-he found Milly and Tai too, and we all got on really well.' She turned to stare out of the bright window. 'I just can't believe they're gone...'

An awkward silence followed.

Eventually Mei Hui said, 'Please – forgive me for saying. But it was not wise for the Professor and the children to go.'

Jemima thought about this and made some quick mental calculations. 'I agree. The odds were stacked against them.'

The PM responded, 'They had very little time to make a decision – you see, the lives of the sick students hung in the balance. We thought we would get the cure to save them. Also, the person behind the disease threatened to infect others...'

Mei Hui spoke out now, her voice small in comparison to the PM's. 'This bad person is...' She turned quickly toward Jemima, asking something in Chinese, to which Jemima replied, 'psychopathic.'

'Thank you. From what you say, this person is psychopathic, and... unbalanced. They cannot be trusted. He, or she, infected university students likely because that person is not only threatened by their intelligence but also because he thinks nothing of life, and will stamp it out if he desires, like walking on stray ants that cross one's path. I am sorry to say, but I think the Professor and children are in danger.'

Someone choked, and everyone turned to find Calista bursting into fresh tears. Jake put an arm around her and pulled her closer.

Looking grave, the PM got up suddenly and motioned for the others to follow him. 'Please, come with me.'

They were led down a series of corridors, until they reached glass doors that automatically slid open into a large room, buzzing with life. Inside, there were three rows of desks with men and women working at computers. At the far end was a huge screen on the wall. They walked behind them and were taken into one of two small offices, separated by glass. Inside was a man working at a computer.

'I want to introduce you to chief of operations here, Rory Sanderson,' said the PM. 'He's overseeing investigations into the Oxford Uni students.' Brief introductions were made, and the man stood and nodded to them. He had piercing blue eyes and a hooked nose. 'Rory,' said the PM, 'what's the latest?'

'As you know, Sir, our scientists started working immediately on putting together an antidote – and given the urgency, it was administered to the most critical student right away... But I'm sorry to report that it had no effect, and the young lady died earlier today... That leaves only two students alive, but barely.' He shook his head. 'Their chances of survival are very slim.'

There was silence as they absorbed this awful news.

Eventually, Calista asked, 'And what about the Professor, Milly, and Tai – any news on where they are?'

'They were taken in some kind of underwater vessel. But nothing's showing up on any of our radars, nothing spotted on Thames cameras, or satellite cameras. Before he left, we kitted out the Professor with a transmitter, but the signal won't reach us until the submarine is in shallow water, or surfaces. I've been liaising closely with the police, because it turned into a murder investigation when the first student died – but unfortunately they, and we, don't have a lot to go on.'

'Terrible news,' said the PM. He looked around at everyone. 'But we mustn't give up hope – not just yet.'

Jemima scratched her head. 'But what was the Professor thinking?' she asked. 'Everyone knows you can't negotiate with terrorists...'

Calista thought about this. 'I've just remembered. The night before he left, the Prof was working on something all night in the computer room. It looked important...'

'Do you know what it was?' asked Jemima.

'No...' But then she had an idea. 'Will you lend me your computer?' she asked Sanderson.

The PM nodded his consent, and Sanderson tapped open the guest user account and pulled out a seat for her.

Calista sat down, and logged into Avernus remotely. Then she spoke out loud into the computer's microphone. 'Hello Jasmine.' She spun round to face Jake, bragging, 'I built a computer for the Professor with voice recognition – and programmed her myself. All my own work.'

A beautiful voice responded from the speakers. 'Hello Calista. How may I help you?'

Jake whistled. 'Cute interface, Cal, well done!'

'Thanks,' she said, and then turned back to face the screen. 'Right, Jasmine, can you show us what the Professor was working on last night?'

There was a pause. 'Negative, Calista. The Professor marked it as confidential. Only he has the authority to access it. Is there anything else I can help you with?'

Calista sat up, annoyed. 'Override, Jasmine. As main administrator, I need to have access to those files. Now.'

Again, another delay. 'Negative, Calista,' Jasmine repeated. 'You do not have authority.'

Calista harrumphed, 'Cheek of it!' Annoyed, she began pounding at the keyboard, murmuring, 'Can't believe he locked me out of my own computer. Why would he do that?...'

Jake watched over her shoulder as she typed – amazed at the skill of her programming, which had improved since they'd last seen each other.

Calista was mumbling to herself as she typed, 'I wrote in back-door access, just in case... Good job I did.' Eventually she said, 'Right, we're in!' She sat back and crossed her arms, no-nonsense. 'Jasmine, you know what I want...'

Jasmine's smooth voice answered without hesitation, 'Opening Professor Wolff's last files.' Sanderson's screen flickered to life, and about 20 thumbnail pages appeared. Calista zoomed into the first one, and the screen filled with lines and lines of numbers and symbols – a mass of complicated equations. 'What on earth's all this?!' said Calista, eyes zigzagging across the screen. 'Looks like... hieroglyphics.' She quickly scrolled through the pages and stopped at the last one. A single, lone number filled the screen. 2.07.

Jemima, the mathematician, drew closer, and the two swapped places without a word. She went back to the beginning and speed-read her way through, hardly believing what she saw. 'No, no, no...' she kept saying with increasing force, turning white when she reached the last figure.

'What is it?' asked Calista, impatient.

When at last Jemima looked up, she searched for the Prime Minister. She tried to speak, but closed her eyes to compose herself, then opened them again. 'Please tell me you're not going through with this?'

The PM stared at her intensely. 'If you're talking about the Professor's plan, then I'm afraid he was adamant...'

Calista looked from one to the other, alarmed. 'Will someone tell us what's going on?!'

Jemima waved at the screen and swivelled round in the chair to face her. 'These are all probability equations. The Professor used these to identify several courses of action that could be taken in light of developments with the infected students... These calculations were made to assess risk for any given event. An event tree, if you like, where various paths are analysed. And he's factored in different possibilities, for example, containment of the disease affecting just those seven uni students, to the other extreme, that the disease spreads, and causes a worldwide pandemic...' Here, Jemima pointed to the stark final figure on the screen. 'And this number, 2.07, is what the analysis has led to. You see, the Professor used all this to determine the solution with the lowest risk to human life, and the lowest number of casualties. And that outcome is the one you see here...'

Calista raised an eyebrow. 'Which is...?'

'That he sacrifice himself,' Jemima said quietly.

Trembling, Calista felt for a chair and sat down.

The PM looked at her, his small eyes creasing. 'This was the only way, Cali. You see, the Professor knows how dangerous this person is. But considering his own... disadvantage, there's very little he'd be able to do to turn things around. So he devised a plan that, whenever he found the perpetrator, he would transmit a signal back to England, in order to initiate a missile strike, targeting his signal. Of course I was loathe to go along with such a plan – any loss of life is to be avoided in my books. But we had absolutely nothing else to go on. And so it was our only chance of containing the worst possible scenario. Unfortunately, Milly Bythaway and Tai Jones turned up at the last moment, and went with him. Which wasn't what the Professor – or we – wanted...'

Mei Hui looked up at the PM. 'The Professor... he is like a Japanese kami kaze.'

He nodded. 'I suppose he is.'

'What do you mean?' asked Calista, looking very pale.

'Kami kaze means "divine wind",' explained Mei Hui. 'In the Second Great War, there were famous tokubetsu kōgeki tai – special attack units of pilots trained to crash their planes into strategic enemy targets, with them inside.'

Calista stared at her, and then at the PM. 'Boz... Please tell me you're not going ahead with this?!'

Sanderson answered for him. 'The Professor himself convinced the Prime Minister. It was, to all intents and purposes, the quickest and most effective way possible of striking back at the person behind this disease, before anyone else is infected. You see, the entire human race is in danger. The PM and we have next to nothing to go on, so this was all we could do. Sure, if we had the chance to send in special ops to sabotage the perp's plans, and take him down without harming anyone else, we would've. But the Prof was taken on a submarine that disappeared. And being a helpless blind old man – what can he accomplish realistically? It's a noble act by the Professor, for the greater good...' Here, Sanderson turned back to Mei Hui. 'So yes, if the Professor is successful in finding the perp, then it will be a suicide mission. And I'm afraid it's the only way.'

Jemima swivelled back to the computer and started typing in her own equations. 'I'm just factoring Tai and Milly into the Professor's equations...' She hit the enter button, and a modified number appeared onscreen. 'This is what we get. It's only marginally different to the previous number, which means it's the same conclusion. Sorry, but the Prof was right. The numbers don't lie,' she said, eyebrows creasing with concern. 'I hate to say it, but statistically, it's better for all three of them to die, to ensure the death of the person behind the disease...'

Mei Hui's heart skipped a beat when she saw the revised result – it added the number '4' at the end. In Chinese, '4' is considered extremely unlucky because it sounds like the word for 'death'. She felt sick.

They stared at the screen in silence.

The PM made one more mental note, a grim look on his face: the deaths of the Professor and the two children were surely inevitable.

## 26 BLIND

Professor Harald Wolff sat on the wet deck, hugging his legs to his chest, rocking back and forth, back and forth. Paralysed by fear.

Great juddering shivers wracked his body – both from the cold of his waterlogged clothes, and from panic. His teeth chattered uncontrollably, and it was all he could do not to bite his tongue. After years of rebuilding his life, adapting to the disability of blindness, and cushioning himself in the comfort of the familiar, he found himself now in the worst possible place. The unknown.

Freezing water lapped at his feet, and the air swirled with a mix of both warm and cold eddies, blasting a strange mix of tastes and smells at him – diesel, chemicals, salt... fear. He flinched at every sound and sensation, the dull plink of constant dripping, the creak of metal framework, the hollow reverberation of pipework.

Desperately, he tried to focus inwardly, to control his thoughts, and thence his fears. But his mind betrayed him – kept bringing him back to a savage memory. One that growled quietly as it lurked inside of him for over a decade. He shook his head vigorously, trying to purge it from his mind, but it was no use. Eventually he could only resign to it, bracing himself as he sunk deeper and deeper into its dark, twisted arms:

*He was waking up feeling strangled, groggy, drugged. Around his head was some kind of tight, cloying, wrapping; it mirrored the braiding sense of fear inside his chest. The linings of his throat and nostrils were so sore that breathing pained him – and every inch of skin ached.*

*There was a stench in the air.*

*It was a chemical, smoky smell.*

*His hands tore at the bandages wrapped around his head – pulling and scraping them off. Yet, with his eyes uncovered now, it made no difference. He was still blinded by white.*

*Bewildered, he slumped against the pillow, and snapped his eyelids shut. In his mind's eye, he saw floating across that snowy blank canvas, dark, wraith-like images.*

*Dense black pillars of smoke.*

*Waves of blistering, billowing air.*

*Charred shoes, kicking down door after door.*

*Searching frantically.*

*Coughing and spluttering.*

*And finally, there, in front of him, that hellish image.*

*His Chiara's blackened body, motionless, and sprawled on the ground. Fumes rising from her form, specked with ash-grey particles – parts of her – disappearing into the air. Clutched in her arms, a small body. His head buried into her chest. Melting into her.*

*That was the last thing he saw.*

*Indelibly imprinted in his mind.*

*Seared into his being.*

*It was a curse for his sins. A punishment. That awful, macabre image locked inside of him for the rest of his life. So cruel, the juxtaposition of reality with nightmare, past with future. Life with death.*

Chiara's voice pleaded with him now. *'Don't give up, mein Schatz!'*

With a jarring jolt, the Professor's mind leapt out of that savage memory, to find himself once again huddled shaking on a cold, watery deck. Blind and helpless.

Taking quick breaths, he mustered every effort, forcing himself to think externally, to sense his surroundings. He clenched his teeth, pressed fingers onto the floor, and stretched toes inside waterlogged shoes.

And then he remembered the children. Gasping to control his breathing, he eventually managed to call out to them. 'M-Milly, Tai! Christian!! Are you there?'

He was answered only by the mechanical thrum of an engine, and he realised they must still be underwater.

Again he called out to them, and from the hollow echo of his voice, he understood that the compartment was small, bare, metallic.

That was when he heard the sound of a door lock, the smooth turning of oiled hinges, footsteps approaching.

'Get up,' came the growly voice of a middle-aged man.

The Professor struggled with numb limbs, floundering.

Impatient, rough hands grabbed his lapels and pull him up with ease.

The old man's bones creaked as he stood, and he was jostled out of the compartment, stumbling, feet squelching with every step.

The gruff man pushed him again and again, directing him down several passageways until they went through doors into a place that felt light and cool on his skin.

The door was shut behind him – clunking cylinders tumbled into place, and bolts hit strike plates, locking him firmly in.

The Professor strained to hear, but discerned nothing.

*Hello, Professor.*

The man's voice came out of nowhere. And the hair on the Professor's skin bristled. Did he hear right? Or had he imagined it? He twisted his head this way and that, ears straining, heart racing. 'Wh-who are you?!' he said.

Silence and then, *You look well, considering... The children – they are well too. Alive and well.*

It was a voice that was like low, rumbling thunder – so pervasive it reverberated through the Professor's bones. He could not detect movement, no sound of anyone else in the room – as if the voice was inside his head, disembodied and impalpable. It chilled his heart. 'Who a-are you?!' he repeated, more forcefully. 'W-were you behind the project?'

*Please, Professor. Stop asking. My identity is not relevant. There is however much we need to discuss... about the project, the children.*

'You want to talk?!' said the Professor, incredulous. 'While innocent young men and women are dying in Oxford. D-did you infect them? Is there even a cure? Or was that just a ploy to draw us out?!'

*You need to calm down, Professor. You're becoming hysterical. Those students are... coincidental. The real matter we should be talking about is–*

'Coincidental?!' repeated the Professor in disbelief. 'A-are they so inconsequential to you?'

There was a pause.

*You are fixated on these students. Please don't bother yourself with them – they are hardly worth it. Inconsequential, as you say. But, I see where you're coming from. This whole thing brings up the question of the value of life, doesn't it? It's a topic I would very much like to discuss with you. Human life.*

'W-what do you mean? Those students are suffering horribly. Dying. Their families are beside themselves. Don't you care?'

*Mmm,* the person murmured, as if distracted. *Mmm-maybe. Isn't life merely energy... like the sun, like electricity. It can be made through a simple act of procreation, and snuffed out, just as easily. Yet life continues in a constant and never-ending stream, throughout time, through our bodies, our family lines. It's here, then it's gone. Easy come, easy go.*

The Professor was horrified. 'So...' he said quietly, daring himself to say the next words. 'So – without compunction – you infected them, sentenced them to death, simply because you could?!'

*You... you think my behaviour... psychopathic? Well, that is just a matter of opinion, a viewpoint. Most everything is, just opinion. For example, how do you define moralism, really? How do you judge what is right and wrong? Just for a moment, Professor, indulge me. Could it be that the inverse is true. Could it be that amoralism is the standard, the norm, and you and your ideals, the aberration.*

'You're mad!' exclaimed the Professor, struggling with such illogicality, such absurdity.

*As I said, that is a matter of opinion. Which conveniently leads back to my questions – the things I'd like to discuss with you. And there are many. About life and death, health and sickness, intellect and inanity. Which of these are right, and which are wrong, Professor? Could we really appreciate health, if there were no disease? Is it better to have intellect, or be stupid? Can we even find the answers in this life, or will we find them in death? An afterlife, perhaps.'*

'W-what are you talking about?'

*Just humour me, Professor. I really want to know what you think.*

The Professor turned his head this way and that, searching for coherent thoughts. 'You want to know what I think?!' he said, angered. 'You cannot flip morality with immorality. There are certain truths that are timeless, eternal. We... we're all born with an innate sense of right and wrong, it's part of our DNA. Any deviation from *that* is the aberration! Babies are born yearning for, and thriving in, the love of their parents. Even animals, th-they take care of their young. And... remote tribes are discovered with their own social system, helping each other, taking care of each other. *That* is natural human tendency.' The Professor tried to calm himself. Eventually he said, 'Your amoralism argument... it's just... ludicrous. You're spouting complete and utter nonsense! Over–thinking conjecture!'

*Over-thinking!* There was almost a sneer. *Over-thinking now... Well, that may be. But humans as a whole hardly think enough, do they?!*

'I don't know what you're alluding to, but... what you said before – any sane person would choose intelligence over senselessness, health over sickness. It is love that conquers – not hate.'

*As you say, Professor. As you say.*

There was a sense of withered tiredness.

*I mentioned that humans hardly think enough - so tell me about Project Ingenious. Seven babies, born out of so much suffering. Could you really say that it was a good cause? Considering all the casualties, all the deformities, all the deaths...*

The Professor froze.

*I have to say that your gushing sentiments, your spouting on about love – love! – such an ineffectual emotion, it does absolutely nothing for me. Nothing! On the other hand, I want to talk instead about id – our gut, primal instinct. That of the human race in general. I want to talk about the holocaust, where everyday people became systematic murderers of millions of Jewish men, women, and children. Mass participants of mass murder – without even batting an eyelid. And in times of famine, parents have been known to eat their own children – starvation tearing into and ripping apart what should have been the strongest bond of all, parental love. Their belly, their own existence, chosen over and above the lives of their progeny. Then there's the Cambodian killing fields, the Rwandan massacre of the Tutsi, Native Americans massacred or killed by forced labour or war, the Circassian genocide, Nanking. Hiroshima. Nagasaki. The list goes on and on and on. That is the reality. It's almost as if humans have a... fascination for death and destruction. And so why should anybody be surprised that, well, Project Ingenious is any different. It followed the same pattern of brutality in their single-minded goal. Life created, malformed, and snuffed out – all in the name of science...*

The Professor's ears tingled; felt all at once sick and indignant; had neither the strength nor the will to refute this madman. His own irritation, exhaustion, and frustration compounded the confusion. He just needed one thing: to find out if this was the person who had caused the cancerous outbreak. Needed him to admit it. But how? His mind raced...

There came a sigh. *I... I'm tired. I need to rest. But first, I just wanted to tell you why I did what I did to those students. Why I gave them a disease that would ultimately end in their certain death. You probably know by now, there is no cure, not yet anyway, and not for them.* There was a pause, followed by a barely audible sigh. *There were many reasons for my actions. The simplest one is that I did it because I could. Because I wanted to test my ability to manipulate the disease and infect other humans – a kind of experimental science if you will. Another reason is that I wanted to flush the children, your children, out into the open. And thanks to you, Professor, you have brought two of them to me.*

The Professor froze. 'W-why do you want the children? What could you possibly want with them? They've done nothing to you. They just want to be left alone to live normal lives.'

*Ah, there's that word 'normal' again... They will never be normal, Professor. They have a vastly superior intellect – a rare and special thing. Yet you have surrounded them with m-mundanity, and given them to mm-mediocre parents, people who cannot possibly understand how to provide the appropriate guidance and nurturing for their abilities. The children, they're dying a slow brain-death in the hands of their parents, their carers. It's like... like a masterpiece given to an imbecile who only defaces it with childish scribbles. Or a priceless Ming vase in the hands of an idiot who uses it as a latrine...*

The Professor stiffened, simmering with rage. He'd had enough! Hearing the man's admission of guilt, that it was him who unleashed that disease into the world – one that could bring awful, catastrophic consequences – that was all he needed to know. The man was a monster. And in a knee-jerk reaction, he stepped forward, stumbled, and collapsed on the floor in a heap.

*Professor! Are you alright?*

But nobody rushed to help him. The Professor sat up on the floor, rubbing his ankle. Trembling, he moved his hand over his shoe, and brushed the tiny device on the inside edge of the heel – triggering the transmitter.

'I'm fine,' said the Professor, terse. He got up.

*O-okay. Anyway, another thing I wanted to tell you... The main reason why I wanted the children is... haven't you already seen it in the two that you brought me? They are dying, Professor. Slowly, but surely.*

The Professor stopped. 'W-what do you mean?'

*I was sure you would have realised by now. It starts out with very bad migraines that become more frequent. Then there's fitting, hallucinations, and even... hearing voices. After that sets in, their minds, their bodies, will begin to deteriorate very quickly.*

The Professor felt queasy again.

*You might grimace from the irony of it – but the cancer given to the seven university students was actually created from the disease inherent within your special children. You see, a mutation has developed from the genetic alteration of their DNA, which, in time, becomes cancerous, and affects the mind. Though for the Oxford students, I managed to speed up the lytic cycle of the disease, accelerating its development. And so, by infecting them, I was curious to see if your top scientists could create a cure, not only for the university students, but also for your genius children. But it's clear to me now, even your top scientists have nothing substantial to offer...*

The Professor felt the blood drain from his head. 'How... how do you know all this? Are you a doctor? Were you behind the project?'

*I've actually been working on a cure for a long, long time, and I've made good progress. In fact, I'm almost there. Almost. But I wanted to see if I was missing anything, if your scientists came up with something I hadn't thought of. But that turned out to be a dead end...* There was a smirk. *No pun intended. Anyway, considering your children are still healthy, they will be invaluable in helping to complete the cure. In a way, they'll be saving themselves...*

A chill seeped through the Professor's bones. Could it be that by securing this man's death, he was also destroying the only hope of a cure for the children, the other children too? What had he done?!

He had already set off the signal, and there was no way to switch it off. They were trapped on the submarine, making it impossible to escape.

Had their roles now transposed?

Was this person trying to save the children, and he, the Professor, had become their executioner?

He tugged at the stiff shirt collar around his neck – it felt suddenly tight. He flushed hot then cold. Became light-headed. Dizzy.

And then, in a long, low exhalation, his lungs emptied. His eyes rolled back. He found that he was falling. Fainting in a heap on the floor.

•••————————————————————•••

When the Professor slowly came to, he could sense that he was in a different place. Some time had passed because his soaked clothes had dried a little and were stiff with salt, sticking to his skin. He realised that he was not alone – there was another presence...

'Professor?' chimed a familiar voice.

'Tai!' exclaimed the Professor, turning in his direction. He struggled to sit up, realising that he was on a soft surface, a sofa.

Somebody else stepped closer and threw their arms around him, hugging him. 'Thank goodness!' came Milly's voice, her breath warm on his neck. 'I was so worried. Are you okay, Professor?'

He didn't know. 'I... I think so.'

'You look like you're... in shock.'

He was. Sweat and guilt exuded from every pore. He crumpled back.

Milly took his hand – he was trembling – and she gripped it within both of hers. Eventually she said, 'I know about 2.07.'

The Professor closed his eyes, casting his mind back to that last night in Avernus. He remembered now, the sound of something in the corridor, though at the time he thought it was just one of the animals. 'You saw my analysis...?'

'Yes, I did. That's why I told Tai before we joined you that we might not be coming back.' She paused, wondering at how strangely composed she was in the face of death. 'I explained that you would do whatever you needed to, to make sure this... this horrible disease was stopped.'

The Professor blinked, absorbing this. 'And yet, you still came? What about your father, Milly? Tai, your mother might well be alive. You both have something... someone to live for. I don't. You should have stayed away. Both of you. I never wanted you to be part of this.' Frustration hardened his tone. There were three pawns in this game of life where there should only have been one – offering themselves on the altar of what they thought was the greater good.

Tai broke the awkward silence. 'Do you think that person is here – the one who made those students sick?'

'He is,' said the Professor. 'I was just with him. We talked.'

'And... what did he say?!' asked Milly.

The Professor felt suddenly perplexed. So many questions, so little time. The futility of it all was too much for him. He turned away, as if looking for words, looking for a way out of this madness. 'H-he said...' But he could not bring himself to repeat it. 'I'm sorry,' was all he managed, his voice cracking. 'I was so incensed, so mad at that person... that thing... that I already activated the transmitter.' He had finally said it! 'As we speak, it's sending a signal back to British intelligence. And when they receive it, they'll lock their missiles onto it – onto me – and initiate an attack. I... I am ground zero.' He shifted away from them, as if distancing himself made any difference. 'I'm sorry,' he said, lowering his head.

A silence descended on them as they absorbed the finality of the situation.

Their last moments.

After a long while, Milly spoke, sadness tingeing her voice. 'You... you don't know what we look like, do you, Professor?'

He was caught off-guard. 'I... well, no.'

Milly took his hand again and gently lifted it to her cheek. It was damp. The old man felt his heart bursting. Cracking with pain.

It was bad enough knowing that he was responsible for their impending death, now he had to put a face to the people he was killing. Yet he couldn't help closing his eyes, breathing long and hard. Couldn't help resigning to her last wish.

He moved his hand slowly upward. It trembled as he felt long silky eyelashes, the delicate skin of her eyelid and the curved indent of the eye socket – large, pretty eyes that he had somehow already imagined her having. Moving up and around, his fingers brushed over eyebrows, a creased forehead, wide cheekbones, and then sweeping down, he felt her jawline. A single tear splashed on the back of his hand as he did so. Finally, he felt the thickness of messy, unkempt hair.

In his mind's eye, he saw her now, appearing out of a blurry vagueness, like a camera sharpening focus. Just a young, innocent girl. Quietly crying.

Milly squeezed his hand gently, then got up, and Tai took her place.

Where Milly released her feelings through tears, Tai simply held his in. The Professor's hand reached upward – but as soon as it touched the boy's cheek, they both jumped – stung by an electric shock.

The old man blinked, in a daze.

'What... what happened?' asked Tai, stunned.

Bewildered, the Professor took a few moments to process. 'I... I thought I *saw* something.' He shook his head, as if trying to purge madness from him.

Both Tai and Milly looked at each other.

The Professor's eyes floated downward. 'This is going to sound strange. But for a split second, when I touched Tai, it was like... like looking in a mirror. Seeing *myself*!'

Tentatively, Tai reached for the Professor's hand. And when skin touched skin, a pulse flowed from one to the other, blooming and growing in the Professor's body. It seemed to tunnel through every nerve, coursing in unstoppable waves through tendons and ligaments, cartilage, muscle, and bone – through every fibre of his being.

The Professor watched in astonishment as a dim haze appeared out of the whiteness. And as both of Tai's hands clenched his, the image clarified, so that shapes, and lines, and details came into focus. While Tai stared at him, the old man found that he was looking at his own face. At those dark, empty eyes. Thick eyebrows set against sallow skin. A head of grey, silver-streaked hair.

Suddenly, Tai let go, and the image disappeared with a whoosh. The Professor was speechless, his mouth open in disbelief. Eventually he said, quietly: 'I-I saw myself – through *your* eyes.'

Milly drew closer, amazed. 'Tai. Do it again. Hold his hand.'

The boy did as he was instructed, and he turned to look at Milly.

The Professor went quiet as tears welled up. 'Th-that t-shirt you're wearing, Milly. Michelangelo's "Creation of Adam".'

Milly looked down at the picture on her chest. It had always been one of her favourites.

The Professor continued, 'During the project, there were Da Vinci posters hung up all over your bedroom – you stared at them endlessly before falling asleep. And that was one of them...'

Milly gasped. 'This... your seeing... it's incredible!!'

The Professor stood up, his eyes glistening. He held out a tremulous hand. 'Please, Tai, show me around.'

Tai took it, and together they walked across the room, stopping just in front of the viewing glass that covered most of the outer hull; it gave a spectacular panorama of the deep sea. The soft internal lighting bounced back a clear reflection of the three of them standing there.

Milly joined them, and hooked her arm in the Professor's. 'How is this possible?' she asked with wonder.

The Professor thought about it. 'Tai's abilities...' he started with awe, 'they seem to be getting stronger, much stronger. First, empathic powers... and now... this.' He caught a choke in his throat. 'But it's too late, I–'

Milly squeezed his arm. 'You did the right thing, Professor. We all know it's for the best.'

They stood huddled together, looking out into the deep sea.

The rich blue water rippled gently – catching glimmers of light that refracted into a dazzling spectrum.

Fresh tears welled up in the Professor's eyes, as he quietly absorbed the exhilarating colours and sheer beauty before them.

As the submarine ascended into shallower waters, they watched shafts of light from the setting sun blaze through like celestial spotlights. The seawater melted gradually from deep blues to a lighter, clearer colour. Soon they reached a cliff edge plateau, covered by an enchanted forest of brown and gold algae, interspersed with stems of emerald eel grass, bobbing and swaying in a dance. Phytoplankton bloomed purple here and there, and when the vessel halted on a level bed of shale, they waited for glittering billows of quartzite sand to settle, until there was once again lucidity.

A red crab scuttled quickly through the sediment, from one hiding place to another – its stalked, black eyes twitching. Several eelpout fish slithered in amber flashes, wide mouths hungrily gulping as they went. And then in the distance they noticed a faint orange stain moving and shifting in the water. As it drew closer and larger, it passed under the strong external submarine lights, and they realised that it was a shoal of krill – tiny shrimp-like creatures with dots for eyes. They gambolled all around in their millions, legs rippling beneath them in a blur. From their midst emerged a detached fish-head that was jostled here and there before floating downwards and away. The shoal spread and swarmed until their view was completely obscured. But then suddenly it swept apart to reveal something round and dark from behind. It was a huge eye.

The three jumped back with fright.

The dull-black eye was the size of a dinnerplate, and as the orange swarm of krill dissipated, huge folds of thick whiskered skin was revealed. An immense mouth, slightly opened, was lined with sieve-like baleen, used to filter food from the water. Below the mouth were fluid grooves radiating outwards – ventral pleats that could expand with every gulp of food. Its body was mottled, barnacled, and scarred – stark evidence of past battles.

'It's a whale! A blue whale!' said Milly, excited. She drew closer. 'The largest animal on the planet. This could mean we're in the Pacific.'

Tai stood right in front of the glass and pressed a hand where the whale's cheek rested. He remained still, staring in wonder, quietly absorbing – and in turn the prodigious creature watched them. Its huge eye blinked, shifting from Tai to Milly to the Professor, and back again. But after some time the whale began to retreat, swimming backwards slowly – a lumbering gentle giant.

'It's beautiful,' said Milly, entranced.

They watched the whale swim away, until it was just a hazy shape in the distance.

Tai looked at the others. 'She's sad,' he said, matter-of-fact. 'In pain...'

Milly turned to him. 'Why?'

'I don't know. I need time to think... sift through her memories...' He suddenly turned back to the viewing glass. 'Can you hear that?'

They stopped to listen.

'She's calling out.'

It was a low, deep, wailing – the very epitome of pain itself, filtering through the water and into the room.

Tai realised. 'She's calling out for her baby. She doesn't know where it is. It's lost.'

Milly felt tears well up – for the sadness of the whale, a mother's loss, and their own impending death...

Together they listened to the whale call. It resonated with their own helplessness and despair. Seconds and minutes ticked by. Meanwhile, Tai's mind drifted back to the thoughts he had absorbed from the huge creature. So immense was its energy, so strong were its brainwaves, that Tai could read her effortlessly; the signal was a powerful yet clear one.

He saw her life now, relived her past. And watched the pretty colours of her memories...

•••———————————————•••

The whale cow was just nine years old when it had reached physical maturity. And a growing urge turned into an overwhelming need – to find a partner. It was so strong that it even pushed her to leave the safety and affection of her mother. And so she set off by herself on a long journey southward, migrating thousands of miles, over months. She eventually arrived at her destination, tired and starving, and missing her mother.

Basking in the shallower, warmer waters, somehow comforted her and lifted her spirits. It was night, and the dark meant that she could find food near the water's surface, which was preferable to the deeper and exhausting day-time feeding, when she had to dive hundreds of metres down. The sight of dull orange stoked her hunger, and she swam like an automaton into the heart of the shoal of krill, lunging with her mouth stretched open. Her gular pouch expanded from the sheer volume, and she flicked her tongue back to squeeze the water through her ventral pouch, gulping down the delicious crustacea.

She spent several days replenishing her energies by lunging, gulping, and basking, over and over – feeding on up to three tons of krill a day, until, at last, she felt strong enough to mate. And right on cue, just a few days later, a pod of five males appeared. She rolled around and nudged them flirtatiously – and the five responded by vying for her attention, jostling and bumping against each other.

They even sang to her – beguiling signature songs, which mesmerised her, and wooed her. She swam around them, listening quietly. At times the bulls puffed themselves up to appear bigger, and at times they broke out in violent fighting, male against male – pushing and shoving, pounding barnacled fins, and bashing each other with their tail flukes. They sometimes glided smoothly against her, caressing her gently with their brown spotted bellies. Sometimes leapt out of the water to impress her, arching gracefully up and over, their flanks slapping heavily on the surface. Sometimes charged into each other, to show off their immense strength.

The whale cow took her time, for the thrill was in the choosing – but after ten days of courtship, a verdict was made. And to increase her chances of conceiving, she chose two males.

She swam around and nudged and courted with the first chosen bull – eventually pairing off and swimming down together, down into the deep abyss. All the while calling out, one to the other, as if cajoling each other onward. It was calmer and quieter in the deep, the waters heavy and dense around them. They waited for as long as they could bear, until their lungs were near bursting, and then, driven by thrashing flukes, they sped up and up to the surface, piercing the watery divide in union, and leaping out. They sliced through the air together – triumphant! – expelling a plume of water from one blowhole, and inhaling air through the other – before arching round and back into the water. Hearts thundering, pulses racing.

Finally the couple swam off, and then at last came together. A thin stream of bubbles escaped from her mouth until, before long, her partner rolled quietly away. And in time he swam off, never to be seen again.

Later, she approached the second male, and repeated the ritual once more.

Eleven months later, her round, ripe belly was ready to burst. The convulsions startled her – tight, contracting sensations which grew stronger and more painful. She groaned in agony, a low rumbling that swelled into a wailing cry. Her pain heard for miles around.

Swimming around and around at top speed was all she could do to distract herself, thrashing her fluke against the water, beating away the agony. And at last, when the time came, she propelled herself close to the surface, squeezing her belly as she moved – moving and squeezing, moving and squeezing. Until the calf's fluke scratched and scraped inside her, inching its way out. And then, with one last mighty squeeze, she expelled the calf in a flush of placental blood. Circling back round, the whale searched for a glimpse of her baby, only to find it gliding slowly downwards, unable to swim... And though faint from hours of labour, she mustered every last strength to speed underneath, curving below her calf, and nudging it upward again and again until they reached the surface. She rolled underneath it, balancing baby on her back, in the hope that it would take its first breath, as she in turn held hers. At last, the calf began flapping fins, and spouting water, to her great relief.

The baby suckled milk from its mother for many months. And mother loved her calf dearly. It swam faithfully by her side, and they roamed the seas together, hardly out of each other's sight. Sometimes the calf would play with other young whales they happened upon, or it would race with dolphins, swimming frantically alongside them. Mischievously, it jumped up amidst unsuspecting flocks of seagulls that sat bobbing up and down on the surface, and then the calf rolled vertically through the air, watching with a twinkle in its eye as the birds scattered and squawked. Or it sliced through thick shoals of fish, just for the fun of it.

Mother taught her calf how to hunt for krill, and if there was little to be found in shallow waters, they dived down together to find plenty far below. The calf was vulnerable to shark attacks, and so it was taught how to charge and head-butt their enemies, and use its powerful fluke to bash in defence.

But one day, the calf swam further away than it ought, distracted by a particularly elusive shoal of krill. When it turned to look for mother, she was nowhere to be found.

Mother searched for her child day and night. She grew weak, not feeding herself – forever calling out in a long, low wail. Swimming around and around, with a heart heavy.

When she saw a long, dark shape in the distance, she raced toward it, only to find that it was a huge, rigid mechanical object, even larger than herself – that had neither head nor tail. She rested her cheek against the transparent skin that ran down its flank, and peered inside. Somehow she sensed that her baby was close, so close she could almost smell it in the water...

●●●━━━━━━━━━━━━━━━━━━━━━●●

As Tai silently relived the whale cow's memories, he felt every contraction, every labour pain, that the mother endured in childbirth. And he began to understand the maternal bond – a bond so strong, that even pain and the threat of death could not break it.

Tai felt flooded by the sadness of the mother losing her calf – and he winced from it. He knew that she would keep searching till the day she died.

And then he thought of his own mother.

Was she alive, he wondered.

Had she come searching for him, only to find their home locked up and empty – her only child nowhere to be found.

He breathed in all these thoughts.

And – as three F-35 Lightning fighter planes hurtled toward them, with just minutes until the first missile strike – ironically, Tai felt a sudden glimmer of hope. Hope that his mother might come searching for him...

The mother whale's last memory came to him now: she was gliding along the length of the submarine, looking inside, room by room, object by object, until she rested her cheek against the last transparent window, to find the three of them staring out at her. Tai examined each image in detail, and he gasped. He spun round to face Milly, the Professor. 'The submarine – it has these... these... round glass escape things, that can drive through the water!' he said excitedly.

Milly looked at him. 'Escape pods?!'

Tai nodded.

'But how do you know?'

'The whale,' was all he said.

There was no time to wonder, they had to act fast. 'We have to get to them right away,' said the Professor.

Milly ran to the door, but it was locked.

That was when they heard it. A hissing sound outside as the first missiles streaked through the water toward them. Those seconds, waiting, were the worst. Finally there came the deafening boom of an explosion hitting the rocky plateau just a few metres away. The entire submarine juddered, throwing the three of them onto the deck. Subsequent shockwaves radiated through the submarine, and it was all they could do to scramble on all fours.

Large cracks crazed the viewing glass – branching out into yet finer cracks – until water began to seep and spurt inside.

The submarine alarm blared out, two high-pitched notes repeating shrilly, like panicked screams. The Professor covered his ears.

Outside, came frantic shouting as the submarine went into high alert, and the crew ran to their stations, following emergency protocol.

The prisoners heard the clunk of the door mechanism, and they realised that all internal doors had been automatically unlocked; Tai managed to pull himself up, and he wrenched on the dog lever. The door was flung open, and then he helped the others up. Grabbing the Professor's hand, he shouted for Milly to follow. 'It's this way!' he said, and turned toward the stern, running down the passageway.

The submarine crew had gone into meltdown, rushing in all directions, hardly caring that the prisoners were loose. It was all the crew could do to get to their emergency positions in the bridge, the boiler room, the engine room, the manoeuvring room, and the radio office.

Pulsating lights soaked them in red as they hurried – but then the hissing sound came again, and they stopped. Milly and Tai stared fretfully at each other, until the missile nicked the hull of the bow, and a second explosion flared. The submarine reeled back on the starboard side, flinging the three against the wall. They winced from the impact, but before they could recover there came another explosion, and another.

The last one damaged the sound system, so that the clangourous alarm fizzled and stopped – though the echo of it still rung in the Professor's ears.

Tai fell awkwardly against his leg, spraining his ankle. He pushed himself up, hobbling, and urged Milly and the Professor to go ahead, saying that he would be right behind.

Milly grabbed the Professor's hand and practically dragged him along, as Tai limped behind them, wincing, yet keeping his eyes ahead. He shouted, 'Try the door on your right!'

Quickly Milly threw herself on the door wheel, and tugged at it – the squelching rim eventually gave way. But it was just a supply compartment, with boxes and containers strewn everywhere.

'It's not this one!' she shouted back. She grabbed the Professor and led him to the next door. This time, when she opened it, the lights were not working, and Milly took a while before her eyes adjusted to the dark. From the little she could make out, it was completely bare, with only a flat piece of furniture at its centre. 'Not here either,' she said, and turned to go.

But the Professor stopped her. 'Wait,' he said, turning his head. 'I hear something.'

Tai caught up with them, and as he stood in the doorway, the hairs on his skin bristled. He suddenly felt afraid. 'Let's go. Please.' He tugged on Milly's arm, but the Professor pulled away.

'Can't you hear? Someone's calling for help,' said the Professor.

Reluctantly, Milly and Tai stopped to listen.

'Please, help me...' came a small weak voice, barely audible above the din and chaos. 'Over here...'

Instinctively the Professor entered the compartment, disappearing into the vacuum of darkness. 'I'm coming,' he called out, feeling his way. His feet bumped into a wooden furniture leg, and he bent down to discover someone lying in front of him. It was a young, painfully thin person, strapped down on the table. The Professor felt buckles around each limb, and he managed to untie them one by one.

When the old man eventually emerged into the light again, Milly and Tai saw that he was supporting a pale, emaciated teenage boy. His body was that of a young man's, but his face looked old, with sunken cheeks and dark rings underneath his eyes. He was wearing beige pyjamas, and his unkempt brassy blond hair had alarming bald patches. Where the Professor was holding onto his stick-like arms, the sleeve had lifted to reveal multiple needle punctures ringed by yellow and purple bruising – so vivid they were like tattoos. The hunched, sickly boy looked up at them with startling clear-grey eyes.

Tai hobbled closer to help, taking the boy's other arm, but he recoiled suddenly and stumbled back. His eyes widened with the sight of scattered images – of being subjected to torturous experiments, the gouging of biopsy samples, drawing blood, numerous injections, starvation diets, brain electroshocks. Each image rose out of fog – as if the boy was constantly in a drugged, hallucinogenic state.

The last images were the bloodiest – experiments on animals, monkeys, sea creatures – so brutal they made Tai gasp. And finally, one last awful picture: a young whale, lying lifeless on the top deck of the surfaced submarine. Split in two. Red rivulets leaking out from it, disappearing down floor drains, and trickling into the sea.

Tai gasped with horror. And when he opened his eyes, and steadied himself, he found that Milly had already grabbed the boy's arm, leading him out and further along, to the next door. She peered inside the room. 'They're here!!' she shouted, just before disappearing inside. Tai limped after them, head reeling with shock.

They discovered three large pods with wide bulbous bodies against the outer hull. Milly bashed on a square green button on one of them, and the door slid open with a whoosh. Peaking inside, she could see that the control area, with the helm and navigation instruments, protruded out of the submarine hull, like a glass bubble, allowing an almost 180-degree view. Up front were two seats, with benches running along the length, and rows of hanging seatbelts. The Professor wrenched on Milly's hand, and she stopped; quickly he pulled off his right shoe and threw it back into the room. Then Milly guided him inside the pod.

The sickly boy watched him curiously, before he too was bundled into the escape pod.

Inside, Milly bashed an internal red button which closed the door, then ran to the pilot seat, shouting out to the others that they should strap themselves in – quickly. She sat down and stretched forward to look at the controls. But out of nowhere came a cracking throb in her head, her stomach churned, and she doubled over with pain so strong it almost blinded her. Gritting her teeth, she instinctively felt her pocket for the bottle of painkillers, but it was not there – and she groaned.

Her face flushed bright red, and in a cloud of pain Milly blinked through tears to try and focus on the confusing array of buttons, dials, gauges, digital displays, levers, foot controls, and wheels, in front of her. She must have pressed on something that automatically powered up the escape pod – and the instrument panel lit up, blinking and beeping, as if conspiring to confuse her.

With the helicopter, she had watched, learnt, and memorised everything V2 did – but now, she had nothing to go on. Given time, she might have been able to work out the controls, but it was impossible to think through the searing pain. Milly dropped her head, taking short deep breaths to oxygenate her brain. 'You've got this, Milly,' whispered her mother in her ear. 'I believe in you.'

Milly sobbed. 'I... I can't do it.'

The sickly boy glared at her, veins bulging through translucent skin at his temple. 'Auto launch!' he shouted weakly. 'There must be some kind of auto-launch sequence, some kind of auto-pilot!' He broke off, gasping for breath.

Milly blinked through the white pain, scanning over the controls. Her eyes locked onto a section to the far right, surrounded in a red border, labelled, 'Emergency Launch Sequence'. She bashed against the central red button, and the engine came to life, vibrating under their feet. The pod juddered as locking mechanisms were released and power surged. Finally, it heaved forward, and the vessel wrenched away from the submarine and was thrust out, into the sea.

Just then, missiles rained down from above, and one of them was an almost perfect hit with the shoe the Professor had thrown back into the submarine. The ensuing explosion of sizzling orange flames hurled the pod downwards against a large rock protruding from the sand. The pod spun out of control – skidding and rolling for what seemed like an eternity, bouncing off a group of rocks, glass shattering, and at last coming to a halt in the sand, upside down.

The pod was cracked wide open, and fissures in the hull began leaking lines of hissing smoke and bubbles. It rocked and creaked as it filled with water – an efflux of spewing sparks briefly lighting up the darkness inside.

It was completely empty...

There was an enormous pop inside the Professor's ears and everything fell suddenly silent.

He was floating, arms and legs extended in a slow cartwheel – water so cold it was unreal. His clothes billowed with trapped air, chest heaved with the squeeze of pressure, lungs burst with tightness. Panic jarred his empty eyes wide open – the sting of the salt so strong it was like acid. He did not know which way was up, and which was down. All he knew was that there was no hope. At last.

Something large came gliding against him. It had cold, sandpaper-like skin, and was long and stocky; the merest touch sent him careening in another direction. From the Professor's blue lips, reluctant bubbles escaped – his last breath – casually floating heavenward to join the great atmosphere above.

As the breath left him, the Professor felt that his spirit was departing too, chasing after those bubbles on one last journey. To meet his maker.

Tai had somehow managed to gulp in a lungful of air before being thrown out of the escape pod. He found himself now sprawled amongst the sea-grass that carpeted the floor. His entire body throbbed with pain after being pounded inside the pod as it spiralled out of control. A dazed mind finally grasped what had happened – and panic crushed him just as the force of the sea crushed down on his body.

He noticed a plethora of things in the ensuing seconds: the massive submarine, further away from him now, lighting up like fireworks as missiles continued to streak down on it, tearing away great chunks. Detritus and debris hurtled, raining all around. The smashed escape pod, rocking to a halt. A murky gloom gathering above him.

Tai looked up, and froze. It was a group of sharks that appeared from the far, dark side of the submarine – a mass so great in number that, as they swam nearer, they cast a vast shadow right across him, plunging him into darkness.

Tai remembered the fish in the tank, attacking his fingers as he fed them, though he had done nothing to provoke. Instinctively he looked around in terror for somewhere to hide. Yet he could not fully understand the impossibility of his situation. He would need at least 17 minutes to swim to the surface, let alone have time to hide, or even search for the others. And his lungs were already giving out.

Seconds ticked uselessly away.

Air bubbles slipped out like liquid mercury from the side of his mouth.

And at long last, tears finally welled up, though he did not know it – dissolving into the seawater as though they were nothing.

---

The fearsome creature was attracted by the great thunderous sounds that boomed again and again through the water. Tiny fibres lining its ear canals tingled, though it was miles away – and whilst it was not particularly hungry (the balmy waters were already rich with food), curiosity got the better of this inquisitive, intelligent beast, and it was drawn to this most unusual disturbance. And so, like a slick, well-oiled machine, its powerful body careened through the water towards the deafening noises.

A lone hunter, it found itself merging with a great shoal of others of its kind, already in the hundreds, and more were still being added. It buzzed with the power of their vast numbers uniting as one throbbing being, daring to swim on together.

The cataclysmic scene that appeared before it made its eyes roll.

A long, giant object lay destroyed on the sand – flaring with blinding flashes. Spiralling upwards came streams of huge bubbles and dense columns of black smoke. The creature's lateral lines (drawn along the full breadth of both flanks) tingled as they picked up delicate electromagnetic waves radiating through the water – so sensitive that even the dwindling heartbeats of scattered prey could be felt from many hundreds of metres away. And there were many hearts all around, each with its own unique signal.

The creature did not like what it was seeing.

Gliding along with the silvery mass of other sharks, it skirted the perimeter of this bizarre scene, jaws grinding. It flared with anger. These were their waters, and theirs alone – and this noisy, huge thing was not welcome! Incensed, it bumped away debris that crossed its path. Lips parting to reveal sharp, pointed teeth.

But then, it smelled the one thing that whipped it into a frenzy. Fresh blood. Blossoming in the water, greeny-blue. And as it swam through it, it sparked within the beast an innate physical reaction. It fixed a beady black eye on the source of the blood, and, increasing speed, it rammed the prey from behind – the full force concentrated into its blunt snout.

The old man, who had been furiously peddling the water in panic, was stunned to unconsciousness by the blow. Smoothly, the beast doubled back and, in a flash, headed for the kill, crunching powerful jaws into flesh and bone. Feverishly the shark shook its head, tearing the limb clean away. Then zigzagged off, munching on the food with a bloody, macabre grin.

When the others of its kind smelled the blood, a feeding frenzy ensued, and they worked together systematically tearing and ripping and gouging and chewing, until there was left nothing but a stain. A stain that slowly disbursed – leaving just a single slipper floating bleakly downwards.

From afar, Tai watched with horror as the sharks ate the man. He could not make out who the victim was, and hoped upon hope that it was not the Professor.

In the corner of his eye he spotted something a few metres away behind a piece of wreckage – a thin arm sticking out from a clump of swaying seagrass. Cautiously, and with a thundering heart, he swam over. It was an unconscious Milly – and he quickly scooped her up into his arms.

The sharks were circling away from them now, and he started to swim upwards with her, when something else caught his eye. It was a single, dark figure, twitching and floating aimlessly about 30 metres away. Squinting, Tai saw that it was the Professor. And then, just below him, he noticed the limp body of the boy they found, lying on the sand, completely still.

Tai glanced from the old man, to the boy, perplexed – instinctively knowing that there would not be enough time to save them both. He himself was struggling to stay conscious. Panic broiled inside him. And at the same time, he somehow sensed that the sharks had spotted him. He turned to see them sweeping back round, swimming toward him at breakneck speed. Noticed the light plume of blood billowing from Milly's arm. Blackness seeping across his vision. Consciousness slipping away.

Tai's eyes locked onto those of the first shark as it sped toward him.

In those last moments, the Professor's words – steady and seemingly omnipresent – echoed in his ears.

*'They sense your fear. Attracted to it like magnets.'*

Tai's eyes closed.

*'Because of it, they fear you.'*

Felt himself passing out.

*'Learn to control your feelings.'*

*'You can influence them.'*

*'Control them...'*

And suddenly, Tai's mind detonated with one last thought just before he lost consciousness. It burst out of him, like an electromagnetic pulse. The force of it exploding and bellowing through the waters, as a single concept, a palpable intention. A shockwave of pure emotion so intense that it boomed through skin and scales, through fat and muscle, cartilage and bone. Sizzling through neurons, axons, capillaries, and synapses. Sparking a new, abstract thought right inside the base carnal minds of those beasts of the sea, those sharks. Willing them with one, pure animus:

SAVE US!

---

They were masters of the sea, those great white sharks. But as all 576 of them stared at the stick-like creatures, half buried in the sand and seagrass, they collectively absorbed the electromagnetic field echoing from their puny hearts, as they beat slower and slower – small, light hearts, that pumped with four chambers, compared to the sharks' two. It was the first organ that sparked to life in a foetus, and somehow the sharks knew that, at death, it was the first to stop. When they sensed the human hearts becoming fainter, weaker, the sharks immediately sped closer, knowing collectively that they must do one thing. Make them beat again.

Dividing into four groups, they swam outward in lines, towards each of the near-dead creatures. Massing around and underneath them in a circular motion, they whipped the water into vortices, stirring the limp creatures upwards. When they were lifted up from the seabed, the sharks unitedly scooped underneath each human and began swimming upwards at top speed – the four bodies slack against their snouts. Powerful, interdigitating muscles, bound to a cartilaginous skeleton, thrashed and pumped, thrashed and pumped, punching through the water at 45 miles an hour. Their teeth bared and bloody.

With stereoscopic vision fixed ahead, they glimpsed the twinkling light on the firmament above. Marking the great divide between two worlds. And as they neared it, they slowed right down, knowing that they could go no further. The humans were deposited safely on the divide – and left floating. When the sharks turned to leave, several of them splashed their caudal fins, as if to revive and kickstart those hearts. But they did not realise that two of the humans were face-down in the water, unable to breathe.

The sharks left. They had done their part.

Having worked up an appetite, they turned back to the place undersea where they could feast on plenty more fresh meat, just lying around – easy pickings and ready for the taking.

<hr />

The whale had watched the spectacle from a distance.

Booming noises and frightening lights had scared her away, but she felt somehow compelled to remain close-by – as if a force, an energy, were beckoning her...

She followed the activity of the sharks with curiosity, watching them swim to the surface, one and all, and deposit four of those tiny creatures at the divide. Wondering why they had not torn them to shreds. The whale knew that the four humans were the same ones she had spied earlier within the giant metal object, and again, she felt particularly drawn to them, though she could not understand how or why.

When the sharks swam away, and she felt it was safe, the whale drew steadily closer to inspect them as they floated limp on the surface. Waves lapped against her eye, as she spied them as close as she could – but still they did not move. Then, she remembered. Remembered how, after giving birth, her own calf's body floated motionless, unable to breathe. She recalled the instinctive action of rolling baby on her back and bringing it to the surface, so that its blowhole could suck in life-giving air.

And so the huge whale swam round and dove down into the water – then shimmied upward directly underneath the four. Slowly, steadily, she broke the divide – with the bodies washed up on her back, swaying this way and that from sloshing water. The whale waited, hoping that their blowholes too could suck in air. She spurted out an encouraging plume of water, which showered down on them, making them stir softly. And at last she felt their faint heartbeats on her skin, getting stronger. The rhythmic beat of life. Heard them wheezing and spluttering.

Slowly, the gentle giant swam away from the frightening sharks – the warmth of her huge body in turn warming the little creatures.

It heartened the sad, lonely whale to feel them on her back, just as she had felt her precious calf there when it had been birthed. And so she sang the same whale song she had sung to her baby. A deep, haunting song that both echoed far and wide through the waters, and vibrated through her bones, stirring the humans awake.

She hoped upon hope that her calf would hear her song too. Hoped that her baby would come swimming back to her.

## 27 AFTERMATH

Since Milly had left, her father, Brian, was beside himself.

Though, to observe him, one would not know it.

He found solace in following the same mindless motions – the repetition, like oil to his bones, soothed him.

Mindless was good.

It was better than thinking – thinking about the worst.

When his beloved Savannah had died so many years ago, he would easily have given up on life, were it not for his little daughter. She would grab his hand and look up at him with those large tearful eyes, mirroring the sorrow in his own. Bound up in that one expression, he saw her despair and confusion – wondering why her mother had abandoned them. Why dad didn't fix it, like he fixed everything else, and make mum come back.

And now, after all that they had gone through together over the years, all the toil and the tears, the sacrifices and sleepless nights, his daughter had left him. Just like that. And he was alone.

In her place was left a paltry scrap of paper, scrawled like an afterthought. *'I'm sorry, Dad, but please understand that I have to go. I love you... more than life itself.'*

He thought of those words over and over again.

As he hand-washed the dishes despite the dishwasher. When he wiped the tables, two or three or sometimes four times, even though they were perfectly clean. And he scrubbed and scrubbed at the sink with scouring powder, then bleach, then disinfectant, until it sparkled. He thought about that sentence, *'I love you more than life itself'*, and wondered what on earth it meant. If she loved him that much, why was she putting others before him? Why did she abandon him, so that he was left alone, in an aimless limbo, day after perplexing day? It just made no sense.

It came as a brutal blow, the realisation that he was no longer the centre of his daughter's universe.

When she was small, she idolised him, depended on him. And reciprocally, he had given Milly so much of himself, 24 hours a day, seven days a week, year after year – only to watch her grow emotionally further apart from him, just as surely as she grew physically. He could only come to terms with it – his daughter blossoming into the strong, independent young lady she was always meant to be.

That was, if she didn't die...

Brian caught a choke in his throat as he thought of this.
Quickly he threw himself back into his mindless work.

•••————————————————————•••

5,000 miles away, in the middle of the North Atlantic Ocean, more or less equidistant between the north-eastern coast of South America and the west of Africa, the pilots of three F-35 Lightning fighter planes, having completed their sortie, saw below them blackened submarine debris that bobbed up and down in the water. With their pylons and weapon bays completely emptied of their payloads, the stealth planes carved a u-turn through the air, as they looked for survivors in a routine sensor sweep. Though they were not expecting to find a single soul. Latest technology radars and electro-optical systems provided 360-degree thermal imaging, so their target would have been obliterated. At last, all three pilots agreed that they were picking up only a large body in the water in the immediate vicinity – visually confirmed as a whale. There were no other signs of life. And so they radioed back to base that the target had been neutralised, their mission was accomplished – requesting permission to return. It was soon granted, and the slick silver machines swung around, one after another, in perfect synchronisation. They readied themselves to punch through the clouds at over 1,000 miles an hour.

But then one of the pilots urgently called out to the others, shouting, 'Lance 1 to Lance leader, hold back! I repeat, hold back!!'

The leader pilot glanced through the port window at his companion. 'You better have good reason...'

'The whale!' came his reply. 'Just off my starboard wing. There's something on the back of the whale – can't you see?' He was answered only by the crackle of radio waves. 'Civvies! Lying on top of it. On the whale's back! Please confirm you can see them too...' The pilot was doubting his own eyes – doubting his sanity.

By now, the other pilots had made appropriate manoeuvres, swooping down as low as they dared to get a good visual. 'Roger that. Just moving in now to get eyes on...' And then after a few seconds: 'Affirmative! I repeat, that's an affirmative!! I can see four bodies on the whale's back,' came the leader's stunned reply, and then the third pilot added his confirmation.

The leader immediately radioed back to the controller a request for 'a dust-off casevac' – to which, shortly after, a reply was given that the navy were sending a helicopter with a doctor and a 'dope on a rope', to winch down and pick up the wounded.

•••————————————————•••

Back in Downing Street HQ, they all watched, silently dumbfounded, as the screen displayed the images from the stealth planes' cameras: three teenagers and an old man lying sprawled on the back of a whale... The Prime Minister was absent, and so Sanderson was calling him on a direct line. 'A-are you seeing this, Sir?' he asked, wide-eyed.

There was a delay, and at last the Prime Minister finally answered. 'I am. I'm seeing, Mr Sanderson, but not quite believing...'

•••————————————————•••

A dazed young man found himself waking up in a room he did not recognise. Around him medical machinery flashed and beeped quietly, an intravenous drip hanging loosely from his arm. He gasped, struggling to breathe; his chest felt as if it had been filled with sludge. And despite being cleaned up, he was still in a sorry state, with clipped brassy hair near-bald in patches, dark shadows under droopy grey eyes, skin so pale and translucent that blue veins were clearly visible in places. His thin limbs were reminiscent of concentration camp prisoners', bruised purple and green. He looked around with glazed eyes, woozy from a cocktail of drugs. An old man was sitting silently at his bedside, staring vacantly into space.

'W-water,' he gasped.

The Professor got up, wincing from his own bandages, and felt for the water bottle that had been left on the bedside cabinet, and held it out to him. But the boy was too weak even to lift it. Just at that moment, the nurse came rushing in, and immediately took the cup, holding the straw to the boy's lips. He sipped slow and long, eventually lying back and gasping for air.

The nurse beamed at the boy, happy to see him awake, before rushing off to fetch Dr Fargo.

The Professor waited until the rhythm of the boy's breathing returned to normal, before speaking. 'Hello, Alpha,' he said, warmly. 'Es ist so schön dich wiederzusehen. It's so, so good to see you again...'

'Professor,' breathed the young man, looking around, confused. 'Was ist passiert? Wo sind wir?' His German accent was mild yet clear – asking in a daze what had happened, where they were. The last he remembered was launching from the submarine in the escape pod.

The Professor sat forward and held out a hand. 'Bitte sei nicht beunruhigt,' he reassured him, telling him not to be alarmed. 'Amazingly, we survived despite the escape pod crashing. Tai and Milly came out in one piece as well, with only superficial wounds and small fractures.'

'A-and... the submarine?'

The Professor's face clouded over, and he shook his head. 'I-I'm afraid there weren't any survivors beside us.'

The boy took a moment to absorb this, his expression nondescript. 'No survivors at all?'

'None... Which is why I need to ask you some questions. Es ist sehr wichtig. Denkst du, du schaffst das?' He was telling him about the importance of the questions, and hoped he felt up to them.

The young man mustered a dazed smile. 'Ja, ich denke schon. I'm okay, I think.'

'Do you know if there were any other children on the submarine, beside you?'

The boy thought for a moment, his brow creasing. 'Nein, I didn't see any others. But then, I was kept locked up...'

'Of course, of course,' said the Professor, masking how troubled he was. Since he had returned, the Professor pondered on the possibility that there might have been other Project Ingenious children on the submarine, but it was the tragic truth that there would be no way of knowing now. There was also another reason for the Professor's troubled conscience. 'You've been unconscious for just over two days, and meanwhile we've been doing tests. And... I'm afraid the outlook isn't good.'

The boy looked at him. Registering the sadness in the old man's eyes. 'I already know,' he said. 'I've known for quite a while, Professor. That I'm dying. I've been living one day at a time... for a long time.'

'I'm so sorry,' said the Professor. 'Our... our doctors are doing everything they can as we speak.' He dared not give too much hope. 'But, this disease that you have, Alpha, it's completely new. Which means that it may take years, if they can help at all...'

'I understand... By the way, my name is Karl now. Karl König.'

Just then, Dr Fargo came rushing into the room. 'Ah, you're awake!' he said, beaming. 'I'm very pleased.' But then he noticed their gloomy expressions. 'Um, you should really be resting, recuperating – *both* of you. You've been through an extraordinary ordeal.'

The Professor nodded. 'He's right. Karl. Thank you for talking with me – and we will no doubt speak another time. It really is very good to have you here with us.' He smiled warmly, and got up. 'I'll leave you in Dr Fargo's capable hands. Thanks, Dan,' he told the doctor, before leaving. The Professor tapped his way out of the room, wincing both from the pain of what seemed like a hundred cuts and sprains all over his body, and the awful knowledge that the boy was dying.

He had so many more questions. But they would have to wait.

Walking along the corridor, he ran into Gaia.

'Ah, Harry, I'm glad I found you,' she said. 'I've done us all some hearty beef stifado – my yiayia's recipe, with plenty of red wine and cinnamon. Very good for the bones. I've taken the liberty of bringing yours to the den, so we can talk...'

The Professor blinked. He had forgotten what it was like to have someone fussing over him, and he realised he could do with some food. Since they had returned to Avernus the day before yesterday, he had barely eaten from anxiety. 'Thank you, Gaia,' he said, trying to sound light despite his fatigue. They walked along side by side. 'How is Axel today?'

Gaia sighed. 'Still up and down. He's terribly confused most of the time. There were a couple of moments when he went quiet, and I realised that he was back. He was my Xeli again – his mind returned. Though it was just for a short time. The last one lasted about 10 minutes or so. 10 wonderful minutes, where I could talk to him like old times!' She smiled, though her eyes were sad.

'A-are you sorry that we did the treatment? Did we do the right thing?'

Gaia stopped and said firmly, 'I'm not sorry at all, Harry. Absolutely not.'

'I just wondered... are we dangling the proverbial carrot in front of him, only to keep snatching it cruelly away? Is he tormented by... by losing his mind over and over again?'

They had entered the den, and Gaia helped the Professor settle into his chair, setting a small table of food at his side. She placed a napkin over his lap, and straightened. 'Well, when he comes back to us, he's rather stunned, so it's hard to gauge. But I don't think so. I don't think it's made him feel worse.' She sat down opposite him. 'The stew is on the table to your left, and at 2 o'clock there's a glass of wine.'

'Ah, just what the doctor ordered,' he smiled. She had intuited his needs perfectly. He felt for the glass and took a long sip – it was a warming mellow red.

Gaia watched quietly as he swapped the glass for the bowl, and began eating. She told him, 'You've said hardly a word since you returned, Harry. I-it must've been traumatic. But... is it true – that you'd been found on the back of a whale?!'

The Professor wiped his mouth with the napkin, and blinked, nodding. 'I can hardly believe it myself, Gaia,' he said. 'As we attempted to escape from the submarine, an explosion made us crash... and the next thing I knew, I was floating in ice-cold water, not knowing where I was, what to do. My one thought was that... well, I was going to die. And then I blacked out. Found myself waking up in a hospital bed. So I don't remember the whale at all. I can only imagine it had something to do with the rather remarkable young Tai, and his quite amazing affinity with animals!'

Gaia clasped her hands together. 'How wonderful – very hard to believe, but wonderful!' She paused. 'But you mentioned a submarine – what happened there?'

The Professor put down his spoon. Remembering that voice brought a shiver down his spine. 'Yes, someone talked to me on the submarine, a man. He had a strange voice that was like... like nothing I'd ever heard before. We talked. And I realised he was depraved, psychotic, unreasonable. He thought nothing of inflicting pain and suffering, and snuffing out human life at a whim. I-I think he's linked to Project Ingenious somehow, because he knew things about it.' The Professor stared into space for several seconds, the crease in his brow etched an expression of worry and fear. 'I'm ashamed to say that I'm glad that psychopath is dead. I know, it sounds extreme, and believe me I've had sleepless nights about the great, great cost to human life... But the world is a better place without him.' He waited for a reaction. 'Is that harsh of me?' He turned toward Gaia, hoping for what, he wasn't sure. Perhaps absolution.

Gaia said nothing for some time.

Her silence was agonising. Unconsciously, the Professor gripped the arms of his chair, fingernails digging into the deep plush of the velvet.

There was a faint hum of the aircon above them. The fire warm against his calf.

At last, Gaia said, 'You did what you had to do.'

'Yes. I suppose. I had to.'

It was perhaps as simple as that.

He paused. 'Except that... he told me the children were dying. From a disease that came from a genetic mutation of their DNA.' He looked down, overwhelmed.

'So all the children have this disease too?'

'Yes,' he said quietly. 'Milly's already starting to show symptoms, but Karl, being the first-born, is already quite far advanced...'

'That's awful!' gasped Gaia, covering her mouth with a hand.

'I have to tell the children somehow. Break it to them...' He closed his eyes momentarily, ruing the day that he was ever brought into this accursed Project Ingenious. The very experimental science that had made them so brilliant, was also killing them. The Professor was in torment.

'H-had I known, Gaia. Had I known that bringing them into this world would create so much suffering... I... I would have stopped the project. Immediately.'

There was a long silence, until Gaia said quietly, 'But then, they would not have been born.'

Her words made him remember the awful musings of that person on the submarine – and though he hated to admit it, he found, to his disgust, that he was beginning to understand that there might be an element of truth to them. That the value of life could be seen to be relative. Was it so, that some life could be deemed more worthy? That it was justifiable to sacrifice others' lives for theirs? The Professor had, by his actions, approved the destruction of all those souls on the submarine for what he thought was the greater good... Did that make him the same as the man on the submarine?

The thought of it made the Professor's heart race, his hands hot and clammy. It felt as if his conscience had been smashed with a sledgehammer – it throbbed now with pain, guilt, anxiety. '"The damned rest not day nor night",' he mumbled under his breath.

Gaia looked up at him. 'What was that?'

The Professor hadn't realised he had spoken out loud. He felt the blood drain from his face. 'I-I was quoting Nathanael Emmons,' he admitted weakly. 'He once wrote, "The damned rest not day nor night".' His cheeks plumed with heat. *He* was the damned.

His hands were so sweaty it felt like they were dripping. He wiped them nervously on the side of his trousers.

In his mind's eye, he looked down at them now, trembling. They were dripping with blood – bright red and viscous, between his fingers.

•••————————————————————————•••

Milly, like the Professor, had multiple gashes and cuts, as well as a couple of bruised ribs, held tight by a bandage around her torso – though no great physical harm had been done, considering what they had been through.

The first person that greeted her as she was trundled urgently out of the ambulance on a gurney was her father, Brian. His expression was the epitome of anxiety, and as she was rushed into the hospital A&E, he grasped her hand so tightly that it hurt almost as much as her bruises. He refused to leave her, standing back to watch in bewilderment as a mass of medics poured around his little girl, shouting urgently to each other – clamping an oxygen mask over her face, sliding needles into her flesh, connecting machines, taking blood.

He stood back, helpless – a bewildered hand combing through messy hair, struggling to hold back the tears.

She looked so fragile, so pitiful.

In time, the doctors and nurses left, and Milly was left to sleep – but still, her father dared not close his eyes, lest she vanish from before him as easily as she had disappeared two days ago. But in time he found himself waking to see that she was sitting up in bed and wolfing down some food. She glanced at him and smiled, before continuing to eat. And suddenly all was right with the world.

Tai on the other hand was still unconscious in the room next to Milly's. The doctor had declared a hairline fracture in his arm, bruised ribs, and cuts and gashes – nothing irreparable physically. Yet they could not understand why he wasn't waking up. Brain scans revealed nothing unusual, and all his tests came back negative. And so they could only wait and hope. The Professor organised for him to be transferred to Avernus, together with Milly and Karl, discharged to the care of Dr Fargo and his nurse. It was also much more secure now with the police patrolling the surrounding area, together with the invisible agents.

Dog had taken to waiting outside Tai's room, in the corridor. She wanted to go in, but the door kept closing shut behind a continuous stream of people entering and exiting. By the time the flurry of people had died down, several of the kittens had joined her in the corridor, play-fighting each other, or snoozing around her paws. At last, when it had quietened down, Dog jumped up and pressed on the handle, releasing the catch. She nudged the door open with her head, allowing the three kittens to pad inside. They looked around warily as they entered.

Instinctively, they crowded around the bed. Dog stood on her hind legs to survey what had happened to the boy, while the kittens sniffed the chair, then scrambled up onto the seat, one by one, finally jumping onto the bed. As they trundled past their mother, Dog licked one of them distractedly, in between whining for the boy. The grey kitten they had named Olly, began kneading the cotton cover that was draped over Tai's chest. Fat little Pasha sniffed Tai's hand and then licked it, and the third kitten, Max, nestled in the space between Tai's shoulder and neck, settling down to sleep.

Dog's constant whining merged with the whirring, beeping machinery surrounding them.

That evening, the door opened and Milly, Jemima, and Mei Hui, walked in to find Dog sleeping on the floor, and the kittens playing and jumping on the intravenous tubing. Quickly they ran over and grabbed a kitten each. 'Naughty babies. You can't be playing with the wires, you might pull them out!' scolded Milly. Thankfully the tubing was still intact. They drew up chairs around the bed, and with one hand Milly gently took Tai's, and with the other she held the kitten on her lap. 'So this is Tai,' said Milly to Jemima and Mei Hui, her eyes lined with worry. 'The doctor says there's nothing seriously wrong with him, but he's not sure why he's not waking up...'

'Don't worry, Milly,' said Jemima reassuringly. 'Whatever happened with the submarine – and that whale! – it obviously took a lot out of him, so he probably just needs to rest.'

Mei Hui nodded her agreement. 'It might be his body's way of recovering.'

Milly sighed. 'You're right.' She glanced at Tai's face – he looked so peaceful, so tranquil, as if he was just napping and could wake up at any moment. Then she thought of something. 'By the way, I was talking to the Professor the other day about Project Ingenious, and he told me that I was born in the third year. Tai and you, Mei Hui, were born in the fourth. And Jemima was born in the very last year, the fifth. So, Jemima, you were just a baby when we left the project. And Mei Hui, you and Tai were between a year and two years old. Toddlers. I was about three. And Karl,' she nodded over to the wall, 'he's the oldest of us all. He's 17, and was about 5 when we left.'

Jemima thought about this. 'I don't remember anything at all about it. Actually, tell a lie. One memory's coming back: being fed the bottle by one of the staff, and holding her finger as I drank, watching her face. Funny the things you remember, isn't it? How about you, Mei? Do you remember anything?'

Mei Hui thought about it. 'No memories like that – just some images like white walls, shiny objects, other children running around. Not much really.'

'Hmm, what about you Mills?' asked Jemima.

Milly stroked Olly on her lap. 'A bit like Mei, nothing outstanding. But I do remember pictures – lots of pictures, like snapshots.' Milly's eyes glazed over, as if she were seeing images right in front of her. 'I also remember them putting us through loads of tests. With picture cards, word cards, numbers. And now I think about it, we had to listen to music, and watch videos. It seemed to go on forever.'

Mei Hui chimed in suddenly – 'Actually, I remember something... the dark. I do not know why, but I really hated the dark.'

Milly nodded profusely. 'Yes! I remember too. It's because they turned off the lights at bedtime, with no night lights, nothing. Just pitch black. I used to lie in bed, terrified. They'd put those glowing stars on the walls and ceiling – so I fixated on them, until I fell asleep. We were left alone in our rooms quite often from what I remember...'

'Ah, that explains a lot!' said Jemima. 'I've always hated the dark, and even now I have to leave a night light on, even if it's just the screensaver on my laptop.'

'And do you remember *him*?' asked Mei Hui, glancing at the far wall.

'Karl?' said Milly. 'Sort of. I saw him around, but we never really had anything to do with each other. Maybe... we should go say hi.'

Mei Hui and Jemima looked at each other, and Jemima shrugged.

'Yeah, sure.'

But Mei Hui asked, 'Are you feeling alright, Milly? You look tired.'

It was true, she was very pale. 'I'm okay. Dr Fargo's increased my dose of painkillers, so I'm good for now. Really.'

'If you're sure then,' said Jemima.

They all got up, and Milly gently squeezed Tai's hand before they left.

They bundled out and across to the next room. Oddly, there was a discarded slipper just outside his door, and Mei Hui picked it up. Karl was sitting up in bed, staring blankly ahead, like he was just about to fall asleep.

'Hello,' Mei Hui called out to him. 'Is this yours?' But he did not respond.

Jemima stepped into the room. 'Hey!' she shouted. Pasha, who was cradled against Jemima's chest, suddenly yowled and scrambled out, falling to the floor and then disappearing out of the door in a flash. Olly and Max followed suit. 'Ow!!' yelled Jemima, rubbing the scratches on her arm.

Karl blinked and looked at the visitors. 'Wh-who are you?' he said, wheezing.

Milly stepped out from behind. 'Hi again,' she said. 'Sorry about the kittens. Not sure why they ran off like that, they're usually chill... Anyway, how are you?'

'It's you!' said Karl. 'I-I'm okay. It's good to see you!'

Milly introduced herself properly, as well as the girls, explaining that they were all from the project too. Karl stared at them as if he were dreaming. 'Meine Güte! Is it true? All of you?'

'Yes!' smiled Jemima.

Karl beamed. 'Komm rein. Please come in. My name is Karl – Karl König. I'm really, really pleased to meet you.'

Just then the nurse came into the room. 'I'm sorry girls, but our patient's been given strict orders by Dr Fargo to rest. So no visitors allowed until tomorrow, okay?'

'Oh, okay. Sure,' said Jemima.

The three waved goodbye before disappearing.

The nurse turned toward the boy and winked. 'You're a popular young man today, aren't you?'

Karl stared at her without saying a word.

Calista could hardly believe it. To have both the Professor and Jake returned, as if nothing had happened, seemed too good to be true. She kept pinching herself, even as she sat next to her boyfriend.

Jake saw that she was staring at him, and frowned. 'Cal! I'm trying to concentrate here.'

'I'm not doing anything.'

'You're staring.'

Calista thought about this. 'But I'm not *doing* anything!'

Jake sighed, stopped typing, and turned to face her. 'I know you're not doing anything per se, but it's hard to concentrate with you sitting there staring at me non-stop. Don't get me wrong – I love being around you. But it's distracting.'

Calista beamed, fixating on the 'loving her' part.

'Haven't you got stuff to do?' he asked, raising his eyebrows expectantly. 'Are the others okay? Does the Prof need anything?'

'Well... I kept bringing everyone pot noodles, cups of tea, and chocolate digestives,' she said. 'But... they've asked me to stop.'

Jake couldn't help but grin. 'My girlfriend's turned into Hyper Caring Godzilla!' He stopped to really look at her now. She was beautiful, despite the biscuit crumbs on her lips. He gently wiped them off, and couldn't help leaning in to kiss them – a long, smooth kiss.

When they separated, Calista smiled dreamily.

'You see how distracting you are!' Jake got up and grabbed his empty mug. 'I'm going to get a refill–'

'I'll get it!'

'No. Thanks. I also need a toilet break, and to clear my head.' Jake stopped just before he left, half expecting another interjection, but Calista remained silent. And he turned to leave.

When Jake walked into the kitchen, the Professor was just finishing talking to the Chauffeur, and so Jake went about making his coffee quietly.

'Brian, is that you?' asked the Professor when the Chauffeur left.

Jake looked up just as he was getting the milk from the fridge. 'No, it's me, Jake,' he said. And then he thought for a moment. 'Actually, have you got a minute, Prof? I'd like to talk with you.'

The Professor drew closer. 'Yes of course.' He felt for the table and chair, and sat down.

'D'you want a coffee?' Jake offered.

'Thanks, but no. Calista has, um, well she's been fussing a lot, and I think I've had enough tea and coffee to last a lifetime!'

Jake laughed. 'That sounds about right!' He drew up a chair and sat opposite the old man, clinking his mug down on the table. 'My sister, Kara,' he said eventually. He stopped to compose his thoughts. 'She's been missing for nearly 12 years... I know we've already talked about it – but please, Professor. Please think hard. Are you sure you don't remember her from the project?' He was still eaten up by her disappearance. 'She was 20 years old at the time, and had short curly black hair,' he ventured. 'Blue eyes. Slim. About five foot five.' And then he remembered something. 'She always wore a necklace – a sapphire on a silver chain. I'm sure she must've stood out.'

'I've already thought about it. A lot,' said the Professor, his voice softening. 'I really, really wish I could tell you something, Jake. But you see, the project lasted five years, and during that time there must have been hundreds of women passing through for one reason or another. Added to that, the powers that be put us under immense pressure to produce as many babies as possible, so much so that, well, every day we were in a kind of distracted frenzy from the stress of it all. There were records – but... the fire at the end of the project destroyed them all. In those days there was no cloud storage, and, for security, we couldn't make off-site backups, couldn't even take data CDs out of the buildings. So I'm afraid there's no way of finding out.' The Professor paused for a moment. 'I'm sorry to say, but after all this time...'

'I know,' Jake said, curt. He had heard the same thing from his parents over and over again. *They* had come to terms with the likelihood that she was dead, and so should he. 'But I just can't,' he said at last – a hint of the years of torment flickering on his face. 'Until we find a body, until we know for sure – I just can't give up... I *won't* give up.'

They sat in silence for some time.

The Professor spoke up at last. 'I understand,' he said. 'Really. If it were my family, I'd probably do the same... And I don't blame you for searching. I gather from Calista that you're tweaking her program, to use it to look for your sister.'

'Yes – first I'm coding a program to simulate her appearance to what she might look like now, working from family photos.'

'Okay,' nodded the Professor. 'Good.'

Jake heaved a sigh, and reached for his cup. 'Well, I'd better get back to work.'

As the Professor listened to Jake's footsteps fade, he felt numb again, staring blankly into the distance.

••• ———————————————————————— •••

The next morning Milly and Mei Hui visited Karl with breakfast they had made themselves – scrambled eggs on toast, beans, and orange juice. The nurse was just finishing inputting his vitals on her tablet. 'Come on in girls!' she smiled. She looked over the tray they were holding. 'Ooh, that looks delicious. I'm sure it'll be appreciated,' she said as she left.

Karl struggled to sit up in bed, panting from the effort. He caught his breath. 'What is this?' he asked sleepily, rubbing his eyes.

'We made you breakfast,' said Mei Hui.

Karl looked over the tray with appreciation. 'This... this is amazing. Thank you!'

Mei Hui looked at the boy with equanimity. 'It is good to see you, Karl. You seem better.'

'I slept quite well, which helps...' He picked up the fork and stabbed some beans.

The girls sat down next to each other.

'You... you must've been through such an ordeal,' said Milly. 'Taken hostage and everything.'

Karl stopped. 'I did. It was awful. Terrifying.' He closed his eyes momentarily, as if trying to block it out.

'You... you don't have to talk about it,' said Milly, worried. She quickly changed subject. 'What about your family? I'm sure you've been in contact to tell them you survived. Are they okay?'

The boy put down his fork and stared at the plate. 'My parents... they died two years ago. Both of them. In a car crash.'

'Oh no!' said Milly. 'That's awful! You must've been devastated.'

Karl's hand dropped, sadness in his eyes. 'Yes, I was. Words can't describe how you feel after losing the people you love most in the world. They were everything to me. I still haven't gotten over it... They were the best parents. Kind, loving, caring. No matter how busy they were, they always made time for me. Always. And my father... he gave me something very precious, very special – a little golden pocket-watch.' Karl motioned toward his bedside cabinet. 'Would you believe, it didn't fall out of my pocket in the sea. It's not valuable, but I will treasure it until the day I die. You see, us Germans are strict timekeepers. You could say we're pathologically punctual. And he and I were very much so. I really miss them!'

'I'm sorry,' said Milly, becoming upset herself. 'I... I lost my mother too. It was quite a few years ago. She knitted me a hat just before she died, but, unfortunately, it's gone. Lost forever...' She was heartbroken. 'After the explosion, I must've lost it in the water. So I understand. I really do...'

They remained quiet for a while, as if paying homage to their parents.

Mei Hui thought of something. 'Then, after your parents died, did you stay with relatives? They must be worried about you.'

'I was cared for by guardians after... after the crash. But... I don't really want to talk about them.'

Milly felt hugely sympathetic. 'Well, if you ever want to talk, we're here for you,' she offered. 'It's one of the reasons why I'm glad we've found each other. We don't have to go through anything alone anymore.'

'Thank you,' said Karl, wheezing. 'That means a lot.' He stopped to take some deep breaths. 'By the way, I've been meaning to ask – where are we? What is this place? Why are there no windows?'

Milly went on to tell Karl about Avernus – but then, to put that in context, she also had to explain about Professor Wolff, and how he had found both her and Tai. One thing led to another, and they went on to tell him their own stories, as well as Jemima's. Milly also explained how Calista and Jake had come into the picture, describing how Calista had built Jasmine, the super-computer that controls all Avernus' automated tasks. And finally, she explained about Dr Kendra and his wife Gaia.

Karl listened, and at the end, he sat up. 'Dr Kendra is here as well?'

Milly nodded. 'Although he's suffering from Alzheimer's – has been for years now.'

On hearing this, Karl slumped back against his pillow.

'You are tired?' asked Mei Hui.

'Yes,' said Karl wearily. He reached for the oxygen mask by his side, and gulped in air.

'Then we will leave you to rest,' Mei Hui retorted, looking at Milly.

'Yes, of course. You still look quite weak – you need to rest,' Milly echoed. And they both got up.

'I'm sorry,' said Karl, his voice hollow behind the mask. He looked from the girls to the tray of food, and pushed it away. 'I'm not very hungry.'

'Oh, no problem,' Milly said. She picked up the tray.

Mei Hui glanced toward the doorway, 'I am sure the dogs won't let it go to waste.'

They followed her gaze to find Acuzio sitting just outside in the corridor, looking into the room. Milly offered him a sausage, but unusually the dog refused to come in. Turning to Karl, she frowned. 'I don't think he's great with strangers... Well, we'll leave you then,' she said.

'Yes, thanks. See you later,' said Karl.

As they passed Acuzio, the tray clattering in Milly's arms, they realised that he was growling.

The girls looked at each other, and Milly shrugged it off. But Mei Hui did not dismiss it so lightly.

•••————————————————•••

Gaia must have watched her husband pack and unpack his suitcase a hundred times, that dull look still in his eyes. She sighed wearily.

But then Dr Kendra stopped, and looked up from the suitcase opened flat on the bed. 'It's gone!' he exclaimed, panicked. He started searching around his room, frantic, mumbling to himself, 'The train tickets, they should be here, I put them in the lining pocket, specially, tucked away, but they're gone, someone must have stolen them. A thief!'

He caught his reflection in the mirror, and narrowed suspicious eyes.

Gaia got up, frowning and shaking her head.

The old man harrumphed and threw everything out of the suitcase on the floor, scrambling through it all.

'Oh, Xeli, the mess! And what on earth are you talking about?!' she said, exasperated. She stood over him, hands on hips. 'What train tickets?'

Dr Kendra turned the empty suitcase upside down, and bashed it with his hand, checking underneath. He straightened, scratched his head, and continued searching. 'The tickets! They're missing I tell you. And we have to leave tonight!!' He was in a frenzy, which in turn was upsetting Gaia. He started throwing things around the room in anger, and she darted to the door, dodging projectiles as she went. She cried out, 'Nurse! Nurse!'

The sound of footsteps were already coming from outside, and the door opened, just as Gaia had reached it. Dr Fargo burst in, followed shortly by the Professor.

Gaia gasped. 'Thank goodness!' she said, eyes pleading. 'He's going berserk looking for... for train tickets. I don't understand why he's getting so mad!'

Dr Fargo narrowly dodged a flying book, and he rushed toward Dr Kendra, grappling with him and pushing him firmly onto the bed. At last the old man submitted. He curled into a ball and grabbed a corner of the bedsheet, sobbing into it. 'I'm sorry,' he cried. 'So sorry...' He blew his nose into the sheet.

Dr Fargo stepped back, heaving a sigh of relief. He pulled his lab coat straight, and went to look at the tablet PC left at the end of the bed. 'I couldn't find the nurse today, and she's not answering her phone,' he said as he looked through the notes – and then he frowned. 'And it seems she didn't give him his afternoon medication. Which would explain the outburst.' Quickly, he went over to the medicine cabinet, unlocked it, and extracted a phial of bright yellow liquid and a syringe. He strode over to Dr Kendra, and before he could protest, Fargo pulled up his sleeve and sunk the needle into his upper arm.

'Oww!' cried Dr Kendra, glaring at his offender.

Dr Fargo smiled apologetically at him. 'I'm sorry if that hurt a little.' He rolled down the man's sleeve gently.

'Oww!' Dr Kendra cried again.

Dr Fargo stepped back. 'But I barely touched you...'

'Oww, oww!!!'

The Professor, who had been standing by Gaia, drew nearer. 'Don't worry, Dan. I can take it from here.'

Exasperated, the doctor looked from his patient to the Professor, and nodded. 'Okay, he probably just needs some rest while the medication takes effect.' He went to throw away the syringe and phial in the pedal bin, then headed to the door. 'It'll kick in very soon, which should calm him. But call me if you need anything,' he said, as he opened the door.

'I will,' the Professor assured him.

Gaia started picking things up and putting them back into the suitcase, but her husband protested. 'No, no, no! Stop it. You're doing it all wrong, woman. All wrong!!'

But she was near tears, and the Professor sensed that she was upset.

'Gaia...' he said gently.

When she heard the warm concern in the Professor's voice, she broke down, sobbing, 'I'm sorry. It's been a bad day. I... I just need a break.' She pulled a tissue from her sleeve and wiped her eyes.

'Yes of course,' said the Professor. 'I'll stay with him. Go. Take as long as you need.'

Gaia nodded, sniffing. 'Thank you, Harry. I-I'll be okay, just need a breather...' She picked up her things, mumbled about going to her room, and then left in a fluster.

The Professor sat down on the bed next to his old friend, and listened for some time to the squeak of bedsprings, the soft rustle of sheets, and Dr Kendra's continual ramblings.

The Professor soon became lost in his own thoughts, losing track of time.

And then he realised that it was completely quiet.

There came a whimper.

A sniffle.

Springs creaking, as Dr Kendra sat up on his bed, drawing his legs in, and hugging them.

'Axel?' said the Professor.

Dr Kendra looked across at him, as if only just realising he was there. 'H-Harry,' he replied, surprised. 'Is... is that you?' His voice was different – measured and calm.

The Professor shifted round, realising that his friend had returned. 'Yes, Axel,' he said, melting. 'It's me.'

Dr Kendra stared at him. 'You... you look so old.'

The Professor smiled. 'We've both aged quite a bit, Axel,' he said softly. 'But it's okay. We're okay.' He reached a tentative hand. 'And you... how are you feeling?'

Dr Kendra looked wearily at his hand, then the floor, as if he had just awoken from a long night of bad dreams. 'Tired, and... confused.'

'You don't need to worry, Axel. Everything's going to be fine. We're looking after you.'

Dr Kendra looked at him oddly. 'Why are you saying that?'

'No reason,' said the Professor quickly. 'Just letting you know.'

Dr Kendra looked down, trying to make sense of everything. 'I... I feel as if I've been away. For a while.'

The Professor thought about this. 'Yes, you have. But we're together now.'

Dr Kendra thought for a moment. 'And the children? Are they safe, are they well?'

The Professor remembered. 'I... I've been meaning to ask you, Axel. About the children. You knew the identities and whereabouts of my children, didn't you? All along...'

Dr Kendra's head dropped. 'I'm s-sorry, Harry,' he said. 'I was... weak. The children, they mean everything to me. Like they're *my* children. I couldn't bear not knowing where they went. Couldn't bear leaving them. In the end, I... I had them followed. I just wanted to make sure they were safe.' The doctor hung his head and sighed. 'Do you... do you hate me?'

The Professor shook his head. 'No. I don't.'

Dr Kendra started to look agitated. 'B-but the night we left the project, I had a heart attack.'

'Oh, Axel! That must've been awful.'

Dr Kendra fingered the corner of the bedsheet, puzzled as to why it was damp. 'Yes, it was. It was a mild one, but still, it was frightening. Took me a while to recover.'

The Professor listened to the sound of his friend's voice, wondering at those precious minutes of clarity. How long would it last? 'We've been through a lot together, Axel. The project. The escape...'

Dr Kendra started mumbling just under his breath, though the Professor barely noticed as he continued, '...But, we still don't know where two of the children are. Two of *your* children. And we need to bring them into safety, because–'

'The tickets,' said Dr Kendra, as if remembering for the first time.

The Professor stopped. 'What tickets?'

'The train tickets!' he said, eyes darting around the room. 'I have to find them. Oh no! No, no, no... Where are they?!'

The Professor sighed. 'Axel?'

'Must find them!!'

'Axel.'

'Where could they be?! I had them, they were here just yesterday!'

But it was no use.

The Professor closed his eyes, listening to the man as he ranted. Despairing at how fleeting their time together had been. And he kicked himself for the missed opportunity.

•••———————————————————•••

Avernus was usually a place of calm and tranquillity, and so when a cacophony of barking erupted, everyone heard.

It was coming from Tai's hospital room.

Running, Dr Fargo arrived first to find Dog standing up on her hind legs, scraping at the bed covers, tail whipping the air in a frenzy.

Next came Brian, panting. 'What on earth's going on?' he breathed.

Dr Fargo turned to him, smiling. 'Looks like our young man has come round!'

Brian drew closer. 'Fantastic!'

Tai had managed to push himself up, and was lying against the pillows, dazed. The doctor drew closer. 'Tai, we're so pleased you're back with us! You've been unconscious for three days now. How are you feeling?'

Tai looked at him through droopy eyes. 'M-my arm hurts,' he said, looking down at his bandaged elbow.

'You've got a hairline fracture, but nothing serious,' said Dr Fargo. 'Should be right as rain before too long.'

Tai shivered. 'I'm c-cold.'

'Actually, I've been feeling cold too,' Brian remarked. He took the blanket lying at the end of the bed, and draped it around Tai's shoulders. 'I was wondering if the heating or the thermostat had broken... I'll look into that.'

'Hmm,' said Dr Fargo. 'I'll give you a quick check-up, just in case.' He took several minutes going through the motions of checking Tai's pupil dilation, breathing pattern, and sensory systems. When he was satisfied, he clicked his pen, and popped it into his lab coat pocket. 'Well, so far so good. We'll get some bloodwork done for routine tests, though I don't think there's anything to worry about,' he said.

When Brian heard bloodwork mentioned, he went over to the storage cabinets, picked out several items, and returned with a small metal tray filled with medical supplies.

'Ah, thank you, Brian,' said Dr Fargo.

'Still no sign of the nurse?'

Dr Fargo stopped, and went quite pale. 'I... I'm sorry, I forgot to tell you. This is hard to believe, but I got a call from her mother a few hours ago. Shauna collapsed in the street yesterday – suddenly, and for no apparent reason. She was rushed to hospital, but... it was too late. She died.'

Brian looked at him with disbelief. 'Oh no, that's awful!' he said. 'But I saw her yesterday, she was as cheery as ever, and looked fit as a fiddle. Do they know what happened?'

The doctor shook his head. 'Not yet. But I'm sure they're going to do a post-mortem. It's tragic – really, tragic.'

Brian sighed. 'I'm so sorry... Well, I'm willing to help out, as you know. Whatever you need.'

'Thanks. I've already called a friend who does locum nursing, and at least she'll be able to fill in. But until then, I appreciate your help. You're a fast learner!'

Just then, Milly appeared – and when she saw that Tai was conscious, she ran over and threw herself onto him. 'Tai, thank goodness you're alright!' she said.

The boy winced from the hug.

'Oops, sorry,' said Milly sheepishly, separating. 'A-are you okay?'

He cleared his throat and smiled at her weakly. 'Think so.'

Milly looked from the doctor, back to him. 'You must be hungry? Thirsty? What can I get you?'

'Actually,' said Tai, his voice raspy, 'I wouldn't mind one of Calista's pot noodles.'

Milly smiled, 'Oh she'll be rapt! In fact, she's learnt how to make ramen now, with the Chauffeur's help.' She then spoke out loud into the air. 'Jasmine. Can you please tell Calista that Tai's awake, and wants her to deliver a number 46.' It was a standing joke between the girls, a code for Calista's signature soup noodle.

Jasmine replied in her usual dulcet tones. 'Your message has been delivered.'

Seconds later they heard a faraway scream, and then someone running down the corridor. Calista burst into the room, looked at Tai in the bed, and then ran over and threw herself onto him. Tai winced again, but Calista paid no heed. She was just glad he was okay.

•••———————————————•••

As the Professor continued throughout the day, the cuts and bumps on his body throbbed persistently, to distraction, as if his conscience were physically prodding him. In the end, he could bear it no longer.

That evening, after dinner, he stood up and requested everyone's attention. He was clearly anxious. 'By now, most of you have met or know about Karl König – the young man in the room next to Tai's. He's in quite a bad shape... because... because... he's ill. Very ill.' He paused, suddenly looking exhausted. 'Dr Fargo and I have run various medical tests, but the outlook is not good. From what we can tell, his health will only decline even more, until... the worst. We're not sure how long he has. It could be months or years. Maybe even just weeks. Nobody knows.'

Everyone gasped, and looked at each other.

'But that's not all,' said the Professor quickly. He braced himself, feeling nauseous. The admission, that his life's work was crumbling after years of toil, was hard to accept, let alone speak out loud. And the toll. The toll on their health, their lives, was just too unbearable for words. But he had to tell them. 'It appears Karl has a disease – one that came about from the genetic manipulation of his DNA. Which means that, in all likelihood, everyone born to the project has it too.'

The ensuing silence was deafening.

Finally someone choked, another shuffled awkwardly, a chair creaked.

Mei Hui was the first to speak, though even her usual equanimity was clearly cracking. 'W-will the disease develop quickly?'

The Professor stiffened; he realised there was no way to sugar-coat this, especially with these teenagers. 'We don't know for sure at this stage. It might take years... But it won't develop as fast as the Oxford students...'

'Wait,' said Milly. 'What have they got to do with this?...'

'It seems,' said the Professor, his voice quivering, 'that they were given the same disease, likely taken from Karl – somehow made more potent, made to progress much faster. I was told by the man on the submarine that infecting the students was a way – a very sick way – of seeing whether our own scientists could contribute indirectly to the cure he'd been working on. You see, I think the man may be the original person behind the project – and this could be his way of salvaging his... investment, and continuing it. I-I don't know for sure, but I'm guessing that's the case...' he said, trailing off.

'All those poor students...' gasped Calista, 'they all died didn't they?'

'Yes, they did,' he said softly.

They all took a while to absorb this horrible news.

'So there's no cure?' asked Brian, gulping, looking at his daughter sitting next to him.

'That's the thing. Our scientists are working on something as we speak – but it's a totally new disease, so it'll take some time to complete–'

Impatient, Brian interrupted. 'How long?'

The Professor sighed. 'We don't know. But... the person I spoke to on the submarine told me that *they* had made progress toward developing a cure. And they were nearly there, so at least we know a cure is possible.'

'But the sub was destroyed, and the man killed,' said Brian. 'Or is there another way of getting the formula, or whatever it's called?'

'No way that we know of...'

After a pause, a tremulous voice spoke up from the back.

'So... if it's not made in time, we could die.'

Everyone turned round to find Jemima, sitting by herself, her blue eyes brimming with tears. She seemed so small, like an injured bird. Mei Hui moved across to her, and they hugged.

The Professor was unable to answer.

•••————————————————————————•••

Later that evening, the Professor tapped his way quietly to his room, completely spent, and needing solitude. But as he passed Karl König's door, he heard a weak voice call out to him. 'Professor, sind Sie da?'

The old man stopped, and entered his room. 'Ja, ich bin es. It's me. A- are you okay? Do you need anything?'

There was a pause, the sound of laboured wheezing. 'I'm... the same. And no, I don't need anything, thanks. But you look tired, Professor. A- are you alright?'

The old man sighed. No, he wasn't. He felt ill, felt like he'd just pronounced a death sentence. 'Not really, Karl. I... I just told the children about the disease – and that they might have it too. They were devastated as you can imagine. So, it's been a difficult evening.' He thought of something and drew closer. 'I need to ask you, Karl. When I was on the submarine, the person that spoke to me said they were very close to finalising a cure. Do you... know anything about it? Did you see anything they were working on?'

Karl thought about it. 'No, I didn't. But I don't remember much. They drugged me, kept me locked up. I was not very... zurechnungsfähig. Wasn't very clear-headed.'

'I understand,' said the Professor, his voice softening. 'I'm sorry to have to bring it up. It must have been an awful ordeal'

'Y-yes, it was.'

'Do you think that, in time, you might be able to talk about it?'

There was a short silence, before he stuttered, 'Mmm-maybe.'

The Professor blinked. Could not understand why his heart skipped a beat. Something nagged him, but perhaps it was just fatigue. 'Well, if you're sure you don't need anything further, Karl, I'll leave you to rest. Are you managing to sleep at least?'

'Not really,' said Karl, breathless. 'I get snatches here and there. But it's always been like that. I've learnt to live on little Nickerchen. Little cat naps.'

The Professor remembered from the project that sleep had always been difficult for the boy, since babyhood. 'If you want, I can get you something to help you sleep, Karl. It may give you some vivid dreams, but at least you'll have a good night's rest.'

'Thanks, but no,' said Karl. 'I'm okay.'

'Well, if you change your mind, let me know.' The Professor got up. 'Gute nacht.'

'Gute nacht, Professor.'

The old man tapped his way to his room in silent contemplation. Inside, he stopped for a few seconds to breathe in the warming familiarity of it. But it was silent, too silent. And so he moved across to a chest of drawers, where there was an antique marble clock. He felt around the back of it for the key, slipped it out, then opened the hinged glass window housing the clock face. He slid his fingers over the etched dial, careful not to displace the delicate steel serpentine hands, and found a keyhole just at the side of the IV numerals. Inserting the key, he wound it slowly so that the mainspring coil tightened, after which he lifted its padded foot, tilting it, to set the pendulum in motion. The mechanism whirred to life, and the Professor listened quietly to the warm, solid sound, as if the antique were echoing the ancientness of time itself.

Tick-tock, tick-tock.

The Professor turned to flick off his shoes, got on the bed, and lay back. He closed his eyes – honing into that staccato rhythm, allowing the soporific sound to wash right through him.

Tick-tock, tick-tock, tick-tock.

Dreams slipped over the old man like the gentle lapping of waves. They seeped into him, and drenched his thoughts – a strange miscellany of fragmented and recent memories, let loose from the constraints of normality, churning around and around in a watery mass. Soon, his imaginings ran wilder, grew stronger, more vivid and frightening, and before long he was tossing and turning in a cold, frantic sweat. Lost and helpless to the savage whims of his mind.

He was floating now, deep under sea. The canvas white.

Gliding past him came a dark ominous behemoth – it brushed his hand, its skin rough as sandpaper yet warm against the icy coldness of the sea. A barrage of other objects slid by, like a litany of awful prayers floating upwards: burnt wreckage, sharks, seaweed glistening in pops of light, fish, corals, limp cadavers. Rejected by even God himself, they floated by him in an aimless limbo, bashing him, dragging him, cutting him.

His lungs were bursting, black eyes popping.

At last he expired.

*At last!*

His body floating away in an agonisingly slow cartwheel, gently disappearing into the murky depths. Never to be seen again.

All that was left was a voice.

It was a voice that rumbled like thunder.

How could that be?

Who was it?!

*Me?* came the voice, hollow and as bloodcurdlingly chilling as the first time he'd heard it. *Who am I?*

In between the words came a throaty rasping, a struggle for breath. Wheezing.

Then came the Professor's own tremulous voice. Don't you care? Don't you care that they're suffering horribly, dying the worst death?

Silence, and then a stuttered response. *Mmm-maybe.*

Tick-tock, tick-tock, tick-tock.

The Professor woke with a start, and he lay still for several hazy seconds, before realising it was a dream – a horrible dream. His pillow was damp, and he wiped the sweat from his brow with a sleeve. Agitated to the extreme, he knew that he wouldn't be able to get back to sleep straight away. A shaky hand flipped his watch open, feeling for the time. It was 4.26 am. His mouth was bone dry, and so he swung his legs out of bed, felt for his slippers, and shuffled out of the room – to get some water. He silently made his way through the dark corridors, nerves still frayed from the nightmare. His form dissolving into the blackness like a shadow.

As he passed an open door, he heard a sound, and stopped to listen. It was the hushed tones of someone whispering.

'Wh-who's there?' called out the Professor feebly.

Silence.

Against his every inclination, he shuffled sideways, closer to the source. He bumped into a trolley with a discarded plate left on it, and his hand felt cutlery, a knife, and he grabbed it.

He stood still, ears straining.

And then he heard it. The voice of the man of the submarine.

He froze. Panicked.

Was he going mad?! Was he still dreaming?

And the Professor started shaking uncontrollably. 'Wh-who are you?' he said, louder.

Nothing.

'Who are you?!'

Inching forward, his legs bumped against something.

There came a soft shuffling right in front of him, the light rustle of bedsheets.

Terrified, the Professor felt his arm rising of its own accord, the knife gripped firmly in his hand. The beat of his heart, like a chant, urged him to plunge the blade into the lying figure in front of him. His entire body shook – but he could not do it. And his arm dropped down, knife clanging on the floor.

And then came Karl König's sleepy voice. From the bed, right in front of him. 'Professor?' he murmured. 'Was ist es, stimmt was nicht?'

Quickly, the old man turned and felt his way back out of the room, closing the door behind him. He leant firmly against it. 'Jasmine,' he hissed into the air. 'Lock this door! And don't let anyone override.'

He heard the bolts click into place, and the Professor felt his legs buckling beneath him, as he slumped to the ground.

## 28   A DEATH BELL TOLLS

The Professor sat very still in his chair, eyes closed, listening with absolute concentration to the night. The beep of hospital machinery, the light snoring from the bed next to him, a pulse funnelling through his ears. And then there was a snort, rustling sheets – and quiet. The Professor held his breath.

'Professor?' came Karl's sleepy voice, and the old man stiffened. He did not reply, he merely waited, biding his time.

'Professor,' said Karl again, louder. 'I dreamt that you came, in the middle of the night. But...' There was a jangling of chains. 'Why are my hands tied?'

The old man breathed deeply. 'I... I heard you talking in your sleep, Karl.'

Silence.

'What... what did I say?' he asked, without a hint of emotion – his voice perfectly controlled.

'Many things. And somehow your voice had altered... changed. It was the same voice of the man I spoke to on the submarine...' There was a pause. 'It was *you* speaking to me on the submarine, wasn't it? You were the person who infected the Oxford students.'

The boy struggled to sit upright – the sound of metal on metal, clinking and sliding – handcuffs straining against the siderail.

The Professor moved back, wary.

'Bitte, Herr Professor,' said Karl, wheezing. 'You're not making much sense. How can I have done that terrible thing? I... I can barely breathe, can hardly move...'

'I don't know,' replied the Professor, confused, momentarily doubting himself.

'You're not making much sense. If... if I talk in my sleep reciting... Hitler's Reichstag speech – does that make me him?'

'No...' The Professor shook his head, shaking away his doubt. 'I-it *was* you. I know it was you,' he said, adamant. 'I've been sitting here, listening to you talk in your sleep. With that same voice. You... you tried to kill the children. And on the submarine, you performed horrible, torturous experiments on animals, and even yourself. You infected the Oxford students with the disease in you.' The old man paused. 'I heard it. Your own voice betrayed you...'

The boy breathed a long sigh, like an adult tired of the nonsensical ramblings of a child. He shuffled awkwardly. 'Are you really accusing me? What if... if I'd talked about something else... about infecting people with the cancer, right here, in this place you call Avernus. What if I'd talked about slipping something into the drinking water. That could just be a fantastic dream, couldn't it? Or then again, it might not.'

The Professor blinked, alarmed at the suggestion. The boy was surely playing mind games. He had to keep his nerve. 'W-why would you say that?' No, he would not be sucked in by this nonsense as he had been on the submarine. 'No!!' he shouted. 'Enough of your games. You mentioned things as you slept, Karl – facts and details that only the perpetrator could have known. It was you.'

There was a long silence before Karl finally responded, his small pathetic voice hardening to smooth coldness. 'Ah, are you sure about that? Let's imagine that you're right. That you've discovered me, Professor. Discovered that I have an alter ego. A mental illness. Realistically, could I be held accountable for my crimes?' There was absurdity in his tone. 'Perhaps I have a dissociative identity disorder? Or a multiple personality disorder? The forensic psychologists would have a field day...'

'And they would know if it's all a pretence!' said the Professor, unconvinced.

'But how could they know, for sure? I might have had a tortured childhood. I might be a lost soul. A lost cause, even. What if I'd suffered years of abuse as a child? Or, I was simply misunderstood?' Karl paused. 'You know, it's extremely tiring being the most intelligent person in the world, Professor. How is that expression... ah yes, I can "run rings" around the best intellectuals, the highest academics, literati, scholars. In my sleep. Do you know that with every question posed, my mind buzzes with a hundred thoughts and possibilities and scenarios. It's... exhausting. I may be just 17, but my brain feels like it's a thousand times older.'

'Do you expect me to feel sorry for you?' asked the Professor, indignant.

'Shouldn't you?' he replied. 'After all, you made me like this.'

He could not respond to that. Instead, he changed tack. 'Those seven students,' he said. 'Why did you have to kill them? They did nothing to you.'

There was a silence for some time, and then Karl lay back, weary. Everything made him tired, even the pretence. At last, he gave in from exhaustion – though it was still a calculated decision, like a manoeuvre in a game of chess. 'What did you expect me to do, Professor?' said Karl quietly. 'I'm dying. Should I just sit around and wait for death to take me? My intellect won't allow me to do that. I have the ability to make the cure myself – and I have. Almost. After the animal trials, I now need human subjects to test it on. Ones with my same genetic make-up. That's all.'

'Human subjects?' repeated the Professor, and then he realised. 'The children.'

'Yes, the children,' Karl repeated. 'They would make perfect lab rats.'

The Professor was indignant. 'What makes you think you have the right to... to just do what you want with them? To experiment on them?'

'Simply because I can. Having this rather exceptional brain, should I not use it? Otherwise, what's it for? What's the use of a 1600 horsepower Koenigsegg that can do 300 miles an hour, when you're only going to tootle along at 20?' he said sarcastically. The chains rattled again. 'Aargh, these handcuffs! Won't you release me? I can barely lift a cup, let alone hurt anyone.'

The Professor hardly believed him.

Karl flopped his hands down in resignation. 'I'm dying, Professor! Your tests have confirmed it.' He huffed with frustration. 'If only I were lucky enough to have a quick, painless death. But no. This one's a slow-burner – interminable years of excruciating pain and slow degeneration. I started life as a painkiller junkie, as you know. Trying to survive from day to day. All thanks to you, and your genetics experiments. So-called scientists!! Playing with the stuff of life, playing with our DNA, like little children smashing play-dough together. Genetic fumbling and muddling. And now look what we have – a mutational disease that will be the end of me. Bravo, Professor. Well done!' He snorted with contempt. 'You know, there's nothing worse than a continuous aching pain that nibbles and gnaws and eats away at the very core of you. It destroys your very soul, shatters any little enjoyment that might be squeezed out of this miserable life.' The boy blinked, his eyes damp. 'Project Ingenious!' he sneered, as if it were profanity. 'I'm sure you can't have forgotten all those foetuses aborted in the process of creating your master race? All the surrogate mothers who died either giving birth, or from botched operations harvesting their eggs? What about the deformities – babies without lungs, limbs, heads. Everything swept quietly under the rug, for the greater cause of scientific advancement! So, Professor, you can hardly blame me if I'm a little desensitised to your "sanctity" of life nonsense, and if I make use of human life as you also once did. Can you?' But the outburst exhausted him, and he snapped his eyes shut, lying back. There was a flicker of pain at his temple – the first spark of a migraine. 'I'm tired now,' he said, his body slumping sideways. 'I was born old, Professor. Born tired. Dying from the moment I was delivered into this god-forsaken world,' he said quietly. 'Death shadowing me... every second of every minute of every day. And these past months, the pain has gotten much worse. Almost unbearable. I... don't think I have long to live now, maybe less than a month. Perhaps weeks. Or days.'

He exhaled, as if exhaling life itself, trembling at the thought of the end... of non-existence. Hot tears fell silently onto the stiff white sheets, and when he looked down, he saw with alarm that the droplets were tinged pink – mingled with blood. He groaned, both from the pain and from hopelessness.

Smarting from the boy's condemnation, the Professor had neither the strength nor the will to argue. He quietened, in time, mellowing. 'Let us work together, Karl,' he said softly. 'We can help each other. Let our scientists work on your cure.'

Barely able to hold himself up, Karl slipped down into the bed. 'It's too late,' was all he said, turning his back to the Professor.

'We can at least try. There might still be time for you. Think too of the children.'

Karl laughed weakly, which turned into a fit of coughing. Eventually he said, 'Do you think I care about the children?'

'W-why not? In a way, they're like your brothers, your sisters. Have you no compassion for them?'

'Professor,' said Karl, his strength weakening. 'How can you ask that? It was *you* that left out the "compassion" gene when you made me...' Karl's breathing slowed and became heavier – and just as the Professor wondered whether he had fallen asleep, the boy said weakly, 'Oppenheimer quoted Hindu scripture, when... he said, "I am become death, the destroyer... of worlds" – and the father of the atomic bomb stood idly by... as he watched his creation kill hundreds of thousands of...

civilians in Hiroshima and Nagasaki. So I too... Have. Become. Death.' He was rapidly fading. 'If I die... why should the children... live?'

As the boy lost consciousness, and his body went limp, the chains from his handcuffs jangled starkly in the still, charged air.

The sound rang in the Professor's ears.

His face pale.

It was as if he were hearing the ominous chime of a death bell.

# 29 THE MADNESS OF PEERING INTO THE MIND OF A MADMAN

In the octagonal display room, where the children's classes had been held, Mei Hui, Jemima, and Milly were sitting in the front row of chairs, and Tai and the Professor sat facing them, the Professor's hand on Tai's shoulder. The old man still found it hard to believe that he could see, through Tai's eyes. And the boy's sense of knowing even predicted where he wanted to look. Tai gazed around the room – at the crystal screens, the jagged edges of the stone walls, the three girls.

Their faces were grim.

The Professor turned his attention to them. 'Karl is weakening, dying,' he told them. 'And he won't give us the cure he's developed. If we had to start from scratch on formulating it ourselves, it could take us years. And as you know, Milly is already displaying symptoms... migraines, nausea. Which, so far, thankfully, we've been able to control with medication. But I've been thinking.' He shifted slightly toward Tai. 'Tai, you have a unique... ability. Not only can you help me see, somehow – but you're also able to see inside people's minds. Read their thoughts.' Tai glanced at the Professor, and the old man was surprised to see himself, the tiredness in his face. He looked exactly like he felt. Tai turned back to the girls, and the Professor continued. 'It will take courage, Tai, but if you can look inside Karl's mind, you can search for and extract the formula of this all-important cure–' he stopped suddenly, feeling Tai tense up.

'But... he terrifies me,' Tai interjected, glancing from the old man by his side, to the girls. Fear in his eyes. 'I can't even go near his room. He makes me feel... sick.'

Mei Hui sat up, stunned. 'Tai. You also have this divining gift?'

Everybody turned to her. 'Wait,' said Jemima. 'What do you mean by "also"?'

Mei Hui paused to gather her thoughts, her heart thudding. 'At my home village, there was a woman called Yin. She came to our house once, not long ago, for a... a family funeral. I gave her a cup of tea, and when our hands touched, I felt a jolt of electricity – through my fingers, right into my body. It shocked me. It was so distressing that I needed to lie down. But when I closed my eyes, I... I saw her memories in my mind. Her recent memories. Every detail. Like I was watching one of those films on the airplane, but inside my head. I even heard her thoughts, and felt how she felt.'

'Woah!' said Jemima, her mouth open in amazement. 'So it was like a brain download?'

'In a way,' said Mei Hui. She paused for a moment. 'But there is something more... I can somehow sense good in people. And bad. I knew that Yin was inherently a good person – it is as powerful as the force between magnets. Badness, on the other hand, repels me. I know who to trust, and who not to.'

'Wait,' said Jemima. 'You can *sense* whether someone's good?!'

Mei Hui nodded. 'Yes,' she said quietly.

'Wow!!' exclaimed Jemima, her eyes round with amazement.

'But you can take things one step further, can't you Tai?' said Milly. 'After the submarine explosion, when we were in the water, you somehow managed to manipulate those sharks, the whale...'

Tai looked self-conscious with all eyes trained on him. 'I thought we were going to die – and so, in my head, I shouted. But then I blacked out.'

No matter how many times she heard it, Milly couldn't stop being awed by the whole thing. 'And look what you're doing for the Professor right now!' she said. 'You're much more powerful than you realise, Tai!'

The Professor nodded thoughtfully.

'So the experiments,' said Jemima to the Professor. 'Project Ingenious. It gave both Tai and Mei Hui some kind of sixth sense. But not me? Not Milly?'

The Professor thought about this, shuffling in his chair. 'The science used in the project was in a constant state of flux. We were continually refining and improving. While each child was grafted with a common set of DNA coding for intelligence traits – the same basic mix for all of you – at the same time, additional genetic tweakings and enhancements were made for each embryo, each baby. That was because we'd learnt so much more in between births, and so we applied those extra, unique refinements to each individual foetus as we went along.'

Jemima remembered what Milly had told her about the order of their births. 'So Karl was the first born to the project, and then?'

'The Beta,' said the Professor. 'Who we've yet to find.'

Jemima continued. 'Then Milly was born, then...'

'Zeta – again, missing.'

Milly took over Jemima's line of thought. 'Tai came after that, followed by Mei Hui, and then, last of all, Jemima.'

'So,' said Jemima. 'If Tai and Mei Hui have all these really neat mind-bending abilities – Tai can mind-control, and Mei Hui can sense good and bad – and the Professor's genetic refinements were different for each baby, then surely me and Milly have some sort of ability too?' she asked, hopeful.

He thought about it. 'It makes sense,' was all he could say.

Milly piped up, 'I've just thought of something. Do you remember the day I had that argument with Dad, when I had a really bad migraine?' she said. 'Calista brought me some painkillers, because my head felt like it was splitting. But when she handed me the tablets, and our hands touched, I felt a jolt of something too. I... I didn't understand it at the time, because I was so distracted by the pain. But now I think about it, when I touched Cal's hand, I felt a wave of... of... something I can't explain. It kind of calmed me down.' She paused. 'Is it possible that taking painkillers suppresses whatever ability I have?' she said, turning to the Professor.

'Maybe,' he said.

Milly thought of something else. 'After the argument, when I made up with Dad, I'd stopped taking the painkillers for a while... Anyway, we talked about mum – and he told me he wanted to get our photos from the house. Of course, I remember every photo in detail, so I started describing his favourite picture – and, while he was holding my hand, he told me that it was like he could see it in his mind... He was amazed.' Milly's eyes widened as she realised. 'I... I think I can put images and memories in people's heads!'

They all went quiet as they absorbed this revelation.

The Professor broke the silence. 'Mei Hui, if you only discovered this thing recently, and you too, Milly – then it may be that Jemima's ability has yet to develop...'

Jemima sat up with excitement, grinning. 'Wow! We have super powers!!'

———

Even though there were two guards standing at Karl's locked door, day and night, Tai moved his sleeping duvet and pillow out of his own room and as far away as possible – ending up settling in a corner of the den. Later, needing to distract himself, he went to the BC with reams of sheet music clutched against his chest.

Mei Hui and Milly were already there – Milly, as was her custom after lunch, sat on the couch with a stack of books, and Mei Hui was leaning against her, plugged into a laptop.

'Hey,' said Tai in greeting. He sat down at the piano, stretched his arms and fingers, and began playing various pieces with relative ease. But one particular piece pained him to distraction, and when he placed the music on the rack, he stared at the flurry of notes with creased brows, before turning to the black and white keys. Positioning his fingers over them, he closed his eyes, emptied himself, and imagined the first three opening chords of Rachmaninov's ***Prelude in C-sharp minor***: A, G-sharp, C-sharp. He pressed down decisively on the keys, the notes clanging like sonorous bells  that rang out a grim, stark warning – the third note tenuto, sustained and gradually fading. He switched to playing the softer, melancholic chords, his hands dancing in repeated variations one above another. Bass notes followed, that jarred between wistful chords; like guilt, heavy against the lightness of innocence. The middle section transformed to agitato and waves of freneticism, verging on hysteria. Instability. Mania. And then the last section returned to the same foreboding – descending, spiralling, tumbling back to the jagged edges of doom. At last the coda exhaled staggered dying breaths. In and out. In and out. All at once introspective, exquisite, seemingly incomplete. And then gone.

As the final note disappeared into the air, Tai opened his eyes and found himself back in the BC. Milly and Mei Hui were staring at him.

'Beautiful!' breathed Mei Hui.

'But dark,' added Milly, her expression mirroring his. 'Really dark.'

Tai looked away, and shuffled his music sheets together, though he hadn't needed them. 'That's how I feel.'

Milly had already guessed this. 'About tomorrow?'

'Yes.' He went over to sit on the couch next to Mei Hui, clutching his hands in his lap, as if he didn't know what to do with them after playing. Since the Professor's suggestion of going into Karl's mind, he had been wrestling with himself, agonising over abstract thoughts: if he stared at madness, directly in the face, could he be infected by that madness? And if he were light, faced with darkness – a thick wall of it – would that darkness swallow him whole, so that he disappeared completely? The wretched boy turned to them both, and told them simply, 'I'm scared.' He looked down at his hands. 'I'm scared that if I look into his mind, I'll lose myself. I won't be able to get out.'

Milly was both surprised and hesitant. 'I get that you're worried, Tai,' she said quietly. 'It... it reminds me of Nietzsche. He said, "He who fights with monsters might take care lest he thereby become a monster. And if you gaze for long into an abyss, the abyss gazes also into you."' She sighed. A few months ago, she thought she had all the answers, knew everything, could work anything out. But she had learnt the hard way that, even though she was a genius, there were some things she just didn't know. She had to come to terms with that. V1, dead in his grave, and V3 lying comatose a few rooms away, underscored one of the hardest lessons she ever had to learn. She caught a choke in her throat, and gulped. 'Y-your question. If I'm honest, Tai, I really don't know... I wish I had the answers, but I don't.'

Tai looked like a frightened deer, caught in the headlights of a speeding car – paralysed by terror.

Mei Hui thought quietly, before saying, 'Then you don't have to do it alone...' They looked at her. 'We can join you!' she told him. 'We will need to experiment, to test, but I think we can join together and look into Karl's mind with you.'

'Yes!' said Milly, sitting up. 'You're so powerful, Tai, you'll be able to take us with you as you do the mind meld thingy. All of us – me, Jemima, Mei Hui – we can be with you. And we'll do everything possible to look out for each other, protect each other. And protect you.' She grinned, looking at them both. 'I really think we can do this. And once we get the formula, we'll be out like a shot! I promise.'

Tai looked quietly from one to the other, feeling at last the tightness in his chest begin to ease.

That very afternoon, the four teenagers experimented. They began in the swimming pool, lying on their backs in a circle, holding onto each other's hands, and gliding round slowly as they closed their eyes and concentrated. They were hesitant at first, awkward, until Tai's thoughts echoed in their heads.

*Empty yourselves*, he told them. *Don't think of anything, don't feel anything. Just be.*

They had to force themselves to relax, force their minds to stop over-thinking. Until at last they felt the connection, felt energy flow, not as individuals, but as one single being – the ultimate baring of souls. Their minds, open between them, so that there were no inhibitions, no obstructions. Just thoughts. It was so intimate, so colourful, so beautiful – like slithers of rainbows wrapping around them, winding through, and between them. The serenity and calm and tranquillity that they felt was overwhelming. And it was then that they realised. They were never meant to be apart; they should always have been together, right from the beginning.

When they opened their eyes, floating weightless in the water, they saw the large shoal of koi looking down at them – hovering in a single mass. And the four finally understood how such creatures existed together, and swam together, and moved in unison. Because, now, they too felt the same.

•••————————————————•••

At last the day came. Deep within Avernus, Karl slept serenely – in a drug-induced coma – while all around him was a beehive of activity as they began preparing the room.

Karl's bed was right at the centre of the octagonal space, and they trundled in four recliners, positioning them in a close circle around him.

Dr Fargo, the locum nurse, and Brian were setting up the life-support system for each bed, including Karl's, which consisted of ventilators, monitors, lines, tubing, and catheters. And to the side were ultrasound and echocardiography machines, as well as rows of cabinets filled with supplies and medical food bags. The room temperature was maintained at 35 degrees celsius, body warmth, and they tilted Karl's bed to a 30-degree angle, to keep his neurological functions optimal.

They laid out the phials of drugs that would keep the teenagers heavily sedated, also to relieve Karl's pain, and to optimise the constancy of his body functions.

Toward the end, the Professor came in and quietly went around the room, feeling all the equipment, checking that everything was in place.

Dr Fargo appeared beside him. 'We've already triple-checked the entire set-up, Harry,' he said.

The Professor nodded. 'I know. I just can't help...'

'I get it,' said the doctor gently, placing a hand on his shoulder. 'I won't stop you.'

The Professor turned to him. 'Please remember, Dan. It's imperative to keep Karl's neurological functions going. If he should by some chance become brain dead, I... I don't know what effect that would have on the children...'

'Of course,' said Dr Fargo. 'I'll do my best.'

At last, everything was ready, and the teenagers came into the room dressed in light cotton pyjamas. Tai looking warily at Karl's sleeping form. And Milly reminded Dr Fargo that they should not administer her with any pain medication, at all.

Then they each lay down on a recliner, whereupon Dr Fargo and his helper took some surgical tape and bound their hands not only to the next person – to form a circle around Karl – but also bound their other hand to one of Karl's ankles or wrists. Tai was on Karl's right side, and so, rather tentatively, he gripped the boy's right wrist.

Then each of the four were connected to the monitoring equipment, and Dr Fargo and the nurse commenced administering the first sleep-inducing drug.

Meanwhile, the Professor, with every intention of camping there until this whole thing was over, withdrew to the armchair that had been placed at the side of the room, and waited. Minutes and hours stretched like elastic, and the Professor's keen ears homed in on every sound – his own chest rising and falling in synchrony with the teenagers' unified breathing.

The four eventually entered deep sleep, their minds coalescing, merging.

Karl lay spread-eagle in the centre of the circle of teenagers, like Da Vinci's *Vitruvian Man.* They all fit together in a perfect biological, physical, chemical mass – a living sculpture of arms and legs, torsos and heads, hair fanning out, bare feet, and splayed hands. Thin wires and tubing criss-crossed over them like fine craquelure.

Where there were five persons, they became fused into one.

Karl's weak heart beat for them all, as the four teenagers descended deeper and deeper into the abyss of a single consciousness.

Their minds homing into the one nervous system.

A frail, sickly boy at their centre.

•••——————————————————•••

All at once their inner selves collapsed, like the death of a star, leaving behind a single core so heavy that it folded into itself, sucked inward by the pull of gravity, to a nothingness – eventually slumping into a black hole, where matter became non-matter, and where space and time were void.

Inside there was nothing but black.

And within this blackness, Tai was the first to become aware of himself, and the overwhelming feeling of fear. It was not just his fear; he sensed it from the others as well.

It was a blind panic – not being able to see, to move, to think.

*Breathe,* Tai told them in his mind.

*Just take a moment.*

*Latch onto my voice.*

*Find me,* he said.

In time he sensed that Mei Hui was near.

*I... I feel like I'm close to you,* she told him.

Tai tried to search for her, to see her, but it was like looking for a black figure, inside a black hole, within a black universe.

And then he heard Milly's thoughts. *I'm here,* she said.

*Me too,* said Jemima.

And their fear began to subside a little.

Yet Tai – whose ability to see inside people's minds was the strongest – still battled with feeling his way around. Karl's mind was incredibly difficult to penetrate, like swimming in syrup, or struggling in quicksand. And as such, Tai's every sense was on high alert.

Yet strangely, the thing that overwhelmed him the most was the peculiar taste in his mouth – an overpowering acridity. It made Tai gag, and he struggled to stop the reflex of dry-heaving. He gritted his teeth, and held his breath, in the back of his mind wondering whether this was how evil tasted. Vile and bilious.

It took Tai every iota of willpower to fight the nausea. But he focused himself, and concentrated his thoughts, just as he sensed that Milly, Mei Hui, and Jemima did also. They could all sense each other. Huddled together, and uncertain. Four specks in an unknown universe.

It was dark. So dark.

But in time, they made out a pinprick of something in the distance, like the light at the end of a tunnel – though they were neither in a tunnel, nor was the thing light.

They all stared at it, trying to make out what it was.

It was a memory. A molten mass of sounds and images, hurtling toward them like a tumbling snowball, growing larger, and larger, and larger, until the colossal mass slammed right into them with blinding pain.

The memory exploded into a hundred thousand million fragments.

Engulfing them completely.

They shivered uncontrollably, and found that they were freezing. So cold that their teeth juddered.

They looked around.

To their surprise and joy, they could see each other, feel each other. Instinctively they drew closer and held hands or linked arms, as if their lives depended on it. Tai blinked several times as he tried to make sense of what he was seeing.

There was snow, lots of it, everywhere, even as it was snowing. Flat arctic tundra as far as the eye could see.

The clarity was amazing – from the vast white-blue landscape, to the tiny, geometric snowflakes that landed on their outstretched hands. Tai's bare feet crunched into the snow, but when he turned, he saw that there were no footprints.

'I'm cold,' said Jemima through chattering teeth.

Milly turned to her, her head already covered with an inch of white flakes. 'It feels real, but it isn't. I think... I think it's like a dream. Or a memory.'

'Then,' said Mei Hui, turning toward them, her skin almost as white as the snow, 'we should be able to control the projection of ourselves, how we are, in this memory.' She closed her eyes and concentrated. When she opened them again, she looked down at herself – she was no longer barefoot in thin pyjamas, but wearing snow boots, a thickly insulated ski suit, mittens, and a woolly hat.

'Woah!' exclaimed Jemima. 'Me next.'

The others followed suit, and, as if by magic, they all became dressed in thick, warm clothing. Milly had even imagined her mother's beanie. She took it off her head, stared at it for several seconds, kissed it, and put it back. 'At least I have my hat!' she beamed. 'Even if it is imaginary.'

Tai scanned the horizon – there was nothing discernible for miles. He looked up at the looming sky. A waning pink sun was just about discernible through the clouds and snowfall. 'I don't get it,' he told the others. 'What is this place, and why are we here?'

'There must be a reason,' said Mei Hui.

'Well, if we can imagine clothes, can't we imagine flying as well, so that we can look around?' Milly suggested. She dared to let go – break her link with the others – and she jumped up into the air. To her astonishment she found that there was no gravity to pull her back down. She levitated higher and higher until the others were like small ants below her. She motioned for them to follow. And they looked up at her with awe, let go of each other, and raised themselves up slowly, like an uncanny end-of-days rapture.

'Whoooaaaa!' shouted Jemima, exhilarated.

About 500 metres above ground, they surveyed the landscape. But there was still nothing.

'Let's fly around,' said Tai. 'See what we can find.'

They agreed, and burst out in four directions, soaring over the snow for miles and miles – a Siberian wind slapping their faces, snowflakes collecting on their hats, and ice crystals frosting their eyelashes with white clumps.

Suddenly they heard Jemima's voice in their heads. 'Over here!' she said excitedly. And in an instant, the next thing they knew, they were next to her, grouped together hovering over something.

They descended slowly down to the ground, and looked up at it. It was an immense man-made structure, cantilevered out of the incline of a sandstone mountain that rose ominously above, casting a broad angular shadow to the side. The structure itself was of a simple but brutalist design: a cuboid concrete wedge, about eight metres high and two-and-a-half metres wide, like a rectangular tunnel, slicing into the mountain-face. The entrance was marked by a work of art above the large door – crystalline, mirrored shards that both glowed with an eerie turquoise hue from internal fibre-optics, and glistened in the sunlight. The teenagers looked at each other. They were after the cure, and the entrance boded well, hinting of something precious hidden deep within the mountain.

'I've seen this scene somewhere...' said Milly thoughtfully. And then she remembered. 'It's the Doomsday Vault! I read about it in the National Geographic a couple of years ago. It's located on one of the islands that formed the remote Arctic Svalbard archipelago, about 800 miles from the North Pole. It was specifically designed with security in mind: a remote island, sub-zero temperatures, snowy plains where polar bears roamed freely, steel fencing and airlock doors, motion detectors, and an impenetrable mountain.'

'Karl came here?!' asked Jemima.

Milly shook her head. 'I doubt it,' she said. 'It's too remote.'

'Then how come we're seeing this in Karl's mind?'

Milly shrugged. 'The facility is used to store hundreds of thousands of the world's seed samples, in the event of global catastrophe. A sort of agricultural Noah's ark. Insurance against an apocalypse.'

Mei Hui looked up and around at the vast structure. 'It seems impenetrable,' she said thoughtfully. 'And we are after the cure. I believe that this structure in Karl's mind, this Doomsday Vault, is his way of keeping the formula hidden and secure, so that it cannot be stolen.'

They drew closer to the entrance.

Milly nodded to the double doors. 'I read that they're dual blast-proof doors, embedded in concrete walls, reinforced with thick steel girders.' She turned to Mei Hui. 'So I think you're right, Mei. What better place to hide the cure than one of the most secure buildings in the world...'

Tai pressed against the door with his entire body, heaving. But it did not budge.

'How on earth can we get in?!' asked Jemima, flummoxed.

Mei Hui looked up at the steel structure. 'Physically, we would never be able to break into the real Doomsday Vault, but this is an *imagined* structure in Karl's mind. Could it be possible to break into it with *our* combined minds?'

Jemima nodded enthusiastically. 'I like that idea! He's only one person, but the four of us could pit our strength together, our mental strength, and break in.'

'Interesting,' said Milly. 'Breaking through with sheer willpower... like an earthquake.'

'A mind-quake!' Jemima exclaimed. 'Definitely worth a try.'

Instinctively they huddled together in a rugby scrum. Heads touching, arms intertwined, minds coalescing. They closed their eyes and creased their faces as they concentrated hard.

Without a word, and in complete unison, they thought the same thing – a thought that sparked and flashed through their bodies.

Need.

That.

Cure.

In their minds, they imagined tremors that increased in magnitude, and before they knew it, coursing waves shook the ground underneath their feet. They held onto each other, levitating into the air, and revolving slowly, as the force of the tremors built and built.

In time, the entire structure began to vibrate, the snowy ground convulsed in waves, and the air shimmered like the haze of a mirage. A deafening rumbling cracked through the air, making them flinch, but still they did not allow it to break their concentration.

So tremendous was the upheaval that it felt as if the whole world was about to implode.

Above them, great boulders from the mountain teetered and then toppled down the slope – tumbling toward them at speed. An avalanche of giant stones smashed right on top of them, until they were completely buried.

There remained just a huge pile of stones and rubble, in a cloud of dust.

Once again, it was dark.

And the four teenagers made a last concerted effort to focus their thoughts, to see through the blackness of Karl König's mind. With a tremendous explosion, and a deafening roar, the mound of rubble catapulted outward in all directions, disappearing in a flash.

As the dust began to settle, the teenagers' coughing subsided, and they were soon able to see. They let go of each other, and turned toward the Doomsday Vault. But it was still standing – sparkling in the haze of the sun. Completely untouched.

For miles and miles around, an immaculate blanket of snow surrounded them. Above loomed an azure-smudged sky, with a waning pink sun just discernible through the clouds. Heavy snowfall descended silently in thick diagonal sheets.

Nothing had changed.

They had failed.

And their hope of finding the cure was crushed.

'No!!' cried Jemima, slumping into the snow. Milly bent down to comfort her, and Tai stood at her side, both equally deflated.

Mei Hui turned from Jemima to stare up at the hazy golden sun, contemplating. In real life, she knew never to look directly at the sun; but this was not real. The perfect sphere glared back down at her, winking through a thin canopy of clouds.

It was painfully beautiful.

She closed her almond eyes, and felt the wind rustling her hair, snowflakes falling softly against her skin. Behind her eyelids she saw the same disc burning, surrounded by a halo of powdery white light. Its pattern resembled the Taijitu of yin and yang – a circle filled with both black and white elements. The symbol of duality, and contrary and complementary forces. Each force existing with a kernel of the opposing force at its heart.

As she stared at this image behind closed eyes, she suddenly realised something. 'I think I understand,' she said, opening her eyes suddenly. 'We have entered Karl König's mind, but we have not yet touched his heart. We have not yet touched the thing that makes Karl, Karl.'

Milly thought about this, and joined in. 'That's true. The heart is the deepest, most emotive part of him – his inner feelings, moods, motivations, the driving force that fuels his mind.'

'It is the very nature of him,' said Mei Hui. 'His soul.' She nodded up toward the glorious sun, shining perfectly above them. 'Do you see?' she said, looking round at them. 'Karl has beauty in him.'

The three stared at the glowing orb in the sky.

'The sun... it is like the white dot embedded in the black heart of yin and yang,' said Mei Hui.

Jemima looked away, wiping the tears of frustration from her eyes. 'Yeah right,' she said. 'He has a funny way of showing that "beauty" – by killing people!'

'That is true,' said Mei Hui. 'But I wonder, what it is that *moulded* his thinking in such a way that made him murderous? Why does he not have feelings and empathy for others, as we do? Why is his detachment so extreme?'

'I doubt we'll ever know,' said Jemima.

Milly was rubbing her temple distractedly. 'Well, actually, we can find out,' she said, spreading out her arms and looking around. 'We're in Karl's mind. We can find out whatever we want from his memories, right through his childhood.'

Tai shivered involuntarily; it was not from the cold. 'Please, no,' he said, so quietly that they did not notice.

Jemima got up and dusted herself down. 'But why would we ever want to see what made him the way he is?'

Mei Hui motioned toward the sun. 'In every force, there is the seed of the opposing force at its heart,' she said. 'Karl is all things dark and evil, but I believe there is a grain of purity deep within. I believe that, if we just search for the good in him, and draw it out, then it is possible he will himself offer the cure to us.'

They all thought about this.

'No,' said Tai, louder, shaking his head. He felt sick. 'I don't want to stay here. It's like... like my worst nightmare.' His eyes pleaded with them. 'In the submarine, when we first found him, I touched him briefly, and... and my head became filled with horrors. Images full of blood and death. He's done really, really bad things.'

'I understand,' said Milly quietly. 'To peer into the mind of a madman is insanity itself.' Then she thought of what Mei Hui said. 'But I agree with Mei. We can search for the good in him – and maybe even go one step further... Tai has the ability to manipulate minds, and I know it works. We're here because of it. So what if we build on that grain of goodness he has. And *make* him into a better person.' She thought for a moment. 'What if... what if we inject *our* own memories and experiences into him. All the good that we've learnt from our families, our parents, our friends. And merge them with *his* memories? We might be able to influence him. For good. Make him a better person, even if it's just a little bit better. And in turn, that might just push him to *want* to give us the cure.'

Jemima looked at Milly, incredulous. 'Is such a thing possible?'

'I hope so,' she said.

'So, in precise terms,' said Jemima thoughtfully, 'how would we do this?'

'Maybe we could go back through Karl's childhood, from his formative years,' Milly replied.

'Time travel, in a way?' asked Jemima.

Milly nodded. 'Kind of. We need to travel back in his memories, to the very beginning...'

'Yes,' agreed Mei Hui. 'To his earliest childhood. I can search for all the bad memories – and from there, we can expose him to good, not bad.'

Tai thought about this. He desperately wanted to get out of this situation – but he looked at Milly now, thought of her constant headaches, her nausea, how sick she was going to get without the cure, and knew deep down that they had to at least try. 'We're going to be here for a while, aren't we?' he said quietly, gulping.

'Yes,' responded Mei Hui.

'Then we should get to work,' said Milly.

They looked at each other, fearful of what they might find inside Karl's dark mind, knowing that the most frightening things are those that aren't immediately visible. Those that are hidden.

'Remember, we're doing this together. We're not alone,' said Milly, determination welling up inside of her. 'We can do this!'

But Tai could not feel so positive. He remembered something, and he told them of it with his small, chiming voice. 'When I was really little,' he said quietly, 'my father took me to a fair, where there was a hall of mirrors. My dad was laughing. But I looked at the reflections and saw lots and lots of deformed, ugly, misshapen Tais, trailing off, and going on forever and ever. I thought I was losing my mind. And I hated what I saw. Hated the fact that I couldn't see where those reflections ended...' He paused. 'I... I kind of feel like that now.'

They all thought about it.

Tai sighed long and hard, a sound that faded and was soon drowned out by the eerie, hollow howl of the biting wind.

Then, in the blink of an eye, they were gone.

In their wake was left just the hint of a question. Could they traverse a lifetime in a second? Or would wading through the minutiae of every single thought and imagining, every dream and memory, take them an age?

They had no way of knowing. But it was conceivable they could be inside Karl's mind, in limbo, for days, or weeks, or even much, much longer...

# 30  THE ALPHA

It didn't look like much.

It was a dot, barely a tenth of a millimetre in diameter.

The single-celled zygote, intelligent life in its simplest form.

Yet within, it held a wealth of secret instructions and information that encoded life itself.

Any normal zygote was the product of a sperm fertilising an egg, perfectly combining the DNA of two separate gametes to create a new, unique organism.

Except this zygote contained genes from a third source.

Rudely inserted through the tip of a micropipette, trans-genetic material knocked into a particular segment of the host's DNA. The zygote shivered from the violation, but then in time, it settled, stiffened, and began dividing. Into two, then four, eight, 16, and 32 – it did this rapidly over the course of four days; a transparent mulberry surging within a wall of skin.

The resulting blastocyst continued its transformation – expanding, contracting, expanding, compacting – as if readying itself, building momentum. It was then inserted into the mother's uterus, and on day 10, it burst out of the zona pellucida, and hatched, implanting itself into the uterine wall. Finger-like projections plunged deep into the mucous membrane, pulling itself in even further so that it sunk entirely within the flesh of the endometrium. Those roots searched all around, until they latched onto the mother's blood supply, and began sucking in from her much-needed gases and nutrients for growth.

It was like a parasite feeding off a host, yet the mother's body welcomed it, and did everything possible to protect this new passenger – sending hormonal signals to tame her own immune response, so that it did not attack and reject the tiny entity. Other hormones switched off the ovaries, preventing egg production, and yet others loosened the mother's joints and ligaments in time. And much later, chemical signals would transform her pear-sized uterus so that it readied itself to expand and accommodate a growing baby.

Slowly it fed and grew.

At week five, the embryo was the size of a sesame seed, its cells organising and arranging themselves into primal organs – the brain and spinal column, fine veins, and a tiny heart pumping energetically at its centre.

By week nine, it was grape-sized and beginning to look more like a baby, with digits at the end of limbs, an alien face with tiny eyes, nose, mouth, ear buds, and in the next week, minute tooth buds also formed. It curled toes and clenched fists, as if flexing itself in readiness for the tremendous growth ahead.

At week 12, baby was about 2.5 inches long, and many of its vital organs and major body systems had already formed. Mother soon began to feel its reflexive movements as flutters deep inside her womb – as it kicked, swallowed, yawned, blinked, smiled, and even practised breathing.

Baby liked to listen. The deafening drumbeat of mother's enormous heart, the rush of blood, the gloopy, bubbly sounds of amniotic fluid. And most of all it listened keenly to the outside world – strange and exotic muffled noises. Mother's voice, in particular, stilled and soothed it.

By the sixth month, baby's cerebral cortex split spontaneously into two separate hemispheres, and by the seventh month, electrical brain impulses burst into regular and consistent wave patterns. Baby's brain grew an astounding 25 million neurons per minute, so that, at birth, there would be 100 billion neurons, with 50 trillion synapses.

Most babies slept entirely in utero, but not this one.

Nine weeks before it was born, it became self-aware.

Its vague consciousness wondered at the muted light filtering in from the outside, illuminating ruby blood vessels that crazed the sphere of its world. It wondered at the smooth and comforting massage of mother's hand rubbing her bump – and it kicked legs, and jerked arms, to elicit a repeat of that soothing sensation. It smelled and tasted the variation of flavour molecules in the amniotic fluid as mother ate different foods.

And when a thumb found its way to its mouth, a peculiar sucking reflex was sparked, which was wonderfully calming.

But then, one day, baby found that it was slowly, inexorably rolling backward, so that its head pointed downwards. It had never liked the odd sensation of upside-down – its eyes bulged, ears tingled, and its head felt tight, so tight. But it did not fight it, did not try to twist upright again.

And then, before long, new and unusual convulsing waves began to flow right through it. At first the waves were irregular and infrequent, but they soon became stronger, closer together, and so powerful that baby felt like it might burst. Ears popped, it peed involuntarily, fidgeting and struggling with discomfort.

Each compression made baby quiver, and it lurched at the loud crying noises from outside. Dread soaked through it, just as amniotic fluid soaked its lungs – its heartbeat pounding thunderously.

Then there came the sense of sliding, slipping, immense pressure, a hiccough, a spark of fear – all as it descended slowly, slowly, inch by inch.

And then, in the blink of an eye, baby slithered out head-first, and the world exploded onto him in a sudden burst of sensory overload: bright lights, noises that pained the ears, a hollow feeling in his chest.

The shock of it made his arms jerk outward.

He gasped, and cried.

Swallowed great gulps of air.

He needed comfort, he was distressed, wanted to suckle, needed to be held.

But instead, he was taken away.

And he cried, and cried, and cried.

The crumpled infant fluttered its eyelids and eventually opened them, taking in the vague form of Dr Axel Kendra's blurred, giant head. The man's eyes were damp with emotion and triumph, his brown hair ruffled, with a gloss of sweat on his forehead.

As baby blinked up at him, his little mouth formed an o, and he frowned. Shivering suddenly from the freshness of air against skin, he clicked his tongue on the roof of his mouth, just as his head flopped helplessly to one side.

Dr Kendra caught the infant's head with his hand, and gently, carefully, passed the miracle baby to the nurse. They drained his mouth and nose, wiped off the waxy vernix and blood, and checked breathing, reflexes, muscle tone, heart rate, and colour.

But all baby wanted was to bond. He craned his neck, and turned his head, as if looking for the thing it ought to bond with. But it never came.

In the first weeks, baby hardly cried.

It lay in the cot – alone – swaddled tight within a cotton blanket, inside a sterile, perspex cot.

He stared and stared, even though he could barely see. But there was only a white ceiling, grey walls, and otherworldly masked figures that wafted by, bringing milk, changing nappies, checking temperature, giving baths.

He longed more than anything to be held.

But even when he was being fed, the medical staff simply propped him up in the cot with gloved hands – following strict instructions not to handle the baby for fear of transmitting pathogens and disease. They were not paediatric nurses, and so they forgot to wind the baby after each feed, and he would writhe with agony, his little chest taut from the discomfort of trapped air.

Baby was naturally drawn to other people, and his eyes would follow the nurses as they went to and fro – though there was no baby-talk, no interaction, no cuddles.

At two months old, things became a little more interesting.

Baby's sight was perfect by now, and he avidly watched the screen on the wall next to the cot – a camera, like a steely eye, recording his reactions. The screen showed videos of human faces talking, singing, shouting, and whispering. Music of all kinds was played. As well as documentaries about every sort of animal, insects, birds, and their habitats, stars and space, sea and land. Vivid portraits and works of art glowed onscreen. And sometimes baby gurgled, or smiled, quietened, or cooed in response to what he saw. When human faces appeared, with varying expressions, baby seemed to mimic these, widening eyes, and poking out his tongue. When there were angry, shouting people, he turned his head away, as if in avoidance.

By six months, baby started to cry. Not just when he was hungry, or needed changing – but almost all the time. Shrill, siren-like cries that seemed to go on for hours, making both its throat hoarse and the staff frazzled. Frantically the doctors performed test after test, but could find nothing physically wrong, and so eventually they resorted to administering liquid paracetamol, which at last had the desired effect of calming him.

Baby was not interested in food, turning his pale face away from the bottle, and either sucked his thumb instead, or reached up to pull at tufts of golden hair – comforting himself. His vivid grey eyes bored holes as he stared at the nurses, defying their attempts to feed him. Consequently, there was no chubbiness, no ruddy cheeks – he was pale, gaunt, and weak.

'Child prodigy!' scoffed a nurse once. 'What a laugh. He's an absolute terror!' That pretty much summed up how most of the medical staff felt about the boy.

When baby was able to sit upright in front of a table, scientists engaged him in various tests. Confronted with plastic stacking rings, baby immediately picked one up, mouthed it, and banged it on the table, startling himself in the process. A middle-aged female scientist slowly took the rings and stacked them in decreasing size order, unstacking and restacking the pyramid several times as baby watched transfixed. For the fourth time, the scientist placed the rings in a line in front of the infant, in mixed order, with the wooden pole in the middle. Baby looked from the rings to the woman, bashing its arms at its side, impatient. Finally baby reached out for a ring – at first picking up the smallest one and mouthing it thoughtfully. But then it exchanged it for the largest ring and started stacking them exactly as it had observed the scientist – in perfect order. The woman clapped with enthusiasm, hardly believing that the child could get it right the very first time.

As the months passed, they found that the baby had excellent practical, puzzle-solving skills. But his temper tantrums were phenomenal, and sometimes the smallest thing would set him off, so that he screeched and raged, and threw things, bashing his fists so hard that he even hurt himself. It was not unusual to find bruises, wheals, and cuts on his emaciated body.

Bedtime was a nightmare. Often the child was grizzly, and the sleep-deprived nurses would furiously bounce him up and down in their arms, muttering, 'Sleep, you little demon, sleep.' Something he heard almost nightly. Some of the nurses even added an extra dose of painkiller into his evening drink; a little chemical fix to give him – and them – a good night's sleep.

By the time the child was a toddler, the scientists had regrouped – their heads already distracted with engineering the next baby. They needed to improve the science of an altered and improved set of genes, as well as their care and tuition methods and practices. They needed to right the wrongs of their first attempt.

So that was what the Alpha had become – an experiment gone wrong.

And while they did not intentionally project their feelings of failure onto the infant, subliminally the child absorbed them.

They were the world's top scientists, but they did not understand how to care for and nurture a baby...

Despite all of this, and testament to the enduring capacity of human nature, the baby miraculously managed to form a bond of sorts with three people in the facility. Dr Kendra was the first person baby saw at birth, and so an affinity grew between them. But it was only a part-time relationship, as the doctor's availability was so limited. Whenever he passed the baby's cot, the man would give a jovial wave, or read a few lines from a storybook, or chat animatedly with him about some scientific process, before being called away on some urgent matter.

The toddler also became attached to Professor Wolff, who came every now and again to speak German to the child – curious as to how quickly their prodigy could absorb languages.

Yet the strongest bond he formed was, unusually, with Carey the janitor.

Carey was a quiet man in his sixties, and despite being po-faced, he was kind and thoughtful and caring, to a fault – going about his chores in overalls and boots, and never without something in his hand: a toolbox, or a broom, or other equipment. Always there in the background. And though he spoke hardly a word, the old man had a preternatural ability to appear whenever the carers were at their wits' end with the Alpha. When Carey heard a commotion, he would simply discard whatever he was carrying, and whisk away the cantankerous child in his arms. Nobody ever asked where he was being taken, they were just grateful to be rid of the little terror, telling Carey that he was an absolute saint.

Carey had never had children of his own. But he remembered how he himself once was a rather active little tearaway, always wanting attention, and to play, and run, and shout, and explore. Yet his mother's almost angelic serenity and endless patience never faltered. Not even for a second. And so Carey mimicked those qualities with the Alpha, distracting the child with other things when he was in the worst of moods.

While the Alpha had been provided with complex and expensive learning toys and puzzles by the scientists, Carey gave him everyday household objects to play with – a wooden spoon, a brush, a pan, an old box. And whatever Carey did, the Alpha watched and mimicked with his own pretend tools. They fixed boilers together, mended broken furniture, mopped floors, changed fuses, hung blinds, and cleaned out the ashes from the incinerator.

The two barely exchanged words, and would mostly work and play together in silence. They had a good if unusual affinity.

But before long, the second baby was on its way, and Alpha, to his silent dismay, was no longer the centre of everyone's world.

There was a communal room which had a long aquarium spanning nearly the entire side of a wall. It was only half filled, housing two diamondback terrapins and a handful of exotic fish – yellow ciclids, tetras, and zebrafish. The Alpha, two-and-a-half years old by now, would often press his little nose against the cold glass, and stare at the creatures in silent fascination, wiping the glass vigorously when it fogged up with breath.

A little terrapin eyed him suspiciously, craning a grey and white neck, observing its onlooker with equal curiosity. But when it retreated behind a stack of rocks half immersed in water, Alpha shouted and stamped his feet, annoyed. He wanted it to come back – now! Fuming with impatience, Alpha bashed the tank with his fist – but was answered only by a reflection of his own face in the glass, warped with anger.

Alpha looked around the room, thinking. He pushed a small coffee table from the side of the room to the tank, and arranged a pile of books on top, against the glass – like the plastic stacking rings, with the biggest book at the bottom and the others in decreasing size, forming a step. The boy climbed onto the table, put a foot on the precarious book pile, and rolled the other leg over the top of the tank. But his foot caught on the rim, and he fell clumsily inside with a splash, grazing his knee on one of the craggy rocks. Blood trickled down his leg, but he paid no heed, distracted as he was by the thrill of the water. He squealed with delight, stamping, laughing, splashing, and scooping up and throwing handfuls of water into the air – again and again. But soon he noticed that the heel of his shoe felt funny – something squishy and slimy underfoot. Looking down, he discovered that the terrapin was smashed to pieces – and so he hunched over his knees to inspect the macabre remains with morbid fascination.

When the grown-ups rushed in, shouting at him with red, angry faces, this was the part Alpha loved best. He had everyone's attention. And he grinned mischievously at them from inside the tank. Two of the staff pulled him forcefully out of the tank, and set him on the floor with a heavy jolt. But he slipped, lost balance, and fell backwards – hitting his head on the edge of the table.

As he lay on the floor, his eyes rolled back, and he began to fit – his body jerking and convulsing in alarming waves. The staff crowded around him in panic.

When Alpha turned three, the all-consuming anger that fired him began to mellow by degrees, so that in time he subdued, spending most of his day reading, playing with electronic games, puzzles, and cryptic crosswords. His pain medication had changed from clear, colourless liquid hidden in his nightly drink of warm milk, to Smartie-red tablets – which were grabbed greedily from the nurse's hand and gulped down with long swigs from his sippy-cup. Lying back in bed, he lay still as he waited for the throbbing pain in his head to subside.

Sleep came as a sweet reprieve.

By the time Alpha was four, he shunned the other children – two toddlers, and a baby. The toddlers crashed into him and seemed to be everywhere, waddling, shouting, screaming. Instead he sought out quiet solace, playing by himself, or watching them from afar – observing how the staff laughed and chatted with the children, hugging and fussing over them. So very different from the way they treated him.

When the Alpha got bored, he would search out Carey, and entertain himself by running rings round the man – easy enough for the whip-smart rogue to do. Yet Carey hardly reacted, only on occasion scolding him mildly. He was too distracted by his caretaking work – fixing things, clearing out the incinerator, and disposing of rubbish, which took up all of his time.

On incinerator days, the old man would take the big round-headed brush and sweep right up the flue – eventually emerging looking like a dusty apparition, and blinking away the powdery soot. He would sweep out the inside of the furnace, removing clinkers, ashes, and other debris, and shovelling it all into a grinder. Alpha was always honoured with the exciting task of pressing the big green 'on' button, and he would watch in silent fascination as the machine smashed and crushed everything into sand-sized grains. The old man spent almost two days every month in the incinerator room, cleaning, burning, and crushing – sweat dripping from his temples as he worked.

There were six tall barrels that stood neatly against the wall next to the grinder, and the Alpha watched as each one was filled – balling his hands into excited fists, as the rising levels counted down to a much-anticipated day trip. When they were at last full, Carey would have them loaded onto a truck, then he readied the little boy with shoes, a jacket, and a neatly packed lunch – and he'd swing him up onto the passenger seat. It was just a 20-minute drive to the field, but to the Alpha it took forever as he looked out from the bottom of the window with bated breath, watching the passing landscape as they trundled along snaking country lanes.

They hadn't always been there, the cornflowers.

Alpha could remember a time when it was just a plain, brown field, with no distinguishing features, which Carey worked tirelessly – digging furrows the full breadth of the land, while Alpha sat at the edge with his little green beach bucket and spade, mimicking him, or digging for worms, searching for spiders, or chasing butterflies – and he even caught a stray frog once, so small it was barely the size of his hand.

Carey huffed and panted as he rolled the barrels out to the field, and then shovelled the contents into furrows. It took him all day. And the boy sometimes looked up to see the old man slowly lifting out the ashes in his shovel, extremely carefully, so as not to spill a thing. When Carey wasn't looking, the boy would reach up on his tiptoes to take a bucketful of the fine grey dust from the barrels, sitting down right in the dirt to make patterns with it in the soil – only to have Carey's heedless feet smash it as he trudged back and forth.

They made the same trip every six months or so – and the following year, when the Alpha was five, the two arrived at the field during a hot, humid July. To their astonishment, they found a shock of bright blue cornflowers in the field – tall and spindly, with delicate pointed petals, like rays of tissue-paper.

Carey rarely reacted, but he stopped when he saw the flowers, took off his hat, scratched his head, and couldn't help snorting in amazement.

The boy didn't have to tiptoe to reach the barrel that year. He easily filled his battered old plastic bucket with his spade, so that the receptacle swung heavily with the weight, ash drifting to the ground like fine snow. But as Alpha made his usual patterns, he noticed that it was not as fine and even as it had been before. He bent down, squinting to inspect the dust. It was much coarser, and scattered with tiny bones, some of which flaked into powder in his hands. Eagerly, Alpha sifted through the rest of the ash to see what else he might discover, imagining he was an archaeologist at a dig, searching for fossils.

The boy collected a small pile of these tiny 'fossils' in a matchbox, and he studied them meticulously. He wondered what they were, and thought about it all the way home, and for days after. Wondered that Carey was getting more forgetful and not grinding the ashes properly. Wondered also where the little bones came from...

In time, the entire field was filled with blazing cornflowers, and Alpha loved picking the heads, breathing in their peppery earthiness, and then throwing them as high as he could, like floral fireworks. Or he would tear them into tiny shreds, and run around, letting the remnants drift between his fingers – the wind lifting and tossing the purple-blue petals across the field.

At the end of the day, Carey would pause to stretch an aching back, and stamp out the rheumatism in his knees – as he did so, he looked over the natural beauty of the cornflowers, hardly believing that, years before, there was just a smudge of bare land, like a Barbizon painting in muddy shades of brown. Yet now, the lea was bursting with vibrancy, mirroring the bluest of Monet's impressions.

Carey absorbed every detail of the picture-perfect field, a pained look on his face, moisture gleaming in his eyes. He stood there for ages, it seemed to the boy – quiet, and lost in thought. Every now and again the old man swiped at his eyes with his sleeve, unable to stop looking at the glorious swathe of cornflowers before him. Mesmerised by its beautiful morbidity.

One day, back in the facility, Alpha noticed a pretty young woman sitting in the waiting room. And at the same time, he saw something sparkle around her neck. He ran up to her unreservedly and stretched out his hands to be picked up, even though they had never before met. The young woman was surprised to find the boy appear out of nowhere, but still, she smiled graciously and picked him up, resting him on her hip. 'Hello there!' she said brightly.

Alpha latched a hand around her shoulder, and with the other he gently fingered the small blue jewel nestled in her collarbone. He looked with amazement from the necklace to the young woman – together they were the most beautiful things he had ever seen.

'You like my necklace?' she said animatedly, her eyes wide and engaging. 'It's sapphire. And it's super special, because my little brother wanted to get it for me, so my parents bought it as a present. We're really close.'

But all the child could do was stare.

The young woman laughed at him. 'You're so cute!' she smiled, lightly touching his little button nose.

Nobody had ever called Alpha cute before – he was not an attractive child, had a sickly pallor, and stringy hair. But the boy liked her even more for it.

'What's your name?' she asked, bouncing him gently on her hip.

'Alphie,' he said.

'Hello, Alphie!' she smiled brightly. 'And how old are you?'

He let go of the necklace and held up a splayed hand right before her face.

'Five?' she said, looking him over. He was small for his age. 'Then you're a year older than my brother, Jake. He's four.'

A voice came from outside in the corridor. 'Ah, Miss Winters. I see you've met the first of our wunderkind – very good!'

They both turned to find Dr Kendra entering in his usual white lab coat, a clipboard tucked under one arm. He was beaming at her, but then mock-frowned at the boy. 'Alphie, I know she's lovely, but you need to let Kara go. She has to sign some forms, and it's going to be quite a long day for her, so she needs to rest.'

'No!!' shouted Alpha, clinging on to her even tighter. His eyes darkened.

'Hey, it's okay, Alphie,' said Kara, trying to reassure the boy. Even her voice was lovely. 'I'm gonna be here for a while – nine months in fact, so I'm sure we'll see each other again soon.'

Alpha looked up at her with hopeful eyes. 'Promise?' he begged, lips quivering, near tears. But he caught himself, blinked, and consciously stopped himself from crying. He gazed at her hopefully.

Kara pecked his forehead, and nodded. 'I promise, Alphie. I have a feeling we're going to become really good friends.' She gently lowered him to the ground, and he uncurled his arms from around her.

The Alpha could only stare as she and Dr Kendra walked away together, already deep in conversation. But just before they turned out of sight, Kara glanced back at him and waved.

Alpha did not wave back; he was too busy thinking about how he could engineer seeing her again. The boy held a hand over the precious spot where she kissed him, but then, realising how stupid he was being, vigorously wiped his forehead clean, then wiped his hand on his shirt. He turned and skipped away.

A few months later, a hairline crack appeared in Alpha's sheltered world. When Dr Kendra approached the boy in the gardens, holding a plate of his favourite Kartoffelpuffer – pancakes topped with treacly apple sauce – the wily boy knew straight away that something was wrong.

Dr Kendra beamed at him. 'Look what I asked cook to whip up for you, Alphie.'

But Alpha knew very well that such rare treats were only for special occasions. He felt a plump droplet splodge on his arm, and he tore his eyes from the pastry to look up at broody grey clouds heavy with rain. Dr Kendra ushered him beneath the covered pergola, where they sat at the wrought-iron table and chairs.

Alpha glanced at the pastry. 'Is there something wrong?' he asked the doctor, wary.

Dr Kendra looked at the child and took a deep breath. 'It's a secret, Alphie. But...' his voice became hushed. 'If I tell you, you must promise not to tell a soul.'

Alpha stared at him, not realising that the doctor was waiting for consent.

'Will you promise me you'll keep the secret?' repeated Dr Kendra.

Impatient, the boy said, 'Yes, yes.'

The doctor drew closer. 'We're going to leave the facility,' he said in barely a whisper. 'You, me, the children, Professor Wolff, and the staff...'

'And Carey?' asked the boy.

The doctor nodded. 'Yes, of course, Carey too.'

The boy thought about this. 'But why? Why do we need to leave?' It was his home after all.

The doctor had already prepared for the plethora of questions Alpha was bound to ask. 'It's because, well, the project didn't go as... smoothly as we'd hoped. It's turned out to be much, much harder than we ever imagined. There have been more... failures than we anticipated.'

Alpha thought about this. For a while, he had known that the project was all about him and the other children, and so he looked up at the doctor, his brow creased, and asked, 'Am I a failure?'

Surprised, Dr Kendra said quickly, 'No, no, of course not, Alphie. That's not what I meant. I'm talking about the project itself, the science, the experiments.' He waved toward the facility buildings. 'It has flaws and consequences that have become... untenable.' The doctor knew that he didn't need to simplify things for the Alpha; the child understood almost everything.

Large droplets of rain began bombing the lawn, throwing scents of mud and grass into the air. The Alpha picked up the fork and helped himself to a portion of the Kartoffelpuffer.

Dr Kendra watched him, raising his eyebrows in anticipation. 'Good?'

'It needs more honey,' said Alpha bluntly, and he put the fork down. 'Where will we go?' he asked, his composure belying his worry.

Dr Kendra handed him a paper towel, and the boy scrubbed at his mouth vigorously. 'Don't worry, I've got everything arranged,' he said. 'And I'd like you to come with me, me and my wife, Gaia – we'll look after you. Would that be okay, Alphie?'

The boy looked at him and blinked. He was very happy to hear this, though his inscrutable expression gave nothing away. 'If Carey can come too, I'd like that,' was all he said. He began eating again.

The doctor continued. 'Yes, of course. Carey can come if he wants. But first, I will leave shortly to arrange things, and I'll be gone for some time – but you must remember that I'll come back to get you. Okay?'

Alpha looked at him and nodded as he ate.

'I just need to see some people... get things prepared. And when it's time, you and Carey must meet us at a specific location – a train station – where I'll come and pick you up. I'll meet you there at night-time. Carey will have the details...'

Alpha stopped. He didn't like this. 'Tell *me*,' he said firmly, knowing how forgetful Carey was getting. 'I want to know.'

Dr Kendra blinked at him, and then nodded. 'Very well.' He looked over his shoulder, and huddled closer. 'On 28 May,' he whispered, 'we'll arrange for a group of the staff to go away on a training course, leaving us alone here. Then, later that night, at 3 am precisely, I'll meet you and Carey in the carpark of Rocheford Station. It's nearly an hour's drive from here, so you need to leave in good time.' Dr Kendra stopped himself from saying, 'Don't forget'; the boy never forgot a thing.

Alpha thought about all of this. 'Why is it a big secret?'

The doctor took a deep breath. 'Because... because we've worked on the project for nearly six years now, and... it's become... questionable, ethically. It needs to stop, and we can't go on like this. Unfortunately, the person who conceived the project, and is funding it, doesn't want us to stop. He's forbidden us from leaving. So, the only way to end this, is for us to simply... disappear.'

The boy absorbed all this. 'Who is "he"?'

The doctor sighed. 'I can't tell you that, Alpha. It's better that you don't know.'

But the Alpha did not give up easily; his face contorted into anger, and he gripped the fork in a fist, bashing it against the table. 'I want to know!'

Dr Kendra glanced over his shoulder, looking troubled. 'I-I can only say that he's... well, you could say that he's a sort of relative. Kind of. But not in the usual sense. Anyway, as I said, I can't tell you more than that. For your own good.' He paused for a moment. 'I know you want answers to everything, Alphie. But sometimes it's best to keep quiet. Sometimes the less we know, the better. So... please just trust me, okay?'

The boy opened his mouth, hesitated, and the flash of red anger on his face slowly melted away. Eventually he nodded.

Relieved, the doctor said quietly, 'You... you're a very special boy, Alphie, and I care about you very much.'

Nobody had spoken like that to him before, and the boy stared at the doctor with a peculiar expression.

Dr Kendra softened. 'You were the first baby born to the project – and I suppose that, because of that, I feel a special connection with you.' His smile was bitter-sweet. He patted the boy's head awkwardly. 'I really mean that, Alphie.' He got up and glanced at his watch. 'I'd better go now. Remember, you can't talk about this with anyone, not even Carey – in case someone overhears. It's very important.' When at last the boy consented, Dr Kendra patted him again, and turned to run back to the laboratories, hunching from the rain.

But instead of following him, the Alpha got up and walked slowly in the opposite direction, distracted. The rain did not bother him, in fact, he enjoyed the fresh droplets soaking his skin, his hair, his clothes, making him shiver. Rivulets traced down his face and dripped like crystal orbs from his chin. He walked and walked until he reached the barbed wire fence – three metres high, and encircling the entire perimeter of the facility. Clasping the old mesh between his fingers, he squeezed so hard it nearly pierced his skin. The wire was rough with orange rust, and the dampness released a metallic odour that smelled like blood.

He stared quietly at the other side through the fence, drenched in rain, as he thought about everything the doctor had told him.

Just as he had said, Dr Kendra disappeared a few days later. And for Alpha, waiting for 28 May to roll closer was like watching the sun set, its movement barely discernible, the days interminably long.

At last it arrived, and then there was yet more waiting for night to descend. The Alpha sat on his bed, tapping an impatient foot on the floor – already coated, and with his shoes on. He glanced at the clock too often; its ticking marked the inevitability of their departure.

Quietly he slid off the mattress and crept out of his bedroom without a single look back. He kept to the shadows in the hallway, knowing from memory exactly where the blind spots in the security cameras were. He did not switch on any lights; his steps were guided only by the faint gleam of moonlight through the tall windows that silvered his path. He held his breath as he passed the other children's rooms, cringing from the idea that one of the little brats might wake up at any moment. But then he noticed that, unusually, one of the doors had been left ajar – and peering inside, he found the bed dishevelled, drawers left open, clothing scattered, and no sign of life.

Curious, he went inside, looked around, and then wandered to the window on the far wall. He looked outside, waiting for his eyes to become accustomed to the dark. Eventually he was able to make out, in the distance, a line of small shadowy figures. He squinted, trying to understand what he was seeing. It dawned on him that it was the children with adults by their side, looking around nervously, waiting to climb into what appeared to be a minibus. He stared at them for some time, stepping aside from the condensation of his breath on the glass, and staring again. Someone accidentally switched on the light inside the bus, illuminating them in a faint white glow – but it was enough for the Alpha to see the adults' faces, a couple, male and female, bearing a striking similarity to the child next to them, before the light quickly went out again.

It dawned on him who they were. And the Alpha felt rage begin to boil inside of him. But he knew he needed to rein in his emotions – he'd learnt by now to control them as easily as turning off or on a tap. Instead, he turned, left the room, and made his way to Carey's living quarters in the basement. He hoped that the old man had remembered. But when he arrived, he found that Carey was fast asleep in bed with his mouth wide open, dribbling saliva.

The boy shook him, and he awoke, snorting. The Alpha held an index finger to his lips, glancing behind him warily. 'It's time to go,' he whispered emphatically. Carey blinked away the sleep, then got up without a word – and there followed a silent dance as they moved around the small room, the old man getting ready, and the boy helping him. When at last everything was done, their two rucksacks, already packed, were extracted from the wardrobe and placed on their backs.

Again, keeping to the shadows and avoiding cameras, they both made their way to the back entrance, across the grounds, and finally crawled under a clipped break in the fence. They were leaving the facility forever, but only Carey turned to look back.

A dirt path led them several hundred metres away to a road with a car hidden behind a spray of overgrowth. They deposited their backpacks in the boot, climbed in, and drove off – the outer gates having been left open. 56 minutes later, they arrived at Rocheford station, and both the building and carpark were dark and deserted. The car's tyres crunched over gravel as they parked by some bushes at an angle where they could watch the entrance from their seats.

They were in good time, it was only 2.38 am, and so they waited with anticipation for 3 am to arrive. A single weak lamp above the ticket office window was the only illumination, and the Alpha watched the flies and moths fluttering in the triangle of light, mesmerised, just as the insects in turn were mesmerised by the lamp.

The time arrived and the boy glanced expectantly from his watch, to the entrance, to Carey, who was beginning to nod off.

But no-one came.

An hour passed, then two, three.

And at last, Alpha slumped back with despondency. His lips trembling, his eyes damp with tears, angered by the weakness of his emotions. Angered at Dr Kendra. Angered by the old man snoring beside him.

Anyone else would be doubting their memory, the instructions, the time, the place. But not the Alpha. He never misremembered.

Soon, slithers of suppressed thoughts came to mind, like tiny silverfish emerging from the damp. And he thought about what he'd seen earlier: the line of adults queuing with the children to get on the minibus. Their parents had come to take them. But not his. And though he didn't even know who his parents were, or where they were, he hated them with a passion. A hatred that broiled and simmered and stewed in his gut. And he wondered why Dr Kendra had not turned up as promised. And now that they had been abandoned, what would they do? Where would they go?

Alpha's body began to shake – whether it was from the cold night air or from despair, he could not tell. He waited and waited, while Carey slept, night yielding gradually to dawn. A haze of light appearing from nowhere – like a trick, pulled out of the dark cloak of night.

The Alpha looked across at Carey, a crumpled old man – himself, a straggly boy. And he felt tired. He shook Carey awake for the second time that night. 'He didn't show up,' was all he told him, his voice wooden.

Carey sat, absorbing the news, scratching his silver beard and harrumphing. He took a swig of water from the flask stored in the door, wiped his mouth, then motioned for the boy to copy him putting on his seatbelt. He turned on the car, and when the fuel gauge jumped to life, he saw that the tank was three-quarters full. He drove slowly back across the gravel, and they turned out of the carpark toward the motorway. The two of them staring ahead at the road, their eyes empty and soulless.

The thrum of the engine and the steady vibrations soon lulled the Alpha to sleep – his body drooping slowly sideways, his head of messy hair thudding dully against the window.

The Alpha was by no means irredeemable at this point in his life. He was just five.

But as Carey slowed along the A-road, to double-check the large green motorway sign that showed both northerly and southerly directions, the boy roused just in time to see the momentary indecision in Carey's face.

The old man did not like to dally when it came to making choices. Life was too short. And so he took just seconds to make up his mind, as easily as flipping a coin.

'What's wrong?' asked the Alpha.

'Nothing,' said Carey. 'Just deciding which relatives to go to.'

'And...?'

'I think, my sister. We'll go to my sister.' He had no particular reason for choosing his sibling in the north, over his cousin in the south. He'd decided on a whim. 'Go back to sleep,' the old man said. 'It's a long way.'

Five hours later, they arrived at the house of Carey's sister, Ambrosia. They had barely parked when the house door flew open and she lumbered up to the car, rosy-cheeked. The Alpha looked at her, and at Carey, not understanding how the two could be related, let alone siblings – they were opposites in every way. Carey was pale, with thinning silver hair, and a wiry frame, while she was taller and stouter with a shock of short brown waves framing a plump face. His nose was thin and pointed, hers was flat and round. He barely spoke, whereas she turned out to be verbose.

Ambrosia peered through the window. 'You're in trouble,' she said, eyes narrowing. 'I can tell – and don't try to convince me otherwise. I don't want to know what shady business you've got yourself into. The less I know the better.' She rolled her eyes. 'Honestly! I don't hear from you for years and then you just turn up unannounced at my doorstep. I see nothing's changed, Carey. Nothing. Actually, no. I take it back. I want to hear everything, every last detail – why on earth you're coming here out of the blue like this.' And then she noticed the child in the seat next to him, and her eyes almost popped.

Carey looked slightly embarrassed, tinged with guilt, shame. She always made him feel that way, even when there was nothing to be guilty about.

'What's going on, Carey? Whose is this child?!'

'It's a long story, Amb,' was all Carey offered. 'But don't get any funny ideas in that head of yours – I ain't done nothing bad. I'm minding the boy... for a while. And he just needs somewhere to stay.'

She glared at the child, and glared at him.

Carey looked down sheepishly. '*We* need somewhere to stay,' he corrected himself.

Ambrosia rolled her eyes, and waved them out. 'You'd better come in then. You too,' she said to the boy.

And just like that, the Alpha, a multi-million-pound government secret, came to be in the care of a simple old man and his foolish younger sister.

In time, Ambrosia learnt about the project, and the need to keep under the radar, so she insisted that they stay together and move to the country, changing their names. She had been alone for far too long, and though she didn't admit it, their arrival brought a frisson of excitement to her otherwise lonely existence. The boy took on the name 'Karl König', marking the beginning of a new chapter in his life. Though he was soon to find out that there was nothing worse for someone of his intelligence, imagination, and brilliance, than to be condemned to a life fraught with tedium and mundanity.

And so, Karl found himself waking up every morning in a strange bed, in an unfamiliar room, with puke-coloured wallpaper and curtains heavy with dust and cobwebs – a far cry from the gleaming, white lines of the laboratories. And he would go to bed at night, staring at that same hideous wallpaper, shrinking into his bed as he watched the shadows from the outside branches transform into ghoul-like hands. Wishing that he was anywhere else, but there.

Ambrosia came to dote on the boy.

She brought him breakfast, granted him a second-hand IBM computer, affordable books, and indulged his whims in a way that bordered on veneration. One morning, she sat on the side of his bed and eyed him affectionately, licking a finger and sticking down a stray tuft of his brassy-blond hair. Karl squirmed. 'I think it's about time you called me "Mother" or "Mum" – don't you? And you should call Carey "Dad".'

The boy eyed the woman curiously. 'But... you're siblings. And you're old enough to be my grandparents.'

Ambrosia batted the air between them. 'Age doesn't mean anything, Karl,' she said, not in the least bit offended. 'We look after you, don't we? Just like parents would. And a boy needs a mother and a father to call his own. So I insist. I do. I insist that you call us Mum and Dad. Besides, it would make Carey happy.'

Karl knew that was a lie; he'd been calling Carey by his name since forever, with not one objection from him. But a sickening revulsion began to blister in Karl's chest. Like the nauseating whiff of boiled sprouts or cabbage – it made his stomach turn. He felt the same sickening dread now.

Completely oblivious to the boy's inner turmoil, Ambrosia took his silence as acceptance, and clasped delighted hands to her chest. 'Right, that's settled then! Now, I'm off to make some breakfast, son. I've got some nice rashers of streaky bacon, fresh eggs from the chickens, and some lovely cherry tomatoes from the allotment.'

'I'm... not really hungry, Ambrosia.'

The woman stopped with a jolt, her face transforming to a squinched glare, sharp as a flicked-out switchblade. 'Mum! Not Ambrosia. Mum!! And we'll have none of this not eating lark. Look at the state of you, you need fattening up. You look like something out of Auschwitz. Now...' – she paused, tipping her head at him, eyes narrowed – '...what do you say?'

The boy closed his eyes, drawing strength.

'What do you say?!' she growled through clenched teeth.

Karl realised she wasn't going to let this go. He pinched his lips together. 'Mmm...' He could not say it. It made him sick just thinking about it. It was a lie. She was not his mother! And he hated his real mother, hated both his parents for not wanting him, not taking him with them after the project.

'I'm waiting,' she said darkly.

'Mmm-Mum!' He spat out the word with distaste, sweat beading on his forehead.

A slow smile crept across Ambrosia's smug face. 'That's it,' she said, satisfied, and turned to leave. 'It'll come easier in time. You'll see...'

Karl slumped back against his pillow, exhausted, knowing that it never, ever would.

At nine years old, Karl took to long, rambling walks through the fields by himself. Not just to escape Ambrosia's foolhardy ways, but also because he was inquisitive, explorative, and was discovering a passion for nature, though not in a healthy, respectful way. The boy was only interested in what he could get. He found a dusty old naturalist's handbook shoved in one of Ambrosia's haphazard bookshelves. It taught him about plants and herbs, and their medicinal and chemical properties. He took the book with him on his walks, disappearing for hours, and using it to find and identify various flora. He brought home bunches of marigolds, with their bright orange heads, which were good for the skin and insect bites. He discovered swathes of creamy white elderflower, an excellent antiseptic. The bristly, purple borage was a remedy for fever, cough, and depression. And even the ubiquitous dandelion had excellent diuretic properties.

He made traps to catch insects and animals, then performed horrible experiments on them, and dissected them, to learn about anatomy. Even the neighbours' wandering cats or dogs were not safe from his morbid curiosity... The countryside became his playground, and everything in it his playthings.

When Karl was nearly 10, his health grew progressively worse. He realised how purifying the tall, constantly whirring air-conditioning units at the laboratory buildings were – filtering out bacteria and germs, and screening them from viruses common to populous towns and cities. During his five years in the project, he had only caught an infection twice – but now, he came down with something every few weeks. The constant nausea, aching bones, malaise, loss of appetite, and pounding headaches were awful. And so he resorted to even heavier doses of painkillers and medication. They brought not only relief, but also loss of memory – swallowing up great chunks of his life, like mental sinkholes.

Ambrosia fussed over him in her usual overbearing manner, imagining she was being the perfect mother. She plied him with vitamins and supplements, practically stuffing them down his throat. And whenever he was admitted to hospital, she battled with doctors and nurses and porters, demanding and complaining, as if they alone were responsible for the boy's pains. And then she moaned at Karl to distraction, saying that he wasn't getting enough sunlight, should be taking more exercise, wasn't eating enough, or drinking enough, and scolding him for messing the bed just when she'd changed the sheets.

Yet despite all of this, the boy's health began to improve by degrees.

And by the time he turned 12, the balance of sickness tipped in favour of better health.

And with a renewed clarity of thinking, he turned to books. Reading everything he could lay his hands on to improve his health. Medical journals, research papers, and experimental studies found on the internet. He read about the human body, its processes and functions, nutritional requirements, and chemical reactions. He read books by revered scientists, doctors, professors. So that by the time Karl turned 15, he had attained doctor-level understanding in most fields of medicine and nutrition. Especially on his own condition.

Such knowledge in the hands of a boy was dangerous. He had learnt how to change his own internal chemistry with drugs and hormones, enzymes and compounds – the chemical factory of the body manipulated with such ease that it was like flicking switches, on and off, within his body.

But with none of them earning a living, Ambrosia's savings soon began to dwindle – and the couple's scant pensions were certainly unable to sustain them. Carey could not find any decent work in the area. And this financial hardship marked a sea-change in Ambrosia's already unstable personality. Her moods and emotions began to unravel and fray even more.

'More books!' she growled, whenever the familiar thud of a parcel hit the doormat. 'We're not made of money you know! We need to economise. Winter's coming, and this house is practically sucking me dry! And you,' she sneered, glaring at the boy, 'ordering expensive books willy-nilly like there's no tomorrow!' Her face creased with anger. 'You only care about your stupid books! You're selfish. And wicked. A selfish, wicked boy!!'

And as she ranted on and on, Karl would look at her in silence, wondering more and more how he could get away from her, pondering thoughts of running away, or suicide, or even fantasising what it would be like without her around... She swung so easily from one mood to another, that it was like walking on eggshells.

'You left the light on again, young man!' she would snarl, flicking off his bedside lamp first thing in the morning.

'I-I'm sorry. I just fell asleep,' he would reply, rubbing tired eyes, and tensing from the familiar first pains of the day gunning through his head.

'Sorry? Sorry?!! If you were really sorry you wouldn't keep doing it. That makes four times this week – not that I'm counting or anything. Just... don't do it again!!'

But Karl was on a daily cocktail of drugs that often made him black out. He could only glare at Ambrosia, aching with pain, and frustrated at the impossibility of living with her.

Yet Karl had only the blunt edge of her anger; Carey was the one who felt its sharp end more often than not. So much so that, after several months, the old man could take it no longer. In quiet desperation, he widened his job searches to further afield, and, at last, found handyman work at a large stately home 170 miles away. The distance meant that he would have to stay away during the week, returning on weekends. He was only sorry that it meant leaving Karl alone with his sister for five whole days, and he hoped that with one less person to look after, she might in time calm down. That is what he convinced himself. But, for Karl, things went from bad to worse. With Carey gone, there was nothing to rein her in.

'Look!!!' she screamed. 'Look at the cost of this shopping bill!!' She balled the receipt and threw it at Karl's head. 'You're bleeding me dry. Dry, I tell you!! What more do you want from me – a pound of flesh?' Cheeks burned red as she eyed the boy lying limp in his bed. But Karl did not react. 'Well a pound of flesh it is!' she shouted, storming off to the kitchen. She returned brandishing a knife.

Karl froze. Looked from the knife to Ambrosia. The rabid madness in her eyes told him that the slightest wrong move could be fatal. And with an amazing ability to control his body, he consciously calmed himself, rearranged his facial features, and controlled his voice. His mind whirred through every possible scenario, every eventuality, and seconds later he looked up at her with a perfectly calculated look. It was a blend of guilt and remorse and childish innocence, as he forced, yet again, that vile word out of his mouth. 'Mmm-Mum. P-please. I'll be more careful. I promise.' With flawless control, he made tears flow from his eyes, made his lips tremble and quiver.

Ambrosia stopped in her tracks. Slowly, she dropped the hand that held the knife, her shoulders slumping.

The boy looked at her, and understood what it was like to come face to face with raw, mindless rage. And he learnt from this. Learnt that such mindless outbursts were like a flame to an explosive. And so, if he had to live with her, he needed to control his every word and action – for self-preservation. 'I promise,' he repeated pathetically.

Ambrosia blinked at him. 'Too right,' she said, her voice cracking. And she turned to leave.

Carey's homecoming every Friday evening was the silver lining to Karl's week. The old man appeared at the doorstep laden with gifts of pork pies the size of plates, bags of shiny red apples, slices of cake, and bottles of wine. He brought home cast-offs of a perfectly good cricket bat, and bags and bags of unwanted books. Karl was delighted, and lined his room with neat stacks that hugged the walls.

Karl didn't mention, and Carey never asked about, Ambrosia's worsening moods. There was no point. The two simply stole silent glances at each other, which communicated everything they needed to know.

As the months went by, Ambrosia's mood continued to wax and wane, making the tension in the house palpable. In the mornings she almost always nursed a hangover, and blamed the boy for the mess that she herself left the night before. But at night, her blind drunkenness made her throw things in rage – black marks and dents in the wall were silent testimony of her wrath.

Karl soon asked Carey to put a lock on his bedroom door. He was just over 15 years old now, and though still scrawny, he was much taller – with acne on his nose and forehead, and a shadow of stubble on his chin.

It was on a day of non-stop rain – which started as a fine drizzle hugging the air, and loosened by the afternoon into thundery storms – that things came to a head. Karl confined himself to the house in fear of catching pneumonia, carefully pulling out a book from one of the stacks and taking it into bed. But the pages felt oddly wet and powdery, and on closer inspection, he saw that it was caked with a fine green-black mould. Looking across at the stacks of books, and then around at the walls and ceiling, he noticed patches of mildew blooming just below the coving, where peeling wallpaper curled.

The boy knew that mould and damp would be disastrous for his health, his lungs being already weak, and so he quickly wrote a note to Ambrosia – his preferred method of communication, because it avoided her mercurial temperament, and meant he didn't have to say that word out loud. He wrote:

'There's mildew and mould growing all over the place, which is really bad for the house, my books, and especially my health. So can you please call someone to come over and fix it? K.'

He slipped out of bed, tiptoed down the hall, avoiding the creaking floorboards, and shoved the folded note under her bedroom door. Quickly, he returned to his room and locked the door. 16 minutes later, Karl heard a muffled commotion from her room, followed by stamping feet in the hallway. He took a deep breath.

'Karl!!' she screamed from the other side, yanking on the handle and banging the door. 'Karl!!' The lock rattled weakly. She began fighting with it – kicking and beating the wood with animalistic rage, heedless of the damage she was doing both to the door and herself. 'Open the door!!!' She paused, caught her breath. 'You're bleeding me dry, you ungrateful little worm!' Her shouts were muffled through the wood. 'Little Lord Fancypants ordering me around. Do you even know how many sacrifices I've made for you? Do you?! I gave up a good job, a *really* good job in the London Stock Exchange, to move to this god-forsaken house in the middle of nowhere. And for what? For you to bleed me dry!! So what if there's damp?! I don't care. I don't care one bit if you die from mould spores. Huh! Mould spores!! Well, if you died, at least I'd be rid of you, you little brat!!'

The lock rattled weakly, and Karl caught his breath, knowing that it could give in at any moment. He heaved himself out of bed, grabbed the heavy cricket bat left leaning against his wardrobe, and stood behind the door. Closing his eyes, he braced himself, tried to control the judders of fear that wracked his body.

There was a loud crack of splitting wood, and the door flew open. Ambrosia stepped in, a bright red face contorted with rage, nostrils flaring, hands balled into tight fists. Karl swung the bat with all his strength, turning his head away as the club connected with her skull.

Ambrosia crumpled to the floor in a heap.

Karl steadied himself, and stared at her lying there – his heart thudding. Inching closer, he extended a hand, but it shook so much that he snatched it back, holding it to his chest. He closed his eyes and consciously calmed himself. This time his hand was perfectly steady as he stooped to place two fingers just inside her wrist. She was alive.

His mind whirred with an array of possibilities, and in just seconds he settled on a plan – wasting no time in swiftly carrying it out.

First, he took the cricket bat outside to the garden hose tap, and scrubbed it under the freezing cold water, and then he hid the bat in the shed, burying it under a pile of junk. He shook his hands from the chilblains as he returned to his room. Stooping down he pushed and heaved the unconscious Ambrosia with all his might, positioning her body and her limbs in a specific way. Next he took a tissue, caught a little of the blood dripping from her forehead, and rubbed it onto the rusty base of his iron bedstead.

Stepping over her legs, he grabbed a bottle of his own liquid sedative, eyed her bodyweight, and then syringed out three times the usual dosage. He popped the syringe into her mouth, right at the back of her tongue, and ejected the medicine down her throat so that she swallowed it by reflex. Karl made a note of the time, and estimated that he had about five hours while she slept it off.

He got rid of the bloody tissue by flushing it down the toilet, and tidied his room, re-stacking the books as they were before. He also retrieved the note that he found on her bedroom floor, and burnt it in the hearth. When he saw that everything was back to the way it was, he sat down, exhausted. He could take his time now.

He went back to Ambrosia's room and carefully looked through her array of supplement bottles. He picked out the bottles of capsules and liquid, and brought them all into the kitchen. Then, rifling through the drawers and cabinets, he set out on the table a mortar and pestle, a knife and chopping board, several clean bowls, saucepans, oven trays, a sieve, digital scales, and more syringe dispensers. He also took a selection of his own medicine, and brought them to the kitchen. Finally, he went outside and spent time picking out a variety of herbs, plants, leaves, and berries from their allotment – then laid them all out on the large wooden table.

He paused to look over it all, eyes glazing over as, in his mind, he configured elements, compounds, and formulae. Karl saw before him a perfect chemistry, a druggery, mentally juggling the elements – as if he were a god with the ability to ply with nature itself, deconstructing and reconstructing matter, transforming them into different forms. He rolled up his sleeves, and set to work – meticulously making potent decoctions of herbal extracts, and mixing them in with Ambrosia's bottles of liquids. Then he dried leaves and mushrooms in the oven, grinding them to a fine powder, carefully replacing the contents of the capsules.

In the end, he scooped up the doctored supplement bottles, and returned them to Ambrosia's room, placing them in exactly the same ring-marks on her cabinet.

After glancing at her sleeping form, he checked the time. He had at least another couple of hours to play with, and there was one thing in particular that he needed to find. He rifled through Ambrosia's bedroom – searching in drawers, shelves, cupboards, her wardrobe. He spotted something wedged under a messy pile of sweaters: a large cloth-bound volume with handsome gold lettering. 'Beating the Stock Market at its Own Game', published by the London Stock Exchange. Karl lifted it out and lay it on the bed. There was neatly written cursive handwriting on the first page: 'To our wonderful char-lady, Amber, we'll miss you! Hands down the best tea-maker in town. And as you're quite the aspiring little stock trader, we thought you might like this, our latest. Wishing you every success in your new adventures. The LSET.' Karl knew that Amber was a name she gave to friends and acquaintances – and he snorted to himself. She was a char-lady! So much for the 'really good job' she gave up to look after him. Still, the book was an excellent find.

He continued his searches, and at last found what he was looking for. Her bank books. They were in a used brown envelope, hidden underneath a tatty old jewellery box. He knew she did all her banking by telephone because she couldn't get to grips with the computer, and then he saw with amazement that the telephone number, as well as her passcode and security answers, were scrawled neatly on the back of the envelope. Karl laughed out loud, wondering how incredibly stupid the woman was! He found himself parroting Ambrosia's voice out loud, something he'd heard her say on the telephone to the bank, once: 'So many questions – and they're all daft! I mean, it's impossible to get into my own account!' Karl had managed to mimic her voice flawlessly, and he chuckled at her idiocy. But then he realised the perfect control he had over his own voicebox, the ability to impersonate; another string in his bow of self-mastery.

He took the envelope, and, after peaking inside his room to check that Ambrosia was still out, went to the computer and navigated to the bank website. He had all the information he needed to set up online accounts, and in this way, he was able to take complete control over her money.

Half an hour later, he returned the envelope of bank books, and then calmly went to the telephone in the hall. As he dialled the number, he deliberately quickened his breathing, and made his whole body shake. He blinked, and pushed tears out of his eyes. When Carey answered, Karl effected a small, frightened, voice. 'H-hello? Carey? S-something terrible has happened,' he sobbed, sounding convincingly distressed. 'Ambrosia got mad at me, a-and broke down my door. But she tripped on the rug, and fell, and banged her head. I... I think she's been drinking... No, I'm fine... Yes, she's breathing, but not moving. Please, please, come quickly!'

He put down the receiver, pleased with his performance. The face that had been twisted with anguish and tears, now returned to wooden indifference. He stopped shaking, dried his eyes, and blew his nose – then got up and went to the kitchen, calm as day. He started making himself a nice cup of tea, before stopping, remembering something.

He returned to his room, stooped down, and hooked the edge of the rug over Ambrosia's foot, then doused some tissue with wine from the bottle, and dabbed it around Ambrosia's mouth and clothes. He put everything back, and washed his hands. Satisfied, he went back to his tea.

Nearly two hours later, Carey arrived all in a rush and saw his sister lying there. He stooped down to look her over, but grimaced from the stench of alcohol, shaking his head with despair. He saw too the stain of blood on the bedstead where she hit her head. Sighing, he grabbed hold of her shoulders and dragged her, unceremoniously, to her bedroom. It took several heaves to pull her into bed, and then he went about cleaning her up with a damp cloth and towel. Afterward, he went to Karl, and found the boy sitting in his bed, red-eyed and whimpering, shaken and upset. Carey did his best to console him.

The next day, Ambrosia woke up with a thumping headache, remembering nothing of the damp note, or the cricket bat. There was no reason for her not to believe Carey when he told her in earnest that, in a fit of rage, she had tripped over Karl's rug and hit her head. Her migraine was so intense, her nerves so raw, that she hardly cared – and she just shuffled to the toilet, took her vitamins with a glass of water, burped, and promptly fell back to sleep.

Carey made sure to repair Karl's bedroom door, setting replacement hardwood jambs in thick plaster, and fitting a stronger lock, together with a couple of bolts for extra reinforcement. Karl also mentioned the damp in his room, and Carey – ever the handyman – immediately wiped down the surfaces with disinfectant, then bleached and white-washed the walls. A temporary fix until they could afford a damp course.

The next days for Karl were halcyon. Ambrosia slept for most of them, and so he was able to read the stock market book in peace, without fear of her storming in. The trading business was fascinating, and, incentivised by the need to make enough money to fix the damp for his health, he became obsessed with learning about investments. It took him just a day to speed-read and memorise the entire book. It was a simple enough concept, to buy stocks low and later sell them at the highest price possible – but the key was identifying which stocks had potential, knowing when they were on the up, and monitoring the market to anticipate and predict growth. The book taught him to analyse past and present market data, financial news on global markets, economies of individual countries, oil prices, and interest rates.

And while Ambrosia continued taking her vitamins, going straight back to bed to sleep off what she thought was probably flu, Karl commandeered the desktop, and set up online banking for Ambrosia's accounts, then registered at eight of the top stock-trading websites. He started by investing small amounts of Ambrosia's money in several companies that his research led him to believe were on the up. Safety was key – he knew that one stupid mistake could make him lose all his bargaining chips. And in just a short time, he was encouraged by the returns, even though they were small. Every penny that he made, was re-invested, gradually growing his portfolio – and by keeping a strict eye on tracking every single stock, it seemed the more Karl invested, the more money he made.

One weekend, Carey returned home looking particularly pleased with himself. Unusually, he asked Karl to go out to the car to fetch something from the boot. The boy hesitated, wondering why, but resigned to doing as he was told. In a few moments he returned to the house carrying a large bell-shaped object about 10 inches high, not too heavy, and covered with a cloth. 'Is this what you wanted?' asked Karl, curious.

Carey beamed. 'It is, it is. The mistress asked me to dispose of them.

Too noisy, she said...'

The boy set it down on the sideboard and pulled off the cloth to reveal a white ornamental cage, with three bright yellow canaries inside. Karl stared at them for some time. They in turn stared up at him with shiny black eyes, huddled together in a corner, heads tilting this way and that. Karl bent closer to look through the thin struts at the little creatures. They shrank back, quivering.

'For me?' asked Karl, glancing at Carey but then magnetising back to the birds.

'Mm,' Carey grunted.

'Thank you!' he beamed.

Carey disappeared for a bit, then returned trundling an old wooden serving trolley into his room – he placed it next to the window, and Karl set the bird cage on top. It was the perfect aspect. The natural light shone on the birds' vivid feathers, and the canaries could look out at the rich blue of the sky, and the rustling, overhanging trees.

In time, Karl came to love the little creatures. Just looking at them calmed him. He often sat next to the cage, and watched as the birds hopped closer, tilting their heads, and waiting for food. He exchanged knowing glances with them, sensing an affinity, their situations parallel – the boy too was captive, in a cage of illness.

Karl took painstaking care of his new pets, cleaning their cage regularly, and providing the best food, treats, and mineral salts. He was often rewarded for his care by their spontaneous singing – trill, and light, and evocative of the great outdoors, and the boundless height of the sky. It was a sad reminder of the liberation that neither he, nor they, would experience. Often, the boy huddled close to the cage and whistled to them. The canaries would listen respectfully, eyeing Karl with mild curiosity, and then answer him with demonstrations of how real songs ought to be sung. In this way, slowly, slowly, Karl's heart began to thaw. Both his love of Carey, and his growing love for the birds, brought seeds of change that might well have redeemed him from his current path. But then, one morning, everything changed.

Karl was jarred awake by a heavy fist banging angrily against his door. He was sleepy, and didn't realise that the bolts had been left unlocked.

Ambrosia flung the door open with such force that it cracked the plaster on the wall.

She was dishevelled, sickly, her hair a mess; months of illness had taken its toll. Her eyes bored into him. 'I couldn't sleep last night,' she growled. 'And just when I started to nod off, those darned birds started their raucous screeching!' She fumed with anger as she looked menacingly from the boy to the cage. 'I'm going to *kill* them!!' she hissed.

Karl pushed himself out of bed, and stood in front of the cage – but Ambrosia thrust him aside as though he were nothing. He fell to the ground like a crumpled leaf, hitting his head against the trolley.

Carey suddenly appeared at the door, and saw the boy bleeding on the floor, his crazed sister fumbling with the lock of the cage. He ran to her, pulled her off, and she fell onto the bed. Then he swivelled round, standing between her and the boy.

Ambrosia turned. Shadows of evil in her eyes. She looked as if she could kill. And like a thing possessed, she launched onto her brother, throwing him to the ground, and pinning him down with her knee. She began slapping at him again and again, while he lifted feeble arms over his head in weak protection. But the slaps turned to punches, raining down on him in fury. Smashing through flesh, crunching into bone.

Karl tried to pull her off, shouting, 'Stop it!!' over and over. But she shrugged him off, continuing to pound down into Carey, who seemed to sink deeper and deeper into the ground.

Karl hung back, horrified, trembling, his mind buzzing. He wiped the blood from his eyes, and looked around. Saw that the birds were squawking hysterically, flying about in blind panic, smashing themselves against the bars. Closing his eyes, he squeezed tears onto pale cheeks, then opened the cage and took out a bird. As he twisted it within both hands – the faint cracking sound inaudible above Ambrosia's onslaught – Karl felt as though he were tearing his own heart in two. Wrenching it asunder like a dry twig.

When he tossed the bird onto the floor, Ambrosia noticed a flash of yellow fall next to her. And she stopped. The canary lay there – immoveable – its tiny chest rising and falling in panic... Eventually coming to a stop. Another bird tumbled next to it, then another. Piled in a pathetic heap. Their stillness a stark reminder of the still body that lay beneath her. She caught her breath. Blinked in disbelief. Tore her eyes away, and forced herself to look down at Carey – emitting a guttural sob that rent the air in two.

'THERE!!!' screamed Karl, barely able to see through his tears. 'They're dead!! Now leave us alone!!'

The woman looked at her brother's bloody, swollen face, then stared at her dripping hands, as if she hardly knew their power. And in a trance, she stood up, stepped over her brother, over the birds, and walked out.

Karl immediately fell to his knees next to Carey, scrambling to check for signs of life. He grabbed a pillow and gently, tenderly placed it under the old man's head. Getting up, he quickly ran to the telephone and picked up the handset – but then he stopped, and slowly put it down. He thought for several seconds. Then got up, walked to Ambrosia's room, and found her lying on her side on the bed. She was shaking and whimpering pathetically, her arms cradling her head. Trying to block out the world, trying to block out the nightmare she was in.

Karl looked from the woman to the cabinet, and he walked over to it, picking out a small brown pill bottle. He went to sit on the bed, letting out a series of agonising sobs. 'Carey's dead!' he cried. 'Y-you killed him...'

The silence that reigned over them was thunderous.

Ambrosia's arms shifted, and she eyed the boy, the torment in his face, and shook her head in disbelief.

Karl dropped his hand on the bed, and uncurled his fingers. The bottle rolled out next to her, rattling lightly. 'I... I think you know what you have to do,' he said in a low voice. 'Now. Before I call the police.' He paused, then got up and left the room. As he passed through the doorway, he crossed an invisible threshold that marked the point of no return. His bitter heart had turned. Hardened. There was no longer any chance of redemption. His soul lost to the darkness.

Ambrosia's eyes gravitated to the pills, as if they held a special power. She stared at the bottle's peeling label, the ink smudged grey. She heard, from the corridor, the faint dialling of only three numbers on the telephone, then Karl's distraught, tremulous voice begging the operator for help. He cried words that stabbed her. 'She beat him to a pulp.' 'He's stopped breathing.' 'He's dead!'

Ambrosia sat up, barely able to breathe. She unscrewed the pill bottle with hands crusted in her brother's blood. Tilting her head back, she gulped them down, greedy for the relief they would bring. The empty bottle fell to the floor as she drank from the glass on her bedside table. When she wiped her mouth with the back of her hand, a smear of crimson stained her face.

She shivered, and hiccoughed, and lay back down on the bed. Feeling the tepid liquid slip down her throat.

Closing her eyes, she willed and willed for it all to be over.

She exhaled.

And like a grim, macabre fable, her one last wish came true.

•••————————————————•••

Karl's eyes snapped opened, and he saw that he was in bed. Somehow he knew it was morning, though it was impossible to tell with no natural light.

The water on the other side of the hull viewing glass cast dappled, undulating shadows on the bulkhead wall – and he stared blankly at the shifting blue waves for some time.

Eventually he yawned, scratched his neck, then sat up and swung his legs out of bed. Closing his eyes, he waited. Ah, there it was – that familiar first pang of a migraine. He breathed it in as it thundered through his head. He had a strange relationship with pain. He kind of liked it. After all, it fed the addiction to the painkillers, and you couldn't have one without the other. He reached for the tablets – blister packs neatly stacked in a glass container. The movement spiked the pain, bringing tears to his eyes. He gulped down a handful of pills with a glass of water.

As he waited for them to take effect, he watched the ripple of the sea on the other side of the viewing glass. It was hypnotic. He knew that water covered 70% of the planet, yet the vast oceans were 95% unexplored. And now that he had amassed wealth from his stock exchange wheelings and dealings, it afforded him the luxury of exploring that vast unknown. And so he had spent months scouring the seas – searching, plundering, experimenting.

He was just 17 years old, and his face was longer and more defined – though his eyes, underlined by dark rings, were still old and knowing. His brassy blond hair was thick in parts, yet patched with baldness in others, his adam's apple large against a scrawny neck. And although he had not grown a great deal in height, his limbs were long and gangly.

When at last the pain had dissipated, he got up and padded into the en-suite bathroom – his mind whirring with a flurry of abstract thoughts despite the blank expression on his face. Distractedly, he went to the toilet – but forgot to flush, or wash his hands. He brushed his teeth, wet his face, and quickly hand-combed what was left of his hair into some semblance of tidiness.

Later he met with Carey in the mess hall, and they ate breakfast together as was their custom. Carey's hair was whiter, his wrinkles more pronounced – a broken, crooked nose now his defining feature. The old man's mind was going, and he wore slippers all the time, even when he went outside. And as he ate his porridge, he drummed a restless foot against the table leg in a steady beat.

Karl talked to him, though Carey didn't register a thing he said.

'I'm nearly there,' Karl told him, looking over his own plate of food and pushing it away. Instead he sipped on his drink. 'The cure is almost complete. Almost.'

Carey smiled, but only from the satisfaction of letting off silent wind.

'I've done the animal testing,' Karl continued. 'All successful.' He paused, tilting his head slightly. 'What was that?' he asked.

But the old man had said not a word. Just stared blankly at him.

Karl nodded thoughtfully. 'Yes, yes. You're right, Carey. Can you believe it! We have those two Neanderthal children from the project right here, locked in a cabin, which is good news! It means I can start experimenting on them. Today.' Karl smirked, and wiped a smudge of juice from his mouth. He got up, scraping back the chair loudly.

The old man looked up at Karl, frowning. 'You haven't finished your breakfast, Alphie,' he said, his voice gravelly, as if there was sand in his throat. 'You should eat it.'

Karl patted the old man on the back, sighing. Then he left. He walked along several passageways, and whenever someone came past him, they stepped aside dutifully, and nodded to the boy, though he ignored them. A few minutes later Karl entered a code into the keypad of his cabin, and he stepped inside, dogging the door down behind him.

He sat at his computer, logged in, and stopped to admire the screensaver. At first glance, it looked like a serene image of two sleeping figures – a man and a woman, their skin pale, eyes closed, lying on a ruby red bedspread printed with small, delicate rosebuds. But they were not sleeping.

Karl glared at them with contempt. *Mr and Mrs Schäfer*. His Mutter and

Vater, his 'geliebten' richtigen Eltern – so called, 'beloved' natural parents. Yet they had refused to come for him after the project. They had abandoned him when he needed them the most. And for that, he smouldered with barely contained hatred, even now, as he stared at the image of their dead bodies.

He wondered. Should he watch the video again? Hesitating, he pulled out his pocket watch – there was still time. And with a frisson of excitement he clicked on the file right in the middle of his desktop, hit the 'play' button, and grabbed a packet of gummy bears as he sat back to watch.

The ghost of Penny Thompson appeared onscreen.

Her image was grainy and out of focus in night-vision shades of grey and white. She was a woman of many faces, and in the video, her hair was scraped back in a severe bun, with thick-rimmed glasses, and a pale face devoid of make-up. Her forehead was creased with concentration as she stooped down to fiddle with the body camera, and when done, she picked up the garment it was strapped to – a black utility gilet – and put it on, fastening the velcro strips at her side. The camera now turned outward from her shoulder, in first-person view. She reached into the car boot for her cross-body bag, carefully checking inside for her usual medical bottles, rag-cloth, syringes, and a 7-inch knife that glinted as she slid it back in its sheath. The boot was closed with a light thwunk, and the car locked remotely. It was an eye-catching car with contrasting squares printed at the side, and bold lettering underneath.

Penny Thompson turned toward the house – a large Edwardian detached building, with sprawling, perfectly-manicured lawns. A Land Rover Discovery gleamed in the driveway. She walked casually up the path, and knocked. A rather haggard looking man, in his late forties, opened. He had Karl's cheekbones, as well as his sunken, grey eyes. He was surprised to see her.

'Is there something wrong, officer?' Hanno Schäfer asked, glancing at her police car parked in the road.

She stopped chewing her gum. 'There've been sightings of a dangerous criminal in the area, Sir,' she said, her voice flat.

(Karl laughed out loud as he reached for more sweets, casually popping one in his mouth.)

'And I just wanted to ask you some questions,' continued Penny

Thompson. 'About whether you've seen anything unusual or suspicious. So, er, can I come in, Sir? It won't take long.'

The man hesitated momentarily, but then opened the door.

He took her into the living room. 'Please, take a seat,' he said. 'Although, I really don't have much time, I have lots of work.' He pulled out an old-fashioned pocket-watch, and glanced at it briefly. The chain drooping between his fingers.

'Like I said, I won't be long,' said Penny Thompson with a sneer. In one smooth movement she took a step closer, reached inside her bag, and extracted a knife. Just as the man's eyes widened with shock, she swivelled behind, and pulled his chin up, exposing his neck to the cut – in one smooth movement.

The man dropped to his knees, hands crossed at his throat, gurgling.

'Hanno?' came a voice from the hall. 'Who was at the d-?'

Penny Thompson spun round just as the woman appeared at the doorway.

Mallory Schäfer froze as she took in the scene, horrified – and she screamed. She turned and ran. Flying up the stairs, stumbling, and then getting up again – still screaming.

Penny Thompson bounded after her like a thing possessed, up the stairs, down the hallway, and past two bedroom doors. She saw her dart inside the third.

Just as Penny Thompson got to the door she heard the sound of a lock turning, then pathetic whimpering from the other side, some commotion, and something breaking. She started kicking in the door. Each bang was echoed by a muffled scream from inside, until the wood caved, and Penny Thompson stumbled in.

Mrs Schäfer was standing, quivering, in the far corner of the room next to the bed. And as her assailant marched round to grab her, the terrified woman produced a table lamp from behind her back, with the bulb smashed and the filament glowing. She jabbed it into her face. Penny Thompson stumbled back, screaming with pain. Pausing for several seconds, she shook her head, grunting, and recovered. The side of her face smeared with bloody black burns. Advancing again, she grabbed Schäfer's hair and pulled it back, so that her chin was thrust upwards, her neck open to the thin red line that was drawn silently across it.

The woman slumped onto the bed. The white duvet gradually seeping with red, its pattern of pink rosebuds fading.

Penny Thompson pulled out a rag-cloth and wiped her hands and face, catching her breath. There was no time to wait for the woman to die, with two more things on her checklist. A memento, and photos. She needed to hurry before the real police came, and so she turned and marched out purposefully.

Karl suddenly stiffened and lunged forward, pausing video playback. The frame twitched nervously. He stared at the screen, puzzled. Rewinding the video several seconds, he pressed play, this time hitting the pause button at just the right frame. He leant closer and scrutinised the image for several seconds trying to work out what he was seeing. And when he realised, his eyebrows shot up and he leant back in his chair, dumbfounded.

The freeze-frame showed the wardrobe door slightly ajar by about a centimetre, and low down, close to the floor, was the shadowy face of someone hiding. An unmistakeable eye wide with horror, strands of fallen hair, a slanted eyebrow.

Quickly he switched screens to open a messenger program. Then he typed: 'Neutralisation command. Target: the daughter of Hanno and Mallory Schäfer.'

He would have called on his trusted Penny Thompson for such a request. But she had been sent to China, along with several others, to bring back another one of those Neanderthal children. So instead, he had to rely on the back-up hitman.

Karl sat back, still amazed at the thought – that he had a half-sister.

Well, not for much longer...

He suddenly wondered about the time, and so pulled out his father's pocket-watch, gliding fingers across the warm smoothness of it, coiling the weight of the chain in his palm. He was fond of that watch. It helped him keep to his meticulous schedules. And today was special, very special, so he needed to keep to perfect time.

It would start after lunch, at exactly 1 pm. When he planned to talk to the recently captured Professor. He thought it amusing that he was now blind. And he wanted to have some fun befuddling the pathetic old man, and making him squirm with impossible questions.

Then at 2 pm he would take the Professor to the same cabin where those nasty little primates were being held. And he would watch as the children were dragged away, with the old man surely being tormented by their screams – the very last time he would hear their stupid voices. Karl chuckled at the thought.

At 3 pm, Karl was to take his usual cocktail of afternoon drugs, the highlight of his day – he wouldn't be able to function otherwise. Followed by a nap in the empty cabin. He'd set the room out specially, a single bed being the only furniture in an otherwise empty room – ensuring peace and quiet for his acid trip. The respite would give him the energy to work into the night. There was much to do. Tweaking and fine-tuning the formula to the cure. The experimentation would inevitably lead to the children's deaths – just as all those other animals had died before them. But at least he will have brought the cure to completion. His life's work, or at least, most of what he had been working on for the past two years. His own exhaustion and sickness was increasing every day, and he would need it soon.

There was still time before his schedule commenced. And so Karl decided to go to his laboratory, to prepare.

When he arrived, and went in, he locked the door behind him. There was an over-powering stench that came in putrid waves – of animals, chemicals, rotting flesh, urine, faeces, hay, bleach, and sawdust. Anyone else would have gagged, but Karl was used to it by now, and only twitched his nose as he put on a once-white lab coat. He switched the lights on, revealing row upon row of cages inside a vast cabin. In the middle of the room was a long, narrow table, strewn haphazardly with medical equipment and instruments, stained brown. At the side were dusty shelves, crammed full with glass jars containing organs preserved in yellowing formaldehyde, and in the far corner was the thick iron door of a waste disposal unit.

Some cages contained heaps of dead animals, but the majority of them held live ones. When the boy passed, the animals immediately quietened and cowered in fear, pressing their quaking bodies away from him against steel bars. Karl whistled a tune to himself as he walked across to the large industrial refrigerator – but stopped suddenly. The three dead canaries sang back to him. And he looked up, and saw the memory of them perched on top of a cage – bright yellow feathers and shiny eyes staring down at him with mild curiosity. He listened to them momentarily as they sung.

Then he went to the refrigerator, searching inside amongst grubby bottles, phials, and containers, and he picked out a half-eaten pork pie – dropping the cellophane on the floor, before biting into it.

When he reached the central table, he distractedly set the remains of his pork pie on the damp, cruddy surface, then tidied everything away so that it was completely clear. Except for the stains. Accidentally knocking the pie on the floor, he tutted, then picked it up and casually popped it in his mouth. As he chewed, cheeks bulging, he stood back and surveyed the empty surface with satisfaction.

Now that he was going to experiment on the children, he would need the full operating table to work on.

Karl only made it through half of his perfectly-planned schedule. He'd just injected himself with the afternoon cocktail of drugs, and a crew member had strapped him onto the bed in the empty cabin. He lay back and closed his eyes. There was a numb tingle in his arm at the injection site, and he waited as the aches and pains in his body slowly began to dissipate. The weak thud of his heartbeat and a rush of blood filled his ears. Sweat eked out of every pore, cooling him.

At last the full force of the drugs hit him like crashing waves – each successive surge giving him an overwhelming sense of power and euphoria. His spine arced. Hands balled into fists. He felt as if he were soaring, flying, rising so high that he was like a god – invincible and indestructible.

And then the missiles came.

Through the fog and giddiness of his acid trip, he was aware only of being led out of the room amidst a maelstrom of confusion and panic and booming explosions. With him were the children and the Professor. Their shouts ringing in his ears. It felt like his body had turned inside out, his consciousness disbursed, yet hovering close by. The sound of his breathing thundered in his head. He was no longer singular, but having an uncertain plurality – he was flying, yet buried, shrieking, yet gagged. He was everything at once, and nothing. And he found that he was in a bubble, a white bubble. Being strapped in. His voice a distant echo as he shouted for the emergency launch. Then the very last explosion burst into a raging monster of red and orange flames.

And he blacked out.

—————————————————

Karl's eyes snapped opened, and he realised he was in bed. He had no idea of the time; it was impossible to tell with no natural light.

By reflex, his hand patted a pocket for the watch, but he found that there was no pocket, and no watch.

When his sight came into focus, he saw that he was not in his cabin. And the Professor was sitting next to his bed, inexplicably smiling. The boy tried to speak, but his mouth and throat were scorched. He gasped for water, and someone held a straw to his mouth. He gulped the liquid down, then caught his breath, waiting for it to fill his veins and hydrate him.

The Professor was greeting him warmly, like a long-lost friend.

Groggy as he was, Karl managed to effect a suitably pitiful expression. Meaningless words exchanged.

And then the Professor told him that awful thing.

The submarine had been destroyed.

Everyone on it was dead.

Karl blinked, absorbing the full hideous truth of it.

All his crew, gone.

The progress he had made on his cure.

Carey.

And he wanted to scream! Wanted to writhe with agony!!

But instead he sat calmly. Quietly told the old man he was fine.

Yet all the Professor was interested in was the other children from the project! Asking question after question about them.

Karl's blood seethed behind that mild façade.

Thankfully another doctor came in and told the old man that he should rest. As he watched the Professor leave the room, heard the pathetic tap-tap of his cane, Karl balled his fists under the cover. And he vowed then and there that he would end the old man and the children, if it was the last thing he did.

Nurse Shauna breezed in and out of his room, always smiling and winking at him, which Karl found incredibly annoying. He could only stare at her in silent indifference. By the third day, Karl was feeling much stronger, and he was already planning how he could stop her enervating cheerfulness.

When he was alone, he searched his bedside cabinet and, to his relief, found the pocket-watch. There was a fine sheen of water misting the inside of the glass face, but amazingly it was still working. He thrust it to the back of the cabinet, behind his swollen sneakers, and closed the door.

Irritatingly, animals were allowed to roam freely, and they came in and out of his room as they pleased. One of the vexatious kittens had even tried climbing onto his bed – but he soon batted it off, cursing. He watched it thud and skid on the floor, until it scrambled up, hissed, and ran off in a flash. A large dog turned up at his doorway and growled at him, and so he threw a slipper at it. But the animal dodged the missile with ease, and left.

Nurse Shauna came to see what all the commotion was about, but Karl made up something about the dog being aggressive for no reason. It turned out to his advantage, because she told him about the CCTV, which was connected to a 'supercomputer' called Jasmine. So if he ever needed her, he just had to say, 'Jasmine, get Nurse Shauna' – and she would come. She even showed him her iPad, which would notify her of his request – explaining how the CCTV app helps her locate everyone. Most of the rooms, and hospital rooms, had cameras, she said, glancing up at the ceiling – but of course, private bedrooms, his included, and bathrooms were off-camera, with only movement and temperature sensors for safety reasons. 'So you can snore away and spend a penny without worrying that Big Brother's watching,' she smiled, remarking, 'Crazy efficient, isn't it? It's what they call a "smart" building. And you wouldn't believe that Calista set it all up! She looks every bit the blonde bimbo, but she's a genius. A beautiful genius!'

Karl was intrigued. 'Calista?' he asked, purposefully making wheezing sounds. And then he realised. 'Ah, I know her! The pretty girl who keeps bringing me tea and cake?'

'That's her,' smiled Shauna, winking. 'Of course you'd notice she's pretty, but I'm afraid she's taken, so don't you be getting any ideas...'

Karl did a double-take, but then went along. 'Yes, yes, what a shame...'

'Well, I've got some rounds to do,' sighed the nurse. 'But I'll be back to check in later. Meanwhile, you know what to do if you want me.' She pointed up at the ceiling.

'Yes,' wheezed Karl. 'Certainly, I will call into the air, and ask this Jasmine to get you if I need.' He put on the oxygen mask, and watched as she left. The CCTV was a problem. It meant that he couldn't move around

Avernus freely without being seen, so he needed to be careful.

And so that night, while everyone was sleeping, and under cover of darkness, he was able to find the supply room which, incredibly, had no lock on it! It was filled to bursting with medicines, drugs, equipment, and bedding. Karl almost laughed to himself. They were that trusting, that stupid.

Early the next day, he waited for Nurse Shauna to arrive. When she came into the room, bright and breezy, she put her iPad on the side table, then administered his usual analgesics. Just before she moved away, suddenly – and with a strength that belied his sickly appearance – Karl grabbed her ponytail, exactly as he had seen Penny Thompson do in the videos, yanking it back. He held a loaded syringe to her neck, its silver needle pressing into her skin. The nurse's wild eyes flitted this way and that, as she snivelled with terror. Karl cradled her head on his shoulder and hissed menacingly, 'Don't. Make. A sound. Don't move. Or you're dead.' The reek of his breath was hot against her skin. He yanked on her hair again. 'Now listen carefully,' he growled. 'I want you to leave this place – right now – and never return. Leave the iPad and take only your belongings. Don't talk to anyone about this, don't say a word. Just go. If I hear otherwise, I will come after you and your family. And I'll obliterate every last member, from young to old. And believe me when I say, they will have long and painful deaths.'

The nurse whimpered.

'Do you understand?!' he hissed, wrenching her hair again.

She nodded quickly, but then panicked and began struggling under his grip. Karl grappled with her, and plunged the syringe into her neck, swearing.

The nurse let out a muffled scream, broke free, and scrambled out of the room as fast as her legs could take her. Stopping only to grab her handbag, she fled Avernus without a word.

Karl quickly jumped out of his bed and took her iPad into the en-suite bathroom, and locked the door. Sitting down on the closed toilet, he discovered that the tablet too had no password on it, and Karl smirked. The tablet gave him a window to almost every room in Avernus... He tapped on the CCTV app, and settled back to watch.

Over the next few days, Karl feigned – with his usual flawless performance – a downturn in his illness, so that he could be left alone to watch Avernus through the tablet, for hours and hours. And then, when he saw the Professor's discussion with Gaia, he sat up, suddenly interested. The old man talked about being glad that the person he spoke to on the submarine had died, despite the cost to human life. And Karl, breathing threats and murder, hated the Professor even more.

Compelling viewing too was Dr Kendra. He watched the demented old man keenly, just as he had watched him in Hope Gardens and was able to glean the names and whereabouts of some of those other children. But Karl learned something even more astonishing: that Dr Kendra had suffered a heart attack the night of the escape! He slumped back, dumbfounded. After all those years of stewing with hatred for the man, wondering why he'd abandoned them – one simple sentence revealed the startling truth. Karl was flabbergasted. The not knowing had slowly eaten away at his soul. It had scarred him. But it was too late now, the damage was already done.

Karl felt compelled to visit the old man one night, tip-toeing silently along the corridors in bare feet. When he entered the room and stood over his bed, the feeble Dr Kendra scrambled up, wondering if he was seeing another vision.

The old man reached out a hesitant hand, and tenderly cupped Karl's cheek. Even in his disturbed state, he knew who it was. After a while, Dr Kendra swung his legs out of bed, went to his suitcase, and pulled out the tickets from the lining pocket. He pressed them in the Alpha's hands, and told him to keep them safe, for the train. It was coming soon, he told the boy, and he needed to stay awake and keep ready.

Karl softened, as he fingered the tickets. Apart from a little yellowing, they were pristine. Quietly, he told the old man that he would keep them safe. That was all he managed to say. And then he left.

The next morning Dr Kendra had completely forgotten about Karl coming, and he went mad searching everywhere for the tickets. It irked his wife to distraction.

So many ideas whirled around in Karl's head as he lay back in bed, staring into space as his mind went over so many possibilities.

First, he would kill off those bothersome dogs and kittens, one by one.

Then he would play around with the medicine cabinet and people's medication; it would be fun to see the hilarious effects. And, ultimately, when he felt that his time was nearly up, he planned to put something in Avernus' water supply – so that with one simple stroke, all of them died with him... After all, the Professor had destroyed his submarine, and killed Carey, and now he would take everything away from the Professor – his friends, the children. His measly life.

All in good time. Perhaps tomorrow he could start with the animals...

But then, the next morning, he woke to find that his hands were constrained, his movements restricted. He struggled to make sense of the situation, and twisted his neck to find the Professor sitting on a chair, bedside. His eyes were closed, his face grim.

'Professor?' said Karl, sleepy and confused. The old man stiffened. 'Why are my hands tied?'

## 31  THE GIFTS THEY GAVE

Milly, Tai, Mei Hui, and Jemima were all at once exhausted, stricken, mortified, and in a state of shock, held inside Karl's mind. The mind of someone who was undeniably mad.

They wholly experienced everything about the boy – his thoughts, his dreams, every action, his speech, and the pure evilness of him. It was as if they had taken on his thinking. Become him.

Before they started, they had blithely thought they could be passive onlookers. But they were inhabiting his body, and wading the mire of his mind, and the longer they stayed, the more blurred the lines of distinction between him and them. They found that when they watched him kill and murder, *they* killed and murdered; when he was angered, *they* became angry too. Each twisted, poisonous thought turned into theirs, so that their minds seemed inextricably bound. Perplexed, the four wondered where Karl's mind stopped, and theirs started. Like unravelled balls of twine that were entangled as one, how could they ever extricate themselves...?

But they had reached the point of no return. They had gone through so much that it was pointless going back now. And somehow they needed to turn this thing on its head, and become the persuaders, not the persuaded.

More often than not, most people yearn to go back in time and right their mistakes, correct their wrongs. And here was the opportunity to do this for Karl – so they knew they must grab it. They did not overthink and become hampered by the ethicality of it; instinctively they knew that, in this situation, where life and death hung in the balance, it was the right course.

Even though they were young – barely teenagers – their higher level of thinking, distilled wisdom, and depth of knowledge, combined, was more like that of a centenarian. At the same time their youthful hope and optimism, meant that they didn't think twice about attempting to do this.

And the only way they could think of accomplishing this was to impart to him their own unique 'gifts', their treasured memories, qualities, and experiences, that – like a kind of metaphysical brain surgery – they hoped would excise the bad from him, and stitch in, imperceptibly, the good. Renewing the very core of his being.

And their gifts could not be token; they were to give of themselves.

Their mind, spirit, and soul. It was who they were, and who they wanted Karl to be.

They also knew that the virtue of goodness was not something that came about casually; it had to be acquired, learned, and ingrained over time, years even. And so exactly how they would do it, they could not say. Did not know. All they knew was that it had to be done in some kind of organic, natural way.

The teenagers could not tell how long they had already been inside Karl's mind, and they also didn't know how much longer they could stay. But they sensed that, despite their mental fatigue, they had the unanimous desire to do this thing. Importantly, Milly was not overly suffering from her migraines – she could not understand why, but being together with the others somehow dissipated her pain. Even more than the drugs. It was a wonderful discovery, and a relief.

Now that they had made up their minds, they could not wait a moment longer. Again, they delved deep into the boy's mind. And instead of waiting for an avalanche of memories to come crashing into them – the four of them flew back together, searching over Karl's mindscape for the earliest possible memory.

At last they found it.

There it was.

The moment when the Alpha was born.

He was the original.

The first viable baby from Project Ingenious.

And the first thing he saw was the huge, masked face of Dr Axel Kendra – the man's eyes full of emotion and triumph, and a forehead shiny from a slick of sweat. Behind him stood a younger Gaia, her hands clasped together, her face a picture of wonderment at having just witnessed the miracle of childbirth.

Baby stared at the doctor, stretched its mouth into an o, and clicked its tongue – experimenting with this new sensation of freedom of movement. It shivered from the freshness of air against its skin.

Meanwhile, Mallory Schäfer, lay back on the hospital bed, exhausted from childbirth, watching with silent relief as the baby was taken away. She felt no emotional connection with it – to her, it was just a business transaction, and once done, she would get her money, pay off their debts, and be done with the financial mess that her husband's crashing business had brought.

The baby was perfectly formed – and after a nurse quickly and professionally went through the usual Apgar test, he was cleaned and wrapped in a cream-coloured blanket printed with little brown bunnies. It was a find that Gaia had bought during one of her Oxfam shop raids – now freshly washed and scented with jasmine. Gaia was given the swaddled baby, and she sat down, holding it close to her, kissing its cheek incessantly. Her eyes sparkling with joy.

The infant instantly felt safe and warm, and, after the tremendous upheaval of childbirth, soon closed its eyes and drifted into a contented sleep.

Its cot had been placed in Dr and Mrs Kendra's room, and their faces were the first thing baby saw on waking, and the last that he saw at night. Gaia took on the motherly role and tended to his every need, promptly and efficiently. She bathed, changed, and fed him the bottle herself. And baby came to cherish feeding time, with Gaia's warm arms wrapped around him, and his tiny hand clutching her finger. The comfort, love, and protection he soaked up, were just as important as the milk he drank and the air he breathed. When the bottle was finished, Gaia gently held him upright, pressed against her shoulder, and she sang to him as she rubbed his back to relieve the pressure in his chest.

Milly, Mei Hui, and Jemima were all bestowing Karl with these new imaginings, particularly Jemima in this instance. She was the last born to the project, and so the staff had by then righted their mistakes, learnt valuable lessons, and provided her with the best care, from childbirth. She was also a writer, a great storyteller, and as such – with more than a little artistic license – she passed these perceptions to Milly, who masterminded the projection of them into Karl's memories. They became an alternate reality, in his mind. One that built and nurtured moral sensibilities that had been so lacking.

And so, baby Alphie became accustomed to falling asleep safe in Gaia's arms – and just as he was drifting off, he would hear her whisper, 'Sleep, my little angel, sleep.' Words they made sure were interlaced through his infantile memories.

Dr Kendra too came to have a more pivotal role, being in charge of the boy's goodnight 'story' every evening, which he fulfilled by reading out loud one of his medical reports in an animated, lively manner – killing two birds with one stone. Baby was enthralled by his reading, but more often than not, the doctor would be the one to fall asleep, well before Alphie.

And as he grew into a toddler, Milly gave him her own memories of attentive parents – helping define both his sense of belonging, and sense of adventure. So, Gaia and Dr Kendra took Karl on daytrips, fun visits to the park, experienced the thrill of the zoo, and journeys of discovery to the seaside.

Jemima also passed on to him her joie de vivre, so that Alphie came to have an infectious laughter, playfulness, and zest for life that charmed and delighted everyone around him.

As before, Alphie developed a rapport with Carey, but in this new version of events, the old man no longer worked in the incinerator room; they ensured that each image and recollection of the horrors of that room were carefully and methodically expunged from his mind. Instead, they filled the voids with Jemima's imaginings, and activities that Milly, the second child born into the project, remembered from her time growing up in the laboratories.

Tai gifted Karl his love of animals – and the warm, fuzzy feeling that came from the affection they gave. And so the diamondback terrapin tank incident was completely rewritten, with Gaia, instead, lifting out the small, slippery turtle, and placing it on two-year-old Karl's eager little hands.

'Now remember, Alphie,' she said firmly. 'These are God's creatures, same as us. So you must always treat them with respect and care – holding them gently, like this. See. He's very delicate, very fragile, and we wouldn't want to hurt him, would we?'

Alphie tore his eyes from the little creature, and looked up at the woman he thought of as mother. He shook his head vigorously.

The terrapin came out of its shell, and craned a striped neck, pacing around slowly. Alphie's eyes widened with delight, giggling from the sensation of small wet feet tickling his palm. He started jumping up and down with excitement, but Gaia put a firm hand on the boy's shoulder, calming him.

'Don't forget, Alphie,' she persisted. 'Gently does it, otherwise you'll scare him. Life is precious – all life – whether it's humans like you and me, little animals like the terrapin, or plants, or insects. We need each other to live.'

The boy thought about this, and then very slowly, very gently, he lifted the terrapin to his pursed lips, and planted a kiss on its head. Startled, the terrapin withdrew quickly into its shell.

Gaia laughed, and so did Alphie.

'Shall we put it back into its home now?' asked Gaia.

Alphie nodded and watched his mother return it to the large flat rock in its tank. The little boy stood on his tiptoes, and pressed his face against the glass, holding his breath. He watched as the little creature turned slowly round and promptly eject a smudgy black poo. Alphie squealed with delight. 'Pwopsy!' he cried, clapping his hands together. 'I wanna call terr-pin, Mr Pwopsy! Mr Pwopsy! Mr Pwopsy!'

Gaia smiled, nodding. 'Okay, okay, Alphie. Mr Plopsy it is.'

Even though three-year-old Alphie still suffered from fits, seizures, and migraines – the four teenagers lessened the frequency, to reduce the traumatic impact.

They also gave him the bare minimum drugs, balancing this out with the perception of healthy eating, lifestyle, and nutritious supplements – so that he no longer became a drug addict. And he developed a healthy love of food.

With Mei Hui's propensity for sensing good and bad, they sifted through Karl's memories methodically, searching for every bad experience. They fast-forwarded through memories that did not need to be changed, and slowed down at moments that did.

And when the other children came on the scene, Alphie was delighted with each one. He now had fellow playmates: Beta, Delta, and Zeta – who they affectionately referred to as Beth, Del, and Zed. And even though they were several years younger, they soon became firm friends, with Alphie taking on a protective big brother role.

They were still given daily lessons to stimulate development of their intellect and intelligence, but this reboot of memories also included just having fun. They loved playing hide-and-seek, Simon says, it, treasure hunt, and piggy in the middle. And they huddled together to chat, with frequent bouts of unbridled laughter. Karl was excellent at mimicking voices, and had the others in hysterics as Dennis the Menace, or as a Dalek from Doctor Who, or a cartoon character.

And in lessons, they helped each other produce intricate and beautiful play-dough models of flowers and animals. They also worked together to make complex and architecturally accurate models of Tower Bridge, or the Eiffel Tower. In their art lessons they painted worthy reproductions of great works – Alphie copied Rothko's abstract expressionism, intensely mixing and smudging blocks of vibrant colours, while Beth was inspired by the soft and moody textures of Degas.

Some of Tai's fondest memories were at the dinner table eating his mother's delicious home-cooking. And so, through Milly, he gave Alphie this same love of food – and the children always sat together at mealtimes to eat jerk pork with rice and peas, or ackee and saltfish, with sides of callaloo, deep-fried plantains, and soft, plump dumplings – amongst many other cuisines.

Of course, with Tai's love of animals, he had to introduce two cats into the facility, who together birthed a litter of five kittens. The children adored them, and watched their comical antics and exploration of the world with great joy and keen interest. Each child was charged with looking after a kitten or a cat, ensuring it had enough food and water, giving it baths, brushing its fur, and playing with it. Alphie even begged the staff to let his little kitten sleep with him in bed, which they did.

Mei Hui had no loving childhood memories that she could offer, because her parents had left to find work when she was little. Yet despite this, like a flower that grows in the harshest desert, young Mei Hui had somehow blossomed with much love to give – so much so, that she was able to shower it on a household of children. It was a miracle that such love could come out of nothing. And so this was her gift to Karl: the knowledge that love, kindness, and affection can be generated from within, and flourish, despite the harshest conditions.

Mei Hui also had been given no formal education in China, yet the lessons life taught gave her a wealth of wisdom that more than made up for it. And so, Mei Hui taught Karl that humility, and humble beginnings, was the seedbed from which truly great thinking grew. And on that seedbed she planted in his mind the very words of wisdom she herself had learnt.

*'The wise one has no concern for himself, but makes the concerns of others his own.'*

*'I have three treasures that I cherish. The first is compassion. The second is moderation. The third is not claiming to be first in the world.'*

*'The reason why rivers and seas are able to be lords over a hundred mountain streams, is that they know how to keep below them. That is why they are able to reign over all the mountain streams.'*

And lastly, for Mei Hui, she had especially learnt that there does not need to be a reason or motivation to do good to others; it can come purely from kindness of heart, with no motive, no hidden agenda. The satisfaction and contentment of knowing that you've made others happy was reward enough. She therefore taught Karl that *'A bird does not sing because it has an answer, it sings because it has a song.'*

And with this, the new, revitalised Alphie picked up and consoled a crying child whenever they fell down. He helped them with their classwork, and gave them pointers on doing better in their tests. He cradled them when they woke up crying from a bad dream. And, when something went wrong, he sat down with them and gently showed them how they could make it right.

In this way, on the night of their leaving the laboratories forever, five-year-old Alphie hugged toddler Delta in his arms, and consoled her. His heart ached as he gazed out of the window, half watching the children outside – obscure black figures in the darkness – lining up to board the minibus that would separate them. Alphie kissed her forehead, and then gently pulled her from him. 'It's time to go,' he whispered, and he stretched a sleeve over his hand to tenderly wipe her tears. 'Remember, Del – whatever happens, I'll always be with you.'

'You promise?' she whimpered, clinging onto Alphie's arm, not wanting to let go.

The boy nodded. 'Of course,' he smiled.

Reassured, Del looked up at him with her bright green eyes. 'I... I love you, stupid,' she whispered.

'Love you too, idiot,' said Alphie softly.

And through all of Karl's 17 years, through all his sickness, and pain, that was the first time he'd heard someone tell him that. That four-letter word.

The teenagers sensed something stir deep inside Karl; something was beginning to change.

From then on, loving someone, and feeling strong in the surety that he was loved in return, became the single most powerful guiding force in Karl's altered life.

As they waited in the car at the train station, and Alphie watched the insects that fluttered in the lamplight, Carey's mobile phone rang loudly, making him jump. He picked it up, and pressed a button awkwardly, not used to such technology. 'Hello?'

It was Gaia, crying. 'Carey,' she sobbed. 'We're in A&E. Xeli... Dr Kendra's had a heart attack – it just came out of nowhere. We had no choice but to go to a local hospital, and the doctors are working on him now. I don't know what's going to happen... if he'll survive. So... so we won't be able to meet you,' she said. And then, 'I'm sorry, so sorry. But we've compromised your security by coming into the hospital. We... we should stop communicating, and you must throw away the phone, and lay low – to keep you and Alphie safe. Please, take good care of him for us, Carey. And tell Alphie... tell him we love him very much.' There was a pause as she tried to control herself. 'I-I have to go now. Please take care.' She stifled a sob, and then hung up.

Carey closed the phone and turned to the boy.

'I heard,' said Alphie, numb. Tears welled up. 'Is he going to be alright, Carey? Is he going to live?'

Carey stared out of the car windscreen. 'I don't know,' was all he said. And then he started the engine.

The car's tyres crunched slowly across the gravel, and before they turned out of the carpark toward the motorway, the old man rolled down the window and threw the mobile into the rubbish bin. Their connection to Project Ingenious, and everyone in it, severed. They drove off – the two of them staring straight ahead in silence.

But when they neared the large green motorway sign on the A-road, Carey slowed down to read it. It showed both northerly and southerly directions, and the boy noticed Carey's momentary indecision.

'What's wrong?' asked Alphie.

'Nothing,' said the old man. 'Just deciding which relatives to go to.'

'And?...'

'I think, my cousin. We'll go to my cousin.' He turned right to head south on the motorway. 'Go back to sleep,' the old man said. 'It's a long way.'

And just like that, the teenagers erased the toxic Ambrosia from Karl's memories. The trauma of years of enduring her personality disorder, having to kill his beloved birds, and then the hand he'd played in her death. All vanished.

Instead, the four teenagers replaced those years with a simulated world, filled with virtual people and events. It was a mountain of a feat, but their brilliant minds buzzed and fizzed with bringing together a new reel of memories to fill the gaping hole in Karl's.

When they arrived at Carey's cousins, they gave him the barn at the perimeter of their land, which also had ample space for growing vegetables. It was a dishevelled building, but with Mei Hui's housebuilding skills, Carey converted it over time into a cosy three-bedroom cottage. Carey stayed home and looked after Karl – and in time Karl grew into adolescence.

The teenagers also rewrote the death of his natural parents: killed in a tragic car crash. An accident. Though Karl was not affected so much by their deaths. And he was home-schooled, just as Jemima had been, so that Karl was still able to study medicine, and the stock market, as a side-line to pay off the loan for the renovation.

The four teenagers knew that they would be unable to alter drastically Karl's recent history. They had to match the new past they had created, so that it joined seamlessly with the reality of the present.

And so, despite all his success, and the nurturing family environment, in this new version of events, the boy's physical health began to decline from day to day – the fits became more frequent, headaches got worse, and he began to hear voices. In time, this spurred him to start work on creating a cure. He locked himself away for hours, days, weeks in his room, furiously working on the chemistry of it. And, convinced that the sea was the organic birthplace of life, he became obsessed with the fact that it harboured all the nutrients essential to health. He therefore increased his stock-market dealings so that, in time, he became rich and powerful enough to procure a submarine and a crew. Exploratory missions brought him new and potent nutrients from the depths of the seas – krill oil, marine plasma, corals, sea cucumbers, algae and chlorella, kelp and bladder-wrack. The teenagers left out the wanton killing of animals; the baby whale, so horribly slaughtered, no longer figured in this new version of events.

This time, Karl was on a mission to save not only himself, but the other Ingenious children too. So it was for this reason that he searched for them, in the hope that he might share the cure he was making. No Oxford University students were infected. And there were no threatening messages.

At last, everything came to an end when, on an exploratory mission in the Pacific, a random explosion in Karl's submarine caused the death of all his crew. He was pulled out of the sea by a nearby fishing trawler responding to their last-minute distress signal – a miracle recovery.

And with this prodigious feat, Karl came to have a whole 'other' past, and altered memories. His mind re-edited, his very make-up revised.

At last, the four teenagers – Milly, Tai, Jemima, and Mei Hui – had completed what they set out to do. Suffering from extreme fatigue.

From now on there was only hope. Hope that what they had done would be enough.

Their task completed, and deep in the underground cavern of Avernus, their pale, sleeping forms finally began to stir.

## 32  NEW BEGINNINGS

Chance is a funny thing. The fortuitous occurrence of unpredictable events, that is so very rare – like dropped toast that almost always lands buttered side down. But sometimes, just sometimes, it lands the right way up.

And so, as they took it in turns to watch over Karl's sleeping form, still in coma, had Gaia been given a different shift, or the watch periods were in any way longer or shorter, things could easily have turned out differently. But it so happened that – by chance – Gaia was the first person Karl saw when he awoke. Which was perfect, because it moved him deeply when he saw her sitting next to his bed, quietly reading.

'Mother!' he breathed, erupting in a fit of coughing.

Surprised, Gaia quickly reached for a cup of water and held the straw to his mouth. 'Drink,' she urged softly.

Karl sucked on the liquid for some time, keeping his eyes fixed firmly on her. When he had finished, and she put the drink aside, Karl fell onto her and hugged her gently, trembling with emotion.

Gaia hesitated, then wrapped her arms around him, knowing she was hugging a psychopath, a murderer. 'Oh, Alphie. My dear Alphie!' she said, acting. 'It's so good to see you, after... after all this time. I... we missed you so much!'

Milly had already briefed her fully on the new role she was to play in Karl's life. She had listened to the girl tell this incredible story, an eyebrow raised – realising the absurdity of it. But she had no choice. It was strange, and incredibly difficult, stepping into the shoes of a devoted mother, especially to him. But for the children, for her husband and the Professor, she put everything she had into it. And so she kissed his messy blonde hair, pulled away, and tenderly stroked his cheek. She even dared to look into his eyes, realising what a beautiful clear grey they were.

Karl asked, 'Und Vater? Is he alright?'

'Yes and no,' she said, genuinely troubled. 'He survived that heart attack years ago, and recovered. But now...' she shook her head. 'He's got dementia, like his father. He's here in Avernus at least, in this safe-house. And I'm sure he would love to see you, Karl.' She squeezed his arm.

'I would like that,' he said.

'In time. First, you must recuperate, and then I promise I'll bring him to you.' She smiled, and then thought of something else. 'And another thing, Alphie, we've also managed to bring together four of the other children. The Project Ingenious children. They're right here with us as well. Together with Professor Wolff... You remember the Professor, and the children?' she asked, wary.

Karl sat up, amazed. 'Really? That is wonderful! Yes, of course I remember them!' he said, bursting with excitement. 'H-how are they? There's so much I want to tell them. You see, I've been working on something that I hope will be of great benefit to them. But... I need to talk to them first.'

Gaia blinked at him, hardly believing what he had just said. She took his hand and squeezed it, truly grateful, saying, 'I'll tell them to come.'

But then Karl thought of something, and he looked around. 'What about Carey? Where is he?'

Gaia shook her head, looking down. 'I... I'm so sorry, Karl. They never recovered his body from the sea.'

Karl stared at her for some time, in disbelief, shock, horror. 'No!' he groaned. 'No!!' He fell back on his pillow and clawed at the blanket at his sides, crying, for a long, long time. Releasing at long last the mourning that he had held inside.

Gaia gripped his hand, and his thin arm, as he sobbed from the loss of his dear Carey. Her doubts that Karl could have changed so drastically were immediately dispelled. Seeing him now, mourning for someone so deeply, surely meant only one thing.

•••————————————————————————•••

Later that day, after Karl had been checked over by Dr Fargo, managed to drink a little soup, and was well rested, Milly, Tai, Mei Hui, and Jemima also went in to see him. Only two days earlier, they had separated from Karl and severed the connection with his mind – and had just about recovered from it. To say they were apprehensive to meet him was an understatement. And so they entered the room, wary not only of Karl himself, but also unsure of their own acting skills.

When Karl saw them, his face twisted with emotion, and again he broke down.

The four drew closer, led by Mei Hui, and without a word, she hugged him. The others watched her face closely as she momentarily closed her eyes and absorbed the sense of him – her discreet nod on parting told them what they needed to know. That she felt only good from him, and he was genuine. With great relief, they took it in turns to hug him.

Before long, the teenagers began talking together, 'catching up' on each other's lives. They remembered perfectly the new version of his story, and their lives together, to keep up the façade. And even though they had woven a web of lies right inside Karl's mind, they cast aside guilt, and feelings of duplicity. They knew they had made Karl into the person he should always have been.

They had just one interruption. A large dog appeared at the door, growling. 'What a beautiful husky!' Karl exclaimed, and he held out his hand to it. 'Come here, boy.'

But Acuzio refused to move, and kept baring his teeth – hackles raised. Karl was taken aback, because he loved animals.

'Ignore him,' said Jemima, waving the dog away. 'He's not great with strangers. He'll be okay once he gets used to you.' She beamed that golden smile at him, and diverted attention by chatting about something else.

But Karl kept glancing at the dog curiously, and he wondered.


In the afternoon, Karl took a turn for the worse, and called Milly to him. With a grave voice, he explained their disease, and the years he had spent developing a cure for it. He then instructed her to take down the details of the formula, and the method, which she recorded on her phone. He described everything in great detail – and even though Milly had learnt some medicine with Dr Fargo, she was awed by his medical knowledge. It took almost two hours for him to go through everything thoroughly, ensuring that nothing was missed. He checked and double-checked with her that she had taken it down correctly. Their lives depended on it. And when at last he had finished, Milly squeezed his hand, thanked him profusely, and got up to take it to Professor Wolff – for his scientists to work on immediately. There might still be time to help him, she said.

But Karl took her hand, shaking his head. 'You haven't changed, Milly,' he said quietly. 'Always looking on the bright side...' He sighed. 'But it's too late for me. I don't have long.'

Milly blinked at him. 'Don't say that, Karl. Y-you don't know that.'

But Karl just looked at her eyes that were like dark green pools. 'It still needs some work, the cure. I'm sure you'll be able to complete it, given time. So, there's hope for you and the others. Just not me... But, knowing that you're okay, and the others – that's all I want.'

Milly caught her breath, her eyes filling with tears. No acting involved. 'Don't cry, Milly,' Karl smiled.

She swiped at the tears with her sleeve. 'I'm not crying,' she said, and turned to leave. She held up her phone. 'I'm going to bring this to the Prof.'

•••————————————————————•••

Jemima had been wringing her hands for days, wondering how she could tell Jake. But despite her mastery of the written word, the ideal phrases eluded her. In the end, she knew she couldn't keep it from him any longer, and she grabbed his hand and dragged him to the den.

'What's going on?' asked Jake, as she sat him down opposite her. He looked worried. 'Please don't tell me you've got a crush on me,' he joked. 'I told you right from the beginning that–'

'Shut up, and stop flattering yourself!' said Jemima. She took a deep breath, and visibly softened. In fact, she started crying.

Jake drew closer and put an arm around her. 'Hey,' he said gently. 'What is it?'

Try as she might, Jemima was still at a loss for words. In the end, she just blurted it out. 'It... it's about your sister.'

Jake stiffened and closed his eyes, bracing himself. 'Just tell me,' he said, his voice cracking.

Jemima swiped at her eyes with a sleeve. 'Karl saw her, when he was about five. In the Ingenious laboratories. And so, through his memories, we saw her too. She told him her name was Kara, and she looked just like you. She... she was beautiful.'

Jake stared vacantly at Jemima's glistening eyes. 'Was?' he said, his tone flat, feeling sick from half knowing what was coming.

'She was supposed to stay there for nine months. That's what she told Karl.'

Jake caught his breath, realising. 'To have a baby...'

Jemima nodded. 'B-but in all that time, Karl never saw her again. And, we know that... well, quite a few people died during the project, giving birth, or on the operating table. So, it looks as if she didn't make it.'

He gulped, barely able to bring himself to ask. 'Did he... see her die?'

'No, no he didn't. He kept looking out for her – I think he was a bit infatuated by her. But like I said, he never saw her again. So I think something went wrong quite early on...'

'So that's it?' said Jake. He had a hard time processing it. After all those years of clinging doggedly to hope, that was it.

Jemima closed her eyes briefly, remembering, squeezing tears onto her cheeks. 'Th-there was a field. A cornflower field, where they sprinkled the ashes – not far from the old laboratories. We think she might be there.'

Still dazed, Jake mumbled something incomprehensible, staring at the floor.

Jemima didn't have the heart to ask him what he said. They just sat together in silence for a long time.

# 33  PATHOLOGICALLY PUNCTUAL

That night, Karl woke with a jolt, mid-nightmare. The images in his head were so real and so frightening that it took him several minutes to understand that he had been dreaming, and for his nerves to settle, his pounding heart to calm. He wondered where he was. On the submarine? At home? In Avernus?

Sitting up, he swung his legs out of bed. The movement triggered a dim light turning on, and he looked around the room, dazed. He was in Avernus. Groggy, and without speaking, he asked Carey what time it was. But the old man didn't respond. And so he reached for his pocket, force of habit, though he couldn't quite remember what he was reaching for.

Scratching his head, he stepped onto the floor and bent down to rummage through the bedside cabinet. He did not know what it was he was looking for. He just knew where it should be. The clothes he wore on the submarine were there, freshly laundered and stacked in neat folds. His swollen sneakers, sitting on the bottom shelf. And he spotted behind them the glint of something thin and snaking. It was a chain.

He reached inside and pulled out a gold pocket-watch, holding it up to the light. Its round body dangled, slowly turning hypnotically. Karl perched on the bed, and instinctively pressed the crown on the stem, releasing the sprung lid, so that it flipped open. There was a fine sheen of water vapour misting the inside of the crystal face. 'Was... ist... das?' he murmured to himself, puzzled. He stared at it for a long time.

He knew immediately that it belonged to his natural father. Yet he had died along with his mother in a freak car accident. And Karl had never met the man, never even talked to him, or exchanged letters – so how did he come to have this?

As he stared at the watch, his fingers stroked over the smoothness of it, as if teasing out confused and jumbled memories. But the memories that came echoed his nightmare. Gashed flesh. The spray of blood. A floral bedcover soaked in red. He saw death in the form of a wall of darkness. A crack appearing in that wall, a thin parting of doors – and inside, a little girl hiding, terrified, and crying for her mother. Her clear grey eyes were like his.

Karl's mind silently imploded. Unable to reconcile these memories. Wondering whether he was mad, or was going mad. Inside of him came a strange feeling – an itch that he could not scratch. A memory, just out of reach. And he balled his fists in frustration.

His legs moved of their own accord, and he stood, the floor rough underneath bare feet. They took him out, into a dim corridor – and somehow he knew which direction to go.

He found himself at a door, pushing down on the handle. It was open. He went inside, and a faint night light switched on.

Milly stirred in her bed, woken by a noise. She turned, and her heart skipped a beat to find Karl standing over her. She scrambled up. 'Karl?...'

He held out his fist, and uncurled his fingers. 'I... I don't understand, Milly,' he said, his voice cracking – looking from her to the watch in his hand. 'I feel strange. I don't recognise myself. Like I'm... fraying. Like I don't know. Who. I. am.' He looked at her now, really looked at her. 'What's wrong with me?' he said, his voice trembling. It felt like his body had turned to dust, and was slowly being blown away by an invisible breeze, cell by cell, atom by atom. Making him disappear.

Milly's heart raced, and her body stiffened. She could barely breathe. But she needed to control herself. She forced herself to look at Karl. At his hollow face, and its pale, thin lines. The wild look in his eyes.

And she caught a choke in her throat, as she understood. What they had done to him.

They had invaded his thoughts and implanted new ones, giving him an altered history, a changed past, new perceptions – with no way to gauge the results, no way to test the effects. She realised now that instead of a delicate surgery, it must have been like a mental blitzkrieg, the land now charred and smoking in the aftermath. Her heart missed a beat as she realised too that his sanity was loosening. He had become unstable.

He took a step closer, and Milly held out an arm, both in instinct to protect herself, and to reach for him.

Karl looked fragile, lost. 'Del,' he breathed. 'Why are you afraid?'

Milly shook her head, struggling to control herself. 'I'm not afraid, Alphie.'

'But... to me, you look scared.' He thought of something and smirked. 'Do you remember. I was always the one you ran to when you were scared, the one who comforted you.' He suddenly doubted himself. 'Wasn't I?'

Milly knew that was an implanted memory, and his mind was unravelling. She barely understood the compulsion, but she found herself standing. They were so close, almost touching. And she put her arms around him – all at once feeling revulsion, fear, turmoil, sadness. 'Karl,' she said. She closed her eyes, and kissed his cheek lightly. Her lips were trembling. 'I... I love you, stupid,' she said, tears dripping onto his neck.

Karl stopped, stiffened. But then at last his shoulders slumped, and he softened in her arms. 'Love you too, idiot,' he whispered.

She did not know how she did it, but somehow Milly was able to lead Karl, who walked as if in a trance, back to his room.

Immediately she alerted the others, and the Professor – once again – arranged for guards to stand outside his room.

They were able to protect themselves from him, but they could not protect Karl from himself.

The next morning they found his body stone cold in the bed, the watch chain wrapped around his throat so tightly it had sunk deep into his flesh – crooked fingers hooked inside the loop, stiff from rigor mortis.

Crumpled on the bed was a handwritten note, in careful pencil scrawls, written so faintly as to be barely there.

*It doesn't really matter who we are, does it? Intelligent, or not. Clever or simple. I know now that what really matters is our humanity. Our soul. The heart that beats inside every single one of us.*

*Maybe that's why things have gone so badly wrong – in the world, and in our own sorry lives. In my life. It's because we keep forgetting – I keep forgetting – that it's the seemingly insignificant, the small, overlooked things, that are actually the most important. Like affection, even from an animal. Like the love of a parent. Or a sister. That is what should compel us.*

*And when it's ripped away, what else is there?*

*I think I've done things... And I can't bear it*

The note stopped abruptly, as if in mid-sentence. As if he were tired of writing, tired of life.

It was not addressed to anyone, and he signed it off simply as 'Karl' – with a full stop, pressed so heavily, that the pencil lead broke.

## 34  THE SIGHING MEADOW

Jake stood feebly before the field, surveying its tragic beauty.

He had been haunted most of his life by the disappearance of his sister. And despite searching for her for years, he had reached a plateau, and was just coming to terms with the thought that he might never know what had happened to her. He wondered whether there was anything worse than the constant pain of an open wound that never heals. A wound so deep it cut through flesh and bone.

He had walked through the field earlier, aimless, and in a daze – a hand stretched out, tumbling through delicate, spindly flowers. Behind him trailed Acuzio, sniffing here and there.

And now Jake just stood on the incline at the perimeter – the dog by his side, at first sitting, then becoming tired, finally lying down. Jake didn't know that he was just inches away from the same spot where Carey had stood, years before, after emptying those barrels of ash for the very last time. Those six, black barrels.

And just as Carey had done, Jake's eyes swept over a meadow that was ablaze with blue, filled to brimming with cornflowers as far as the eye could see. It was breathtakingly beautiful. Yet the impact was lost on him, knowing what those flowers – every single one of them – meant.

In time, Jake fell to the ground, unable to hold himself up any longer, battling to control his emotions. Alarmed at his distress, Acuzio began whimpering, and then licked the boy's hand vigorously. Jake threw himself on the dog and hugged him for a long time. He listened to the soft whining that seemed to come from deep within the animal's chest; the sound passed into his own body, and the dog whined for them both.

At last, he parted, and looked for his rucksack, pulling it closer to search for something inside. He took out a blue cotton cardigan. It was the last thing she wore, casually thrown on the edge of her bed before changing into her 'going out' clothes. It had remained there for years after she went missing, gathering dust. Her parents, paralysed by her disappearance, dared not change a single thing in her room, in case it somehow jinxed her safe return.

Jake hugged the cardigan to his chest.

And the dog sat by his side, and rested his head on Jake's bent knees, burying his wet black nose into the fabric. Breathing it in. But suddenly he caught a whiff of something. A scent. And he sniffed it with interest, his blue eyes sparkling and alert. Then – abruptly and unbidden – the dog turned and ran through the cornflowers, hurtling in all directions, stopping only now and again to sniff something. He did this for ages. And Jake watched him with little regard, distracted by his own misery. Even the sun seemed weighted with grief as it sunk gloomily into the horizon, trawling the last light of day in its wake. It cast Jake in long, dusky shadows.

And then the dog started barking.

Jake scanned the field to find Acuzio's head popping up amidst the flowers that had grown so tall they almost covered him. The dog was at the far northern edge of the field, looking eagerly over at him, and then digging at something in the ground. Sighing, Jake pushed himself up, sure that Acuzio had caught a field mouse or something, which was the last thing he wanted. More death. His heavy feet trudged over to the dog, who was still barking manically.

When Jake reached him, he dropped to his knees at the spot where he was digging, and Acuzio stood up to greet him, his tail whipping the air. Jake parted the clump of cornflowers, and searched, but there was no animal. Relieved, he started to get up – but Acuzio barked loudly at him, bidding him to stay, and then digging even more.

Jake knelt on one knee next to him, wondering what all the commotion was about, and he parted the flowers again, to see. The dog continued scraping up thick clumps of dark, loamy soil – and the boy caught his breath when he saw a faint shimmer of something in the hole. It was a delicate thread. He hesitated, but then stooped down to feel for it with explorative fingers, nails scratching against a thin line of metal. Working his fingers into the soil around it, at last he pulled it out.

He held it up toward the last traces of light, like a prostrated worshipper appeasing the sun, staring at it for some time.

It was a chain, a fine necklace chain, weighted with a small clump of mud. Carefully, he broke the mud away, rubbing it clean between his thumb and index finger. And he saw that it was a gem. He knew instantly what it was. Pained, breathless, tremulous, he closed his eyes, daring himself to remember.

He saw Kara. Laughing at him, and fingering the sapphire that nestled in her collarbone. 'I love it!' she sang. Her beautiful blue eyes sparkling with delight – they were the same colour as the gemstone. 'I'm going to wear it always. And I'm never taking it off, Jakey. Never. Till the day I die...'

Jake opened his eyes just as he felt a chasm of pain cracking inside. He was certain now. His sister's ashes had been buried here. A trembling hand pulled off his rucksack and gently folded the necklace inside the cardigan. Then he reached for the clump of cornflowers that Acuzio had dug up, placing them, carefully, inside. 'Good dog, Acuzio,' he said, eyes damp with tears, his chest heaving with sobs. 'Good dog.'

Jake stood up, and dusted himself down.

When he left, he did not stop to look back at the field. It was a place of astounding beauty by day, yet by night, it transmuted into what it really was – a dark, windswept, graveyard. Within it lay innumerable souls. Hundreds and hundreds of unmarked graves, with no-one to acknowledge they were even there. No-one to mourn them.

All that remained were the gentle ululations of a breeze floating over the field. And if ever a passer-by stopped, and they closed their eyes to really listen, they might hear in that breeze the lingering sighs of a thousand forgotten souls.

## 35 THE COLOUR OF LIFE

All six teenagers sat in an outward facing circle, in the middle of the octagonal classroom in Avernus. But there had been no classes for a long time. Instead, came the sound of crashing special effects with the tinkling background music to a video game, booming from the room's surround-sound speakers. Joysticks and controllers were set upon with frenzied thumbs. Each of them faced a huge 4k screen – the graphics and sound were amazing – and they were excitedly shouting over each other.

'Shoot me, and you're dead!'

'You fight like a chicken.'

'I'm gonna pretend I didn't hear that.'

'Aaargh, you shot me!'

'Sorry, but it's kill or be killed...'

'No, *I* wanna get King Kong!'

'You're sapping my energy.'

'Oops, sorry.'

'You're *still* sapping my energy.'

'Sorry!!'

Brian came in again. 'You lot still at it?!' he said, rolling his eyes. He went around, wearily collecting their cups and empty snack packets – getting in their way.

'Dad!' Milly objected.

'Yeah, Dad!' echoed Jake, ducking this way and that to see past him.

'I thought you said you were just going to play for an hour?' said Brian.

'When was that?'

'About five hours ago,' Brian replied, withered.

'Time flies!' said Jake with a cheeky grin.

Suddenly, their screens froze and the music stopped. And they all groaned.

Jasmine's smooth voice resounded from the ceiling speakers. 'I'm sorry to interrupt, but the Professor would like to see Tai,' she said. 'He's waiting in the den.'

Surprised, Tai said, 'Okay.' He jumped up, put his controller down, and told them to continue without him.

When the boy arrived at the den, the Professor was standing by the door. He looked tired, and serious. 'Ah there you are!' breathed the old man.

'Is something wrong?' asked the boy, worried.

'I've got news for you, Tai. Bad news.' The Professor paused. 'They've found your mother. But she's in hospital, in a coma.'

Tai stepped back, barely able to believe it.

'There was a train crash several months ago. She was on it, and taken immediately to hospital. They found no ID on her, that's why you weren't informed. But up till now she hasn't revived. And, well, she's taken a turn for the worse... They don't think she's got long...'

Tai shook his head, hardly able to believe it.

'The Chauffeur's outside, waiting to take you to her now.'

•••————————————————————•••

Tai entered the sterile hospital room with trepidation – his sneakers squeaking on the floor.

Hesitantly, he drew closer to his mother's sleeping form, eyeing the bed cover that sunk into the crevices of her body. She was pale, as if the sun had bleached her, though the curtains were drawn, and it was dim. Someone had groomed her long, dark hair – tried to tame the fullness of it into messy braids. He reached out a hand and touched those braids, still not quite believing where he was, who was lying in front of him. Sinking into the chair, he took her hand within his – it was light as a feather.

'Ma?...' he said.

Nothing.

He looked around, then got up, and opened the curtains. He didn't expect so much light to flood in, and he squinted as it shone in his eyes. When he turned back round, that's when he saw it. A hazy aura that surrounded her – though barely visible. He drew closer, mesmerised.

It made her glow, as if she were an angel, a sleeping angel, surrounded by ethereal light.

For a long while he just sat there and watched. Watched the halo of soft amber around her. It pulsed and glowed as she breathed. Yet it seemed to be fading gradually even as he stared, and somehow he knew that when the light disappeared, she would die. He squeezed her hand, pleading with her. Don't leave me. And he willed and willed for her to live.

His tears dropped silently onto the cotton cover, the wet stain slowly spreading as he prayed and begged and implored that she wake up – to who or what, he did not know. And then he noticed. He sat up, and took in the yellow light surrounding her. It was glowing brighter, undulating in vibrant waves. He lifted a hand to shield his eyes.

Just then a nurse came in and looked first at Tai, and then at his mother, who was beginning to stir. The nurse gasped, and quickly ran to press the emergency button. A loud alarm resounded, and Tai stood up as doctors rushed in, pushed in front of him, and swarmed around the bed.

'W-what's wrong?' asked Tai, his voice hoarse.

The nurse turned to him, 'Wrong? Nothing's wrong,' she beamed. 'In fact, it's a miracle – she's waking up, after all this time! We thought she wasn't going to make it past the evening. So it's good news. Very good news!' She looked over her shoulder at the doctors. 'They're just making sure she's okay.'

A choke caught in Tai's throat. He was so relieved.

The nurse smiled kindly, and touched his arm. 'Bless you,' she said. 'Are... are you her father?'

Tai looked at her oddly. 'No,' he said. 'I'm her son.'

The nurse stared at him, puzzled.

Feeling suddenly weak and tired, the boy rushed out of the room – gasping for breath. But then he caught his reflection in the glass of a picture hanging on the wall, and he drew closer, not understanding what he was seeing.

His hair was grey. Fine lines etched into his skin.

He looked down at his hands, and saw that they were wrinkled and pale. He staggered back, felt his bones creaking as he moved. His knees aching. Looking down at himself, he stared in amazement at the glow of yellow that surrounded him.

It was faint and weak, and barely there.

# EPILOGUE

Axel Kendra sat in his pyjamas, rocking back and forth, back and forth, in his chair. He murmured a constant stream of gibberish that made little sense, eyes fixed on his wife. She was always close by – hovering around. She was bending over the radio in the far corner of the room, putting on reading glasses, and trying to work out the digital pre-sets. But it only hissed obstinately back at her, and she stood up, grunted with frustration, and banged it with a fist.

The noise jarred Dr Kendra and he glared at her as he rocked.

Suddenly, the radio came to life, and they heard the warm, lilting voice of a male announcer.

'...and just after that, at 8.30 pm, sit back and enjoy the long awaited "Amazing Amazon", presented by naturalist, John Foreman. Prepare to trample through the undergrowth with him, as he explores exotic flora and fauna of the jungle. Hold tight, as he takes you by boat down the Amazon river – and watch out for that larger-than-life anaconda sneaking up from behind... The show is recorded live, straight from the Amazon delta.'

It concluded with a catchy jingle.

Suddenly, Dr Kendra stopped mid-swing

Noticing this, Gaia turned to him, peering over the rim of her glasses. 'Xeli?' she said. 'What is it?'

The old man looked from the radio to his wife, surprised to find her there.

Gaia recognised the clarity in his eyes, and she gasped, and ran to him. 'Oh, Xeli, you're back!' she breathed, throwing her arms around him.

'Gaia?' he said, his voice fragile.

'Thank goodness,' she said, parting. 'It's been such a long time. I was beginning to give up all hope that–'

'Listen!' said Dr Kendra urgently, eyes wide.

His wife stood back in surprise.

'She... she's near the delta. The Amazon.'

It took a few moments for Gaia to understand, and she gasped.

Dr Kendra turned aside, frowning in concentration, trying hard to remember. And then it came to him. 'It... it's where the white meets the black.' He sat back in wonder, his own words surprising him. 'The white and the black, the white and the black,' he chanted to himself.

Gaia shook her head. 'Oh no,' she murmured. 'Don't leave already...'

But then Dr Kendra stopped. Fear clouding his expression. 'We must get her,' he whispered.

Gaia bent down and took his hand. 'Yes of course, Xeli. But–'

'Now!' he said. 'We have to get her before *he* comes.'

Gaia looked scared. 'W-what do you mean? Before who comes for her?'

But the old man suddenly became agitated. He shook his head – all at once frightened, anxious, and frustrated. His mouth opened and shut, trying to get the words out. But they just wouldn't come.

'Before who comes for her?' Gaia repeated gently, knowing that they didn't have long before he was gone again.

The old man struggled with himself – his face reddening, eyes bulging, as he battled to say one more thing. And at last – with enormous willpower – he spat it out. 'Th-th-their father!!' he said.

Gaia looked at him in stunned silence.

But Dr Kendra's eyes were already glazing over, his face reverting to that blank, dead-pan expression.

His chair creaked, as he slowly started rocking again.

Creaking and rocking.

Back and forth, back and forth.

'I have seen something further under the sun, that the swift do not always win the race, nor do the mighty win the battle, nor do the wise always have the food, nor do the intelligent always have the riches, nor do those with knowledge always have success, because time and unexpected events overtake them all.'

Ecclesiastes 9:11

You can order book 2:

## *The Ingenious*

## *and the Heart of Shattered Glass*

on Amazon, Apple Books,

Google Books, or Kobo

or

for updates, follow me on:

Instagram: jysamwriter

Facebook: jysamwriter

Twitter: JYSamwriter

or

subscribe at www.jysamofficial.com


If you enjoyed the book, please leave a review on:

Amazon
or
Goodreads